WORKS BOTH WEYS

(Wey Back in Time 4)

S. J. Blackwell

*Welcome back to the
world of the Weys ...*

... and if you haven't already got it, as a thank you for getting this far in the series, I'd like you to have a free copy of my standalone prequel short story, ***The Wey We Were.***

All you have to do is click on the link at the end of the story, and let me know where to send it.

You can also find me online here or by clicking on the links below.

Twitter

Instagram

Facebook

To all my readers -

We all get to experience multiple lives through reading stories.

There are millions of stories out there, so thank you for choosing to read mine, when you need to take a break from your own life.

Stay safe and well.

FOREWORD

The chapter headings tell a story of their own.

Head over to Spotify, search for Works Both Weys and immerse yourself in the music of the time while you enjoy the story.

CONTENTS

The Extended Fam

(plus even more olds)

2019

Maisie Wharton – Me. Weyfare. Doing my best.

Ani Chowdhury – resident historian, brains of the squad.

Jasper Lau – BFF. Self-professed Guard of mine, working on the claustrophobia.

1987

Lizzy Brookes – Weyfare. My mother in about fifteen years. Doing her best, like me.

Glenda and Henry – my nan and granddad, Lizzy's rents.

Paul – Lizzy's biker big brother, my uncle.

Blake - my big brother.

Rob Bennett – still the hottest thing to pre-date the internet. My bae.

Valerie Bennett – his adopted mother. Weyleigher. Not a good thing.

Eve Bennett- Valerie's mother. Weyleigher.

Scott Kelly – Valerie's boyfriend.

Kim Fox – Lizzy's Guard. So much more than Lizzy's squad.

Brian Walker – Plays guitar and air flute. Hooked up with Ani.

Ian Hills – condemned to revision. Lizzy's squad.

Tracy Rutherford – determined to avoid revision. Lizzy's squad.
Esmé - her Great-Aunt.
Angela - her Aunt.

Ed Mitchell – bassist with Divine Morrissey. Not a bad guy. Not really.

Mary Davenport – Witan, Lady of the Dials.

1972

Helen Davenport – Witan, Lady of the Dials.
Tommy – her eldest son and Chief Guard. Still hench with a capital H. A problem I need to sort out.
Mavis – Helen's Guard, self-proclaimed housekeeper.
Joan and Arthur Bishop – Lizzy's nan and grandpa, my great-grands.

1979

Polly Frobisher – The Mermaid.

Gus, Barry and Clive – her Guard.

Janice – her healer.

Chapter One – Put Yourself In My Place (Kylie Minogue, 1994)

Memories. Some memories are sweet, like the first time you ride a bike without stabilisers, or you're allowed out with your squad after dark, promising your rents you'll be careful while you hide a bottle of Blue WKD in your tote bag. Other memories you'd rather forget, like the fact that you were always the last kid to be picked in a game of rounders, or the time you realised the fit boy in 9S at Fletcher-Clark Academy was only talking to you at the Fundraiser Disco because he wanted to hook up with your BFF. Some memories are precious, like the memories me and Jasper have of our lives in 2019 before we rode the Weys. Here in the hidden caves beneath Stoneford, facing the new Weydoor, our memories might just save us from a paradox. The worst thing is that, to some people, we might not even be a memory.

'Why have we stopped?' Jasper, my blud, bestie and the only person I know whose memories match mine, peers at me through the gloom of the purple glow from the Weydoor. 'Why aren't we riding? Those security guards are going to be here soon!'

'We've ridden to 2019 through this Weydoor before, haven't we?' I ask.

'Too right we have,' he says. 'It felt like we'd been buried alive when we landed. Not cool.'

'The last time we rode to 2019, we used the Old Library Weydoor, not this one.' Ani lets go of my hand. She used to be my blud and my bestie, but her memories don't match Jasper's or mine because we met her on an alternate timeline. 'You need to remember these things if you're going to avoid a paradox, Maisie.'

'Yes, thank you for your kind words of wisdom.' I tell her. 'Let's leave it a minute or so anyway. We don't want to risk meeting ourselves.'

'And I don't want to stay a minute longer in that tomb than we have to, thank you very much,' Jasper adds, with a shiver.

'Awww. Was you all freaked out because of that landfall, baby boy?' Ani coos.

'Hush your gums.' Jasper glares at Ani. I wonder if he'll ever get on as well with this girl as he did with the original.

'We'd better hope all the caves are unblocked when we get

to 1987 then,' I say. 'Crap. They've found us.'

The distant sound of heavy footsteps jogging through the caves shakes me into action. I put my clean hand out, and they take hold of the other, and with me leading, the three of us step forward away from 1994 and there's white heat, purple light, black – nothing.

I just celebrated my 18th birthday in 2019, but we've spent more time in 1987 with my teenage Mum Lizzy and her crew since I discovered I was a Stoneford Weyfare, Guardian of the Weydoor at Drake's School. The Weys are invisible energy paths across the world where the four dimensions meet. A Weydoor is a crack in the energy: a break, a fissure, or whatever else you want to call it that allows people to ride the Weys to other times. Some people, like Lizzy's ex- Scott Kelly, want to make money from the Weys, and others, like Valerie Bennett-Simmons, want power and control over them. The Weyfarere have to protect the Master timeline from being manipulated by lowlifes like those two.

Do I make it sound easy? Don't believe it for a minute.

As we were expecting, we arrive in 2019 because it's the end of my natural timeline, but the caves in 2019 are blocked. Fortunately, we've spent enough time teetering at the edge of the Old Library Weydoor to avoid other versions of ourselves

that were here before. I take hold of the hanky Tommy Davenport gave me as a token, and we ride back to the moment in
Time that we left him in 1987. Me and Jasper flick on our
phone torches, since there's no one around who's going to freak
out at the sight.

'So we're in a loop now, right?' Ani asks, looking out at
caves pretty much the same as we left them in 1994. 'The other
us is up at the Old Library right now - with both of your baes.'

I turn on her. 'You think I'm enjoying this?'

'Don't you start getting all salty with me as well,' she says.
'I wasn't the one getting down and dirty with a new guy before
the old one had left the building.'

'He didn't leave the building, he left the bloody decade,' I
snap back.

Okay, I am salty. My love life's more confusing than dozing
off at the beginning of *Inception* and waking up again halfway
through. On the one hand there's Tommy Davenport, from
1972. He's hench and all snatched smoulder like a 50s movie
star, and he's the eldest son of one of the most important Weyfare in the country at that time: Helen, the Seven Dials Witan.
On the other hand, there's Rob Bennett from 1987. I've known
two versions of Rob and both of them are gentle, thoughtful
and breathtakingly fit. For a while we thought he was the son
of Weyfarere enemies, known as the Weyleighers, but by the

time we discovered Valerie Bennett or Simmons adopted him, Tommy was already taking him to the Bergh. I've not been there, but The Bergh sounds like a cross between Azkaban and Shawshank, and Rob shouldn't be going. He's not a blood relative of the Bennetts - he even said he never felt like part of the family. The Bergh is for people who have betrayed the Weys community , and he hasn't. It's somewhere in Edinburgh, but I'm pretty sure Tommy will take Rob to his mother at the Seven Dials in London, and let her handle it.

Ani looks at one of the three exits from the cave. 'Is it worth seeing if we can get through to the Weyroom while we're here? We could pick up some of the tokens and vials. Lizzy took some. You're Weyfare. They're your property as well as hers. And I could do with a change of clothes.' She peers down at her long grubby knitted coat and her embroidered flared trousers. 'I'm so over looking like a hippy.'

'Just because Lizzy took stuff from there, doesn't mean it's right,' I tell her.

Jasper gives me a sympathetic look. 'You're going to have to clear the air with her eventually.'

'She's just found out I'm her future daughter. How would you feel if you just found out Tommy was your son?'

Jasper's eyes glaze over, and he shakes his head. 'That's just wrong on so many levels, Maisie, but it changes nothing. You and Lizzy will need to get over this.'

He's right of course. Lizzy is my Mum in 2019, but right now in 1987, she's an 18-year-old rule breaker with a volcanic temper and a bad attitude. She didn't take the news of our relationship too well, but I'm hoping she might chill about it once she's got used to the idea. I had to.

'Fine – I'll get over it,' I tell him, 'but like I say, Lizzy's busy trying to work out what happened to her Gran. My Great-Gran. No one knows about Rob's adoption. We're the only ones who can stop him ending up in the Bergh.'

'Well, if we're not going to the Weyroom and we're not going back to St Pete's, there's only one cave left to take,' Ani says. 'And we'd better get going if you want to stand a chance of heading Tommy off before they catch the train up to London.'

The cave system feels different, both from the Vaults that connect Trinity Church and St Peter's, as well as the tunnel that connects the Weydoor at Drake's School with my home, Travellers' Rest. There is more space and height so, at first, we can walk next to each other through the mossy stone archways and brick supports. In places though, there are piles of dirt and fragments of rock by the walls, as if everything is in the process of a slow collapse, and the sight of them makes me want to walk a bit faster.

The further we walk, the narrower the cave gets. Eventually we're back to single file, and I'm glad me and Jasper are in our under-the-radar uniform of black jeans, black T-shirt and jacket as Ani trips over yet another uneven patch in her platform wedged boots. Abruptly, the passage comes to an end.

'Rock fall?' she says, walking up the back of my trainers.

I wave the phone light around. 'Ladder.'

Jasper reaches forward and adds his torch to the light, so that I can clearly see the metal ladder reaching up into what looks like a wide industrial chimney with no visible top. There are no clues as to where that chimney is going to come out. For all I know, we're going to emerge under a bush in the Railway Gardens.

'You want us to climb up there?' he asks weakly.

'No, I thought we'd fly, tool.' I punch him lightly on the arm. 'It's 1987. Unless you want to turn back and try your chances with Valerie's mob at St Peter's Hotel, we don't have much of a choice.'

One summer when I was young enough to be ordered about but old enough to get salty about it, Mum had taken me and my two older brothers Lucas and Blake up to London to "show us the sights", which translated as dragging the three of us around every bloody landmark, museum and art gallery for the best part of the whole holiday. Being with a history teacher, we got a lecture everywhere we went. As I climb up onto the narrow step, it reminds me of the metal ones we had to go up to get to the outside of the dome of St Paul's Cathedral. This ladder is almost vertical, but it's surprisingly sound. By the time I get to the top, my legs and arms are aching like I've been tasered again, but I'm more worried by the apparent dead end.

'Why have we stopped?' Ani calls up.

'Hang on,' I say, bracing myself to hold onto the ladder with one hand so I can feel around with the other.

'It's blocked, isn't it? My legs are on fire,' Jasper says. 'Oh my God. I can't bear it.'

As he continues to moan and Ani continues to tease him for it, my hands touch upon what feels like a long metal handle over my head. I pull on it several times before it finally gives and starts to turn a circular piece of metal above me like the top of a jar. Trying to keep my balance isn't easy, but eventually the round piece releases and I can push it away, revealing a hole into which daylight streams.

Tentatively, I climb another step or two until my head is just above the level of the hole. We seem to be in the middle of a road with buildings all around us, but it's not busy enough to be a main road; more like an access road behind a row of houses. There's no one around, so I clamber out, and Jasper and Ani follow.

The round metal piece looks like a manhole cover that

might lead to a drain or a sewer, but there is a tiny Weysigil embossed on it along with various other words and numbers. We fix the plate back into place until it's flush with the ground, and have a good look around.

'Any ideas where we are?' I ask.

Jasper shakes his head, no. 'It's familiar though. I think we're still in Stoneford.'

Ani tsks like a teacher. 'How far d'you think we walked?' she asks sarcastically. 'Were you expecting us to end up in Ashbridge?'

'Will you two just give it up with the constant mouth?' I exclaim. 'It's like being back at primary school. You're making my head hurt.'

'Don't have a benny about it,' Ani says, crossing her arms.

Jasper looks around. 'I get the feeling we've seen these houses a lot, but they don't look right, and I can't work out why.'

The access road slopes up through trees and garages until it turns a bend, but it also slopes down towards a railway line, and some tall red brick buildings that I can just see over the top of other houses: some of them brick; some white; all of them large and sprawling. It comes to me as it comes to Ani.

'Town Hill,' we both say at the same time.

'That's the block of flats where Neil Thorpe lives,' I say.

'Down there by the railway.'

'This is the back of the houses on Town Hill,' Ani says. 'This road must run parallel with the main road at the front.'

I turn to look at Jasper, but he is staring at the back of the nearest house to us, his head on one side. 'Jasper, are you okay?'

'I think that's the house from the bombing raid,' he says. 'The one where you, me and Tommy saved that woman and her baby. Remember?'

How could I forget? Thrown through the Weydoor by Weyleigher thugs, we'd ridden to 1940 and the night of Stoneford's worst bomb raid of the Second World War. It was the night the original Drake's, our school, was destroyed. With our bare hands, we'd helped to dig a young woman and her baby out of the burning rubble of her once grand house on Town Hill. I will never forget that night.

'Esmé,' I say out loud. 'They called her Esmé.'

It's hard to be sure from this side, but it does look like the big brick house that replaced the whitewashed pillared one that was destroyed. The manhole doesn't seem to be attached to any of the houses, but I guess it could have been on their land once. Looking at the houses under the fighter-plane-free skies of May 1987, it makes my skin creep to see the scenes from the War in my mind's eye at the same time, overlaid like a transparency on today's reality.

'So what're we waiting for? An invitation?' Ani says. 'There must be a way through to Town Hill if we follow this road down, and then we just need to sprint across to the station.'

We were just about to. Jasper had even broken into a jog, when I hear a familiar voice.

'*Maisie*? What in the name of Sod are you doing climbing out of drains?'

I turn to face the girl standing with her hands on her hips a little further down the road. She's dressed in a cropped white T-Shirt over pink leopard-skin baggy trousers that balloon out from her hips and thighs. A thick black plastic belt sits high over her waist; she wears a pair of purple Converse All-Stars on her feet. Her fluffy backcombed blonde hair is held back from her face with a white plastic headband, and beside her, the guy looks as if he's standing in the shade. Tracy Rutherford is what you imagine when someone says "80s teen". And it looks as thought she just watched us climb out of a manhole.

Awks.

'Where have you been? We've been trying to get hold of Lizzy on the blower since yesterday lunchtime,' Ian says, as they come closer. He looks dressed for study in a plain T-shirt and bleached jeans, carrying a massive bag of books. 'No one's answering at her place. And Brian's Mum didn't know where he was.'

Funny that. 'Hey Ian. It's a bit of a long story,' I say.

Ian sniffs. 'It always is with you three. Well, I reckon we can't sit around partying tonight. We've got to study. Or have we?' he asks Tracy, as if he's hoping for an answer in the negative.

'Not likely.' Tracy puts her hands out in the universal language of enough already. 'Forget that. I saw you. You climbed out of the drains? What are you doing in there? Am I the only one here who wants to ralph? Has Lizzy turfed you out of her caravan? I bet she has, the cow. I bet she's off with Patchouli, isn't she? Please tell me you're not living in the drains. It makes me want to barf.'

The sound of Scott Kelly's nickname brings me up short. Does this mean 1987 is back to the way it was originally? Is Lizzy seeing Scott Kelly, and are we the local runaways again?

Then I remember why we're standing in this little road. Of course things aren't the same.

'We haven't seen Lizzy,' I lie. 'And no, we're not living in the drains, but we've got to get to the station, so we won't get in the way of your plans.'

'Pity. I was hoping for a distraction,' Ian remarks, dropping the bag of books.

'You are going nowhere until you tell us what you were doing down that drain,' Tracy says, crossing her arms. 'Don't deny it; I watched you climb out.' She looks at Ani, and then Jasper and me, and then back to Ani as if she can't quite believe what she's seeing. 'What in the name of Gobshite are you wearing?'

'A coat?' Ani says scathingly.

'That's not a coat, it's a flea blanket for tramps.' Tracy shakes her head. 'I knew this would happen. I love that girl Brookes to death, but she's so bloody unreliable. You were fine at my barby queue and now look at you: you're covered in crap wearing beggars' clothes and sleeping in the drains. You'd better come in and clean up and then,' she adds with a particular look at me, 'you're going to tell us exactly what's been going on, why Ani's wearing clothes from my aunt's dressing-up box and why you're climbing out of the manhole at the bottom of my great-aunt's garden.'

Jasper looks at me. In my head, another bomb drops.

'Did you say your great-aunt's garden?' I ask faintly.

'Mum and Dad have gone to Majorca for the week. I'm staying at my great-aunt's place, so I can concentrate on my revision and not have to worry about things like making food,' Tracy explains.

'Not strictly true, Trace,' Ian says. 'You're here because your olds knew you'd do nothing if you were left to your own devices. I'm here because your mum met mine in Woolworths and told her she should send me over if she had to work.'

Tracy grimaces and leans on the black iron garden gates. 'Fair comment.'

'Look,' I tell them with forced cheerfulness, 'I'm not being salty or anything, but we really need to get to the station before the next train to London.'

'Good luck with that,' Tracy says. 'It's Bank Holiday Monday, so there's a reduced service. Last train to London left about twenty minutes ago, with my olds and their suitcases on it.'

Chapter Two – Live To Tell
(Madonna, 1987 (1986))

Crap. I'd forgotten it was still Bank Holiday Monday here. In 2019, you'd never spot the difference between an ordinary weekday and a Sunday or Bank Holiday if you went to the shops, but back in 1987, it's like a ghost town here in Stoneford. If Tommy and his goons made that last train with Rob, we can't do much about it, and if they didn't, we've got no idea where Tommy might go next. Would he hire a car? Did he have enough money for that? Can he even drive? Would he be taking Rob up to his mother Helen, up in London at the Seven Dials? Will Helen still even be there? I have a link to her as Witan in 1972, but it's 1987 now. And when they get to London, how long will the Witan keep Rob there before moving him to Scotland? Double crap.

'Maisie.' Jasper puts his arm gently on mine. 'We don't even know they made that train. They could be anywhere by now. There's no point in chasing all over town trying to find them. We all need some downtime.' I realise he's read my mind, and

I nod. 'We will find them, blud,' he says, squeezing my arm encouragingly.

FML. This is not going how I planned. No. Who am I trying to kid? Whether I plan anything or not, very little has gone right since Brian Walker knocked me, Jasper and Ani 1.0 over in the Old Library at Drake's, and we fell through the Weydoor into my mother Lizzy's 1987.

'Who are you trying to find?' Tracy pierces the bubble of my muddled thinking. 'Do we know them? Whoever they are, if they've gone up to London, you won't catch them now. Go up in the morning. Come in and have some supper with us. There's pop tarts, and a couple of Vesta curries, and some left-over steak and kidney pud if you're really hungry.' She looks me up and down again. 'There's two shower rooms. And guest bedrooms. Knock yourself out. There are only five of us here tonight. We've got loads of space. You're more than welcome to stay over, but you will need to tell me what the hell you've all been doing down those drains at some point.'

Well, that's all right then. Not.

The ground floor of the house is huge. We enter through a boot room with a washing machine and a tumble dryer, and as we go into the kitchen, it's all pale pinewood doors and black sparkly surfaces, leading to a large kitchen diner, where two women are busy loading dishes and cups into a dishwasher under the counter. They must have some money to have a dishwasher already. I can still remember Mum getting our first one.

'Some of my mates need a room for the night, Granty,' Tracy says. 'And a wash.'

'We're not that dirty,' Jasper says.

'You're entitled to your opinion, of course,' Tracy says. 'You've obviously been living rough. You don't have to pretend with us, you know.'

The older of the two women turn and face us, and I'm struck straight away by how similar they look. Both blonde-haired, both athletic like Tracy, with bright blue eyes and freckles. The older woman has more lines around her eyes and her mouth, with a faint scar across her right eyebrow, and she's the one who wipes her hands on a tea towel first, holding out a hand for one of us to shake.

'Do come in and make yourselves at home,' she says smoothly. 'You are very welcome. I'm Tracy's Great-Aunt Esmé, but for God's sake don't call me that. It makes me feel old.'

'So I call her Granty,' Tracy says, affectionately.

I'm only aware of the world slipping away from me as I stumble onto my knees on the stone floor, and Ani, Jasper and Tracy rush over to help me.

'Poor girl. She needs soup, Mother. Warm her up some chicken soup,' the younger woman says, kneeling down in front of me. She's vaguely familiar, but my brain is fried. 'I'm Angela, Tracy's auntie. How long is it since you last had a meal?'

Well, there's a bloody good question. I had burger and chips in London in 2019? How long ago is that? No, don't go there. 'I am hungry,' I say weakly. Jasper nods in agreement.

'She needs more than soup. I'll heat up some of this meat pudding and do some Smash with it,' Esmé says, heading for a tall white narrow fridge.

They prop me up on a massive sofa overlooking the back garden, and Angela puts the kettle on. I'm annoyed at myself for being such a klutz but I haven't eaten in ages, and now I'm face to face with the woman whose life we helped to save in 1940 – maybe both women's lives if Angela was the baby – and she is a close relation of Tracy Rutherford.

The tea, when it arrives, is strong and sweet. Tracy doesn't bang on about the drains in front of the two older women. Me, Ani and Jasper eat steak and kidney pudding with mash made from a packet with real butter, milk and lots of salt on trays on our laps, watching *Staying Alive* on the TV with a very young John Travolta. Tracy calls him John Revolting. To be fair, he's not revolting, but his clothes are a bit tight and silky. Maybe she'll need to see him in *Pulp Fiction* before she finds him less disgusting.

When the film ends, it's not that late, but we all go to our rooms anyway. Me and Ani have to share while Jasper shares with Ian, but I'm so tired, I'm asleep on the soft, clean sheets before Ani can even begin to cross-examine me about our next move, or what we're going to tell Tracy about our adventures in the drains.

I know what Tracy's like. I saw the way she took Lizzy apart over her relationship with Scott Kelly. Tracy's like a dog with a bone once she gets an idea in her head. We won't just be able to slip away down Town Hill in the morning after a cup of tea and some cereal.

I wake to the smell of coffee and the sound of Ani munching toast in a comfy looking beanbag. Finally free of the long coat and platform boots, she's wearing a blue T-shirt, bleached jeans and a pair of black Reebok Hightops. She's watching a tiny white cube of a television in the corner of the room, with a triangular-shaped aerial on top and a black and white picture showing a kids' programme singing the words "Ready to play? What's the day?" at her.

'Wish I bloody knew,' she mutters to herself.

The coffee and toast on my bedside table are still warm,

and the blocky black-and-white digital alarm clock beside the bed says 10:35 in square infrared numbers. I sit up abruptly. Ani turns away from a guy with a beard telling her to wave at people if she knows them.

10:35? 'Why didn't you wake me up?' I exclaim. 'It's nearly lunchtime!'

'They said I should leave you to rest. To be honest, I've only been awake fifteen minutes or so.' Ani takes another bite of her toast. 'If Rob's left the Dials by the time we get there, the Witan can get him brought back. I've been thinking though.'

I learned a while back that when Ani starts thinking, it's usually worth checking out, even if she can be a bit of a tool. 'About what?'

'You know Tracy's going to bang on until she finds out why we climbed out of her great-aunt's drains. Are you going to come up with another load of spiel about why we need to go running all the way to London after two boys they don't know? Quite honestly, I'm done with all the lies. Look where lying to Lizzy got you.'

I nibble on my toast and marmalade. 'What are you suggesting? We come out with the whole "Maisie's descended from the daughter of a Valkyrie" blah de blah?' I'm about to laugh at my bad joke until I see the humourless face looking back at me. 'You're serious, aren't you?'

'Why not?' she replies, putting her unfinished toast on the plate on her lap. 'Everyone else knows now.'

'It's not my place to spill the tea on Lizzy's secrets. She'll hate me even more.'

'She doesn't hate you,' Ani says calmly. 'She's pissed off that you lied to her, and she needs some time to get her head around things. You can tell Tracy and the others who you are, and what's going on, without bringing Lizzy into it.'

This much is true. This toast is heavenly. 'Did you come up with anything else while you were thinking?' I ask between munches.

'You said you and the boys saved Esmé and her child from a burning building in the War.'

'Can't be sure it's the same Esmé, but it's a bit of a coincidence, don't you think?'

She nods. 'And she has a tunnel leading to a Weydoor at the bottom of her garden.'

'So you think they might be Weyfarere?'

She shrugs. 'I didn't say that. There's a manhole just up the path from my house, but I've never considered going down it to see if it happens to lead to a portal through Time. Why should they know what's down there?'

'I remember Helen saying not all families continue the tradition of the guardian.' I bob my head from side to side, weighing up the comment, and drinking some coffee. 'Or it might've been Glenda that said it. D'you think Tracy's going to accept what we say?'

'She might need some proof,' Ani says cautiously.

'If she needs some proof, I might need something stronger than coffee.' I swing my legs out of bed and finish my breakfast.

'Your clothes are at the end of the bed. Don't ask me what time those women would have had to wake up to get everything clean and dried. Tracy's put another black tee on the pile as well, since you appear to have become a Goth in the last 30 years.' Ani gets up and picks up my now empty plate. 'I'll take these downstairs, and you can have some privacy to wash and dress.'

'You don't have to go,' I say. She stops and raises her eyebrows at me. 'I just mean – look, you aren't the bestie I used to chill with, and I wasn't even your friend. We may not be from the same versions of the timeline, but we've been through a lot together recently and I'd like to think we were over all that.'

She stares at me for a few seconds, and I can't read her expression. Then she smiles, and it's a genuine, open smile, if a bit small. 'Okay. I think we're over all that too. You should still have some privacy though.' She moves over to the doorway, hesitates and turns back. 'And don't expect me to get off Jasper's back anytime soon,' she adds, her brown eyes twinkling.

'That boy is a box of rocks.'

As she walks out the door, I grab a towel; wrap myself in a short, silky pink dressing gown embroidered with dragons from the pile of clothes at the end of the bed, and walk out onto the large sunny landing in search of a shower. I can't help wondering what this place would've looked like before the bomb fell, but whoever redesigned it did a good job. Not like the mess I've made of things so far.

I get where Ani is coming from. Lying to Lizzy about who I am has left her much angrier than I imagined. Even Kim and Brian, our friends from 1987, had looked hurt and confused by our secret. I set out with such good intentions to protect them all, and it's all backfired. I am a total tard, but snorkelling through my own stupidity isn't going to get Rob back. By the time I finish my shower, my mind is made up.

May 26th 1987 is cooler than it was on the day of the Fundraiser Disco, and there are clouds over our heads. I've suggested to Tracy that they still go out in the garden to study and, fortunately, she's got enough sense to get my meaning. So we're sitting on blankets on the lawn with glass bottles of Corona cherryade and limeade in a tin bucket full of water and a plate covered in packets of Salt 'n' Shake, Space Raiders and Chipsticks. Ian has also brought out a huge plain blue hardback book called *Nuffield Advanced Chemistry*. I mean, just looking at it makes me glad I studied something else. Be interesting to see how long it keeps his attention once me, Jasper and Ani get started.

Tracy just has a notebook with her. She's looking slightly less circus act today. The purple Converse are still on her feet but she's in blue and white tight stripy trousers with a baggy, white blouse tied under her boobs. She lights a cigarette, and passes the golden packet around. When we decline, she pulls a face, as if we're the ones making the bad health choices. 'So, the drains. How in hell did you lot end up kipping down there?'

'We never slept down there,' I say, looking straight at Jasper. It's been impossible to communicate my decision to him, as I haven't been able to get him alone; I just hope he catches on.

'Oh - you really are going to do this now?' he asks, taking a packet of crisps. "Let's hope you get a better reaction this time.'

'We aren't runaways like we told you,' I tell Tracy and Ian. 'We're time travellers.'

The words come out much easier than I imagined they would. There is silence for maybe three or four seconds as they smoke, before they both laugh.

'Good one,' Tracy says. 'And the truth?'

'That is the truth.'

Ian snorts and shakes his head. 'Come on, joke over. It's not even that funny.'

'We originally came from 2019. There's a portal in the Old Library at Drake's. We call it a Weydoor. It's like a fracture in the dimensions; it allows people to slip backwards and forwards in Time,' I go on, ignoring Ian's sneer. 'We didn't know how to tell you guys what had happened to us when we met you because we didn't think you'd believe us, but then I found out my family were the Guardians of the Weydoor in Stoneford.'

'Guardians? Like She-Ra?' Ian asks, completely straight-faced.

'I have no idea who She-Ra is,' I say. 'Tracy asked me for the truth and I'm giving you the truth. I didn't say it would be easy to believe.'

'That calculator you had when we met,' Tracy says slowly, looking at Ani. 'It was freaky, I admit.'

'Wasn't this Ani,' Jasper says.

'Wasn't a calculator.' I add, pulling my smartphone out of my bumbag and placing it on the blankets between us all. 'This is an *iPhone TenR*. It's like a mini computer, I guess. It is a calculator, but it's also a phone and it does all sorts of other stuff.'

Tracy picks it up and turns it over in her hands. 'You disappeared,' she says to Ani.

'Apparently,' Ani replies.

'You disappeared at Lizzy's party,' Ian says, 'and then you showed up at Tracy's garden party on Sunday.'

'Not the same person,' I try to explain. 'We did something in 1987 and the first Ani vanished. We call it extinction. This is another Ani.'

'Ani 2.0,' Jasper says.

'You make her sound like *Metal Mickey*,' Tracy says.

'Better than *Ben 10*,' Jasper replies.

'Sitting right here!' Ani snaps.

'So, who's the President of the USA where you come from?' Ian asks.

'Donald Trump,' Ani replies.

'You're expecting us to believe the American President is named after a fart?' Ian asks.

Tracy tucks her knees beneath her and stubs her cigarette out on the grass. 'But you still haven't explained why we saw you climb out of the manhole in the road,' she says. 'If you weren't sleeping down there and you aren't runaways, what were you doing there?'

'We found another Weydoor,' I say.

'Another portal,' she says. 'In the sewer.' I pull a face. ' Okay, not a sewer. And are you in charge of that one as well?'

I shake my head, no. 'We don't know much about it, but it works.'

'Let's get this straight,' Ian says. 'You three are time travellers from the 21st century. There are two time portals here in sleepy old Stoneford that mean you can travel back in Time -'

'Not just us. Anyone,' Jasper interrupts.

Ian frowns at him, '- that mean *anyone* can travel back in Time, and one of them is at the bottom of a sewer drain? Just what kind of pillocks d'you think we are to believe a story like that?'

'To be honest,' Ani says, 'it's a whole lot more complicated than that, but it'll do you for now.'

She looks at Tracy and Ian, and they just snort and giggle at each other. Why would I honestly expect anything less? Would I believe this if I hadn't seen the things I'd seen, and met the people I'd met?

'You can laugh at us,' Jasper says, 'but why would we go to the trouble of making up something so extra and totally unbelievable?'

'Because you are druggies, I bet,' Ian says. 'Taking acid tabs that make you think you're living in an episode of *Dr Who*.'

'So how do you explain that?' Ani says, pointing down at my *iPhone*, still lying on the blanket like an embarrassing photo. 'You think that's a tardis?'

'Like you said at the time, it's just a fancy calculator from Athena,' Tracy replies.

'So if we took you down the manhole and showed you the Weydoor, would you believe us then?' I ask. 'Come with us now, and I'll show you that we're not druggies or liars or whatever else you think of us.' I take a deep breath. 'We lied to Lizzy about it and she threw a benny. That's why she's not here. I don't want to tell any more lies. If you don't want to come and see what we're talking about, that's cool, but you don't have the right to throw shade unless you come see, and then we'll get going after our blud.' Which is what I want to do, but I'm not holding out much hope.

Tracy lights another cigarette. 'Fine,' she says. 'You prove to us this garbage you're spouting is the truth. I don't understand half the crap you say. But Sod help me, if I get these new Converse all mucky just so you get to faff about and play your little pranks on us, I will boot you all the way down Town Hill to where the down 'n' outs kip in the Railway Gardens.'

Whether she's related to a forgotten Weyfare family or not, they live within a shout of an active Weydoor, and someone needs to start guarding it, because if we can ride through it, any one can.

Chapter Three – Break Every Rule
(Tina Turner, 1987 (1986))

'Perhaps you might want to consider changing out of your best shoes then,' Ani says, crossing her arms. 'Have I borrowed anything else you don't wish to get *mucky*?' I don't expect the emphasis on the final word was lost on any of us. 'Or might you think that a joke entailing a wade through Stoneford's sewage is a step too far, even for us?'

Sometimes I could still hug Ani. But I don't feel like that often, and I know she'd punch me if I tried. I pick up my *iPhone* instead, and put it back in my bumbag.

Ian stands up and wipes the crisp crumbs onto the blanket. 'What do you want me to tell your olds?'

Tracy frowns. 'Aren't you coming?'

Ian snorts. 'Got better things to be doing than going on a wild goose chase down your drains.'

'Too gutless to even accept it might be the truth?' I ask.

He makes a noise like he's stifling a sneeze. 'Are you seriously asking me that question?'

'Well, I'm game for a laugh. Anything's got to be better than Geography revision. As long as it doesn't involve sewage,' Tracy says, putting her hands on her hips. 'I told you – these Converse are new. Mum and Dad only gave them to me yesterday. I don't want them covered in shit.'

'I know I said I wanted a distraction, Trace, but this is bloody stupid,' Ian says, taking the cigarette from her and drawing on it.

Tracy pats him on the arm like he's a pet dog. 'Don't throw a pink fit, sweetness. You're a scientist. Don't you want to know if there's a time portal under Town Hill?'

'Of course there bloody isn't,' he replies scathingly, but his face looks less convincing.

'Brian believed us,' Jasper says. 'We took him with us to 2019.'

'*Brian* knows about this?' Ian's face is now as confused.

'And Kim,' Jasper says. 'And Lizzy, obviously.' He glances up at me. 'They've all ridden the Weys with us.'

'Are you people completely off your rockers?' Ian exclaims. 'What's that?' he adds, because I have decided they need to see more evidence before we get them down the rabbit hole, and this is the least icky of the proof in my bumbag.

'This book is called *The Trewthe of the Weyfarere*,' I say, holding the little purple leather-bound book in my hands. 'It's passed from eldest daughter to daughter down through the Weyfare families. It's written in Middle English, but it's been translated.'

'Not particularly well, in places,' Ani adds, with more than a tinge of smug.

Now I have their attention – ironically, even more of it than when I showed them the *iPhone*.

Tracy takes the book from my hands as if it's made of glass.

'Read the front page,' I tell her.

She opens the book, carefully turns the thin pages to the first piece of writing and her eyes scan down the page. Ian reads over her shoulder.

Then she looks at me. 'Where did you get this?'

'It's mine,' I say with conviction. 'I am the youngest of the Stoneford Weyfarere. We guard the Weydoor at Drake's, and help lost people to find their Wey home.'

As the words come out of my mouth, I remember Lizzy saying something similar when she was challenged by Helen Davenport, the Witan of the Seven Dials, and thinking back then that it was the first time she had sounded proud of her family's legacy, and maybe this is the first time I've felt proud saying it.

Tracy hands the book back to me. 'Show us,' she says simply, and suddenly all the mocking and sneering has evaporated into thin air, and it's replaced with a buzz of curiosity. She looks at Ian, and he confirms agreement with a firm nod.

I put *The Truth* back into my bumbag, Jasper grabs the last few packets of crisps and we head out through the iron garden gates onto the access road.

The manhole cover is as we left it; flush against the surface of the road.

'Do we need a crowbar?' Ian asks.

Ani nudges me and points at the Weysigil that we saw earlier, embossed on the surface of the metal disc. I didn't notice before, but there is a keyhole in the top of the ancient symbol that represents the past, present and future.

I pull the silver key that's hanging from a chain around my neck out from below my T-shirt and kneel down.

'Where've I seen that key before?' Tracy asks.

As I push my key into the hole in the metal, I remember that she saw Lizzy's Mum Glenda giving her daughter a similar gift for her 18th birthday. Tracy's not stupid, but right now, I hope she's having a slower day. Before I can think of a reasonable answer to her question, my key turns and the metal disc pops up above the road level so that we can lift it.

Ian and Tracy push the manhole cover aside, revealing the ladder plunging into the depths.

'Well, it doesn't stink, at least,' Tracy says into the silence.

'It doesn't stink, because it's not a sewer,' Ani replies curtly.

It was hard enough getting three of us up the rickety wooden ladder; getting five of us down it poses a few problems, a few near emergencies and borderline panic attacks before we are all on level ground. Me and Jasper click on our phone torches, and I can almost hear the reluctant feelings of wonder when Tracy and Ian finally realise they are seeing technology from the future. How will they ever cope with *Snapchat* and *Facetime*?

In the light from our phones, the passage through the caves weaves away from the ladder. I take the lead, Jasper takes the rear, and we caterpillar our way slowly, somewhere under the streets of Stoneford, through the labyrinth of ancient stone, until I see the telltale purple glow appear faintly in the distance, responding to the approach of my Weyfare blood.

As we turn the final corner into the cavern with the Weydoor, the tension in the air trebles. I turn around to face them all, in front of the glowing purple light that I already know so well. I'm totes impressed by the gaping mouths.

'This is the Weydoor,' I say. 'It's a portal. If you step through it, you could end up anywhere in Time, forward or back, unless you have a token to ground you. Weyfarere are the only ones who can travel the Weys safely. My blood binds me to the end of my natural timeline every time I ride out. I'm in 1987 right now, so my next ride would take me back to 2019.'

'So you protect this time portal?' Ian asks, reaching out a hand towards the purple light. Ani bats it away like an irritating insect.

'This isn't the Weydoor I protect. In 2019, these passages are blocked.'

'So you're saying you can't show us how it works?' Tracy asks, crossing her arms and pulling her mouth to one side. 'Why did you bring us here then?'

'Because *you* wanted to know what we were doing in the drains,' I say evenly. 'This is what we did. We came through this Weydoor, and we followed one of the passages to the ladder that comes out at the bottom of your Granty's garden.'

'Where do the other passages lead?' Ian asks, looking around.

'One leads to the Weyroom, and the other goes down to St Peter's,' Jasper explains.

'What's a Weyroom?' Tracy asks.

'St Peter's? You mean the hotel in Town? Why would this thing be linked to a hotel?' Ian asks.

'Because the hotel is linked with the Weyfarere. The Weyroom is - look, we've shown you the Weydoor. You know we're telling the truth, so can we leave now? We've got a train to catch,' I say, my patience running thin.

'You'll never catch up with them now,' Tracy waves her hand dismissively back at the passage.

'If you don't take us through this portal thing, how do we know you're telling the truth?' Ian asks.

In the light of the phone torches, Ani pivots like a netball pro. 'So would you like to give us your own conclusions as to why there might be a *glowing door hidden in a fucking cave under Stoneford*?'

'Keep your hair on,' Ian says huffily. 'I was just saying.'

'Yes, and if you don't have anything useful to say, save us the bother of hearing it.' Ani steps forward. 'If Maisie takes us through the Weydoor now, two things will happen. One: we will all arrive in 2019, where the cave system has collapsed and there is hardly any room for three people to breathe, let alone five. Two: me, Maisie and Jasper could arrive in 2019 at the same time as another version of ourselves, thus causing a paradox, which means two versions of me, Maisie and Jasper will be laid out cold. The two of you will be abandoned in 2019, with no way of knowing if or when we'll wake up, and no other choice except to ride the Weys and end up in 1356. Or 1729. Take your pick.' She pauses: I'm guessing for effect. 'Maybe Maisie could show you the Weyroom instead.'

'Did anyone else understand what she said?' Ian asks, after a pause.

'You sound like Brian when he goes off on one,' Tracy remarks, eyeing her with a certain amount of respect.

Ani crinkles up her nose. I wonder if she misses him.

'How can this place have been under my house without anyone knowing about it?' Tracy continues, staring into the glow of the Weydoor. 'Okay. Show us this Weyroom.'

I shrug my shoulders. Rob could already be on his way to Scotland by now. They could have taken him to the Dials and arranged for his travel north hours ago. I've got no idea where The Bergh is in Edinburgh. Tommy said it was a place called Boswell's Court but that's no help, and the people that might be able to help me are divided between Lizzy, who isn't talking to me, and Helen, who I only know for certain is in 1972. Where's the harm in delaying the journey to London by going back to the Weyroom? To be honest, I want to see whether we can still get into the weird little space, whether I can salvage anything and whether there is still a way into Drake's School.

We walk away from the Weydoor down the only passage we haven't used.

'So how did you find all this?' Ian asks, 'or do you make a habit of searching underground tunnels when you're a Wayfarer?'

'Weyfare,' Jasper replies. 'She's not a pair of retro sunnies.'

'Okay, smartass. The questions still stands.'

'It's a bit of a long story,' I tell them.

'We all ended up at Drake's in 1902 before it was bombed, and found an escape hatch in the Head's Offices,' Ani says.

'Not such a long story then,' Tracy says.

I should've really learned that lesson by now.

'1902? Seriously? What was that like?' Ian asks.

'The school was more like a stately home,' Ani says. 'We didn't get to see much. The Head looked as if he came from *Downton Abbey*.'

'Where's *Downton Abbey*?' Tracy asks.

'It's a TV show about posh people and their servants,' Jasper says.

'Oh, like *Upstairs Downstairs*,' Tracy replies.

'If you say so.' I can't remember how long this passage is, but I know it's a reasonable walk from Town Hill back to Drake's, and every time we turn a corner, I'm expecting a landfall or some kind of damage that prevents us from going any further, until the passage opens out and I don't know which of us is more surprised; me, Jasper and Ani who saw it over 80 years ago, or Ian and Tracy, who have never seen anything like it in their lives.

The Weyroom, as we've affectionately named it, is a room of unknown origin, full of Weyfarere artefacts, separated into three sections. The first is an open wardrobe rail, filled with hangers of clothing on racks. They are all covered in a thick layer of cobwebs, but Ani takes a plain looking shirt from one end of the rack and wafts it over the clothing, dislodging the grime until we are all coughing in showers of airborne dust. Underneath, the items are surprisingly undamaged: elaborately embroidered velvet coats, long dresses, short skirts and cotton blouses, a few pairs of velvety trousers.

'There's not much stuff here that I could wear,' Jasper says mournfully.

I pat him on the shoulder. 'Weyfarere are women, aren't they.'

He shrugs in unhappy acceptance.

The second section is a little harder to explain to Tracy and Ian. Lots of little glass vials are lined up on shelves, each containing a liquid varying in colour from a vivid scarlet to a deep almost mahogany colour.

Ian takes one down. 'I can't read the label,' he says. '26, does it say?'

I take it from him. The label is similar to the one I watched Tommy sticking onto the vial containing my blood when we were back in 2019. At the time, he knew who I was, but Lizzy and her Mum - my Nan Glenda - they didn't.

The initials are gone but it definitely says 25/1/26. 'I think so.'

'1926? 1826? 1726?' she asks.

'Are we practising counting back in 1000s now?' Tracy walks forward and takes another little bottle from the shelves. She goes to unscrew the top, and instinctively I reach out and stop her. I can't see the look on my face, but she doesn't carry on. 'What's in here?'

'Blood,' I say bluntly.

She hands it back to me. 'Eww! Why hasn't it all dried up? Are you people vampires or something?'

'You're quicker to believe we're vampires than time travellers?' Jasper asks.

'To be fair, there's not a lot in it,' she replies, wiping her dusty hands on her leggings.

'If you mix blood with methanol, it enables the platelets to stay fluid,' Ian says. 'I'm not sure how useful the blood would be in a transfusion, or how much DNA would be preserved.' You never know when you're going to need a chemist for back up. He gives me an appraising look. 'Do you know *why* your blood is special?'

I shake my head, no.

Tracy has moved on from the blood, and is lifting items from the third set of shelves. She's holding a gold brooch, with the silhouette of a woman's head carved in what looks like white stone, with a tag attached. 'So we've got fancy dress, and now we've got props. You sure this isn't some big hoax, and we're just backstage in some old theatre?'

'Except that there's a glowing underground door,' Ian adds, with a nod in Ani's direction. She tuts like an old-school teacher and turns away from him.

'Except that there's vials of blood,' Jasper tells her.

'Except that Maisie has an archaic book handwritten in Middle English,' Ian says. 'I think they're on the level, Trace. Hard as it is to believe, I don't have any other explanation for what we're seeing right now.' He turns back to us. 'I'm sorry I called you druggies.'

'No worries,' Jasper says with a smile.

Tracy nods slowly, and then she grins broadly. 'So as long as we stick with you, we can go anywhere we like in Time and still get back to revise? Can we go to LiveAid? I couldn't get tickets before.'

'It doesn't work like that. See this brooch? This is a token. It was given to someone on-' I shine my torchlight on the dusty label, 'February 14th, 1957. So if we held this when we rode on the Weys, it would take us back to the time when this brooch was given as a gift.'

'And then we come back here, right? So I just need to find something from July 1985.'

'And where do you propose to find that?' Ani asks.

Tracy scowls at her. 'But it works in principle, doesn't it?'

'No, because Maisie couldn't get you back here to 1987 again,' Ian says. 'That's right, isn't it? So to get here in the first place, you needed a … what did you call it? Something that was given to you in 1987?'

I pull Tommy's hanky from my bumbag. 'A token. This was given to me by a friend so that we could find him again,' I say.

Tracy's grin is back but now it's sly. 'This wouldn't happen to be the bloke you're planning on chasing up London?'

'It's complicated,' I say, and everyone laughs.

'Sorry, but after everything you've told us and shown us so far, you choose a hanky to tell us things are complicated?' Tracy says, when she finishes snickering.

'Well, they are,' I say glibly. 'You want a short story? Weyfarere have enemies. Enemies that want to control the Weys and mess about with the Master Timeline. A good friend of ours has been falsely accused of being one of these enemies, and he's being taken to prison.'

'Finally she's getting the hang of the short stories,' Jasper says, pleasantly.

'So he's been arrested?' Ian asks.

'I guess so, though not in the way you think.'

'Where are they taking him?' Tracy asks.

'Somewhere in Edinburgh,' I say, flustered that they're

beginning to see the fatal flaw in my not-so-brilliant plan. 'It's called the Bergh.'

'Edinburgh's a big place,' Ian says.

'The people in London will know where the Bergh is,'

'Will these people be paying for your travel? How much cash have you got on you? Because three train tickets to Scotland are going to cost you an arm and a leg,' Tracy says.

I close my eyes. Why in the name of Sod hasn't that occurred to me? Of course we'll need funds to buy our way to Scotland. Suddenly, Rob feels further and further away, and I feel like I'm letting him down all over again. Just to make things worse, the torch on my iPhone goes off.

My battery has failed, but it kickstarts me out of my self-pity.

'Forget all that,' I tell them. 'We've got to get out of here before Jasper's phone dies as well.' I step back to the shelves of vials, and literally scoop a handful into my bumbag. 'Ani, Jasper; grab as many of those tokens as you can. I don't know if or when we'll be able to get down here again.'

'Shouldn't we all grab something?' Ian asks.

'Three of us is enough.' I zip up my bumbag, and give a few more vials to Jasper.

'17%,' he says, pushing the vials into his jacket pockets.

'Ip dip to choose the passage?' I ask him. 'Drake's or -?'

45

'The "or" might give you another headache if it leads to Travellers' Rest like we think it might,' he points out, his voice low.

Shit. Travellers' Rest is Lizzy's home. Our home. I can't involve Lizzy yet. It's got to be up to her to tell her closest friends that she's Weyfare. If we show them a link between the Weyroom and Travellers' Rest, they'll ask questions I don't want to answer. If I tell them her secrets, she'll have even more reason to treat me like dog muck for the foreseeable future. Or past.

'Surely the passage up to Drake's is blocked?' I ask him. 'After the bombing?'

Jasper gives me an encouraging smile. 'Only one way to find out,' he says.

Chapter Four – Can't Wait Another Minute (Five Star, 1987 (1986))

Of course, it's not even really a passage. I peer over at the ominous dark space that marks either a blocked exit, created after the destruction of the old school building by the war-time bomb, or yet another of Drake's secrets. We first found it through a hidden door in the Head's old office in 1902, and I'm trying to think where that would be in the modern building, but all I keep coming up with is the reception area. I'm sure all the school admin staff over the years would've noticed if weirdoes dressed in crinolines, plastic boots or both kept popping up behind the photocopier. I say as much to Jasper.

'Well, at least we know it won't come out in the new Head's offices,' he says. 'They're on the fourth floor.'

'Copperfield would have a hissy fit,' Tracy says.

'Especially as she caught us snooping around her rooms two days ago,' I point out.

Tracy's eyes widen by half. 'What in the name of Sod were you doing poking around at Drake's at the weekend?'

'Looking for my book. Okay. Jasper, you go first.'

'Why me?' he whines.

'Because you're the only one with a working torch,' I say.

'16%,' he says, and passes it to me. 'You have it then.'

Sighing, I flash the phone torch over to the corner, expecting to see rubble and no way through.

But I'm wrong. When we were here before, there were steep wooden slats, like a short ladder, rising up to where the hatch opened out of the bookcase; now there are no steps left, just a steep slope, and darkness.

'Let's get going then,' Ian says impatiently, 'I want to see where it comes out.'

I'm not claustrophobic but Jasper hates small spaces. I think he's going to have a benny, so I shove him in front of me.

'I am so not going *the fuck* first,' he hisses.

'Yes, you are, or you can stay *the fuck* down here on your own in the dark. 15%.'

I have to push him, but he moves, and it doesn't take long for us to realise that we are not blocked in by bomb damage after all, just moving into a dark space. I can taste the dust in the air. I'm not comfortable, but I'm not going to let Jasper know that, or the others, to be honest. How did I end up leading all of this? I never wanted this; even less so now I have no choice. I'm the one in charge because I'm Weyfare. Now everyone bloody knows about it, I have to step up.

There is rubble but no blockage; there are broken stones here that look very much like the grey stones of the original school, the Old Library and Travellers' Rest. They don't look like they've been moved since the day the bomb exploded.

Why would you go to all the trouble of clearing the site and building a modern new school, and then leave a pile of rocks somewhere like a shrine?

Unless, of course, that's exactly what it is.

'Be careful,' I say out loud, swinging the phone torch around to shine on the floor as the others stumble out. 'I'm not sure what this is, but it might be some kind of memorial.'

Suddenly there is a huge noise in front of us. At first, I think it sounds like machine gunfire, and everyone dives to the floor. I kill the phone torch.

'Is someone shooting at us?' Tracy hisses in my ear, with a hint of hysteria.

'We're in 1987. I wouldn't put it past Valerie to arm her Guard with Kalashnikovs,' Jasper mutters.

The clattering goes on for a few more seconds and then cuts out, with an unmistakable thud. Maybe they shot each other.

'She may not have a Guard now,' Ani whispers. 'Scott never stayed in 1972.'

'Are Valerie and Scott the people you're trying to catch up with?' Ian asks.

'Can I tell you about them when we're confident we're not about to be turned into kitchen sieves?' I ask quietly.

A rectangular beam of light appears, and moments later, the whole area is flooded with light. It seems we are in some kind of room, full of bits of metal machinery large and small, and open shelving not dissimilar to the ones in the Weyroom. A figure in dusty blue overalls comes in and stands with his back to us by one of the larger machines nearest the door, and, as I watch, he starts to tap at a part of it with what I think is a hammer. The electric strip lights above our head flicker but stay on, so I hand the phone back to Jasper, who pockets it. We seem to be hidden from the guy with the hammer by a combination of rocks and old filing cabinets. It's like a graveyard for old school equipment down here, but me and Jasper have seen enough of him to recognise his face. Seems like we're not the only ones.

'It's Mr Bennett,' Tracy says. 'He's the school caretaker.'

'Uncle Frank,' I confirm. 'Rob's uncle.'

'Who's Rob?' Ian asks.

FML. 'One of the guys we're trying to find,' I tell him. Used to be a good friend of yours, now you don't even know he exists, I think to myself.

'Do you think Mr Bennett will dob us in to Copperfield if he finds us?' Tracy asks. 'He always seems okay. My mum thinks I'm revising at Granty's, and if she gets a phone call from Copperfield saying I was monkeying around up here, Esmé'll confine me to my room.'

I've met Frank Bennett twice. Once was here in 1987 two days ago, before Scott Kelly messed up the timeline, and he was an older guy who let us into Drake's so we could search for *The Truth*. The other time was on my nan Glenda's birthday in 1971, when he had long curly hair, ran the bar in the basement of a church and sang in a band. Neither of those guys would think of grassing us up to a Headteacher, but this is Valerie Bennett-Simmons' little brother, and we don't know whether she's still the fake Witan of Stoneford.

'Frank Bennett might not help us,' I tell her. 'His sister's a bit of a biatch.'

'Why do I get the feeling you haven't told us everything?' Tracy asks.

'Because we haven't,' Ani says.

I watch as Frank puts his hands on his hips and mutters to himself, before turning and leaving the room. The light's still on, and he hasn't bothered closing the door.

'He'll be coming back,' I say. 'We have to risk it and leave now.'

We emerge from our hiding place into the room that looks like a cross between a junk room and a factory. The machine that sounded like gunfire has obviously failed because it's quiet now, and the walls are covered in thick padded pipes and wires. When we step out of the room, it's through a door marked "Staff Only" into a corridor I recognise, leading to the staff loos and a staff rest area. There's a door to the outside buildings near to us, and we slip out of it quickly, walking up to the junction where the paths to different school buildings cross.

'Where to now?' Tracy asks. 'Can you take us for a ride from the portal in the Old Library?'

'Weydoor,' I say, 'and no. Too risky. We need to get to London. Scotland. Whatever. I kept my end of the deal. You've seen enough to know we're on the level here.'

She nods. 'I've also seen enough to know there's not a Sod's chance in Hell of me doing any revision knowing you're on a jolly, gallivanting all over the country and time travelling. There's no way you're going on your own.'

'To be honest, it does sound a lot more fun than revising thermodynamic equations,' Ian says. 'But you think Esmé and Angela are going to let you flit off on holiday when they were left strict instructions to keep you on track?'

'No. But they're time travellers, Ian!' She stares at me. 'We could be away for a week, and still come back to today. That's right, isn't it?'

'In theory,' I say carefully.

'With the right token,' Jasper adds.

'You need to have something on you that was given to you today for the token to bring you back to the exact date,' Ani explains. 'The greater the emotional attachment to it, the more likely it is to work.'

'It might not work?' Tracy asks.

'Time travel comes with its own risks and dangers,' Ani replies. 'You need to show it some respect. Don't you, Maisie?'

'It's irrelevant, Tracy,' Ian says. 'You haven't got anything that you were given today.'

'How about yesterday?' Tracy lifts up a slim leg and points at her new purple Converse All-Stars.

She's like a dog with a freaking bone. 'Honestly? The boots should bring you back to the time when you were given them. If you use the Old Library, you'll arrive here yesterday, and create a loop.' I'm making it sound so basic. 'You'll have to lie low until the loop is finished.'

Tracy claps her hands together like a child that's been told it's going to Disneyland. 'And then it'll be like we were never away! Ian? Come *on*.'

She's broken him. 'Sounds like utter madness,' he says, but I can tell he's already caved. 'As long as you can get me back for my Thursday evening shift at the Amber Teapot. I can't afford to lose my summer job.'

It occurs to me that I've had no say in this. Tracy's very like Lizzy in one respect; she gets an idea into her head and nothing can move her off base. I'm not fussed whether they come with us or not, to be honest. There's probably safety in numbers. Other issues are bothering me more now.

'If we don't find a way of getting there, none of us is going anywhere. No funds, remember?' I tell them.

'I thought of that. We could ask Will if he'll take us,' Tracy says. 'Mum gave me some money. I could pay Will to drive us to London. Maybe even Scotland.'

'It's not a trip to the beach! You can't ask him to drive us to *Scotland*!' Ian exclaims.

'We need to get to London, not Scotland,' I say firmly. 'They may be holding our boy at a place we know near Covent Garden, and if not, the people there will know where they've gone.'

'We can't ask Will to help,' Jasper says firmly.

'Why not?' Tracy asks.

'We have a problem with Brian, as well as Lizzy, don't we?' Jasper says, glancing at Ani. She nods once.

'Thinking about it, he'll be working today, anyway,' Tracy remarks, looking up at the Old Library. 'Is there really a time door in our school library? I thought that was just stories the third made up to scare the first years. How come we never noticed it?'

'It's invisible unless it's in the presence of a Weyfare.' I sigh. This is not getting me any closer to Tommy and Rob. 'Look -'

'Oi!' A voice shatters the silence around us. I turn on the spot, not sure what I'm expecting to see: the Guard, the headteacher Marguerite Copperfield, Frank Bennett, Lizzy – but it's none of those.

It's Neil Thorpe's friend Ed.

We first met Ed when he was pissed and we borrowed his car to get up to Trinity, and again when he took us to Travellers' Rest in his van. That last time didn't turn out so well, but he's not running away from us, so I'm wondering how much things have changed for him.

'Ed?' Jasper says. 'You've recovered from our little standoff with the Bennett's then.'

As I suspected, he frowned. 'What standoff? Maisie, isn't it? What you lot doing up here? It's the school holidays, isn't it?' He looks around hopefully. 'Where's your sexy mate?'

'Kim's not here,' I say. 'We just came to collect some books we needed for revision. What're you doing up here?'

'Oh, I've come to collect the food surplus. Anything perishable in storage that'll go bad before the start of the new term, Drake's always donates it to Trinity for the old people and the tramps so it don't go to waste.' He waves back in the direction of the blue Ford Transit van, parked on the side of the access road. Well, who knew?

'I know you,' Tracy says, stepping ever so slightly in front of me. 'You're the bassist with Divine Morrissey. You fellas were kicking it at Lizzy's party.'

He pushes his fingers through the spiky hair on top of his head like a peacock preening itself. 'We always kick it, babe. What's your name?'

'I'm Tracy,' she says, high-key flirt mode engaged.

I need to power her down. 'Couldn't give us a lift into Town, could you?' I ask him sweetly.

'All of you? Thought you said you were revising.'

'Give us girls a break, why don't you?' Tracy says with a grin.

'So are we on for this lift or not?' I ask him.

He gives me a lecherous wink. 'For you, baby, anything.'

He's a fickle sleaze, but it'll give me time to formulate the seed of a plan involving a guy who's a walkover with the girls, his van, Tracy's money and a trip to London to find the guy who might well be my soul mate – if I can work out which one. Yay me.

Chapter Five – Livin' On A Prayer
(Bon Jovi, 1987 (1986))

Ed may be in a band, but there is no musical equipment in the back of the van as we all pile inside, just shallow wooden crates of fruit and vegetables and some cool boxes that I guess must be for meat. Ed says he has to collect a few more of these before he's ready to leave, so we settle down in the back.

I spring my question on him once he returns. 'You know how you just said you'd do anything for me?' I ask.

Ani raises an eyebrow, and Jasper coughs gently. Yeah, I know what they're thinking, just how many boys does she want on her side – but it's not like that; I'm working out my plan of action.

'I thought I was already giving you a lift into Town,' Ed says, grinning as he slides another box into the van.

'We'll pay you for another favour,' I say quickly. I should probably have checked this out with Tracy, but if she was willing to pay Will, it's not so different.

Ed stretches his back out, rolls his head around a couple of times, and looks at me. 'Okay,' he says. 'Shoot.'

'We might need your van.'

'My van?'

'We might need to get to Scotland,' Tracy explains.

'*Scotland*?'

'You know, Ed. Mountains. Bagpipes. Irn-Bru,' Ian says.

'London will do, 'I tell him. 'We'll give you petrol money and a bit more as well, if you like. It's really important, Ed – we have to get there as soon as we can.'

'London's not a problem. I'm not taking you to fucking *Scotland*,' Ed says. 'I'm on my other job tomorrow, babe. Six to twos. There's no way I can get you up to Scotland and back in time for my shift.' He looks at me in confusion. 'What the fuck d'you want to go to Scotland for?'

'We've got to rescue someone,' Jasper says.

'In *Scotland* though?'

I sigh loudly. 'I didn't even say Scotland! They said Scotland! Will you stop saying Scotland like it's in Narnia? I want to go to London!'

'Fair enough then.' He lights a cigarette. 'If it's London, you're in luck. I got to take this food up to Trinity, and then I've got to do a favour for a mate who needs some stuff shifting up to the City. You can bunk down in the back with his gear.'

'Could we borrow the van after that if we need it?' Ani asks.

Everyone looks at her.

Jasper slams his hands down hard on the metal floor. 'I am not driving this van all the way to Scotland on a provisional! It was bad enough driving the Shagmobile through the middle of Stoneford!'

'Not you, tool,' she says thinly. 'I can drive.'

'You can drive?' Tracy asks, with a rare air of admiration.

'Passed my test after thirty lessons,' Ani says proudly. 'Dad helped out with extras, to be fair. I don't need a special licence to drive a Transit, do I? Can we borrow your van, Ed?'

'You can take the Shagmobile to work, can't you?' Jasper asks him.

'The van's yours until Friday. I need it back then 'cos we've got a gig in Ashbridge that evening.' Ed hauls the last of the boxes into the van and eyes Ani doubtfully. 'You sure you got a full licence?'

'I have,' she replies haughtily.

'Are you fully comp?' he asks. 'Because I'm not paying for no shunt if you have a prang halfway up the M1.'

'My insurance is fine,' she says.

I don't see how it can be fine since she's not even been born yet, but if convincing him it's okay makes the difference between us getting the loan of the van for a couple of days or not getting it, I'm game.

It feels like the sun's come out. We may not even need to borrow the van if we find Rob and Tommy at the Dials. I'm not sure about Tracy and her crew tagging along, but what right do I have to tell them what to do when they should be revising? We all know I can get them back here with a token, and Tracy's Converse are as good a token as any. I know I've not got a clue where the Bergh is, but if the Seven Dials is still safe, I can explain what I know to the Witan, whoever she is. I can tell her that Rob isn't related to the Weyleighers. She will sort it out. If Tommy's already left, we'll just wait for him to return. I don't want to think about the possibility that the Dials aren't safe, or that Tommy and Rob didn't go there. I'll worry about that if it happens. It'll be handy to have some wheels.

'We'll have it back to you in a day or two,' I assure Ed out loud.

He nods once, and slams the rear doors of the van closed.

It's a bumpy ride to Trinity in the back of a Ford Transit with the fruit and veg, but eventually the doors reopen, and Ed's grinning in at us again. 'I'll get this job done a lot quicker if you can help me out with carting it over to the storage rooms,' he says.

Another day, another version of Trinity. No longer the Church of the Blessed Holy Trinity as it was in 1972, the building is now a shadow of its former self again – renting out the huge cathedral-like space to local bands for gigs and parties at night, while still providing food and shelter for Stoneford's street community during the day. When we were here in 1972, the vicar was Valerie Bennett-Simmons' dad, and the Bennetts had women like Dolores Umbridge's army in felt hats and cotton scarves, collecting information from Stoneford's Lost over cups of what just about passed for soup. When we were last here in 1987, the Bennetts were like the local mob and no one wanted to mess with them. Things should be different now. Scott's not Valerie Bennett's partner, and Rob's not her son. All the same, as me, Jasper and Ani climb out of the van, I know they are watching their backs as much as I am, and it doesn't go unnoticed.

'Is there something wrong?' Ian asks, dragging a cool box out of the van. 'You look like you're expecting to be arrested or something.'

'Time travel is complicated,' Jasper says, grabbing another crate of fruit. 'You're coming along for the ride, so you'll soon see what we mean.'

I place one of the crates of fresh vegetables on the floor of the storage room. The door at the back is blocked from view by huge shelving units stacked with tinned chopped tomatoes, Campbell's soup and meatballs. It doesn't look like anyone's come through it for a while.

Ed drops a crate of lettuce at my feet.

'Who's the mate moving to London? Any one we know?' I ask casually, just to make conversation.

'Not sure. D'you know Scott Kelly? I heard a rumour he was messing about with your mate Lizzy.'

Tracy looks at me, just arrived at my side with a sack of potatoes. 'Patchouli's moving house?'

I stand up straighter. '*Scott's* the friend who's leaving Town?'

Jasper drops a crate of cabbages on the floor behind me. I can feel his tension. 'He's going to London?'

'Told me he knows some bird up there. He's selling the shop soon as he can get a taker.' Ed looks at us all in surprise. 'Why're you all acting like it's the end of the world?'

Shit. I feel like all the life is draining out of me. My whole existence is suddenly on the edge. 'Doesn't he share the flat with some other guy?'

'Tim, yeah. Tim's going to stay and manage the place until it's off their hands. He's moving on with Scott. Scott reckons they've got work lined up in the West End.'

Tim, yeah. That's Tim Wharton. My dad, Tim Wharton, who meets my mum in Stoneford. Not London. They get together sometime in the early 1990s; they fall in love, get married and eventually, after having my brothers Lucas and Blake, they have me. The first-born daughter. The next daughter in line born to the Stoneford Weyfarere. If Tim goes to London with Scott, he'll never meet my Mum. They'll never have kids. Me, Lucas and Blake will be extinguished. I feel like I've been punched in the , and I can't catch my breath.

'Are you okay?' Tracy asks, dropping the sack beside mine and staring into my face.

'Not really,' I tell her.

She nods. 'They're serving burgers and soup in the canteen. Maybe you need something to eat? I think I do too. Lizzy's going to go right off on one when she hears Patchouli's leaving town.'

'Maybe just a coffee,' I say.

'It's pretty much lunchtime anyway,' Ed says from the doorway. 'The grub's not bad here, and I might even get you a discount.'

So for the second time in three days, we are sitting at one of the metal camping tables on plastic school chairs next to the serving hatch at the back of Trinity. The coffee still looks and tastes like watery mud, but at least Ed's sober this time and the burger is cooked well; it's just my stomach is churning too much to finish it. Knowing what I know now, it's hard not to look around at the street people and check them out for the giveaway signs that they're the Lost: Fitch hoodies, Timber-land boots, bowler hats and long dresses trimmed with grimy lace.

Even with that distraction, I still feel unwell. Jasper is fidgety like a tiny kid; I can tell he's desperate to talk to me about Scott and Tim but I don't want to risk it – it's too close to being Lizzy's story as well as mine. What will happen to me? How soon will I know I'm in danger? Ani was ill for a while before she vanished. I don't feel well now. I thought it was because of the news of Scott and Tim leaving, but suddenly I'm scared that it's more ominous than that.

I knew Tommy was right when he told Lizzy that she needed to take Scott to the Bergh. Now he's taking the wrong guy there, and Scott, with all the knowledge he has of Lizzy's family being Weyfare, is going free. Even if I wasn't worried about my imminent extinction, Scott suddenly deciding to leave Stoneford worries me. Lizzy only bought him back to 1987 yesterday, and he didn't look in good enough shape to be climbing a flight of stairs, let alone packing up and moving out. Is he running away, maybe from the person who stabbed him? Or is he up to something more sinister? Who does he know in London? Could it be something to do with Valerie?

She must be in her late thirties now, like Glenda is in 1987. She jumped back through the Weydoor in 1972 and we've got no idea where she went, or where she is now. In all the chaos that exploded when Rob came back and Lizzy learned I was her daughter, the fact that Valerie had ridden the Weys to an unknown destination dropped under my radar. It suddenly hits me that, since we've been here, no one's mentioned her. The family must still be around, because her brother Frank is still the caretaker at Drake's. Last time we were with Ed, the family were the Stoneford equivalent of the Krays.

I put my half-eaten burger down on the white china plate and turn to face Ed, who is stuffing the end of a hot dog into his mouth. 'Ed, do you know the Bennetts?' I ask, as carelessly as I can.

Ed wipes the tomato sauce and mustard off his mouth with the back of his hand, and shakes his head, no.

'What about the Simmons?' Ani asks.

Ed lights a cigarette. 'Only Simmons I know is the bloke who runs the hotel down by the bottom of St Peter's Hill. Where the old hospital used to be?'

'What's his wife's name again?' Jasper asks carelessly, pouring more HP fruity sauce onto the side of his plate of chips.

Ed looks strangely vacant. 'That's weird. I want to say Val, but I'm sure it's Sheila.'

Ani, me and Jasper exchange looks.

'Robin Simmons is going out with my next door neighbour,' Ian says. 'He was in my form when we were in the 5th.'

Robin Simmons?

'The 5th?' Jasper asks.

'5th form. The year you take your 'O' levels?' Tracy tries to explain.

'Year 11. GCSEs,' Ani explains better.

My head feels like my brain is in a blender. If Robin Simmons is the son that died, how come he's still alive? This gets added to my ever-growing list of things to find out, and now I have to do them all before Scott and Tim get me extinguished. FML.

'You suffering from amnesia or something, forgetting the year you took your 'O' Levels.' Ed checks his black plastic Swatch watch and stands up. 'You lot stay here. I've asked Mandy behind the counter to keep you topped up with tea. Once I've picked Scott and his stuff up, I'll come back for you.'

'No, I want to come with you,' I say, standing up next to him.

'You want to help me shift more boxes in and out of my van?' Ed looks me up and down. 'You nearly keeled over from the effort of carrying a tray of carrots, babe. Best leave the hard labour to the fellas.'

Before Ani attacks him with a fork for being a chauvinistic asscloth, I say, 'I need to speak to Scott before he leaves Town.

Without an audience.'

'He won't appreciate any sob stories,' Ed points out. 'He's never been one for steady girlfriends. Plus he got in a fight the other day, and he's in a bad way.'

You. Have. No. Idea. 'I don't want to talk about that stuff. We've got some unfinished business. And no,' I add, raising my voice as Tracy prepares to launch herself across the little table towards me, 'not that kind of unfinished business. The guy's a tool.'

'If he's in a bad way, you could probably do with some help,' Jasper suggests, finishing off the last of his chips. 'I'm sure you don't want to be lugging his boxes into your van all by yourself.'

Ed regards him thoughtfully. 'Hadn't thought of that. Maybe I could do with a hand.'

'How about you take it as part-payment for the loan of the van?' Ani holds her hand out to shake on the deal.

He laughs, but he shakes on it. 'Cheeky cow.'

I'm hoping that Scott's parents don't still live nearby, as we met them when Glenda rented the flat upstairs, but Stoneford New Age and Natural Health Food Stores and Supplies is back to being Serendipity again, alias the Hippy Shop. The creepy dolls have left the window display, the door to the flat is blue again and there's a little black button next to a name card that I know reads 'Kelly 2b'.

'You do know he lives on the second floor,' I say to Ed as he opens up the back of the van, remembering Lizzy pointing up at the window she knew was Scott's. 'You didn't want to be carrying all of the boxes down that staircase.'

'It's just as well you met us today, isn't it?' Tracy beams out at him. 'While we're here though, I might just pop next door and stock up on my jasmine oil.'

Ed does look a bit salty, but he doesn't comment on it. 'You coming in to help or what?' he asks, pressing the little button. When it clicks, he disappears inside.

Now I'm here, the reality of the situation is a bit clearer, and my hastily formed plan sucks even more. Scott made it obvious that he didn't want to see us again as long as he lived, and I don't think he was planning on it only being two days later. He's not going to be happy about us turning up. We might even be part of the reason he's running. Do we just storm into his flat? Do I get the others to pin him down while I interrogate him? Do I tell him we've got to take him to the Bergh, and he's got to come quietly? Like that's going to happen.

'Let's just play it low-key,' Jasper says, looking at me and once again showing that weirdass knack he has developed of being able to work out what I'm thinking. 'I don't think he's going to tell us anything up front, but if you're shady about it, he might accidentally spill the tea.'

'He might,' I say, with a sideways look at the pretty, dark-eyed girl, who spent the best part of two months holding Scott Kelly's hand while he lay in a coma in a hospital bed in 1972.

Chapter Six – Into The Fire

(Bryan Adams, 1987)

'You know this.' Jasper slips out of the back of the van. 'The last time he saw Ani here, he was screaming that she wanted to kill him. He's not going to want to sit us down with a cup of chai latte while he tells his story.'

'Wrong millennium. The first time he said it, he'd just woken up from a coma in a completely different decade.' I drop to the ground beside him. 'The second was just after he'd been discharged from hospital by a sociopathic Weyleigher and forced to ride the Weys again. You don't think he might've been a tad confused both times?'

'How do you know Scott, anyway?' Ed asks, appearing back from inside the block.

'He was seeing Lizzy Brookes,' I explain. 'The rumours were true.'

'We call him Patchouli because he always smells so good. I knew he was bad news from the outset, though,' Tracy says smugly.

Ed pulls a face. 'She's a bit younger than his usual choices.'

'That sounds right skanky,' Tracy asks, pulling a black purse out of the pocket of her jeans.

'Just the opposite. He likes his girlfriends a bit older usually.' Ed grins. 'He likes them mature. Got no idea why he got off with your mate. He doesn't usually do schoolgirls. No offence. I'm not so fussy,' he adds, leering at Ani.

'Back off, asscloth,' she says, 'I wouldn't touch you with your own bass.'

'Seriously, though,' Ed says, perching on the tailgate of the van, 'everyone at Drake's and FCAB knew about Scott Kelly and his older bird. She used to meet him in her car by the tennis courts when school finished early on a Wednesday.'

'Scott was at FCAB with you?' I ask, frowning.

'Yeah. We was in the Upper Sixth together.' He pulls his mouth to one side. 'I'm sure we were.'

Ani sits beside him. 'Scott's 24 though.'

Ed looks at us. 'Nah, he's not that old. He was at school with me, Paul Brookes, Neil and Will Walker. I think. He's 20, not 24. Isn't he?' He looks confused. '21, maybe?'

I'm watching his thought processes bounce about like a ball on the centre court at Wimbledon. There is something wrong here. Scott Kelly had his 8th birthday in March 1972, so surely he was born in March 1964. That makes Scott 23 now, but I'm sure he told us once he was 24. Why would he get his own age muddled up?

Rob told me Scott had had his 40th birthday in March 1987, which means when he rode back to 1971, he *was* 24. It was how we worked out when he'd been stabbed. And even if he was 23 when he was stabbed and thrown back to 1971, these guys think he was at school with them.

The numbers don't add up. And how do I know this? Because I celebrated my 18th birthday already, but in 2019, at the end of my natural timeline, I haven't had my birthday yet. I'm still 17.

What's more interesting is Ed's reaction. It's like he's trying to retrieve memories about Scott that he expected to find, only to find they aren't there. *Because they are changed.* The time line has changed.

I turn to look at Jasper and Ani, to find them staring at me. 'We have to talk to Scott, whether he likes it or not,' I say.

Ed's eyes roll. 'I thought you came here to help out?'

'The others will. Won't you?' I say, giving them my best pleading puppy eyes.

'Why do we have to do the leg work while you have a cosy cuppa with Patchouli?' Tracy snaps.

'Because you want to come with us to London, and you're not in charge here,' Ani snaps back.

In charge here. It's great to hear she's got my back now, but it's scary as crap.

Tracy pulls a face and goes into the Hippy Shop.

Ian stands in front of me. 'I'm not sure about all this,' he says seriously.

'You and me both, but you have a choice,' I say. 'You want to bail out now, go right ahead. No one will blame you for it. Least of all me.'

He stares at the ground for a few seconds, and then seems to make a decision. 'No, it's fine. It's got to be better than sitting at home wondering what you lot get up to without me.'

'FOMO,' Jasper says, trying to be helpful.

'Bless you,' Ian says, and follows Ed up the stairs.

We follow them. The layout of the flats hasn't changed a great deal. I'm wondering why Scott opted to live in a different flat to his parents, but as I go through the front door of 2b, I have an idea why; it's a lot more spacious than the one Glenda rented, so I'm guessing it's the biggest of the three.

In the large front room, there are lots of boxes, but the bigger furniture is still in position; either the flat comes furnished or Tim is dealing with it once the shop lease is sold. The cardboard packing boxes are piled up in the corners like an oversized game of Jenga, and Scott is sprawled out on the sofa in a white vest and tight bleached jeans, with a bottle of Glenfiddich whisky nestled next to him like a dog, smoking a large joint. There is a white bandage on his side, the dressing just visible through his vest.

Ed and Ian pick up a box each and take them downstairs, but me, Jasper and Ani don't move. It's at least a minute before Scott tears himself away from the news. Apparently, there's going to be another election in a couple of weeks.

'What the fuck are you doing here?' he slurs.

'Come to help you move,' I say calmly. 'We gather you're leaving Stoneford.'

'So what if I am?' he says.

'We wondered why you felt the need to leave Town so quickly,' Ani says.

Scott gazes at her. 'Your voice. It's like an echo. I know you.'

I walk forward, and sit on an armchair across from him. 'This is Ani Chowdhury. She spent a lot of time with you when you were sick.'

'You tried to kill me!' he shouts out suddenly, but there is no one around to react, and strangely, he seems to crumple into himself as the words fade into the smoke.

'No, we didn't,' I say calmly.

'No, you didn't,' he echoes sadly. 'She told me you hurt me. The nurse. You didn't.' He looks up at Ani with bloodshot blue eyes that are somehow still as piercing as ever. 'I remember.

You sat with me.'

Ani nods, just once.

It's not exactly easy having a convo with a guy who's stoned at the best of times, let alone being a total asscloth, but I have to talk to Scott now, for a completely different reason than I first thought.

'My head – it's all mussed up,' he says, holding the joint so close to his head I expect the blond hair to go up in flames.

'I'm not surprised,' I say. 'You've had a hell of a ride. Who stabbed you, Scott?'

'I don't know,' he says, staring back at the guy reading the news. 'I'm not shitting you about; I really don't. I wasn't kidding when I said I never wanted to see you again, either. Especially the redhead.' He takes a long draw on the joint.

'Where did you go?' I ask quietly. 'After you were attacked, I mean.'

I know my instincts are right when he looks at me; there is such fear in his eyes, it's like I've threatened to re-open his stab wound.

'You know where I went,' he whispers. 'You found me.'

I shake my head, no. 'Before that,' I tell him. 'Before you landed on our feet bleeding out in 1971, where did you go?'

He puts the joint on an overflowing white ceramic ashtray, grabs the bottle of Glenfiddich and pours a decent quantity down his throat, coughing wetly like the smoker he is. 'I don't know what you -'

'Yes, you do,' I interrupt him. 'Let me help you out. You were born in 1964. Ani here went to your 8th birthday party in 1972, while the older you was recovering in hospital. I'm sure you told us you were 24 in 1987 at Lizzy's party, but you can't have been. The guy here moving your worldly goods thinks you were at school with him and that makes you 21 tops. Your numbers don't add up. You're older than everyone thinks. There's only one reason for this that I know of.'

Jasper and Ani are now staring at me.

Scott eyes me maliciously from under his long eyelashes. 'So *you* explain it, Einstein.'

'You've gained a year. Maybe two.' I step forward, and take the whisky bottle from his hand. 'So where have you been?'

The news on the TV ends, but for us, it's just beginning.

'I'm not sure,' he says, slumping deeper into the sofa.

'Try to remember,' I say determinedly. Ani sits on the arm of the sofa.

Unexpectedly he reaches out and takes her hand, like it's the most natural thing in the world. 'I've been all over,' he says, shrugging. 'When I got knifed, I got lost.'

At that moment, Ed, Tracy and Ian come back in and pick up a few more boxes. I'm aware of the filthy look Tracy gives me. I choose not to react.

Once they have gone back down to the van, I say, 'Where?'

'I don't know.' He holds his other hand out for the whisky, and I'm not sure I want him more pissed, but I give it to him. He takes a swig. 'It wasn't somewhere I recognised. Like it was a long time ago.'

'Were you a prisoner or something?' Ani asks.

Scott shrugs. 'I wasn't there long enough to be a prisoner.' He lets go of Ani's hand, pulls a squashed black packet from his jeans pocket and lights a cigarette with the lighter stored inside.

'Just spill the tea, Patchouli,' Jasper says impatiently, sitting down cross-legged in front of him on a worn patterned rug.

'All of it,' I say.

'If it gets you tossers off my back, all right. I own a shop full of pagan artefacts,' Scott says. 'My dad passed it on to me a few years back, but I've been working behind that till since I was 14. Most of it is old tat we sell to birds who are pretending to be witches, but me and Dad were at a buyer's convention one day when I found an old manuscript connecting Drake's school and an old house at the edge of The Park with a time portal. I should've told him, but I didn't. I did a bit more research, and I found out the Old Library was the only part of Drake's left standing after the Second World War.'

This much is true. 'Go on,' Ani says. He takes her hand again.

'Then this woman came into the shop. I must've been about 18. She said she was interested in information about the time portals in Stoneford, and she'd pay me well to find it. She called the portals Weydoors. She wanted to find it to smuggle goods from the past to sell at a profit. Smokes, booze – even the odd antique. I worked in a shop up the backside of Stoneford,' he says. 'I needed the money.'

'Who was the woman?' Jasper asks.

'She said her name was Vix.'

'Victoria?' I ask. 'Not Valerie?'

He shrugs, and pulls another level of calm from the cigarette. 'I only knew her as Vix. I bought the caretaker a few drinks in the pub one night, and he let me have a look around Drake's. I found the Weydoor by accident really; I was feeling around the bookshelves in the Old Library and then I just fell through. Vix had already given me a way of getting back to her in 1987. The first time it was the nuts.' He closes his eyes. 'The second time, I went shopping. I did it a lot. I hung around a few places once I realised I could. 1977 was a riot. I enjoyed being a punk that summer.'

'I had you down as more of a rocker,' I tell him.

'That was the summer of 1981. Monsters of Rock at Castle Donington: AC/DC, Whitesnake, Slade. I was into anything with a decent riff, babe,' he replies, shifting a little and wincing.

'So that's where you've gained your time,' I say. 'You've been taking holidays in Time.'

'Can you blame a bloke? I was in my element for a while back there.' The ice in the blue eyes thaws a little. 'I knew wherever that Weydoor took me, I'd come back to Vix where I left her. She always left it a good month between trips. All I had to do was come back with enough gear to make it worth her while. Never knew where I was going, and I didn't care.

'Then I did a bit more research and found out about a book connected with the Weydoor that I reckoned would be worth a decent dollar. Vix was crazy interested in that. I found out that the family who lived in the house at the edge of the Park had a kid daughter who was a looker, and I reckoned if anyone knew about this book, they did. Didn't take much to get her interested in me,' he adds smugly. 'But she didn't seem to know anything about the Weydoor, until the morning after her party.'

'We know. We were there,' I say thinly. 'So you knew about the Weydoor all along. Did you know Lizzy was Weyfare?'

'I guessed the family must have something to do with it because of the manuscript,' Scott says, 'but I didn't know how. I just knew about the Weydoor.'

'You managed to keep that quiet,' I say.

'I did, didn't I?' he replies, with a small smile that makes me shiver.

'And it was this Vix woman who stabbed you?' Ani asks.

He stares at his hands. 'Whoever it was, they were wearing a balaclava. I'd just come back from a shopping run for Vix and someone was waiting for me in the Old Library. They sliced me up and pushed me through the Weydoor and I ended up in Buggerknowswhere. There were fields and mountains. It was warm. If it was Stoneford then it must've been back in the Dark Ages, because there wasn't even a Drake's Manor House. It was nothing like I'd travelled to before. There were people singing and playing instruments. When they found me, they said I didn't belong with them and I had to leave.' He takes a deep breath, and I get the impression he's missing some of this part of the story. 'They put me straight back through the Weydoor, where I ended up at your feet.' He looks up at me, and instead of suspicion I feel an unexpected pang of pity for him. 'I've no idea where I was that last time. I don't know how old I am here. I don't want anything more to do with this now. All I know is I need to get away from Stoneford. I'm sick of being Vix's lackey, and I don't fancy being no one else's pin cushion, neither.'

There was a timeline in 2019 where we faced a dystopian world of pain, where my Mum Lizzy had died because she rode the Weys too much and her body aged quicker than her time-line. If it hadn't been for me knowing that, I'd never have considered the fact that Scott Kelly was really 24 when everyone else thought he was younger. But if he's spent his time raving in some of the 20th century's more entertaining hotspots, I can see it would be easy to lose track of time. Literally. And has he really ridden so far back on the Weys that he's gone back to a time when Stoneford was nothing but hills and fields?

'I only have one more question,' I say. 'You said Vix gave you something, so you could always get back to 1987. Like a silver key?'

He shakes his head, no. 'She didn't have a key like Lizzy. She had a locket.'

'Have you still got it?' Ani asks. I note he's still holding her hand.

'It's in one of the boxes,' he says, turning away. 'You want it – you can go find it.'

I turn and look around the room. Even with the ones that have already been taken down to Ed's van, there must be upwards of fifteen boxes here.

'How much did you tell Valerie about the Weys?'

Scott pulls his mouth down to one side. 'You said no more questions.'

'I lied.'

He shrugs. 'I told her what I knew. She grilled me a bit, after I woke up burbling about 1987. I was wired up in a hospital bed in 1972. What did I have to lose in telling her about the Weydoor? She was the only one I had to talk to.' He leans forward and relights the joint. 'I told her about the Weydoor, the keys and the tokens you need to control time travel. She was well pumped up and excited about it and, as soon as I was well enough, she discharged me and we pretty much went straight up to Drake's.' He offers the joint to Ani, but she shakes her head, no. 'Ria was desperate for me to show her the Weys, but she had a kid so we gave each other things we could use as tokens to make sure we could get back to 1972. I got this cute little clip-on watch that the nurses all wore back then. She got my Parker Pen. We found it at the back of my locker. Some bastard had already nicked my other valuables.'

Yes - that bastard is currently sitting beside him. 'We gave them back. Valerie rode out again after Lizzy brought you back here,' I say. 'Any idea where she might've gone?'

'From 1972? Who knows? We had a few items she could've used for tokens.' Scott sits up, taking hold of Ani's hand again. 'Ria won't do any harm. Let her be. She just wants a better life for herself. You might all think I'm a git, but I never meant for things to get so buggered up.' He looks at her. 'I remember your voice in the hospital. It was like a radio signal that wasn't quite tuned in. It always made me feel better. I want to thank you, for being there for me. You didn't have to do that.' He pulls her hand gently to his lips, kisses it, and lets it go. 'I don't even know your name.'

He has a short memory.

'If you're really that grateful, you can tell us where Vix's locket is,' she says, her eyes sparkling a little.

His eyes narrow, and then he gives a little grunt of a laugh. 'Why? You thinking of setting up your own smuggling business?'

'More like making sure no one else does,' I say. Scott does not need to know I'm Weyfare.

'Look, we're quits,' Scott says into the silence. 'I don't know where that shitty locket is. I'm never going anywhere near that Weydoor again, so I don't need it.'

'You can't ride the Weys any more. We gave you that pill, remember?' Jasper says.

'That's right. Of course you did.' He smiles again, and that small chill hint of foreboding tickles down my back. 'Now piss off and give me some space. I need to make a phone call.' The spell is totally broken when the others come back into the room for more boxes, moaning about us slackers and asking when we're going to do our bit. We pick up some boxes and join the others in clearing the flat.

'Did you believe all that?' Ani asks, as we get to the bottom of the stairs.

'Not all of it, no, but I can't see why he would've bothered to make up the story about this Vix woman.'

Jasper looks at me over the top of his box. 'If that locket is a straightforward grounding token, he could only have used it once,' he says.

I nod, and sigh, pushing my box into the back of Ed's van. 'I'll bet my last pound that there's blood inside it.'

'You think this Vix is Weyfare then?' Ani's eyebrows are arched to extremes. 'A real rogue Weyfare?'

'As opposed to a pretend rogue Weyfare?' Jasper asks. She gives him one of her best shrivelling looks. 'Thanks for coming. I'm here all week.'

'Whoever she is, she knows about blood tokens.'

Tim comes to help us with the final few boxes. I try to keep from looking at the big pink Band-Aid that's now on his neck. I wonder if he's part of the reason they're leaving. It must've been Vix we heard threatening him that day when we were hiding at the back of the shop.

Don't misunderstand me, I don't trust anything that comes out of Scott's mouth, especially now he's admitted he was riding the Weys long before he met Lizzy, and I don't know how much he really knows about the Weys and their communities.

I decide that if we ever make up, I will never ever be the one to tell Lizzy why Scott asked her out. But it surely would've bothered even an asscloth like him that this woman Vix was now going after his friends. It must've bothered Tim as well.

As for Tim, I want to jump on him and tell him he's not to leave Stoneford with Scott. He must stay here and run the Hippy Shop until he falls in love with Lizzy so they can make Lucas, and Blake and me, but doing that seems like taking a fast train to Insanityville, so I keep my mouth shut and try not to stare too hard at the face of the man I hope will still become my dad.

Chapter Seven – Sledgehammer
(Peter Gabriel, 1987)

Once all the boxes are in the van, and Ed and Ian have helped Scott down the stairs with a final bag of clothing and got him into the passenger seat, it's a tight squeeze for the rest of us in the back.

'Remind me why I thought this was a good idea?' Tracy asks, as Ed takes a corner a bit quickly and a red case of records slides into her for the third time.

'You would've done anything to get out of revision today,' Ian says, pushing the box back into place. 'And muggins here went along with it.'

'And remind me why we're doing this?' she says, turning to look at me. 'And what was the big chinwag with Patchouli about while we were doing all the heavy work?'

'I told you why I need to come to London,' I say. 'And the rest of it is Weyfarere business.'

'Is that what it is?' she says, with a small smile that practically screams, Liar.

'I told you. We need to go to London to find our friends,' I say.

'Do I look like a moron?' she asks.

'Don't make us answer that honestly,' Jasper says from a corner filled with boxes of mugs and plates.

She bares her teeth at him, and turns back to me. 'Well? And spare me the goody-goody bullshit.'

Bring back mad Lizzy and her spontaneous outbursts. I'm going off the bossy one. 'I want to see where Scott's going to live.'

Tracy nods. 'Here it comes. So you're stalking him. Can't be for Lizzy if the two of you aren't talking. Fancy him for yourself? Just how many blokes are you stringing along?'

'Don't be a biatch,' I snap back, carefully avoiding Ani's eyes, as for her, fancying Scott Kelly wasn't so far from the truth.

Of course, Tracy's right about me being a liar. Knowing where Scott ends up is less than half the story, and that's only because I'm not finished with him yet. He belongs in the Bergh, and, as long as the Witan aren't corrupt in these parts, I'm planning on shopping him to the one who's now in charge of the Seven Dials. But it's not the main reason I'm rolling around in the back of a grubby transit van. I want to see where Scott goes, because I *have* to see where Tim goes. If I lose Tim completely, I'm lost. Extinguished. Gone for good. I need to keep track of Tim Wharton, or else Maisie Wharton is toast.

We've been on the road about an hour when the van begins stopping and starting as if it's caught in traffic. There are no windows in the back of Ed's van, and although I got a bit of sleep, I'm now feeling queasy from the smell of petrol and being hemmed in with four sweaty people. Jasper is curled up asleep like a cat. Blud can sleep through anything. Knowing his dislike of confined spaces, I figure it's best for him to stay as he is.

Ani, ever resourceful, yanks open the hidden metal hatchway that I'd forgotten between us and the driver's seat. A blast of air rushes in from the open windows.

'You couldn't have remembered that earlier?' I say, breathing in great lungfuls of fresh oxygen.

'I thought you might want to talk to us privately,' she says primly.

'Are we there yet?' Tracy calls through the hole, sounding a lot like a toddler on a road trip.

'Just around the next corner,' I say. She scowls at me.

'We're just passing the docks, so probably another half hour,' Ed calls back. 'Bloody mess this part of London is. Be good when they actually do something with this whole area, rather than just sticking in a railway that leads to the back of beyond.'

'I heard that the money was planning on moving up here from the City,' Scott says.

'Those yuppie boys? They wouldn't be seen dead on the Dogs with their bloody handheld telephones and sharp suits. It'll be a big flop, and tax payers will have to pick up the tab for buildings that no one wants.' Ed says, swerving so violently that everyone in the back slides to the right. 'And no one knows how to drive in this frigging city!'

'So Patchouli, I guess you'll have a few quid behind you once the shop has been sold on,' Tracy says, adjusting herself. 'Got any plans for it?'

Scott snorts. 'Dosh from the shop? You mean what's left after I've paid all the red bills, rent and rates? I'm selling a dump where people come to buy a packet of jossticks and perfume oils and get change out of a fiver; I'm not selling the bloody A&N.'

Poor Dillon. I wonder where him and Nora are, and if they know Scott's selling his inheritance. Dillon Kelly loved that shop.

'You've not come up here to live the life of Riley then,' Ian says.

'Some hope. I'm up here to get away from a witch and make a new start,' he says. 'Give the cross-examination a rest.'

'Be nice to us, or we'll dump you and your boxes outside your new pad and watch while you rupture your innards trying to carry them inside,' I say pleasantly.

Ed laughs. Scott doesn't.

By the time the van comes to a final stop, my stomach is churning and my head is splitting. We open the back doors onto a London street that feels vaguely familiar.

Jasper, having finally woken up about five minutes ago, leaps out onto the tarmac as if there's someone behind him with another stun gun. He looks around, eyes narrowed, a little startled. 'Where is this?'

'Back end of Covent Garden,' Ed says, from the driver's seat. 'We haven't got long; I'm in a loading zone but if something commercial shows up, I'll have to shift.'

Jasper comes back to the van and pulls out a box. 'You can walk to Seven Dials from here easily,' he says, into my ear. 'Remember we walked up from the Tube in 1971?'

'I know.'

'No,' he hisses, 'I mean, *anyone* could walk to Seven Dials from here.'

I know what he means. 'Bruh, I can't get caught up in this paranoia of seeing Scott as the source of all of our problems. He's back in 1987 where he belongs, in a flat above a ropey bookshop. He never got Lizzy's key and he never stole *The*

Truth, but I'll get the Witan to come pick him up once we've found Tommy and Rob.'

'It's not all about Rob and Tommy either, you know,' he says, with an unusual display of disloyalty. I let it go; he's as entitled to a sketchy day as the rest of us, and he has just spent an hour and a half folded up in the back of a van with no windows.

The bookshop, which looks like it might do better trade in Knockturn Alley, has a tatty black door with a shiny silver letterbox. There are four flats here, according to the list at the side of the bell, but I don't recognise any of the names. There are no Weysigils or links to the Seven Dials or anything else connecting it to the Weyfarere community. Scott's new place is a one-bedroom bedsit with a private bathroom. Someone clearly already lives there, by the look of the dirty mugs on a low coffee table, and the TV in the corner.

'I've got no idea what they're going to do with all that crockery,' Tracy says, putting down the box full of mugs and plates. 'When I get my own place, I'm just going to use paper plates so I never have to do the washing up.'

'That's incredibly bad for the environment,' Ani says sternly.

'Don't be daft,' Tracy says, flouncing the blonde hair as she turns back towards the front door of the flat; 'paper decomposes, doesn't it?'

'Don't fight battles we still haven't won 30 years later,' I tell Ani.

Ed has to wait in the van in case the wardens turn up, so he's yelling at us to go faster every time we emerge on to the street for more boxes, but we manage to get everything offloaded before he's moved on. Scott shakes Ed's hand, pushes a brown note into his hand and grunts his gratitude at us before disappearing into his new life.

I turn back to Ed. 'We're not far here from where we needed to get to,' I tell him.

'I can't hang around while you lot catch up with your mates,' he says.
'What about getting home?'

'Have you got enough money to get us all back to Stoneford?' I ask Tracy.

She shrugs. 'I checked. Ian won't believe it, but they probably did give me enough to get us to Scotland.'

Ian pokes his tongue out at her. I remember the massive townhouse with a pool, where her family held the barbeque the day after Lizzy's 18th, and decide she's likely right.

'We'll be okay, Ed,' I say. 'If we need the van, we'll come back for it.'

'Well, if you decide you need it, it's yours until Friday. I live in the same block as Thorpe.'

'I know it,' I say.

'I'm on the floor above him, number four. Come after two-thirty and knock bloody loud,' he says. "If you can't get me to come to the door, go downstairs and see if Thorpe's in. Get him to play his northern soul at volume ten. That'll wake me up. Gotta motor,' he adds, looking in his wing mirror. We turn as one to see a traffic warden coming down the road, armed with a notebook, and Ed screeches off.

'Where now?' Tracy asks. 'I love Covent Garden. Can we go and look around the jewellery stalls?'

'We're not on a day trip,' I say. 'There's a woman who lives on the Seven Dials. She's like the leader of the Weyfarere. We need to go and see her, because the guys we're trying to catch up with might have gone there.'

'You know, it's a lot like being in an episode of *Jamie and the Magic Torch*,' Ian says. Everyone looks at him.

'Pop culture reference completely lost on us?' Ani asks.

'He goes on a helter skelter to Cuckoo Land,' Ian says.

'That clears things up,' Jasper says.

'You're in sodding Cuckoo Land, mate,' Tracy says. 'This is nothing like *Jamie and the Magic Torch*. There's no helter skelter and we don't have a dog called Wordsworth. If you've been smoking weed, why didn't you share?'

'It just feels freaky,' he says. 'Like a parallel universe.'

'Are you coming or not?' I ask, knowing I sound a bit salty but to be honest, I'm over these guys delaying me any longer than they have already.

The traffic warden is pissed off that she missed a ticketing opportunity, but she still gives us directions to the Dials. Jasper's right – it's little more than a ten minute walk from Scott's new place, and although when we arrive it's clearly not as trendy as the Seven Dials we saw in 2019, they've done a lot of work on it since 1972 and it's far from the dereliction we saw back then or in 1940, when we were here during the Blitz. We approach from another way, past Neal's Yard and the Cambridge Theatre, which is advertising *Peter Pan*, with Lulu starring as Tinkerbell. The Crown doesn't look quite as good as it did in 2019 or as rough as it did in 1940, but there are still people hanging around where the roads cross, and there is no sundial pillar.

'This is well bohemian,' Tracy says. 'Look at that bloke's clothes! He looks like an extra from *Mutiny on the Bounty*. And that woman has a coat just like the one you were wearing yesterday, Ani,' she adds.

'She's probably from 1972,' Ani replies calmly.

Tracy gives her the wide eyes. 'You mean these people are all time travellers?'

'No,' I tell her. 'Well, probably not. Some of them will be.

The Seven Dials Weydoor is one of the most powerful on the Weys.'

'Neat,' she remarks. 'They all look like they've been to a festival. Like Reading. Or the ones where all the Greenham Common women go. Glastonbury, that's the place.'

What a difference a decade or three makes. 'We're going over there,' I say, pointing to where Earlham Street continues beyond the little roundabout.

I feel my insides churning as we walk up to number seven, Earlham Street. It could be the end of a journey or the start of another. It's crazy to be hoping for two outcomes at the same time: I want Tommy and Rob to be here, but I don't. If they are here, we don't have to chase them across the country in a borrowed transit van driven by an uninsured girl, but then I have to face them both, and make a decision that I'm not ready to make.

The Weysigil is still written next to the button that rings the bell to the flat. I think that's a good thing.

'Maisie, what are we going to do if Valerie opens this door?' Jasper asks suddenly.

'Run?' I say feebly. I haven't really thought this through.

The voice that comes through the tinny speaker is vaguely familiar. 'Yes?'

'We need to speak to the Lady of the Dials,' I say, with more confidence than I feel. I'd already decided not to use the word Witan. Just in case.

'I'll come down,' she says, and the speaker cuts out.

'That didn't sound like Valerie,' Ani says.

'Why are you both expecting Valerie to be here?' I snap at them. 'Why would she come to the Dials? She was lording it over Stoneford, sure, but we have no reason to think she might come up here and stir things up. We have no idea where she went after she left us in 1972.'

'Exactly,' Ani replies thinly. 'We have no idea where she is. The last thing we knew is that she'd worked out who the Stoneford Weyfare was.' That brings me up short. She's not talking about me; she's talking about Lizzy.

'But the last thing Tommy told me was that Joan was missing,' I say. 'What would Valerie come all the way up to London for if she was the one who got rid of Joan? She was all about controlling the Stoneford Weydoor.'

'Glenda showed her *The Truth*,' Ani says. 'Tommy told us. Am I the only one who remembers any of these details?'

I'm struggling to come out with an answer but my words have run dry. My memories are woolly and trying to tease any information from them is proving pretty impossible. I feel like everything I'm trying to work out is getting more knotted up.

'Perhaps you should've ironed out these problems before

you brought us all the way up here,' Ian says.

The door opens inwards, and the woman who opens it makes me feel like I can cope with whatever is coming, because I've already met her.

'Maisie?' Mary Davenport stands in front of us, a cigarette burning between her fingers. She's older now, maybe in her thirties, with loose curls of hair falling over her shoulders, a cropped cream blouse that ends just above her waist and pink leggings. 'We thought you might show up. There's a chap upstairs that's going to be over the moon to see you.'

Chapter Eight –Dancing On
Glass (Motley Crüe, 1987)

Chap? Singular?

As I'm walking past the door that still looks like it leads to a housekeeper's flat and not a Weydoor, I'm wondering which chap, and how old will he be? Turns out my questions are answered sooner rather than later, because as we're about to climb the stairs, a familiar dark-haired tornado dressed from head to foot in black thunders down and wraps his arms around me.

'I knew you wouldn't let me down,' he mutters into my neck. 'I knew you'd come.'

It's great to see him, of course it is. He's snatched and he makes me feel safe, but right now, in front of everyone, he's making me feel sketchy, so I peel him away and ignore the laser beams from Tracy's eyes.

'Introduce us. Now,' she says, although it sounds more like a purr.

'Tracy, Ian; this is Tommy, and that's his sister, Mary

Davenport. Tommy, where's Rob?'

He pushes the bank of long straight hair away from his eyes. 'You trust them with our secrets?'

'Only one way to find out,' Jasper says.

'You'd better come on up,' Mary says. 'Things have moved on a bit.'

So has the flat. The low wooden record player unit has been replaced by a silver stack of buttons, dials, turntables and rectangular glass windows, with big black speakers either side, the words 'Amstrad' printed on each in black and white letters on a silver badge. There are little shelf units underneath; one side is full of vinyl records, the other with tapes in clear plastic boxes covered in handwriting. The TV is larger, and there's a big cabinet displaying a tea set like it's something special, similar to the one at Travellers' Rest. The sofas don't have cloths draped over the back any more, and in front of a fake coal fire, there is literally a sheep's skin on the floor like a rug. Ani eyes it as if it might bite her, but thankfully decides that's not a battle for today, either.

'Coffee?' Mary asks, but she doesn't ring a little bell like her mother Helen did when we were here before. I guess Mavis is with Helen, wherever Helen is. Hopefully all will be explained to us. Well, I can dream of a world where things make sense again, can't I? Where people don't skin animals and put them on their carpets.

'That one's fake,' Tommy says, following my gaze as Mary leaves the room, 'but Mum used to have a deerskin on the wall in her bedroom that Dad shot. You could still see the puncture holes.'

'D'you mind if we change the subject?' Ani asks thinly.

'Not at all.' He holds out a hand to Jasper. 'Good to see you again, dude.'

'Same, blud.' Jasper shakes his hand, and then makes a fist, which Tommy copies after a couple of blinks, and they bump.

'Did you come straight here from Stoneford?' I ask, sitting down on one of the sofas. 'Where did Rob go? Where is the other you? You're already here in 1987 somewhere, aren't you? You must be what – 35? Where's your Mum?'

Tommy blinks slowly once, and lights a cigarette. 'Sorry, chica, but I'm going to need a smoke before I can answer all those questions, and we'd better wait until the Witan gets back. How much do your new mates know about us?' he adds, after taking the first drag.

'Weyfare 101,' Ani says.

'Is that like a room where they put everything that frightens you people?' Tracy asks. 'I've read *1984*. Blimey! That room with all the blood and creepy old clothes! Was that Weyfare 101?'

'Not even remotely,' I say. 'It just means we told you the basics.'

'You showed them the Weyroom under the school?' Tommy asks. When I nod, he says, 'Looks like you're going to have to answer a few questions yourself.'

Mary walks in with a large cream and brown contraption. She opens the top and puts what looks like a piece of filter paper from a chemistry lesson inside, folded into a cone and covered with fine brown granules. The water jug, full of boiled water, is poured on top filling the room with the smell of Starbucks, and I realise I'm looking at an early filter machine. The second time, she comes back with a tray with a toucan advertising Guinness printed on it, and lots of mugs.

'It's called a percolator,' Mary says, shutting the lid on the filter paper. 'I reckon this one's probably an antique in your time.'

'Mary, we're from 2019, not the 25th century,' Jasper says. 'We know what a percolator is.'

'You know they're time travellers?' Ian asks.

Mary laughs. 'You poor lamb. It's all a bit much to take it at first, isn't it? The coffee will help. Hot Lava Java, this one's called. And I'm called the Witan.' She tilts her head. 'Where shall we start with sharing our stories?'

'With me. I decided not to keep my birthright a secret any

more,' I explain. 'Especially after the whole secrecy thing went so well with Lizzy. They know I'm Weyfare.'

Crap. Mary and Tommy know Lizzy is Weyfare, and my Mum. Forget about the power to control the Weys, right now I'm wishing I had the power of telepathy so I can make sure neither of the Davenports spills the tea. I guess if they do, it won't be my brain Lizzy'll want to hang like a flag from the roof of Travellers' Rest.

'Tommy tells me you and Lizzy parted ways on bad terms,' Mary says, taking the now familiar golden packet from the table, and offering them to Tracy and Ian.

'Maybe Tommy can tell us what happened to Rob,' I say, desperate to pull the conversation away from me and Lizzy.

'I overstepped my duties,' he says, not meeting my eyes.

'No one's said that, Tom,' Mary says to him, her voice gentle.

'No one needed to.' He looks at me then. 'When Joan went missing, I knew I had to find you and Lizzy, and when I saw that Rob was back-' He stops, and draws on the cigarette. 'When I saw him, I lost my cool. I was angry that'd he'd come back to try and worm his way in with you again. I decided to take matters into my own hands, as I had Isaac and Abraham with me. I should've contacted the Witan. I should've asked for backup. We got as far as the station in Stoneford, but the platform was packed solid; it was the last train to London as it was a bank holiday. He got away from us in the crowds.'

So Rob might never even have made it as far as here, or he could've got on that train without them. 'He's good at disappearing into the crowds,' I tell him, thinking back to New Year's Eve 1971.

'Tommy, we've had this conversation.' Mary leans back against the sofa. 'I don't hold you to blame. For all you knew, if you'd rung this number, your other self might've answered the phone – you could've taken each other out and then we'd have lost the Weyleigher anyway.'

'Where are you, anyway?' Jasper asks. 'I mean the older you. Where are Helen and Mavis?'

'Back in Dartmoor,' Tommy says. 'Mum retired and went home; Mavis went with her. I run the farm.' He looks a bit shady as he says this. I get the feeling he's not telling us something. There's something I'm not telling them, either.

'Rob's not a Weyleigher,' I blurt out.

'Not technically, no, since he's male,' Mary says, putting the cigarette in a clear glass ashtray and pouring the now percolated coffee into milk-primed mugs.

'Not at all,' I persist. 'My story, remember?' And I tell them about how we rode to 1994 using Rob's original signet ring, ending up at his birthday party, only to discover that he'd been missing for the previous seven years. How his mother Valerie revealed that her first-born son Robin had died, and Rob was adopted.

When I finish speaking, the only sound is the tinkling of Jasper's spoon stirring sugar into his coffee mug.

'You have to trust me,' I say, looking at Mary, but directing my words at Tommy. 'I can't take you there because the token's been used. A long time ago, Rob told me to use the ring as a token when I needed answers I couldn't find anywhere else. He's not born of Weyleigher blood, so he's not a threat to us.'

'I beg to differ,' Tommy mutters. I pull my mouth to one side.

'And this is the reason we came to London,' Tracy says. 'This is the reason we were going to travel all the way to Scotland?'

Mary and Tommy look at me, blue smoke blurring their features. 'Were you?' Mary asks.

'You can't send an innocent person to the Bergh,' I say shortly. 'I was just trying to do the right thing.'

'Absolutely,' Mary replies. 'However, to be fair, the fact that Rob is adopted doesn't entirely solve the dilemma.'

'Why not? They aren't related by blood,' I say.

'Weyleigher blood is not like Weyfarere blood. They have to use tokens to travel the Weys like any other bystander. Rob is still Valerie's son by law. She can't track him, but she would never have been able to. But we must assume she will still love him and want him back, as much as if she were his biological mother,' Tommy says firmly.

'So it is still a problem,' Mary agrees.

I hadn't thought of that. How could I have been so naive? Finding out he was adopted may have changed everything for Rob, but why would it have changed anything for Valerie?

'How many problems do we have now?' Ani asks.

'99, but at least going to Scotland isn't one,' Jasper quips with a smile, but when no one joins in, he just sips his coffee.

'We spent a while trying to locate the dude, but once the train left, I knew we'd lucked out, so I used Mum's vial to ride back to 1972. By the time we got back, Joan had returned, and the others had left for 1987, I reckon. Back to the end of Lizzy's timeline.'

Now that's not something I expected to hear. 'So she wasn't kidnapped her after all?' Ani asks.

'I didn't say that. I just said she was returned.'

Some tone in his voice makes my skin crawl. 'Was she okay?' I ask him.

He takes a beat, and shakes his head. 'She wasn't okay at all, Maisie.'

'Tell me,' I insist.

'She was really confused. Kept thinking people were going

to trap her and lock her away. She'd changed physically; she was thinner and the light was gone from her eyes. She kept shouting for help, and then she'd be calm for a time. Glenda in 1972 called a doctor and he gave her a bunch of sedatives, and said it was likely something called premature senility, and there wasn't a lot he could do about it.'

'Dementia,' Ani says.

'That's what I was told she died from,' I say.

'But I don't think she was senile,' he says, stubbing the cigarette out in the ashtray and immediately lighting another. 'She was only in her mid forties in 1972. People don't lose their marbles that young.'

'Actually, they do, but it's a recognised condition in our day, and things can be done to help,' Ani points out.

Tommy shakes his head firmly. 'No. Her eyes looked – *older*. I think she may have been kept in another time against her will.'

'What - you mean trapped?'

'For a while,' he says seriously.

A cold shiver ripples down my arms. First we have Scott, riding out and back across the Weys, moving goods for profit and ageing a couple of years in just a few months, and now Joan, my great grandmother, who we always believed was inflicted with a terrible disease before doctors really understood it, maybe not having it at all. Maybe she spent years banged up in another time, wasting away, going out of her mind. Tears prickle at the edges of my eyes.

Nothing bloody gets past Tracy. 'Who is Joan?' she asks. 'Who is the Glenda in 1972? Is that Lizzy's *Mum* Glenda?'

'Let me guess,' Mary says softly. 'You didn't tell your friends that part of the story.'

'Not mine to tell,' I reply, sticking to my guns.

'Well, this is one way of knowing whether you can trust them, I reckon,' Mary says, turning to face Tracy and Ian. 'Maisie is descended from a long line of Weyfarere. The Stoneford Weyfarere are a quirky bunch, not known for riding the Weys, but Maisie and her mother are proving an exception to the rule. You know them both.'

'We know Maisie's mother?' Ian asks, but Tracy's eyes are glinting.

'It's Lizzy, isn't it,' she says simply.

Ian goes pink. 'You're Lizzy's daughter?' he squeaks.

'Lizzy's a Weyfare too,' Tracy says. 'I bloody knew it! I bloody knew she was keeping secrets from me, the old cow! I bloody well knew – and Patchouli!' she exclaims. 'He's part of it too, isn't he? That's why you chased him up here.'

I nod. There's little point trying to hide it now.

'Scott's in London?' Tommy asks, overriding Tracy's hyper

thinking.

'So Glenda's a Weyfare as well?' Ian asks.

'I have never smoked in my life, but if you guys don't shut the hell up I'm going to break the promise I made to my mother when I was 9 and start smoking!' I shout.

'Your mother being Lizzy Brookes,' Jasper says into the silence. "Ironic, really, since she smokes like a chimney.'

'Gobshite's knackerbag,' Ian says. 'Can I scrounge another fag?'

'Lizzy is my Mum,' I say slowly and calmly. 'She found out. She went apeshit. That's why we aren't talking. Glenda's my Nan, and Joan is my great grandmother. In 2019, I live in Travellers' Rest with Lizzy and my two older brothers Lucas and Blake. I only found out I was Weyfare when Glenda told Lizzy on her 18th birthday. I fell through the Weydoor with Jasper, and ever since then, my life has been like a jigsaw that someone took hold of and tossed all the pieces high up into the air, and I've been trying to put it back together again every day since.' I wave away the cigarette that Mary is offering me. 'I'm not sure I ever will.'

'Sorry, but – Scott's in London?' Tommy asks again. 'Lizzy hasn't contacted a Witan to have him taken to the Bergh?'

'Not that we know of.' I could've done with some sympathy but it's probably not practical. I want to tell him it's a long story but it never is. 'We came back to 1987 and met an old friend. We were going to borrow his van so Ani here could drive us to the Bergh to find you and Rob, then it turned out he was doing a flat removal for a friend, and the friend was Scott. He's in Covent Garden.'

'Have you seen Valerie?' he asks.

I shake my head, no. 'We knew she was back in 1972 at some point because you told us about her meeting Glenda for coffee.' The coffee is bitter, but it's doing its job. 'Tell them about the Simmons family,' I add, turning on Ian.

'You mean the ones that run the restaurant?' he asks, straightening his back as if he's proud to be important enough to be asked. 'Ted Simmons runs it with his wife – Sheila, although I want to say Valerie and I don't know why. Hey!' he adds, the coin dropping, 'that's a weird coincidence.'

'Isn't it just,' Ani says smoothly. 'Tell them about the guy you were at school with.'

'Brian?'

Ani swallows, and gives him a tight little smile. 'The Simmons guy.'

'Oh! Robin Simmons, you mean. Goes out with my next door neighbour.'

'We know Valerie was there in 1994. Ted was with her. There was no Robin when we were there,' I say. 'He was dead.'

'So she must have changed that after we saw that timeline,' Ani says. 'Whatever she did, Robin's now alive and Ted's married to someone else.'

'Blimey,' Mary says. 'Now that will put the cat among the pigeons. If Robin is still alive, then Valerie would never have adopted Rob.'

'I still don't bloody trust him. He's lived with a Weyleigher family for his whole life!' Tommy exclaims.

'So she may not even know who he is?' I ask, ignoring him.

Mary shakes her head, no. Tommy puffs like someone pissed off the tank engine.

We all pause to consider this.

'She's a Weyleigher, and you said she doesn't have the natural ability to control her rides on the Weys,' Ani points out. 'So she could've ridden anywhere after she left 1972.'

'Is there a possibility she could've used Joan's blood as an anchor?' Mary asks.

'Joan's blood would only take her to wherever Joan was,' Tracy says. We all look at her. 'What? I've been listening. You think I'm a cretin?'

'Whatever that is, you're obviously not one,' Mary replies.

'We're pretty sure Valerie's family don't know about the blood tokens,' I say.

'Can we just rewind a bit?' Ian says. 'Could I have the idiot's version, please?'

'Joan, Glenda, Lizzy and Maisie are Weyfarere,' Ani says.

'Valerie is a Weyleigher, sworn enemy of the Weyfarere,' Jasper says.

'Scott knows too much about Weyfarere business,' Tommy says.

'We don't know where Valerie is,' Ani says. "Or Rob.'

'Valerie has probably altered her own timeline to prevent the death of her son,' Mary says.

'We need to find Valerie,' Tommy says. 'We have no way of knowing exactly where she is now.'

'We thought Rob was her son, but he isn't,' I say.

'It doesn't change a lot in my eyes,' Tommy insists. 'He's been part of a Weyleigher family.'

I glare at him, but he won't look at me.

'Thank you,' Ian says. 'That makes things as clear as mud.'

I'm not sure who hears the thud first, but suddenly we are all sitting up, backs straight, and the smokers are putting out their ciggies.

'Someone else seems keen to talk to the Witan this evening,' Jasper remarks.

The second thud is louder, and this time, I'm certain the mugs on the coffee table rattle. Tommy is on his feet.

'You and Maisie go now, Mary. Go to the bedroom and use

the hatch. Do as I say,' he adds as I open my mouth. 'We will join you when this has passed. Mary, you know the procedure.'

Mary nods. I'm about to tell him that I don't know the procedure, and that I'm going nowhere without Jasper and maybe even Ani, when Mary grabs my hand, but there is a third thud followed by a crash and a splintering of timber, and the noise of footsteps coming up the stairs, and suddenly people are shouting and yelling and screaming, and before we can leave the room, it's full of the Lost of the Seven Dials, and they are all screaming at Mary.

Chapter Nine –Lil' Devil (The Cult, 1987)

Tommy reaches down and opens a flap I'd not noticed on the arm of the sofa. Inside, like something out of an early Bond movie, the arm is cut away to reveal a round black plastic button. He smacks it hard with the fist of his hand, but this isn't a Bond movie; nothing blows up and no one is ejected from the room.

Jasper and Ani push me behind them so they form a human wall between me, Mary and the shouters, who just seem to keep coming up the stairs. When I finally make out what they're yelling, I'm confused: they are shouting words like 'witch' and 'devil worshipper' and 'evil'. Tracy and Ian join Tommy in creating another barrier between them and us, but it's no good – we are seven against maybe thirty or forty of them. The sofa behind me is scraping slowly across the carpet as they push us towards the cabinet with the tea set, and I'm finding it harder and harder to stay on my feet, while Mary is hanging onto me as if her life depends on it – and it might, at this rate. These people are crazed; there are women in full-length shapeless dresses and men in tunics that come to their knees, carrying sticks and canes, others dressed like extras from the *Pirates of the Caribbean* films. I wonder if it's significant that they all look so similar, but there's no time to ask Ani; she's grabbed the tray from the coffee table, and I can see she'll not be afraid to use it if they start using those sticks as weapons against us.

Why have they turned so nasty? I know the Dials has been a rough place to hang out over the years, but even at its lowest, the Lost here were always fairly easy-going. Until today, the worst thing that ever happened to me here was someone mistaking me for a prostitute. Mary stumbles beside me; some of the invaders have climbed over the back of the sofa now and grabbed hold of her from behind, pulling her off her feet and almost taking me with her. I land on the sofa awkwardly, and Mary's hand is wrenched out of mine; they haul her away screaming as she's sucked into the heart of the mob. There is a roar of anger as Tommy launches himself over me like an unleashed panther, trying to get them to release his sister, scrambling over the furniture after them as they drag her away. Jasper and Ani are struggling to stop the mob getting to me, but Ani's tray doesn't seem to be having much of a deterrent on any of them. Jasper's trying to fend off a guy with long dirty blond hair tied back with a black velvet ribbon who seems determined to cave his skull in with a particularly hefty stick, Tracy's screaming as a large guy picks her up like a sack of vegetables and shakes her, and Ian is raining ineffective blows down on the chest of another. I realise we're in serious trouble. Again.

I scramble off the sofa and down onto my hands and knees, trying to weave my way around the kicking legs and head in the direction that they were taking Mary. I spot them by the door to the entrance hall, and the dilemma hits me. Do I go after the Witan and Tommy, or do I try and get my friends out of another mess I've got them into?

It's a no-brainer, really.

I stagger to my feet, taking a woman by surprise, so I grab the stick she's carrying and use it to start thrashing my way through the people back to my friends, but it's not long before I notice that most of the intruders are heading out of the door after Mary and Tommy, leaving everyone behind, yelling "Punish the Witch!" and "Send her back where she came from!"

They were never after me in the first place, were they? I'm just a girl caught between them and their actual prize, the Seven Dials Witan. A girl and her friends, who never booked any of this crap as extras when they signed up for the time travel experience.

They are looking at me; their clothes torn and faces

scratched and already bruising. Tracy's lip looks like she's taken a punch to the mouth, Ian's T-shirt is ripped, and Jasper's cheek and neck are slapped bright red.

'I'm so sorry.' The words seem a pathetic reward for what's just happened.

I needn't have worried.

'This is no time to feel sorry for yourself!' Tracy exclaims. 'We have to get Mary and Tommy back!'

'Haven't been in a decent scrap like that since Edward Betts took on our fourth outside the Wimpy,' Ian says, grinning.

'You're bleeding,' Jasper says, pointing at my arm as we jog out after the last of the intruders. I hadn't even registered it in the riot, but there is a big cut near my elbow from some weapon or other.

'It's nothing. Tracy's right, we need to get down there now and stop whatever they're planning on doing to Mary,' I tell them, my breath coming in gasps; I hope that I've not broken a rib or something as well.

The last of the Lost are going down the stairs, but instead of going out through the front door to Earlham Street, they turn right and head towards the other exit – the one that leads to the Weydoor. They're still yelling, and chanting the same three words over and over.

'Holy crap,' Jasper hisses, "*Send her back*?" Are they going to throw her?'

'It's fine,' I say, feeling less confident than I sound, 'she can ride straight back, can't she?'

From a few stairs up, I can just see the heads of Mary and now Tommy, as they are carried like hog roast through the ground floor of their home, struggling to be free of the many arms that hold them up high in the air, bashing them into walls and doorframes, knocking down picture frames and denting plaster surfaces.

The door is closed. As the chanting pack pushes forward, someone reaches up and yanks the chain around Mary's neck so hard that it splits, and her silver key tumbles into waiting hands, and the door is unlocked. Dressed in the woollen hooded tunic coats of so many others, the figure leads the way into the darkness.

I send a prayer up to whichever God is listening, though I doubt any of them could hear me over the chaos.

'How did they know about the key?' Ani is asking.

'It doesn't matter about the key,' Jasper is saying, 'If they throw Mary through the Weydoor, she can come right back. If Tommy still has your vial -'

'But they can't come right straight back though, can they?' Tracy asks, dabbing at her sore mouth. 'I know I'm a late starter on all this Weyfare stuff but, if they come straight back, won't this lot still be here waiting for them? They'll just chuck them straight back through, like a cross-dimension game of catch.'

'We need to get to the front of this lot,' I say. 'We might still be able to do something. Control the ride. If I can go first, and somehow get you all behind me –'

I break off speaking, because even saying it out loud shows me how hopeless it is as a plan, but I've got nothing better in reserve, and Ian is already at the bottom of the stairs, starting to force his way through the chanting marchers.

By the time we pass through the door, we are halfway through the people, who seem much less bothered about us now they know their prime target is being carried at the front. I can still hear her and Tommy yelling, but if what they're saying is important, their attackers are still creating way too much noise for me to make any words out.

By the time we approach the Weydoor cavern, the Weydoor itself beaming its bright purple light over everyone, someone has installed electric lighting and the place is lit up like the London Eye on New Year's Eve. So when I finally stumble to within centimetres of a tall man in a black high hat of the front of the roaring pack, I stop short, and I go no further because of what I see.

'You have got to be fucking joking me,' Ian says.

'One thing you'll realise about time travel is that it's a lot less funny than you'd think,' Jasper remarks.

'But that's –' Tracy begins.

'We know. Shh,' Ani says.

I should've realised, shouldn't I? Every bloody body else would have worked it out. Scott Kelly is as incapable of moving his own stinking garbage as I am likely to win the school award for Historian of the Year 2019. He's a scheming, evil bastard of a man. He didn't tell us anything in the flat back in Stoneford that it wasn't in his plan to tell us. Whatever made me think we could trust him? He'd only been back in 1987 for about 24 hours, so how could he have organised a new place to live? He'd done it with the help of the other scheming evil, present in this cavern right now.

She holds her hands up like a preacher, and the mob all settle like a wave of calm has come over them.

'But who in the name of Gobshite is that when she's at home?' Tracy asks quietly.

'That is Valerie,' I mutter. 'Don't move. We mustn't be seen.'

It may be 1987, but Valerie Bennett or Simmons doesn't look any older than Scott. How is that possible? She lowers her arms, and points at Mary, who is still trying to get free of the guys who hold her, but her struggles are weakening now. Tommy is trying to grab hold of her hand, but the thugs restraining him won't give him the chance.

'This is the witch who has lived amongst you, guarding this portal to Hell!' she exclaims, and the crowd all cheer and shout agreement. 'This is the witch who abandoned you when the devil threw you all across his Weys!'

'Christ on a bike,' Ani whispers, 'it's like being in Pendle in the 1600s.'

'Abandoned you to fend for yourselves in a time of which you had no understanding!' Valerie holds her hands up and the crowd cheers again.

I stagger forward slightly as someone pushes me from behind in their enthusiasm to show their support for her words.

'She is a devil worshipper! The devil sleeps with her and he gives her riches in return for being the protector of his evil Weys! No man, woman or child would leave their own time by the will of your God!' Valerie's voice gets higher and higher until it is a screech.

This time, the roar is deafening. I turn back to the four people standing around me. 'They're going to throw them through the Weydoor without a token. Tommy should have Mary's vial and mine, and I have Helen's. If we are caught and thrown, I'll go back to 2019 and then I'll jump straight to wherever Helen is, and get some help.' I touch my faithful bumbag, bulging with its precious items: *The Truth of the Weyfarere*,

The fake *Book of the Witan*, various vials and tokens from the Weyroom, the serviette with the two pills which prevent any further riding on the Weys, Tommy's hanky and the vial with Helen's name on the label. I have a light bulb moment. 'Touch my elbow.' I say.

'This is our moment of retribution!' Valerie yells. 'This is the moment that we rid ourselves of the Scourge of the Seven Dials!'

'This is not the time or the place for kinky stuff,' Ian hisses.

'It's not kinky,' Jasper says, placing his fingertips gently on my cut arm. 'Maisie's blood is special, remember?'

'Put a little blood from my wound on your fingers, and if we lose each other, touch the Weydoor with those fingers and the blood token should bring you to whichever timeline I land on,' I say.

The other three just manage to catch some of my blood on their fingers when there is another surge forward, like last year when Mum let Uncle Paul take me, Lucas and Blake to the Reading Festival and the crowd all went ape when Kings of Leon came on stage. I lose my footing, and tumble forward past the tall man with the high hat, right onto the stone floor in full view of Scott Kelly and Valerie Bennett-Simmons.

There is silence for a few moments.

'The Gods are with us, my friends,' Valerie says, her voice

suddenly hushed. 'How fortuitous that we should gather here today and be able to rid ourselves of the witch, her brother, and now some of her vile friends.' She claps her hands. 'Hold them.'

I hardly even try to get away from the hands that grab at me. Where am I supposed to go? I wouldn't even get as far as the Crown for a light and mild. Or a Bud.

All five of us are marched forward in front of the chanting group as if we are on parade.

'We meet again.' Valerie steps forward, severe in a woollen shift dress that comes to the floor; she's nothing like the groovy hipster from 1972, the prim hotel manager from one version of 1987 or even the grieving mother from 1994.

How many faces does Valerie have? Just the two, I guess.

'You keep getting under my feet,' I say with more bravery than I feel. 'Everywhere I go lately, you show up like a bad smell.'

Valerie laughs and turns to her muttering audience. 'You hear how the fallen one mocks me, friends? But I am righteous, and I will not stoop to the level of the darkness she inhabits.'

'Since when did you become the Witchfinder General?' Ani hisses angrily.

'Since I found that a large group of the folk who hang out in the Dials have a bit of a thing about witches,' Valerie smiles. 'I've been here three years. That was plenty of time to gather resources and stir up the mob while I waited for Scott to come through.'

She's been here for three years?

'When darling Glenda showed me her precious little book in 1972, I decided I had bigger fish to fry. Why should I settle for a tinpot portal in the sticks, when I can control one of the most powerful Weys in the country?' she adds.

'Send her back!' one of the witch hunters shouts loudly, and some of the others join in. I guess they came here to see some action, not to be an audience on *Question Time*.

Valerie turns to Mary, who is standing like a statue, her face set as if in stone. 'Time for you to depart this world.'

Tommy starts shouting then, and I'm suddenly scared that I've misjudged this whole crazy weird situation and they are going to properly hurt Mary in some way. The crowd start chanting together again: send her back, send her back.

But it's worse than that.

Valerie holds one hand up to silence them, and the other hand out towards Scott. He drops the hood from the blond hair, and he turns to me and smiles; that hideous rictus of a smile like Joker without his make up. Why did I ever think his icy blue eyes were sexy? They are cold, like he has no soul.

He reaches a hand into a pocket of the tunic and pulls it out again in a fist, which he opens with a flourish in front of my face.

A tiny white pill is lying in the palm of his hand. The same tiny white pill we gave him in Stoneford. The pill that was supposed to prevent him ever riding again on the Weys. The pill we'd watched him take into his mouth.

'I knew it!' Jasper mutters beside me. 'I bloody knew it! Everyone hides pills under their tongues.'

'You said when you gave my partner this pill that it stops travel on the Weys,' Valerie says, taking it from Scott.

'Didn't your mummy ever tell you not to accept sweeties from strangers?' Scott asks.

'It was a bluff,' Jasper lies boldly. 'We just wanted him to think he couldn't ride –'

'Is that so?' Valerie asks. 'Let's test that theory out. Behold! The witch is banished!'

She shoves her palm without warning into Mary's mouth and grabs hold of her nose. Mary coughs and chokes, squirming for release and when she eventually swallows, Valerie steps aside, and the guys that have been holding Mary toss her straight into the Weydoor, which flashes bright white and purple.

Did she swallow the pill?

Tommy screams.

The crowd erupts in cheers and bellows of laughter that are soon replaced with "Send him back!"

'He's just a useless boy,' Valerie says. 'The female of their species is more deadly than the male.'

She got that right. I close my eyes as they launch Tommy through the Weydoor and I can't bear to watch; I just hope I can find him again. She steps towards the remaining five of us, but turns to face her avid followers.

'The threat is past.' They all cheer. 'Now you have a leader who will master these pathways of the devil. Return to my quarters and await me.'

Scott moves forward, and the mob start to back off like obedient sheep, leaving just the ones who are holding us. These are the origins of Valerie's Guard, maybe.

'Look at you all. Like something out of an Enid Blyton story,' Valerie sneers into my face as Scott moves the others into the passage back to Number Seven. 'Trying to solve mysteries you have no understanding of. Stupid little children.'

'Leave us out of this missus, we just came along for the ride,' Ian says.

'Three years in London, Valerie? You're looking good for 45,' I snap.

'I'd have been 38,' she snarls. 'Your Maths is as flawed as your decision to interfere in my plans.'

'I don't think so. You've been busy riding about the Weys, and too much time travel ages a girl.'

'I don't know why you keep popping up like this, but it's high time you split.' She steps forward.

'Where else have you been stirring things up then?' I ask. 'In 1972, maybe? Since Robin's still alive?'

She stops moving and her face darkens. 'You leave Robin out of this.'

'I remember a timeline where he died,' I say. 'He died, and you went to a mother and baby home and you adopted another child from a girl hardly old enough to make decisions for herself. The baby's name was Rob.'

'Robin and Ted are safe! I made my baby boy's future secure and I left them!' she hisses. 'My true family have waited decades to find the location of the Stoneford Weydoor!'

'So you found out about the Weydoor, and you left Stoneford?' Tracy asks. 'That makes so much sense. Not.'

Valerie glares at her. 'Who are you?' she sneers. I don't remember seeing you hanging around with Glenda's girl and her mates before.'

'We've been quite busy riding the Weys too,' Ani says.

'So it seems. Well, you're wrong. I didn't leave Stoneford. I was waiting for Scott in 1987 when he got back to his flat.' She reaches into her cloth tunic and pulls out an ornate golden locket. 'Scott gave me this at the hospital. Someone cleared out his valuables locker at the hospital, but they didn't see this at the back. It doesn't work like normal tokens. We spent some time that day planning what we were going to do to secure the Seven Dials.' She smiles at Scott. 'Amongst other things.'

That's just ratchet. My insides are curling up, but I'm trying not to overreact at the sight of the locket. It can't be what I think it is. Jasper coughs. He must think it is. I daren't look at Ani.

'It was Scott who came up with the idea of the witch-hunt. We found something to take me back to 1984 in his little shop. I've spent three years in the Dials after reading Glenda's book planning this, and today of all days, you show up! Scott rang me and said you were coming. You're like bad pennies!'

'And you left your son and husband for a bloke you met for five minutes in a hospital bed?' Tracy says. 'You're a right piece of work, aren't you?'

'No, I left my husband and son because I am a Weyleigher, and my true family's calling is what matters most! I told my mother about the Weydoor in Drake's school, but I am destined for greater things. Like controlling the Great Weys!' she cries defiantly.

'Playing on people's greed,' I sneer. 'Going completely extra and being an asscloth. Messing with people's lives.'

'And yours isn't looking all that great right now!' she sneers.

'So what did you do with Joan?' I yell back.

For the first time, I seem to have said something that confuses her, and she frowns. 'I've got no clue what you're jabbering on about,' she says. 'Give me that belt purse. We don't want you hanging onto any unnecessary tokens.'

'It's a bumbag,' Jasper quips, and he kicks one of the men holding me hard enough for him to let me loose with a yelp, and I manage to wriggle free of the other and for the first time, I leap into the Weydoor alone, and there's white heat, purple light, black – nothing.

Chapter Ten – Solitude Standing
(Suzanne Vega, 1987)

The cut on my arm is deeper than I thought; one of the sticks Valerie's witch hunters were using to bash us must've been a bit sharp. I feel bruised, defeated, let down – but most of all, I feel weak and alone.

This is the first time I've ever been anywhere on the Weys by myself. I've always had someone with me. I've never been separated from Jasper. We've kept each other sane that way; whatever else was going wrong, we always knew we shared the same memories and experiences. We knew we weren't going completely crazy. Now he's not here, I can only hope that the blood the others smeared on their hands will bring them to me.

I ought to be arriving in front of that woman Hannah who's going to send me to bed with no hot milk because I obviously didn't swallow her tablet. I rode out to 1987, so I should have ridden back to the end of my timeline – Monday May 27th, 2019. I guess it could be 2019, but this isn't the Seven Dials Weydoor. I'm sprawled in front of a tall stone, like the ones you see at Stonehenge, but there's only one, and it's glowing purple. In front of me there are green meadows as far as I can see, groups of white ponies running freely and, in the distance, there are mountains with white tops. It's sunset. Or sunrise, I can't really tell.

It's like the place Scott told us about.

He had been on the level about this place; he just hadn't been on the level about anything else. Apart from the fact he rode on the Stoneford Weys, and I came through a different Weydoor, Scott could have been describing what I'm looking at right now.

Ordinary people, or bystanders, get lost on the Weys because they don't have tokens to control their travel, and Weyfare help them get home. But I'm Weyfare. I'm supposed to be anchored to my timeline. I remember Helen telling us that the Seven Dials Weydoor was more like a vortex sucking the people that ride on the Weys into its own energy and spitting them out into random times and places. Helen said it was why the Dials was full of the Lost; people who had travelled in time accidentally, but couldn't or wouldn't risk another ride. But I'm Weyfare. I'm supposed to be anchored to my timeline. So why has this happened to me?

Rob is on the run, Tommy and Mary could now be anywhere in Time and so could all my squad. I'm the only one who's supposed to have this stuff under control and I can't even get that right. FML.

I stand up, and check the contents of my bumbag. There was no way I was going to let Valerie or Scott get their mucky little hands on the precious things I carry, which is why I just went through the Weydoor with no warning to the others. Amazingly, the glass vials are all intact, but there's no sign of the others.

I'm about to step back through the stone Weydoor when it flashes bright purple like violet sheet lightning. I stumble backwards, trip over my own feet and land on my backside again, only to find someone falling over the top of me and knocking the final breaths from my lungs.

When they roll off, and we look at each other, still panting, I can't be sure which of us is more surprised.

'Tracy?'

'Maisie!' She flings her arms around me, and holds on as if she's expecting Valerie's arms to reach through the Weydoor and drag her back away from me. We hold onto each other for a few seconds.

'What in the name of Sod was going on back there?' she says, after she's got her breath back.

'I'm guessing Valerie's been winding up the locals,' I tell her. 'Most of those people looked as though they were Lost from the time of the Witch Trials. Somehow Valerie got three years behind us, and she used their fear of witchcraft and devil worship to launch an attack on the Witan. I've been on a timeline where she controls the Stoneford Weydoor. Now she's got bigger ideas.'

'She wants the Seven Dials,' Tracy says, nodding slowly. Then she looks around her. 'Where are we?'

'That I don't know. We ought to be in 2019. The blood on your fingers brought you to me, but I don't know where the others are.'

'Me neither,' Tracy replies. 'Jasper and Ani were thrown before me. They would be here already if they were connected to you, wouldn't they?' My stomach lurches as I nod, yes. 'And who in the name of Sod is that?'

Her voice has gone up a few notes, and she is staggering to her feet before I can even turn around and see what's got her so shook.

What's got her shook is a woman riding towards us on a white horse. Her hair is long and white, almost silver grey, and it matches her eyes. She's dressed in leggings that look like they're made of black leather or something similar, and a black leather tunic that ties up across her stomach like a corset, over a white collarless shirt. Her black leather boots are carved like the cowboy boots from 1972, but they go way up past her knees. She's wearing some kind of cape that seems to be made from the black feathers of what must have been several big birds. A raven maybe, or even a bird of prey or a swan. Behind her is nothing short of a chariot, with silver cushions inside, and shining metallic wheel spokes.

'What the freaking hell was in that coffee Mary made us?' Tracy says out loud.

'Greetings, Weyfarere,' the woman says. 'I am Reginleif. You came of your own volition. This is unexpected.'

'I was expected?' I ask.

'All Weyfarere are expected, eventually,' she smiles. 'You are hurt, of course. Let me tend to your wounds.'

I look at Tracy, who shrugs and dabs at the cut on her mouth.

She's talking about the Weyfarere, so I risk a leading question. 'I expected to ride to 2019,' I say, as she looks at my arm, 'but I came here instead. Where am I?'

The woman pushes the thick wave of silver hair away from her eyes as she looks at me. 'This is your only wound, sister?'

'As far as I know,' I tell her, 'although my ribs hurt.'

'You chose to come here, and in good health? This will please the gods and stand you in good stead with them. You will both need to be taken to a place of rest until your bodies cease to function.'

'Say what?' Tracy exclaims.

'Cease to function?' I say, my voice a bit squeaky. 'I'm not dying! We were just in a bit of a fight!'

'All the same, you are here,' Reginleif says, the same smile never leaving her flawless face. ' The choice has been made and the wrong is made right. We welcome all the kin of the Vana-heim for their spiritual gifts and knowledge.'

'I'm going to need medicating,' I say, dropping to the floor and crouching there like a rabbit ready to bolt for it. And shit, am I ready to bolt.

'I do not understand,' Reginleif says. 'Some aspects of your tongue are unfamiliar to me.'

Tracy puts her hands on her hips. 'Would someone please tell me what the hell is going on?'

'If you do not know,' Reginleif says, 'your presence here is all the more remarkable.' She holds out a slender hand to me. 'Come. Let me help you board.'

I don't accept the help, but I do get to my feet. I'm beginning to think Tracy's right about Mary's coffee being laced with some hallucinogenic. 'I'm not dying. I'd know if I was dying. I don't know anything about mortal wounds or where the hell this is or whether you're a figment of my – our imagination, but I'm not going anywhere with you and your pretty horse and cart.'

'I'm with her,' Tracy says.

'Nice to meet you,' I say, turning and taking Tracy's arm, 'but if this is Heaven; it's all very nice, but it can wait another 70 years.'

Before Reginleif can answer us, I've leaped towards the Weydoor taking Tracy with me, and instead of stone there's white heat, purple light, black – nothing.

I just about manage to land on my feet, but I trip straight over the body that is on the floor in front of me, and Tracy follows a few seconds later. The cry that comes out of the body we've accidentally kicked is the best thing I've heard in hours.

'Blud!' I fling my arms around him, knowing why Tracy did it now, and although Jasper's not all that touchy feely, he grabs onto me and hugs me right back this time. Over his shoulder I can see them all: Ian pulling Tracy to her feet and Ani scrambling towards us, her face lit up like it used to before she was extinguished. There is no Tommy, and of course, no Mary, but there is a guy with a large black tablet, looking at us as if it's Christmas.

'Welcome to the Seven Dials Weydoor 2019!' he says. 'My name is Noah Short, and I'm here to assist you in reclaiming your timeline! Can I take your names, please?'

I'm pretty sure that if I tell him, Noah Short won't be helping us.

'Hey Noah,' Jasper says. 'What's going down, bro?'

'You're my only bystanders today,' Noah asks, checking his tablet, 'but at least my shift is over soon. And you are -?'

I nudge Jasper.

'I'm ... Gaspar Smith. This is my girlfriend, Dani Jones,' he says, planting a wet kiss on Ani's cheek. She's furious, but she can't react badly and he knows it.

'I'm Paisley Taylor, and these are my friends Gracie and Dean Williams.' I say, adopting Jasper's extra tone. 'Ooooh, are you in charge? What's with the tablet? We've just travelled in Time!' I squeak at him.

'I guess you're incoming,' Noah says, running his fingers down the screen. 'What was the name of the Weyfare who assisted your return ride?'

'Oooh, I can't remember,' I say, putting my hands on my hips. 'Nice old dear though.' I pull my trusty (dead) *iPhone* out of my bumbag. 'She got me to hold this and then we all had to jump into this purple void.' I turn around, and fake surprise. 'Hey! It looks just like that one.'

Noah looks as I'd hoped, like he's tiring fast of my impression of a wired bystander. 'Have you done this before?'

'No way, bro, we were having a drink in the Crown when I needed a wee and some mad guy came up to me and said I should go down the basement for the craic,' I say, sighing dramatically. 'Course, I thought he was being all ratchet so we all went – you know – safety in numbers in case he got his todger out - but we found this door thing and we ended up somewhere completely different! When was it, Dani? – Nope, don't tell me, it's right here on the tip of my tongue – 1979, the old lady in the pub said! And the music was *shite!*'

'I mean! This is lit! What you guys doing hiding secret doors in the West End?' Jasper exclaims.

Noah had closed his eyes briefly at the word 'todger'. After opening them again and having checked that our crazy fictitious names aren't on his list, he looks like he wants us gone, as I'd hoped.

'Leave this place, and do not speak of it again,' he says. 'Do not talk to strangers in these parts. There are still people that will do you harm, even in this day and age. I have registered you. If you return, you will be restrained.'

'You think we're going to go out there and tell people there's a freaking time machine under the Seven Dials?' Ani snaps, finally joining in. 'No way – I *value* my freedom! Which way back to the pub?'

Noah points away from the passage that leads back to the Witan's flat, and we all scamper away from him.

No one speaks until we are opening the door behind the

curtain, and stepping out into the busy pub on the corner of the Seven Dials opposite to Earlham Street. Hardly any one notices us; they are all too busy talking about their own stresses, adventures and issues, and those that do notice just turn away again. The curtain falls back over the hidden door, and we turn to face each other.

'I don't know about you lot, but I could do with a bloody drink,' Ian says.

'I still have some cheddar,' I say, and we go up to the bar.

There's no place to sit inside, and although the weather is cooler than 1987, it's not too cold to sit outside, so we take our drinks and go and sit on the pavement with a good few of the rest of the drinkers.

Ian's pint is half gone before he speaks. 'So we're in the future.'

'Finally,' Tracy says. 'I don't know where I was before I came here but it was freaky.'

'2019. We won't stay long,' I say, 'but we might have to ride out through another Weydoor.'

'We won't end up back with that weirdo woman who thought we were dying, will we?' Tracy asks.

'Excuse me?' Ani asks, over her pint.

'It was cray. Me and Tracy got sideswiped to some place else before we got to you,' I say.

'That's not possible though,' Ani points out. 'That was your return ride. You should've come straight to 2019. *We* did.'

'You're right, but I haven't been able to get my head round it,' I reply, taking a mouthful of cider. 'It must be something to do with the Dials.' I add, remembering what Helen said about the vortex.

'I'm sure I was back in the room with Valerie for a minute as well,' Tracy says, 'but there was shouting and it sounded like there was going to be another riot, so I just jumped back through again.'

'The Dials can chuck you out anywhere. You were lucky.'

'Rewind a bit there, blud. You met a woman who thought you were dying?' Jasper asks.

'She had a white horse. There were fields and flowers, and little birdies. Even mountains. Sweet,' I say.

'Like the place Scott said he went to before he arrived in 1972 all bleeding?' Ani asks, her brown eyes very big and wide.

'You can't trust a word that git says,' Jasper snaps.

'But Maisie went there!' Ani exclaims. ' She saw it! And why did you go there and not the rest of us?' she adds, glaring at Tracy.

'You know what? I have no idea. Deal with it,' Tracy says, glaring back.

'Maybe it was because of your bloody eye,' Ani says.

'This is not helping,' I say. 'Like I said, it was probably just a Dials thing. I was expecting to see Hannah with the pills, but what happened in 1987 has obviously changed something. We're all here now, and we're all okay. We need to decide what to do next.'

'What are our choices?' Ian asks.

'There are quite a few,' Ani says, before I can speak. 'Maisie will tell you that it's a priority to find Rob.'

'Her fella who was a Weyleigher and isn't anymore?' Tracy asks.

Ani nods. 'He's on the run because he believes they still want to lock him up. Then there's Tommy, who is also kind of her bae because Rob disappeared. We don't know where he is, either. Although he might be able to find his way to us, if he's still got her blood token, but he hasn't got here yet.'

'Standing right here!' I cry. 'You think I'd only consider those two options? Thanks for the support – not!' But then I catch Jasper's look, and remember what he said about it not being all about Rob and Tommy. They're not taking a great selfie of me here. I wonder if they're right. 'Okay, so maybe I've been a bit blinkered. There are other important issues.'

'You need to find Lizzy and sort things out with her,' Jasper says firmly.

'You need to find Mary and work out how to help her get back to 1987,' Ani says.

'You need to find out who Vix is,' Jasper adds, 'and why she knows so much about the Weys.'

'You need to get back to 1972 and see if Joan is thrown through the Weydoor, and who by,' Ani adds.

'Oh, is that all *I've* got to do?' I say, wishing I'd ordered something stronger to drink.

'Don't worry, honey,' Tracy says, patting me on the shoulder. 'We're here to help. All for one and one for all.'

'Muskehounds are always ready,' Ian sings back at her, and they laugh. 'Bagsy I'm Dogtanian.'

Jasper and Ani look at each other, and roll their eyes.

Me? I close my eyes, and doubt that how I'm feeling is anything like relief.

'So we can't use this Weydoor at all now?' Tracy asks.

'Big no,' Jasper says. 'We rode forward in Time from 1987, so everything that has happened here since then is affected by that incident with Valerie and Scott.'

'The Dials are probably corrupt now, which is why Maisie and Jasper used false names. I bet our real ones were plastered all over Noah's spreadsheet in bold pink highlighter,' Ani says.

'We can't go back to the point in 1987 where Valerie and the witch hunters would still be waiting for us,' I say, gazing down towards Earlham Street; there's a green painted shop front that sells vintage items from the last half of the 20th century and I wonder idly how much they'd have given us for just one of the long woollen coats we borrowed from Joan. 'And we can only ride out from here if Hannah and Noah aren't playing Gatekeeper.'

'How are we expected to know?' Ian asks.

'Without locking down under the Crown for a stakeout, we don't,' Jasper says. 'We'll have to find another Weydoor.'

'And since they don't tend to have big arrow signposts saying "This Way to the Hole in the Fourth Dimension", it's not as easy as it sounds.' Ani finishes her drink. 'It might be time to check out *The Truth* again; see if it can help us.'

'We have my Converse, remember?' Tracy says, holding one foot out in front of her like Cinderella's glass slipper. 'So we can go back to before the witch hunt happened, can't we?'

'Yes eventually, but there are more important things than getting back to 1987 right now.'

'Like making your peace with Lizzy,' Jasper mutters.

'That can wait as well,' I snap. 'I don't know where Rob is, but I'm hoping Tommy had tokens for his mother and his sister. I can't help Rob if I don't know where he is, or help Tommy sort his fam out.'

'Tommy's mother was the Seven Dials Witan when we met

her in the 70s. Mary's her eldest daughter.' Jasper tells Tracy and Ian, putting his pint glass down beside him on the pavement. 'Tommy's like their bodyguard. He knows the dangers. He'll be prepared for ambushes from Weyleighers. He's like a time travelling Eggsy. What?' he exclaims as I thump him on the arm – I know when he's being snarky.

I finish my Kopperberg cider. 'Right. We need to find where Mary ended up, and we need to stop Valerie throwing Joan through the Drake's Weydoor, and the key to that is in here.' I pat my bumbag.

'What have you got in your belt purse?' Ian asks.

'Bumbag,' Jasper corrects him.

'Asshole,' Ian retorts.

Jasper shakes his head. 'No! - it wasn't an insult – oh, never mind.'

'I have a load of random stuff in here.' I rummage around inside the fabric pocket. I have small trinkets and keepsakes and some vials from the Weyroom, but they're not what I'm looking for. Finally I lay my hands on it; a small vial with the label still clearly written – H 2/1/72. 'This is probably the only thing I need right now.' I throw a large mouthful of cider down my throat, and take a breath. 'I know you're all trying to help and I'm really glad you're all here, but I am totally out of my depth. I need to find someone I can trust. I need some advice. I need to find Helen Davenport, and this is her blood token.'

'I am not wearing any more coats made from sheep fleeces!' Ani says.

'You don't need to. We're not trying to blend in this time, we're trying to sort out a time problem,' I point out.

Tracy takes the vial from me and reads the label. '1972? Groovy, man.'

'Yep, pretty much,' Jasper agrees. 'You should hear some of the stuff they sing about.'

'We have to go backwards to stop this mess,' I say. 'We can't go forward from this point, because this is a timeline where Valerie has already got rid of two Weyfarere.'

And let's face it; they don't know how much mess I'm in. They don't know that, if Tim Wharton leaves Stoneford to be with Scott, me and my brothers are dust, and Valerie will have extinguished three Weyfarere.

Helen will know what to do. Helen will be able to help me. I know, I should be able to sort my own problems out but the truth is; this is a bigger problem than me, and this is what the Weyfarere are supposed to do, isn't it? I know I have no clue where to turn, and that's the precise moment that I see him, leaning on the corner of Earlham Street.

'Maisie, are you okay? You've gone a really weird –' Jasper says, but, before he can finish his sentence, I'm on my feet and running as fast as I can towards the dark-haired figure in the shadows cast by the high overhanging roofs of the Seven Dials.

Chapter Eleven – Just You And I (Tom Walker, 2019)

I can hear the others scrambling to their feet, so I stop halfway across the road next to the Dials pillar, and turn, shaking my head rapidly and looking a bit like a traffic warden with my hand held out towards them. Jasper reads my mind instantly and backs them all up to the kerb where we were sitting moments before. I walk over towards the spot on the corner of Earlham Street; now vacant, as I expected.

'I'm alone,' I call out, which is a bloody stupid thing to say on a Tuesday in the middle of one of the biggest tourist traps in London, and several people look at me as if I'm trying to pick someone up, but he needs to know because we have to have this conversation: just him, and me.

There's obviously an alley or a parking bay hidden down between some of the older buildings on the far side of Earlham Street because after a few minutes he appears on the opposite path. The people pass between us like a river; we are the rocks in the flow of the water, staring at each other.

His hands are in his pockets, his hair is past his shoulders including the spikes that used to be bleached on the ends, and he's still wearing the blue, violet and yellow T-shirt printed with Global Hypercolor, over jeans and black hightops. He looks bloody amazing, but it's those eyes that are freezing me to the spot; those beautiful green eyes, full of questions, full of hurt. FML! Why has it taken me this long to work out that I can't have it both ways? I can't mess this up any more than I have already. It's not the way I planned it, but he's here right now, and Helen will be wherever her blood leads us. I want to run across the road to him like the female lead in every sappy girly film I've ever watched on my tablet on a dull Saturday afternoon: I want to run across the road and throw myself into his arms and kiss him as we kissed at Lizzy's party. But there's not going to be a fanfare of uplifting music as we smile into each other's eyes.

I betrayed him, and I have to answer for that.

We meet in the middle of the road, but a black cab hoots us and others around us out of the way, and we end up standing opposite number seven.

'Did you go?' he asks. 'To the party in 1994?"

I nod. 'I went with Jasper and Ani.'

He nods and pulls a black packet covered in warnings and gory photos from the back of his jeans. 'I didn't see you there,' he remarks, after lighting a cigarette. "I'm still not altogether sure how this works.'

'You and me both,' I say, but he laughs.

'We both know that's not true.' He gives a small smile and stares at his feet before looking up at the top of the highest buildings. 'I'm surprised I found you here.'

'How did you find me?' I ask.

Again with the small smile that doesn't show any happiness. He reaches into his front pocket, and he pulls out a glass vial. I can guess what it is without reading the label, and it explains why Tommy's not shown up.

'I nicked your vial from Tommy's pocket at the station. When Tommy grabbed me, I took a chance. I remember you all saying that Weyfare blood was special. There were loads of people bustling around as it was the last train, so he never noticed. I got away from him into a corridor carriage, and the conductor never found me, either.' He looks at me. 'I decided that if anyone was going to have a direct link to you – it was going to be me. I remembered Helen saying there was an entrance to the Weydoor from the Crown, so I used the vial and it brought me here.' He smiles, but it's a shadow of the one I love. 'Couldn't believe my luck when I saw you were still here at the Dials.'

I nod and swallow hard. My cheeks grow hot. 'Where have

you been, Rob? When we found out ... after the party, we were coming after you but - well,' I finish lamely, 'something came up.'

He takes a deep drag on the cigarette. 'Of course it did. You're Weyfare. Something's always going to come up. After the party, I went down to our rooms at the hotel, and I found that Mu - Valerie still had Glenda and Lizzy's silver keys in the safe. I took them, and I took a wad of money, bought some togs and used a scarf I'd made Ani give me as a token to take me back to 1972. I was hoping to find you there, but I knew I had to wait until after we'd all come up here to see Helen, and after that, you just vanished. I could only find Ani and Brian – and your grandparents.'

'Yeah,' I say, biting my lip. 'We took the long way round.'

'With him.' It's not a question.

'And Jasper,' I say quickly. 'We ended up in the Blitz –' but one look at his face tells me that he's not interested right now in my eyewitness recount of the bombing of Drake's School in 1940, and I stop.

'I don't blame you,' he says quickly back. 'For going with him, I mean. We'd only been together five minutes, and you thought I was a Weyleigher's son.'

'It wasn't like that,' I try to tell him, but I know I'm lying and so does he. 'I was confused. I didn't know if I'd ever see you again, or what we would do if we did meet. He was kind.'

He nods. 'At the time, I had no choice but to leave. Surely you got that?'

'Of course I did, but it didn't make it any easier.'

'No.' He stubs the cigarette end underfoot, earning himself the stink eye from an old couple with a huge camera. 'So I posted Glenda's key through the letterbox at the flat one day, and I slept in the pill box. During the day, I kept an eye on Valerie.'

'Did you follow them when he was discharged from St Peter's?'

'I was pretty sure he'd seen me once or twice. I watched you go into the Old Library, but none of you came out. So I used the only thing I had left, which was Lizzy's key. It took me back to 1987. I just hung out, as close to the Old Library as I could get and hoped you would appear. There was a disco that night; I watched you all go in.' He sighs. 'I slept rough in the Park for a couple of nights, as I didn't want to go to Trinity. Finally, you all appeared back at the school with Scott and Tommy.' That small emotionless smile returns. 'I used your blood token to ride the Weys once I reached London. I've been waiting for you here for a couple of days. If you look hard enough around here, someone helps you out.'

I did a quick mental calculation. 'So you haven't seen me for a few weeks?'

'I've had a lot of time to come to terms with stuff,' he says. 'Finding out that I'm not who I thought I was. That the people I thought were my family are fake. Finding out that I'd lost you. It's allowed me time to think about where I go from here.'

'You haven't lost me, Rob,' I say, my voice hardly registering over the happy chattering of the shoppers and theatregoers.

'You don't have to say that,' he says, and he puts a hand on my shoulder that's so distant, it makes me want to cry. 'You're a perfect match, you and Tommy – the Weyfare and the Weyfare's son. But I'd like to think you and me can still be friends, now you know I'm not about to steal your heritage.'

'Of course we can be friends!' I exclaim, wiping my eyes roughly, and hoping he doesn't notice they've filled with tears because that's not what I want at all. I've been a complete tool.

'That's great then,' he says cheerfully, 'because I need your help.'

'Anything,' I say. Well, let's face it; it's the least I can do after how I've treated him.

'There was a bloke at the party in 1994 who talked about my real mother being sick. He said he was my half-brother. Did you see him?'

'We heard him speak.'

Rob lights another cigarette. 'I want to find my real family.'

'I understand that,' I say. 'But how do you think I can help?'

'I'm not sure you can, but I'm hoping Helen can, and I can't approach her without you. She thinks I'm the enemy.'

I look at him, trying not to lose myself in the depths of green gazing back at me. 'Rob, you need to know a few things before we do anything else.'

As the sun begins to dip behind the tallest buildings of the dials casting long shadows across the roads, I tell him about how we think Valerie might have thrown Joan through the Drake's Weydoor, how we found a new Weydoor leading to the road outside Tracy's aunt's house, about Scott moving to London to escape the mysterious Vix, Valerie's gathering of the witch hunters and the loss of Mary and Tommy.

'Wow.' he says genuinely. 'Something really did come up.'

I take a big breath for the finale. I told myself, don't keep any more secrets from people I care for. That way only leads to pain. 'Rob, Valerie went back to 1972, and she saved her son. Robin, I mean. He's still alive. Valerie would never have adopted you.'

People pass by, walking around us as if we have become part of the street furniture as he stares at me.

'I didn't want there to be any more secrets, Rob –' I begin, but he shakes his head.

'No. No, you did the right thing. So I've never been a Bennett?'

'Or a Simmons. No.'

'Well, I suppose that's a good thing,' he says. 'Bloody hell-fire,' he adds after a while.

'It is a good thing. She won't come after you now,' I say; then I feel bad. 'I'm sorry; that's a shitty thing to say,' I say lamely.

'What is? Telling me the truth? Don't be sorry about that. You'd think it would matter, but I never wanted to be part of that shitty family anyway. Anyway, you must be bricking it,' he says, 'when Tommy could be lost anywhere in time.' This time, the hand squeezes my arm gently.

'Not all that. He'd not be much of a Guard if he didn't carry his sister's blood token on him. Not to mention his mother's. And I have a blood token for Helen.'

'Will you take me to her?' he asks.

My mouth falls open. I can't even. 'You think you have to ask me?'

'I don't want to assume anything of anyone right now. I hear what you're telling me, but I still want to find a way back to my real mother, and Helen is the only person I know who might be able to get me in the right ballpark.'

Maybe if I can do this for him, maybe if I can show that I do still care, then maybe eventually we can see if there is anything left of the amazing connection we felt for each other on two different timelines. Because if this is a timeline where I'm not with Rob, I'm pretty much decided that I don't want to be on it. And Tommy? Will he understand? Maybe I should just swear off boys for a bit. I'm making a right mess of being in a relationship. I can't even face the one I have with my own mother.

'You'd better come back and meet the others,' I say out loud. 'Jasper and Ani know you, but Tracy and Ian don't.'

He nods, stamps another butt into the pavement and follows me back to the Crown.

'It's the perfect plan,' Jasper says, as we all sit on the kerbside again, me having subbed everyone yet another beer. 'Neither one of the gatekeepers will know you, Rob. You can go down there and check out who's on the desk, and if it's not Hannah or Noah –'

'Thunderbirds are go,' Ian finishes for him.

'And if it is Hannah or Noah?' Ani asks.

'Then we're sleeping rough tonight, unless we can find a place to stay in the West End that costs less than I've got left in my pocket,' I tell them. 'I've just blown over 50 quid on three rounds of beer. My mother would have a seizure if she knew how I was spending my Uni savings.'

'Beer and enough for a ride home,' Jasper says. 'I can't see the difference myself.'

'You'll all need to put a dab of this on your fingers.' I pull Helen's vial from my bumbag. 'Wherever she is, this should take us to her.' I pass it to Ian.

'Which version though?' Ian asks, upturning the vial on his palm and passing it on. 'I mean, surely there are loads of versions of her depending on where we show up.'

'No, the blood was given on the date on the label, and that makes it a token,' I tell him, 'but Weyfare blood controls travel on the Weys, so it takes you to the person that gave the blood. It ought to be 1972 but Helen's likely had to ride the Weys.'

Rob swallows the last of his pint, tips the vial onto his fingers, passes it to Tracy and stands up. 'Best motor then,' he says. 'No time like the present for sorting out the future.'

'Tell the barman you want to use the loo in the basement,' I tell him.

He nods and walks back into the Crown, and, like a nest of baby birds wanting worms; all their eyes are on me.

'That is one hot puppy,' Tracy says, smearing the tip of the vial on her hands. 'All I can say, girl, is that when you decide where you're going to lay your hat, I'll have your cast off.'

'Has he forgiven you?' Jasper asks, taking the vial from her.

'It didn't look like much of a reunion from where I was sitting,' Ani says.

'So that's Robin Simmons' adopted brother?' Ian asks.

'No. The Simmons never adopted him on this timeline,' I tell him.

'So he's Rob Bennett?' Jasper asks.

Is he? I put my head in my hands. 'Will you guys give a girl a break?' I exclaim. 'You're giving me a headache!'

'You're always getting headaches lately,' Ani says, more seriously, taking the vial from Jasper.

The lights come on around the theatre across the road, and suddenly the black exit doors open and a steady flow of people drain out onto the street, laughing and talking. They've been watching *Matilda*. It was one of my favourite books when I was a kid; I loved the fact that Matilda had a superpower. I guess I have one now. Some of them go into the Crown, and others disappear down the streets towards Leicester Square.

After a while, Rob reappears from the Crown with a pint in his hand. He squats down in front of me, his long hair flopping over one eye.

'Where'd you get that?' Tracy asks.

'Girl at the bar bought it for me,' he says with a grin, and although I try to grin back, it feels more like a grimace. 'Anyway, we're on. There's a bloke sitting at a computer by the Weydoor, but his name's Ryan, not Noah. Told him I was lost and I ran for it.'

'Thunderbirds really are go then,' Ian says.

'We need new names,' I tell them.

'Can you seriously even think of another name that rhymes with Jasper?' Jasper says, frowning.

'So call yourself Jacob. Jamie. Jay.' I stand up, straightening my bumbag. 'I don't plan to hang around there long enough for him to ask. Tracy, you ask the barman about the loo in the basement this time. The rest of you, keep your heads down and when I say, grab hold of each other behind me and run for it.'

'It's like being in the final episode of *Life on Mars*,' Jasper says.

'No one's jumping off any buildings today,' I tell him, but he's not that wrong. I might as well be jumping into oblivion, as I lose more and more control over my dad's movements and whether he'll ever be around to fall in love with my mum. We might as well be jumping off buildings when every ride on the Weys brings us more problems and more heartache.

The Crown is buzzing, but the barman Tracy latches onto wastes no time in opening the hidden door for us all. We jog down the passage with its bright LED fittings until we meet Ryan, typing into the computer on the desk. Before he's even had a chance to pick up his tablet and introduce himself, I'm past him.

'We know where we're going, thanks very much,' I call, grabbing the hand behind me, hoping they've all remembered to link up hands as I leap into the Weydoor, and there's white heat, purple light, black – nothing.

Chapter Twelve – We Are Family
(Sister Sledge, 1979)

As soon as I land on solid ground, I check to make sure the others have all followed and breathe a sigh of relief as they arrive beside me in varying states of elegance and timing. It's the first time I've had to lead the ride with so many of my squad. Tracy and Ian are a little delayed, but that's the Dials for you. They look a bit confused, but I have to remind myself that relatively speaking, I'm a pro when it comes to this Wey riding now.

Ryan has gone, and so have the computer, tablet, desk and all the other little modern gadgets from 2019, but there are strip lights in the ceiling that I don't remember from 1972. There's a cavernous atmosphere to the place again; the walls are bare rock and it doesn't feel like an airport arrival lounge. There's some rubbish dumped in one corner: a couple of crumpled newspapers, an old tea towel and a broken mug.

'The Crown or Number Seven?' Jasper asks, pointing at each passage away from the glowing Weydoor.

'Number Seven,' I say.

'But what if it's later than 1987?' Tracy asks. 'There's no way of telling from here.'

'If it's post-1987, Valerie would have Guard all over this Weydoor like a rash,' Ani says. 'It's a safe bet we're earlier than that.'

All the same, I'm treading carefully as we head for the door to the flat. I've been jinxed too many times already by believing in something when I had no hard proof. Luckily, the strip lights are placed all the way along because the smartphones are all dead again, but Ian still nearly trips over something on the ground as we approach the door to the basement flat. When I look down to see the large and unexpected rock there, my eye is drawn to a cream envelope that's tucked away behind, wedged between two stones in the wall: it's very nearly hidden. I pull it out. There is an M on it and six numbers.

'It might be M for Mary,' Ani says, peering at it.

'Could be M for Meghan Trainor. And if it is, I'll put it back,' I say.

'Do you read everyone's private letters?' Tracy asks.

'People don't leave private letters hidden in walls in a public thoroughfare,' Rob says. 'That was meant to be found. Someone's put that rock there on purpose.'

'Remind me never to leave my diary lying around when

she's about,' Tracy retorts.

'Yeah, don't do that. She could sell it on the black market. They'd make it into a film. Tracy does Dallas,' Ian says, avoiding a swipe from her as I peel open the envelope.

'What would Tracy be doing in Dallas?' Jasper asks.

'What's 150779 mean?' Rob asks. I try not to react to the closeness of him as he reads the numbers aloud beside me, but it's not easy.

'The date, at a guess,' Ani says. 'Without dots or slashes or hyphens. 15 for the 15th. 07 for July. And 79 for 1979.'

'Clever. We were right about riding back in Time then,' Jasper says. 'What does the message say?'

I read it out loud to them. No more secrets. Secrets just mess with people in the end.

M,

If you ride out to me after what's happened to my M and T, you should get this letter. T sounded the alarm in the lounge at number seven, so rest assured help will have gathered there to restrain the enemy and prevent her from doing any further changes to her timeline, or damage to yours.

T came to me, and we rode to my M. She is in 1979, as are you if you are reading this. T explained to me about the items given to you that prevent our travel. We are travelling to the mermaid on the southeast coast of England. She studied chemistry at Dartmoor

University. It is my hope that she will be able to identify the components of that which was given to my M to see whether there is any legitimacy to the claims. T tells me you should still have more.

I don't know when you will arrive, but we left on the date of this envelope. Hopefully, you will find it sooner rather than later, and us. I have left you another envelope with legal tender in it. Fortunately, here is not so different from seven years ago. You will know where to find it, M – it is something important that links us both. Use it as you need.

Ride safe, little sister.

H.

'I didn't know there was a university on Dartmoor,' Rob says.

'What in the name of Sod is that supposed to mean?' Tracy exclaims. 'It's a load of old codswallop!'

'That's exactly what Helen wanted you to think,' Ani says. 'You being a bystander who might have picked up the letter and read it. It gives nothing away.'

'Okay, but the *mermaid* with a *degree* in *Chemistry* who lives on the south coast?'

'That's not what it says.' There is a distant light bulb flickering at the end of the tunnel of everything that's happened to me in the last couple of weeks. I pull *The Truth* from my bumbag. 'It must be in here somewhere. Give me a minute or two.'

'And what does she mean about something important that links the two of you?' Ian asks.

'That's easy. Blood,' Jasper replies.

'Crap!' I thrust *The Truth* into Ani's hands, and run back towards the Weydoor. 'You're the resident historian. See if you can find us a list of the names of the Great Weydoors. Preferably in English, not middle-feckup.'

'Where are you going?' Rob asks, beginning to follow me.

'I won't be long. Wait there.'

I jog back through the passage to the Weydoor, which starts glowing again as I get nearer. I knew I'd seen something there; something else that triggered a memory. A tea towel abandoned in a pile of litter: like the tea towel Helen used to bind her hand when she cut it breaking a glass, like the tea towel I stole to keep a token of her blood, giving myself away. I pick it up and instantly recognise it: "Greetings from Torcombe." Wrapped inside is another cream envelope, and inside that, a bank of notes tied up in a white ribbon that could get us a lot further from London than the southeast coast.

When I get back to the others, Ani is grinning wider than I think I've ever seen this version manage. She holds forward *The Truth*, open about three-quarters of the way through, and I hold out the wad of money that Helen left for me.

'Christ on a Bike,' Ian says, 'that's a massive amount of dosh by anyone's standards.'

'Rich in three decades, this squad,' Jasper says.

'You were right,' Ani says, as I pocket the notes and take the book from her. 'The Mermaid isn't a who, it's a what. It's listed as one of the doors on the Great Weys. There'll be another Witan protecting it. She'll be the one with the Chemistry degree. There are directions to all of the Great Weydoors. Swallow Falls is in Wales. Dial Post is in West Sussex. I found directions to the Bergh as well.'

'No need to go up there any time soon,' Rob says, thinly. 'Ready to unlock another brave new world, Maisie?'

'No need to unlock,' I tell him and I push on the door.

It opens into a weird mix of hipster chic and plain solid furniture that looks homemade. I wonder if Mavis and Helen are still here, as I look up at a tall grandfather clock and run a finger over a huge bright orange lampshade, sitting on a low wooden sideboard next to a TV on a trolley. The TV is encased in wood, with a small curved blue-grey screen and six labelled silver buttons reading BBC1, BBC2, ITV and AUX along with a random 4 and 5 above other buttons for things like "colour" and "brightness". The pattern on the velvet sofa makes my eyes hurt, the armchairs look boxy and uncomfortable, and, in the middle of the room, there is a huge wooden chest with iron hinges that looks like it was taken from a pirates' ship. Everything is overwhelmingly brown, apart from the wallpaper and the lampshade. I was with someone at a party once, and, when she spewed everywhere, someone called it a multicoloured yawn and the wallpaper makes me remember that.

'That telly looks just like the one I had when I was a kid,' Ian says. 'I used to lay in front of it every morning in the summer holidays with my Coco Pops, watching *Champion the Wonder Horse.*'

'And *Why Don't You -?*' Tracy says, turning to him and grinning.

'Just switch off your television set and go and do something less boring instead,' Rob says.

Tracy claps her hands together like an excited toddler. 'And *Multi-Coloured Swap Shop!*'

'I *loved* that programme,' Ian says wistfully. 'I sent in a swap once, but it didn't work out.'

'What did you want to swap?' Rob asks.

'I had a Matchbox James Bond Aston Martin DB5, and I wanted a Lotus Esprit,' Ian replies mournfully. Rob's face is full of compassion.

'When you lot have finished planning out your *Antiques Roadshow,* we need to bounce before we're seen,' I say, and turn to face Mavis in the doorway.

'Miss Maisie?' she says uncertainly. She doesn't look much

different to how she looked when we met in 1972, except her hair is now in a bun rather than a ponytail, and she wears a black blouse and trousers under her white apron, instead of her severe *Downton Abbey* style servant's dress.

'Yes, Mavis. It's good to see you,' I reply. 'These people are my squad – my friends. You remember Jasper and Rob?'

'You bought a Weyleigher's son back to the Witan's home,' she asks, her eyes latching onto Rob like Gorilla Glue. 'Do you want me to send for the Guard? Mrs Davenport is away.'

'He's not the enemy we thought he was, Mavis. Can you trust me on this?' I ask her, feeling Rob shuffle awkwardly from foot to foot beside me. 'We need to find Helen. She left me a message saying she's gone to The Mermaid.'

Mavis nods, but her eyes still keep flickering back and forward to Rob. 'Three days hence. You should follow her directly. It's not prudent for Mrs Davenport to be away from the Dials for too long.'

'I understand. We'll get out of your hair,' I say, and seeing her confusion, add, 'I mean, we'll leave right away.'

'Catch the next train southeast,' Mavis says. She suddenly stands up very tall and faces Rob. 'Why shouldn't I be alerting the Guard?"

'Because I'm nothing to do with the Weyleighers,' Rob says. 'I was adopted by one.'

Mavis looks at me. 'Is this the truth?' she asks. 'He was taken from his birth mother by the Weyleigher?"

I nod. 'It's the truth.'

'Then I am sorry for you,' Mavis says. 'No babe should be taken from its mother.' She steps forward then, and like some kind of ritual, she puts a hand on Rob's shoulder. 'I wish you Godspeed until you can be with your kin again.'

Rob puts a hand over hers. 'Thanks, Mavis. That means a lot to me.'

With her hand still on him, she turns to me. 'T'is your destiny to ease these troubled times, Miss Maisie. I feel it in my bones. I wish you well on your journeys, and hope we may meet again in more peaceful times,' she says, and she leaves the room as if it is a dismissal.

'Time to go,' Jasper says. 'Can't be sure when we arrived here; if it's late, we might have trouble getting to the station in time for a train south today.'

But when we step out of the door to number seven onto Earlham Street, the sky above our heads is blue with fluffy white clouds. The Dials are looking a bit grubby around the edges again with boarded-up buildings and the colourfully painted walls all grimy brickwork, but the people make up for it. I'm used to the Dials being full of the Lost in all their differ-ent clothing from their timelines, but these guys are different –

boys and girls with painted faces that put *Ru Paul's Drag Race* to shame, huge feathers and glitter and hair slicked into the craziest angles, clothes a mixture of all the Lost – pirates and street workers, neck ruffs, shiny silver-buckled shoes and DMs that reach to the knees - all uber-cool as they walk past us, heading toward Covent Garden.

'Blitz kids,' Tracy breathes, with an air of respect I don't often hear from her. There is no feeling of menace in these people, just style, spotlight and swagger. They don't give us a second glance.

We head off towards Leicester Square to pick up a tube train to take us to the station that will take us to Helen, Mary and Tommy.

The clock in front of the departures board tells us it's the 18th July as I buy our tickets southeast, and the newspaper stand on the entrance tells us it's a Wednesday. London is hot and busy; full of workers and tourists with massive cameras, but it's tarnished again, like it never really got over the War, like it never really got back on its feet. Apart from that little pocket of human rainbow in the Dials, London looks exhausted. I wonder if that's why that group dresses like that.

We pile into a large carriage, not needing to hide from any conductors as legit travellers, and settle down with a large order McDonalds we picked up from Victoria Street. I swear this chocolate milkshake is creamier and sweeter than any I've tasted on my own timeline, and Big Macs are definitely bigger.

'Good to know that some things don't change,' Ian says, biting into his Quarterpounder with Cheese.

To be honest? Things never stay the same, but he'll have to work that one out for himself.

Chapter Thirteen – Up The Junction (Squeeze, 1979)

We have to change trains at a busy resort junction and pick up a little rickety train that goes inland again on a single track. There are no hills around, and then, as the train carriage turns a bend, we see a town that looks like it's clinging onto to a cliff face – except someone's taken the sea away.

Coming out of the station, trying to blend in with the tourists and their hot, squally kids, is a lot like arriving at Stoneford except there's a definite seaside feel to this place.

'Have you ever been here?' I ask Ani.

She nods. 'It's a cinque port.'

'Sync port?' I repeat.

'How can it be a port? There's no sea,' Ian says.

'There was. The land was reclaimed about 400 years ago. Before that, it was one of five ports that defended England against Europe before there was a navy.' Ani points across the road at what is, to be honest, a very obvious sign declaring the town's identity. 'Cinque ports means five ports in Norman French. Or did you think it was something to do with flash drives or kitchen equipment?'

I crinkle my nose at her. I may recommend to the Witan that in future, all Weyfarere should travel with a smug historian. Or not.

'I've been here as well,' Tracy says. 'The nicest bit of the town is the oldest, up at the top by the castle. If we're looking for a place where a Weydoor might be hidden, I'd bet on it being there.'

'Do we know what the Mermaid is? I mean, why is the Weydoor called the Mermaid?' Rob asks. 'Is it worth asking someone?'

It turns out that it is worth asking someone. The first person we find tells us it's a well-known medieval inn in the citadel, which is up on the hill like Tracy told us. We walk for a while and then turn right up a lane that suddenly narrows, and is full of quaint little cottages backed up together with dark wooden shop fronts, quirky little places selling pottery and bits of handmade jewellery, next to grand old stone buildings that look stately and important.

As cutesy as it all is, I can't join Tracy and Ani cooing over the silver bangles in the display windows. I can't think of anything except the fact that we are likely not too far from joining Helen, and that means meeting Tommy again. I mean, I know I've had to get to grips with all this Weyfarere stuff pretty bloody quickly, but I'm still Maisie Wharton and it wasn't that long ago that I was an asscloth who thought taking responsibility meant remembering to put my dirty washing in the basket without being reminded. Tommy will think things with us are the same as they were, and they so aren't. Rob thinks I want to be with Tommy and I don't think I do. I think I want to be with Rob, and his body language is screaming that I've not just missed that train; I've missed the entire timetable. So I've messed up big time with both boys, and now we're all going to be in the same room, and I have to pretend I'm in control while we deal with the fact that Mary was given a drug from the future that we took back to the past. I can't even.

'Maisie? Are you all right?'

I shake off lecturing myself at the sound of Rob's voice. 'Super-fine. What's up?'

'The others were wondering if we could get ice cream or something,' he says.

Now on top of everything else, I feel like Teen Mother. 'Why don't I divvy this cash out and then you can buy whatever you like.'

Jasper shakes his head, no. 'You're in charge of the trip; you carry the moolah,' he says.

'They've got Zooms and I haven't had one of those since I was small!' Tracy exclaims. 'Orange Maids, look! Raspberry

Mivvis!

'Hold me back,' I say, as she literally drags me into the little shop, which is crammed with families who've obviously had the same idea in the sun. While Tracy and Ian go totally extra over the sweets and ice creams, showing Ani, Jasper and Rob their favourites ("Look! It's a Texan!" and "Banjos! I bloody *loved* Banjos!"), I'm looking around. We're at the opposite end of the 1970s now, and the whole hippy vibe has definitely left the decade from what I can see. Although one of the mums has long hair, it has shorter layers flicked back over and over that seem to be glued in place, as they don't move whatever she does. Her jeans are still flared compared to ours, but her blouse is plain, almost like school uniform. Her friend has a long chestnut-brown bob with a heavy fringe, and she's wearing a trouser suit the colour of chicken nuggets over a white crocheted vest top. One of the men is wearing a lemon-yellow jumper with no sleeves over a blue shirt, and his trousers look like they have tiny velvet stripes going down the material. The other guy is in double denim. I'm beginning to think I prefer the platform boots and the freaky colours. The kids are in very short shorts – nothing knee-length in sight. When I realise they are all staring as one at my excited crew raving over the chest freezer, I step in.

'We need to be a bit more basic, guys,' I say quietly. 'The

people here think you're crazy weird.'

'Basic?' Tracy asks, brandishing an orange-wrapped lolly with Cider Quench printed on it.

'Calm the hell down,' Ani says, looking at a plastic cone of pink and white ice cream. 'Is there really gum in the bottom of this ice cream? Won't it be frozen solid?'

At the top of the High Street, we turn into another street, cobbled this time, passing more tourists with huge cameras and women dragging tartan shopping trolleys or guiding flimsy pushchairs that look like toys containing wriggling toddlers, and then, a little way down the next narrow lane is a massive black and white Tudor building, squished between cottages decorated with colourful flower baskets.

The Mermaid Inn looks pretty grand, and more worryingly, pretty busy.

'How in the name of Sod are you lot hiding a time portal in there?' Tracy asks, as at least twenty people pour out onto the stony roadway, laughing and chatting as they snap away at the front of the inn with their huge black and white cameras.

'The Weyfarere manage well enough hiding one in a school,' Jasper says, peering at a white piece of paper behind a glass cabinet on the wall. 'I'm no expert on 1979, but those prices look steep. I don't think Helen's money is going to cover rooms here.'

'If Helen's here, we shouldn't have to pay,' I say, more positively than I feel.

'*If* she's here?' Ani asks. 'How many mermaids are there likely to be in one town?'

'Until we find her, I'm taking nothing for granted.' I step into an archway that travels right through to the rear of the whole building, and there is a doorway to the right, through which I can see a reception area and lots of wooden beams.

A man dressed like he's going to a posh dinner comes up to the counter before I have a chance to ding the little silver bell. 'Good afternoon, Miss. How may I help you?'

'I'm looking for Helen Davenport,' I say.

He blinks twice. ' You are required to tell me the falsehood.'

'Say what?' Ian asks.

Rob's hand reaches towards me, and I get goosebumps as his hand touches the fabric over my stomach seconds before opening my bumbag, taking out the letter from Helen and handing it to me.

'You could be anyone, couldn't you?' he says, shrugging.

I must be getting better at all this, as it doesn't take me long to realise what he's on about. 'There's no such place,' I say, glancing down the letter. 'Dartmoor University.'

The man nods. He's changed from cheerful and welcoming to efficient and professional. 'You will wait in Dr Syn's Lounge, and I will inform them that you have arrived.'

As he walks away from us, Jasper hisses, 'Dr Syn? I thought Soho was back in London?'

Dr Syn's Lounge isn't as it sounds at all; it's all fancy red leather sofas and walls with black beams curving across them showing paintings of rosy-cheeked women in floaty dresses, old men with white beards and pointy hats like Gandalf and local landscapes. The furniture is dark wood and solid. We are the only people in there.

'What are you going to say to Helen?' Rob asks into the silence. 'About me?'

'I don't have to tell her anything if you don't want me to,' I tell him. 'It's your story. It's up to you how much of it you want them to know. I'll just make sure they listen. No one's dragging you off to the Bergh on my watch.'

He looks at me gratefully, my heart melts and I want to throw my arms around him. 'Thank you,' he says, but he doesn't touch me. 'That means a lot.'

When they walk into the lounge, the temperature drops by several degrees as if we've just been joined by three phantoms. We stand and face each other across the room.

'Blimey, it's like *Gunfight at the O.K Corral* without the pistols,' Ian says.

'You caught him!' Tommy exclaims as if I've completed a

very complicated test. 'Far out!'

'No, I didn't catch him,' I say, trying to keep my voice even. 'He's not a Weyleigher, remember? Rob's here because he wants to talk to Helen.' I hope he's going to turn around and tell me that's not the only reason, but he doesn't.

Helen lets her head fall to one side, her dark eyes staring at Rob, who stares straight back at her. 'He isn't?' she asks.

I shake my head, no.

'But he could still be on their side, sugar-'

'My family are not Weyleighers,' Rob says. 'Valerie Bennett, Simmons, or whatever she calls herself, is not my mother. She's never been my mother. I've never been a Bennett. I want nothing to do with her or her family.'

Tommy makes a choking noise and looks at me in exasperation. 'And you *believe* him?'

'Thomas.' Helen says, and he attempts to regain control of himself. She continues to look at Rob. 'Tell us what you have come here to say,' she adds. When Rob has finished, she looks at me. Tommy is going pink with the effort of keeping his mouth shut.

'We rode to 1994. We heard Valerie tell a room full of people that Rob was adopted.' I move my head around, trying to get Tommy to look at me, but he won't. 'I told Mary and Tommy all this in 1987, but he won't believe me.'

Helen opens her arms to me like a long lost relative, which I guess in a way she is. I step forward into them, hugging her briefly and taking in a familiar sharp floral scent that I can't place. She's small, dark-haired and slim and she's not to be messed with; she's the Seven Dials Witan, and that means she outranks everyone in the room, except maybe the younger woman next to her that she's not introduced. The waistcoat of crocheted coloured squares over a shiny cream roll neck jumper and trousers would've told me she rode straight from 1972, even if I hadn't had her blood to track. As she holds me, she whispers, 'Be kind.' I nod my head, yes, and we step away from each other. 'You have new friends with you, Maisie Weyfare,' she says out loud. 'As well as old.'

'This is Tracy and Ian,' I say. 'I got fed up of lying to everyone about who I was.'

'This is Polly Frobisher, the Witan known amongst the Weyfarere as the Mermaid,' Helen says. We nod at each other.

'We know all about the Weyfareres,' Tracy says, proudly pronouncing the word Wayfarers.

'Wayfarers are an overpriced pair of shades. We are Weyfar-air,' the younger woman says, spelling it out like Tracy is five. 'Let's hope you know enough about us to keep your mouth shut.'

Tracy is shocked enough to do it.

'Tommy tells me there is bad feeling between you and Lizzy,' Helen remarks.

'Lizzy's stories aren't mine to tell,' I say firmly. 'They only know mine.'

She nods, glancing at Tracy and Ian.

'And the only thing I do like a fish is drink,' the younger woman says, grinning, and, as she comes closer, I guess she's only a few years older than most of us, wearing a pair of wide-bottomed dark jeans with a bright red Brutus label on the waistband, and a white *Star Wars* T-shirt. 'Welcome to the old place. It's a bit naff, but the punters like it that way. They think it's haunted. Every time a bystander gets away from us and es-capes into one of the guest rooms, we just tell them it was a ghost.' She holds her hand out. 'So you're Maisie from the 21st century. I'm appreciating the off-radar outfit. Hip.'

I take the hand and shake it. 'Thanks, I think.'

'You'd better come up,' Helen says. 'Mary is resting upstairs with Polly's Guard, Barry and Clive.' She takes a deep breath as if she's calming herself down. 'Valerie must've been watching Number Seven for a long time. She knew exactly when Mary's Guard used to go out for their daily jog so she could have them delayed.'

We climb a set of steepish red-carpeted stairs to the first floor, where, next to a door marked Dr Syn's Bedchamber, there is another room labelled 'Bayley – Private.'

Polly takes a key that looks remarkably like mine from under her T-shirt and unlocks the door onto a suite of rooms. 'I live here,' she explains, replacing the necklace.

'So this whole inn is yours?' I ask, taking in the surroundings.

Polly snorts. 'No. My official title is Heritage and Cultural Manager. The owners don't really know what we do, only that it's a part of the deeds that the eldest female in my family line gets the job. We get this suite, and when some weirdly dressed bod pops up in a guest bedroom and the punters sell the story, and it's the Witan's job to convince the press it's just another ghost from an old smuggling gang.'

The room we're standing in looks like a set from *Downton Abbey* with its huge flowery sofas and armchairs, except there's a TV in a corner cabinet and a record player very similar to Helen's at Number Seven. No skinned sheep on the floor, thankfully, just a faded rug that looks like it started life in a Turkish market. An archway to the right opens onto a long corridor that runs parallel to the one outside where the guests are, and three or four more doors lead off it. A large bookcase at the far end of the room is filled with leather-bound books. I wonder if Polly keeps her family's copy of *The Truth* on it as Glenda did.

Polly walks past a tall grandfather clock and flicks a light switch on the wall behind it, but, instead of flooding the room with light, the large bookcase starts sliding to the left like it's on rollers, revealing another room behind it. She steps forward and waves us all after Tommy and Helen, who are already walking into the hidden room.

'It's another Weyroom,' Tracy says, looking around her at the shelves of vials and token objects.

Polly nods. 'Good name. Should use that ourselves, Helen.' Once we are all inside, she clicks on a similar switch and the rear of the bookcase, a plain piece of plastered wall, slides back into place. In the centre of the room, there's a round table like something out of *Merlin*, and we all sit down around it. I'm worried that Mary isn't joining us, and I say as much.

'She's still recovering,' Helen replies, steepling her hands on the carved wooden surface of the table. For the first time, I notice a few extra lines of tension around her eyes. 'We thought it best that she gets plenty of rest. She was in a bad way when we found her three days ago, but she is much better now.'

'She was out cold in a pool of her own chunder,' Tommy says, never taking his stink eye from Rob as if it was somehow his fault. 'She told us she rode through to the Dials in 1979 and then made herself sick trying to get the tablet out of her stomach before it did her any damage.'

'Do you think she ingested any of it?' Jasper asks.

'We don't know.' Tommy stands up, clearly distracted. 'Polly needs to examine the pills so that she can work out whatever that bitch has done to my sister. I'm going to sit with her, Mum. I don't want her waking up with just the Guard for company, while we're down here gassing.'

I'm such a klutz. Here am I, all too big for my kicks thinking Tommy's going to be beside himself about me turning up when he's got so much more important things than me on his mind. As I watch, he eyes Rob, the anger smouldering behind the hard look, and I wonder how long it's going to take for him to believe that Rob is not here on the orders of the woman who might have damaged his sister for good. I'm the last thing on his mind right now.

As he leaves the room, Helen says gently, 'He's taking this situation very hard. He isn't Mary's Guard, but he believes he should've protected her better, regardless of anything we say to him.'

'He didn't stand a chance,' Jasper says. 'None of us could do anything to help her. There were too many of them.'

Helen looks at Rob. 'I'm afraid your news won't be seen as positively by my son.'

'I'm not here to break anyone up,' he says. 'I have a favour to ask you, but it can wait.'

Helen doesn't try to hide her surprise, but when she looks at me for answers, I don't have any, and I just shake my head. 'Tell us more about these tablets,' she says randomly.

I nod, yes. 'We were given them to take in an alternate 2019 at the Dials, but none of us swallowed them. We thought they were some kind of tracker.'

'Like a microchip?' Polly asks.

'You have those?' Ian asks.

'The building's medieval, sweetheart: we aren't,' Polly says.

'They told us it would cause a reaction with the Weydoor if we tried to ride again.' I take the serviette out of my bumbag and carefully open it on the table to reveal two more little white pills. 'I kept them safe, but we gave one to Scott to prevent him from riding the Weys again. Trouble is, he didn't swallow his either, and they gave his pill to Mary.' I meet Helen's gaze. 'I'm so sorry.'

She shakes her head as if to dismiss me. 'Part of a Witan's job is to deal with anomalies that are separated from their timelines.' She waves a hand at the contents of the shelving. 'This is why we have the Heritage Rooms.'

'Tommy says Mary threw up though?' Ani asks.

'She made herself sick, but she was unconscious when we found her,' Helen says. 'Fortunately the 1979 me was upstairs bathing at the time, but Mavis found us and got *The Truth* for me.'

'That must have been well freaky for Mavis,' Jasper says. 'One of you with Mary all vomity, and the other you in the bath.'

'You forget that Mavis has ridden the Weys herself. Although it's still frowned upon because she is a woman, I consider her part of my Guard.' Helen says. 'There was a footnote in *The Truth* saying that The Mermaid of 1979 was a chemist, so I rang Polly, and she sent one of her Guard up in a car for us.'

'I use a pagan healer for identifying ailments and diseases in typical bystanders,' Polly explains. 'The Witan keep most of the major vaccinations on hand; it's easier than explaining to your local hospital why some toff in a top hat just showed up in town with advanced consumption, but I'm not going to pump a load of antibodies into a Weyfare until we know what we're dealing with.' She pulls a red and white packet of cigarettes from her jeans pocket, lights one with a slender golden lighter with the words Dunhill printed on it and tosses the packet to Helen, who catches it.

'So what happens to the Dials while the two of you are down here?' Ian asks.

'My blood returns me to the end of my timeline,' Helen says, passing the packet on. 'The place where I left it. It will be as if I was never away. The 1979 me is still in London. As for 1987,

Tommy had the foresight to sound the alarm as the attack happened, and every Witan close to London would've got their Guard to the Dials as soon as was humanly possible.'

'How will we know if they stopped Valerie and Scott?' Tracy asks.

'You won't know that until you return to the end of your own timeline,' Helen says bleakly.

'And if Mary can't go back to 1987?' Ian asks.

A bell in the corner of the room tinkles into the tumbleweed and Polly gets to her feet. 'Gus has probably left us some tea in the outer rooms. Stay put, and I'll go grab it.'

Gus must be another of Polly's Guard as well as the efficient receptionist we met when we arrived, as they both come into the hidden room with trays laden with silver pots, jugs and solid-looking mugs that don't match at all, and he doesn't react to the rows of blood-filled vials. The plates piled high with sandwiches and foil-wrapped cakes remind me that all I've had to eat recently is an orange ice lolly shaped like a cartoon Dracula, and that's not going to cut it if I'm about to take part in an advanced Chemistry lesson. I put the serviette of pills back into my bumbag. I haven't taken Chemistry since I was 14. FML.

Chapter Fourteen – Are 'Friends' Electric? (Gary Numan, 1979)

The sandwiches are ham and mustard on buttered white sliced bread and they taste amazeballs. Mum buys bread that she says it's good for her gut health, but my gut thinks this bread tastes just fine. The teacakes are little chocolate covered marshmallow domes with a biscuit on the bottom. I'm drowning in a sugar rush when I realise Polly's speaking to me.

'We'll crush one of your tablets and I'll run some overnight tests in the lab,' she says, 'but it'll be at least 24 hours before we get any meaningful results.' She's leaning forward onto the table and grinning at Ani. 'I don't often get company down here in the sticks. Do either of you bystander girls fancy helping me out with an experiment I've been wanting to trial?'

'What kind of experiment?' Tracy asks.

'I want to compare the blood of the Weyfarere with bystanders' blood.' She stubs her cigarette out in an ashtray that looks like it came from the bar downstairs. 'Most bystanders are freaked out already by the time they realise what's happened to them. It wouldn't help much if I said "Oh, and before you go, could I extract some of your blood?"

'No, I can see that would go down like a sack of sick,' Tracy replies, her top lip curling. 'Maybe while you're at it, you can explain to me why me and Ian keep having to ride the Weys twice to get to Maisie.'

'The Seven Dials Weydoor is a bit temperamental,' Helen says. 'Ordinary bystanders get pulled in and thrown out anywhere because it's where all the Great Weys cross.'

'Think what a caper you'd be in if you weren't riding with Weyfare blood to guide you,' Polly adds.

'All this talk of blood is making me feel like an extra in *Twilight*,' Jasper says, with a shiver.

'Riding the Weys isn't for the squeamish. Listen, there's a midweek discothèque at the Town Hall on Wednesdays. If you donate some blood, I'll take you all down for a boogie.'

I've thought before that Polly can't be more than five years older than us, and I can hear in her voice she's lit at the thought of getting out for the night.

'A bogie?' Jasper asks, his lips pursed in disgust.

'A boogie. A dance,' she says impatiently. 'I get maybe five bystanders a month through this Weydoor. It doesn't need watching.' She turns to face Helen. 'I know you'll want to stay with Mary so I wonder –' She lets her voice trail off, and her blue eyes get very big and wide. 'We'd only be up the road.'

Helen has ten years or so on the younger woman, and she gives her the same motherly look she always gives to me. 'We can do nothing until the morning,' she says with a smile, 'and we are safe here. But I like my music a little less frantic. Go cut a dash.'

Polly claps her hands together like a child that's been told it's off to Disneyland Paris for the weekend. 'Let's get this show on the road,' she says, standing up. 'Come down to the lab.'

We leave the hidden room and go back through the archway and down the corridor that leads off the main room. Turns out that acting as a cultural manager for the Mermaid Inn isn't Polly's only job; she's a freelance research assistant for some biochemical company in Brighton, and this goes a long way to explain why there's a room like looks like a set from *Breaking Bad* in this old building. There are racks of test tubes, Bunsen burners, wall cabinets with clear glass windows attached to tubes that run into a vent on the wall, various labelled bottles and Petri dishes on a polished stone worktop.

'I've been working for some time on a theory I have about why the Weyfarere can control their movement on the Weys,' she says, putting on a white coat, some blue gloves and pulling her blonde bobbed hair back from her face with a plastic hair band covered in fake flowers. 'Have you heard of DNA tracking?'

'We call it profiling,' Ani says.

Polly nods. 'I *knew* it would become important. To cut a long story short, women have two X chromosomes, and men only have one, so I thought the Weyfarere gene must be passed down through one of the Xs. Right?"

'Makes sense,' Rob says, reaching to pick up a jar.

Polly bats his hand away. 'So I've recently started trying to identify the component parts of my blood so that I can compare it with bystander blood.' She picks up a syringe sealed in its wrapper. 'That's where you girls come in.'

'Don't worry about making us feel surplus to requirements or anything,' Ian says.

'Don't get on your high horse, stud,' Polly says. 'Anyway, first things first. Hand over one of those pesky little tablets, and I'll dissect it.' She holds up a sharp-looking scalpel, and I decide there and then never to get on the wrong side of Polly Frobisher.

'Don't you want them both?' I ask, taking the serviette back out of my bumbag.

'Not if I can help it. We ought to try to preserve one intact,' she says, taking the little tablet with a pair of tweezers from a new packet, dropping it onto a clear Petri dish, and cutting through it with the blade.

I put the other tablet back, and we all watch as Polly cuts the tablet over and over like she's chopping a very small vegetable so that eventually it is little more than a dish of dust. 'Bring over that rack of test tubes, will you?' Rob, being the nearest, does as he's told. 'I do like a man who can take orders,' she says, sending him an undeniably flirty look, and I don't look to see if he returns it; I feel a pang of jealous pain in my stomach, but of course, he's a free agent and she's not even that much older than him.

After dropping tiny bits of the tablet dust into several test tubes containing different substances ('I could explain what's in all of them to you, but you'd be snoring before I got to Tube Three' she told us, much to Ani and Ian's disgust, and no amount of their insistence would change her mind), she puts the rack in one of the glass cabinets and locks it. 'Sleeves up, ladies,' she says, reaching for new syringes as Ani and Tracy's noses scrunch up.

'Do you think Tommy will want to come to the disco with us?' Tracy asks, wincing as Polly does her work.

Helen looks at me, and I shrug. Do I want to go to a 1970s disco where Rob and Tommy are glaring at each other over their pint glasses? Of course I bloody don't, but it isn't all about me, is it? 'Perhaps it might be nice if you ask him,' she says to Tracy.

'I'll go.' I look across at Rob, but he's way too fixated on a Bunsen burner. 'I need to speak to him anyway.'

'Mary is in the bedroom at the far end of the corridor,' Polly says. 'You can't miss it. If an alarm goes off, you've opened the Fire Exit.'

Polly lives well. Everywhere has that understated look you get on those antiques shows where the owner says he bought a bowl for 50p from Oxfam and the guy from the BBC tells him you better insure it for ten grand. Mum used to love watching *Antiques Roadshow*. I think maybe I get why now.

Tommy is sitting on the edge of the pink quilted double bed, holding his sister's hand. Mary seems to be sleeping. When he sees me in the doorway, he puts a finger over his lips, gently places her hand on the bedspread and comes to meet me in the corridor.

'How is she?'

'Better, but still weak,' he says, pulling the door almost closed behind himself. 'She's pretty bruised and battered regardless of whether or not the pill's done her a mischief.'

The silence is uncomfortable. 'You couldn't have done anything more than you did,' I say quietly.

'Trouble seems to follow you like a magnet, Maisie Weyfare,' he says, without smiling.

'I don't go searching for it.'

'Yet it finds you, doesn't it?'

'Are you suggesting that what happened to you and Mary is my fault?' I ask, trying to stay low key. I wasn't expecting him to be quite so salty with me personally.

'If the cap fits. You gave one of those pills to a known rogue bystander. And now Lover Boy's back on the scene.'

'He's not my lover boy,' I say truthfully.

'Am I?' he asks, catching me off guard. Before I can answer, his face has twisted into a mean smirk. 'No, I thought as much. Dumped for the Weyleigher's son.'

'He's not Valerie's son!' I exclaim. 'Maybe right now I shouldn't be with either of you!' As the words come out of my mouth, the rest of it just follows naturally. 'It feels like I've only known I'm Weyfare for five minutes! If I'd just gone straight back through the Weydoor the first time, Lizzy would have told me what I was when I turned 18, and I would've done my duty and never known either of you! But I didn't go back, and now I'm still fucking here, bouncing from one timeline to another like bloody Bambi with a shedload of shit to clear up, so maybe I don't think having a *lover boy* is a priority!'

His face falls, and he closes the door completely shut behind us. 'Hey, chill. Maybe I was a little sharp - '

'A little? Forget it,' I snap back, torn between anger and hurt. 'I came to ask you if you wanted to come to a disco. Polly's taking the rest of us. Consider yourself asked.'

He does look a bit shamefaced. 'That was nice of you, but I think I ought to stay with Mary. Maisie -' he adds, as I turn to walk away, my cheeks red with irritation and humiliation, 'please, hold up.'

I refuse to turn and look at him, probably because there are tears disloyally leaking onto my cheeks when I'm supposed to be taking a stand, but I do stop walking away.

'Maisie, I'm sorry. It's just I'm worried about Mary. I'm so bloody angry with myself for letting her get hurt, and I'm taking it out on you. I'm the son of a Witan. I'm a man; I'm supposed to protect her, not get her attacked.' He pauses. I still don't turn. 'And when I saw you with Rob, on top of everything else, I just felt betrayed,' he says bleakly.

I take a deep breath, and I turn around, ignoring the tears on my cheeks. 'You didn't need to feel like that. I don't need a man to protect me, Tommy. Where I come from, we all protect each other. What I need right now are friends, not bodyguards. People who will stand by me, warts and all, because they want to, not because they feel it's their duty. People who will help me. People I can trust.'

'You can trust me,' he says firmly.

'I can trust him, too.'

'You really dig that, don't you?'

'Yes, I do.' I tell him. 'You were there when I needed you in London, and it felt right at the time. But maybe I was just looking for a comfort blanket.'

'And that's changed?' he asks.

'I've got to grow a pair,' I say.

'A pair of what?' he asks, looking a bit shocked.

'Cahones.' I put a hand on his shoulder, and as I do, there is a faint voice calling his name from inside the room. 'She wants you. We'll see you tomorrow.'

'Are we friends?' he asks.

I lean forward, kiss him on the cheek, and walk back to the lab.

When I walk in, I can tell immediately that they've all heard the bones of what me and Tommy have said to each other: Polly is busy counting vials and test tubes that probably don't need counting; Helen is gazing at the strip lights that have been cleverly fitted into the ceiling beams; Tracy and Ani are pointedly looking out a window at the landscape of chimneys that tower off into the near distance; Jasper and Ian are reading a book on genetics. Rob is looking at me.

'What time does the disco start?' I ask.

Polly strips off her gloves, hair band and lab coat, dumping them carelessly on the floor as if she knows someone will be in to tidy up after her. 'Eight,' she says. ' Till eleven. This is the sticks, remember? We don't party until dawn like those peeps up in the City.'

'I haven't partied until dawn since I was a teenager in Devon and we used to have a hoedown after the haymaking,' Helen says, with a smile. 'Children tend to put a stop to that sort of life, and Tommy came along quickly.'

'Hoedown?' Jasper and Tracy ask at the same time.

'Shindig. Hootenanny. Barn dance?' Helen tries, until finally, we all nod.

'Everyone who's anyone in Town will be there, and the DJ plays all the latest hits,' Polly says. 'It's only a quid to get in. Do you want to borrow some clothes?' she says, looking uncertainly at Tracy's purple Converse and blue and white stripy trousers. 'I've got a couple of pairs of satin drainpipes, and you look like we're a similar size.'

'Satin drainpipes?' Ani asks faintly.

'Sorry, future girl. Tight-fitting, satin trousers. All the rage since Olivia Neutron Bomb wore a pair in *Grease* last year. You'll probably get away with your outfit,' she goes on, pointing to me, Jasper and Ani, 'but Gus, Barry and Clive will have some things you other fellas can change into. It looks like someone threw a bottle of bleach over your jeans,' she says to Ian. She looks at Rob. 'Why does your T-shirt glow purple in your armpits?'

'To be honest, I never found out,' he says, lifting his arm to investigate. 'I bought this from a Top Man in 1994, and I didn't hang around to ask.'

'I don't reckon much on your top man's taste. T-Shirts that show off your hot and sweaty bits,' Polly says. 'Why would you? It'll never catch on.'

We all leave the lab and go back to the main lounge, where Gus or Barry or Clive have put a three-tiered green trolley in the middle of the room, filled with cocktail glasses full of lettuce, sauce and peeled pink prawns. Polly claps her hands together.

'My fave! I hope it's chicken cordon bleu for main!' she exclaims. I'm thinking chicken anything will be great right now because it might give me some breathing space to process what just happened between me and Tommy, to work out exactly what was going on behind the look that Rob gave me when I went back into the lab, and to work out how long I've got to boogie with Polly in 1979 before my dad leaves Stoneford and extinguishes me.

Chapter Fifteen – Boogie Wonderland
(Earth, Wind And Fire With
The Emotions, 1979)

The Town Hall doesn't look like the kind of place to be holding what Polly calls discothèques, but the people flooding in through the doors don't look like they're here for a poetry reading, either. The clothes are all the colours of the rainbow, silver halter neck jumpsuits and red strappy dresses, skimpy, stretchy gold fabric tops that cling to every curve and shiny satin skinny trousers in gold, black and red above white stiletto heels and sandals. The men are in shirts with collars that spread out to their shoulders unbuttoned way too low, blue and brown and white trousers with waistbands virtually reaching up to their chests. When we were at Tracy's Granty Esmé's house, we watched *Staying Alive*, and I feel like I've been cast as an extra from that film, but in a funeral scene.

We hand over our green one pound notes, and the woman sitting at a table in front of the main doors stamps our hand with a blue P in a circle, and we are in.

This is nothing like the Fundraiser Discos at Drake's.

Although the last disco I went to was in 1987, it wasn't so different to the ones I was used to in 2019; all the boys would hover around the edges of the Main Hall in the darkness, awarding us marks out of ten and thinking we didn't know what they were doing, or that we were judging them the same way. The girls divided their time between the toilets and the dance floor, reapplying makeup and then sweating it off under the lights from the DJ's deck.

Here everyone is dancing, and not the kind of shuffle step that mums and dads do at weddings. Hips are gyrating like they're missing a hula-hoop, hands raised in the air like it's an act of worship; twirling and touching and moving every part of their bodies that I can see in time with the music, which throbs and twists and turns with them. We still call the Fundraisers Discos, but they aren't really – the DJs play chart stuff. This is real disco music; soulful singers and beats that drag you in until you just can't keep your booty still whether you're a guy or a girl. Seeing this lot, it makes me wonder what happened to them to make them go from these amazing movers to the mums and dads shuffling across the floor at weddings. Maybe they don't like the music nowadays, or maybe they just don't have the energy any more.

The music is loud, the singer is telling someone to play

that funky music, and Polly turns to face me, glowing with the flashing lights of the DJ deck behind her in a white halter neck top that barely covers her boobs, a pair of skin-tight red satin trousers and red strappy heels.

She grins as she leans in to speak into my ear. "Let's see your moves then, future girl.'

I have nothing to offer, but Ani loves bhangra music, and her dancing isn't all that far removed from the rest of the hall. Tracy and Jasper copy her with some success. Ian and Rob look uncomfortable, and the three of us head to the bar to buy some drinks as the next song tells us all to burn in a disco inferno.

The bar is in another room to the side of the hall, and it's just about quieter enough to be able to hold a conversation. The queue is long enough too. It's just there's no conversation.

'Ani's a sexy dancer,' Ian remarks after a while. The bleached jeans have gone, and he's wearing a pair of Barry's red Wrangler jeans and a shirt that looks like someone threw five pots of paint at it. I can feel how uneasy he is, and he's not alone. 'I think I'm off for a slash,' he says quickly, and disappears before either of us have registered that we're going to be alone. Relatively.

At least two more people have been served and I still can't think of anything safe to say.

Rob doesn't seem to be bothered about safe. 'I heard what

Tommy said to you,' he says, not looking at me. 'I'm sorry.'

'Why are you saying sorry? It's not your fault,' I say, continuing to stare at the ponytail of the woman in front of me in the queue. 'He's going through a lot.'

'And you aren't?' he points out. We shuffle forward.

'He did apologise,' I say, not sure why I'm defending Tommy because I wasn't all that impressed with his 'tude either.

'If we can get Mary back to 1987, and Helen can help me find my family, what will you do next?' he asks casually. I honestly don't think he realises how brutal that question is, because it states clearly that he believes our paths forward from here won't be together.

'I have to go back to 1972,' I tell him. 'We think someone throws my great-grandma through the Weydoor at Drake's and when she comes back, she's unwell. I want to sort that out. Then I have to try to make things right with Lizzy. We aren't talking, since she found out – ' My voice runs out of fuel.

'We're sort of in the same boat,' he says, as we shuffle a step nearer to the bar. 'Except I don't know my mum, and yours didn't know who you were.' A shiver runs down my arm as I realise he's touching my shoulder. 'I'm sure you'll get things ironed out with her.'

I turn to look into his intense green eyes. 'It's not just that.'

'What else is it then?'

'It's my dad,' I blurt out.

Rob's eyes become very wide. 'You mean –'

'The guy Lizzy's supposed to have kids with. Yes.'

He blows a sigh hard from between his lips. 'You know him then. Here in the past.'

'We met in 1987. It's not anyone we know well yet, don't worry.' I treat myself to a smile as I reassure him. 'But I found out he's leaving Stoneford. Three or four years before Lizzy asks him to meet her for a drink when she comes home from Uni.'

'You think you're going to be extinguished,' he states gravely. 'Maybe he left Town and went back again?'

'He never mentioned anything about moving away. Mum and Dad just told me they didn't get on before Lizzy went away, and when she came back, it all worked out for them.'

'But it's possible he will still be in Stoneford at the right time?'

'I guess. But I'm not even sure whether Lizzy will go to Uni now. This whole shitstorm with Scott and Valerie has turned everything tits up.'

'Things will work out,' he says. 'My timeline changed because of Scott, and we still found each other.' I look down and only notice at this point that he's holding my hand. I think he notices at the same time, and he lets go. 'I'm sorry. I shouldn't have done that. I heard what you said to Tommy about needing some space to work things out.'

I could cry. I want him so much; it's like having a toothache in my whole body. Life *is* just too bloody complicated. I've tried to have a relationship with both Robs, and neither has ended well. What's that old saying – once bitten, twice shy? Then surely three times would just run out of the building screaming.

He lifts my chin gently. 'Things will work out,' he says again.

I think of the little signet ring hanging around my neck with my silver key. 'Like you said. Forevermore.'

He blinks twice. 'I still believe in forever,' he says, but I don't know what would have happened then because Ian comes back with stories of some of the more outrageous outfits he's taken a piss next to, and we are next in line to be served at the bar.

Back in the hall, the music is turning the beat around, and Polly, Tracy, Ani and Jasper are still dancing in the same spot we left them in, but once we turn up with their pints, we all move to the tables at the side of the hall. With everyone at the disco intent on dancing the night away, it's easy to find a seat.

'That's better,' Polly says, 'although it feels a bit strange drinking pints. Doesn't this place blow your mind! Oh, look, it's Trudy! Must go over and catch up! You'll be all right by yourselves for a bit, won't you?' She's halfway across the floor before any of us can reassure her we are big girls and boys now and we don't need a childminder.

'She's a bit different to Helen, isn't she?' Ani says, watching as Polly grabs hold of an older woman in a silver jumpsuit and they hug like they haven't seen each other all year.

'Helen's all right,' I say. 'She's got kids. Polly's younger. She's bound to be a bit extra.'

'A bit?' Ani says, sipping her lager. 'I guess she probably doesn't have a lot to do. People won't stumble much by accident into a Weydoor that's tucked away at the back of a hidden room, in the private quarters of a hotel.'

'So remind us - the Witan are the ones in charge, right?' Tracy asks, taking Polly's packet of cigarettes from the table and lighting one.

'The Witan are kind of senior Weyfarere,' Rob says.

'Polly seems a bit young to be classed as a senior,' Jasper says, drawing a J with his finger on the froth on his pint of Guinness.

'Clever though,' Tracy points out. ' A female research scientist.'

'Quite a rarity, I should think,' Ian agrees. 'Science isn't really a girls' thing.'

'Oh, you think so?' Ani asks. If she'd had fur, it'd be standing all on end.

'It's not his fault he thinks that way; he doesn't know any different.' I say, deliberately patronising and patting his arm. 'It must be hard for her to be in a family of Witan though. Helen said the Witan are voted in, but Polly said her family are always given the job.'

'What I don't get, 'Ani says, 'is why she's doing blood tests to identify the differences between Weyfare and bystander blood.'

'To identify the differences,' I say slowly, not really holding back on the sarcasm.

'But *why*?' Ani persists. 'We all know it must be different. Isn't that enough?'

'Us chemists always want to know why,' Ian says self-importantly.

'Don't look for trouble where there isn't any,' I tell him. 'I've got enough real crap to deal with without adding more things to the list.'

We spend the rest of the night dancing. Rob and Ian aren't keen at first, but Ani teaches them some of her bhangra moves, and they just repeat those to every song, and no one seems to care what anyone is doing as long as they're moving. Polly comes back every now and then, but she's too busy flitting around all her crew to pay much attention to what we're up to, until it's almost the end of the evening. The DJ tells the room excitedly that he's going to play a "smooch for all you lovers out there" which is the "hot new single straight off the press" by KC and the Sunshine Band.

Polly swoops down on us as we hear the slow chords and make our way back to the table. 'Fancy a smooch, lover boy?' she says, taking Rob by the hands and pulling him back to the dance floor.

'I- I-' he stammers, clearly not wanting to dance with her, but enough of a good guy to not want to offend her.

'If you don't smooch with me, you have to smooch with Maisie,' she says smugly. 'I mean, everyone here knows that's what you both want.'

Why is there never a Weydoor under your feet for you to sink through when you need one?

'Maisie?' he asks hesitantly.

However I feel about him, I have to save him from dancing with Polly; he looks freaked AF. I take his hand; Polly claps her usual rhythm and grabs hold of a tall, thin guy on the next table. He laughs and says something about second-best being better than nothing.

On the dance floor, me and Rob hold the other like we're made of glass.

'Thank you for dancing with me,' he says, leaning forward and speaking against my ear, sending goosebumps down my back and arms.

'No worries,' I reply lightly. 'You looked like a rabbit in the headlights. It would've been cruel not to save you.'

'Is that the only reason you agreed?' he asks.

I pause, fighting myself. I lose. 'It's not the only reason,' I say, sighing, leaning my forehead gently against his chest, 'but it doesn't matter now, does it? You're going to go searching for your family, and I have to go looking for mine.'

'Maisie, if that's all I wanted to do, don't you think I would've asked Helen for her help by now? I could be halfway to wherever now, instead of dancing to disco music here with you.'

I want to ask him what else he wants to do, but I'm so enjoying being close to him again after what feels like ages, I don't want it to end. We don't exactly have the greatest record for happy ever after so far. Not even happy until the end of the evening. I try a different approach. 'Do you want to tell me why you haven't asked Helen for her help yet?'

'Do I need to?' he asks, his voice a whisper that's louder than KC asking us please don't go.

The responsible part of me, the one that seemed to kick in once I found out I was Weyfare, is telling me there are more important things in my world than Maisie hearts Rob and Net-flix 'n' chills, but the other me, the one who used to kick off just because I didn't feel like loading the dishwasher, wants to tell him not to go in search of his family. Maybe Forevermore doesn't start for us yet, but for the length of this song, I can pretend.

'Probably not,' I whisper back.

We sway together in an old-fashioned slow dance, and as the song continues, his arms draw me closer, so I can feel the beat of his heart through the black shirt and white jacket Gus lent to him. In this gear, he looks more like the Rob from the Fundraiser in 1987 in his band T-shirt and blazer with the sleeves rolled up. Could three times be worth a try after all? I put my arms around his neck, close my eyes, and wish for a world where KC and the Sunshine Band's music plays on a con-stant loop, and the disco never ends.

The final dance starts slowly, but it soon speeds up, and I think it must be called Last Dance because the singer says it a lot, and let's face it, it's a brilliant way of making sure your song gets played at every club and disco across 1979. Me and Rob stand frozen like a snapshot in the middle of the hall, as everyone dances around us like it's the last dance at the last disco ever.

I look down to where our hands are still linked, and then up into Rob's face. Without warning, he turns and leads us off the dance floor, out of the entrance area past an empty chair where the stamper sat earlier, and into the tropic-like warmth of the July evening.

'I was pissed off when we met in London,' he says, abruptly as we arrive outside. 'I was trying to say all the right things, about understanding why you got off with Tommy, but inside I was jealous. Big time. I was just trying to protect myself when I said it would be best if we were just friends, but I was pretending, and I can't pretend any more. I do have to find out who I am, Maisie -'

'I know that. Listen-' I try to say, but he shakes his head.

'I need to find out who I am, but I need you to tell me the truth. What you said to Tommy back at the Mermaid. Did you mean it? Do you really need some space? Because if you do, you know I'll give you that, Maisie. I'll give you anything. Leaving you in London was the hardest thing I'd ever done in my life, but I had to make sure I didn't lead Valerie to you. And then when I found out she wasn't my mother, the first thing, the very first thing I thought was that we could be together again, and I had to find you.'

So. He loses his entire identity, and his first thought is to find me and tell me. When he disappears, my first action is to snog Tommy on Westminster Bridge. Rob may understand my motives, but I don't like myself all that much at this moment.

'And when you found me, I was already with Tommy,' I say. 'What a biatch I turned out.'

'I told you, I get it,' he says. 'What I need to know is did you tell him you need some space because you do – or because of me?'

I look up into his face, slightly shadowed by the building behind us, the expression so vulnerable as he waits for my answer. The crowds are starting to flow out of the Town Hall now the last dance has finished, and we might only have seconds before the others find us. My head is still repeating what I told Tommy. I don't need any more complications. I need to untangle the web of confusion that's been weaved through my family's timeline, and trying to have any kind of relationship with Rob has always been a loaded rifle. But I'm Maisie Wharton, and I'm still not very reliable when it comes to listening to my head.

'I said it because it's you I want to be with,' I admit, and he kisses me then, as if we're alone and time around us is standing still, and as our lips meet over, I remember a bench near the lych gate at Trinity on Lizzy's 18th birthday, when the Rob I knew then kissed me as if we were alone. I know they are different boys with different experiences of life, but my heart knows now without a shadow of a doubt that somehow, they share the same soul.

'If you're that hungry, I'm sure Gus will fix us all a night-cap,' Polly said loudly in my ear.

We spring apart as she walks away with Tracy and Ian laughing, but when I glance across at Jasper and Ani, they are just smiling at us. Rob kisses my cheek, and we turn hand in hand to walk back to the Mermaid Inn with our friends, the streetlights shining on the cobbled streets and the laughter and chatter of the disco dancers spreading out across Town like a blanket of happiness.

'So Tommy's fair game, right?' Tracy asks, linking her arm through mine. 'Are we staying here for much longer? I might just chance my arm tonight.'

We arrive back at the Inn to find mugs of steaming cocoa left for us in Polly's quarters.

'Gus is my hero, but it's been a long day,' she says. 'I'm going to turn in. I've got three Weyfarere under my roof tonight, so the girls are sleeping in my guest rooms; you blokes can stay in here on the sofas.'

I have a room to myself it seems; Ani and Tracy have to share, and Rob, Ian and Jasper are on the sofas in the lounge with blankets chucked over them. It feels like favouritism, and I'm uncomfortable with it, but Polly's insistent, and I'm too tired to argue with her. I give Rob a smile, which he returns, and I take my cocoa to my room, leaving the others to chat. There's a pair of deep red silk pyjamas on the end of my bed, and it's good to have a change of clothes to sleep in, but I'm more tired than I think I am, and I fall asleep before I've had a chance to drink the cocoa.

When I wake up, it's still dark, and there is a black shadow in my room, sticking something sharp into my arm.

Chapter Sixteen – Gangsters

(The Special Aka, 1979)

I don't know who's the more freaked out; the shadow sitting on the edge of my bed, or me when I sit up and scream. The figure runs from my room before I get a chance to switch on the bedside light. *What the actual fuck?*

For a few seconds, I wonder if I've just had a really vivid and ratchet nightmare but I'm sure I saw someone running out of my room. When I run my hand over the inside of my arm, it's slightly sore. I fumble to turn on the bedside light, and look more closely. There is a small red scratch on the underside of my elbow. It was no nightmare.

On my bedside cabinet, the alarm clock with two silver bells on top tells me it's three twenty. I'm surprised my scream hasn't brought someone to my room, but there is no noise at all from the corridor outside. Helen is in Mary's room with Tommy, and I don't want to wake them up, but I don't want to be on my own any more tonight. I want to talk to Jasper, I want to be with Rob, but I have to do the right thing here – there's potentially an intruder in the Mermaid, and I have to tell Polly.

I peer down the corridor, lit only by a pale nightlight in the ceiling. Polly's room is next to Mary's. There's no noise from the room next door to mine where Ani and Tracy are sleeping. I can't believe my scream didn't wake them, or Gus from Reception, who is sitting down next to Polly's door on a stool; he's obviously on the night shift, except he's not doing much of a job as a Guard because he's fast asleep, the moonlight shining through a window onto his face.

'Gus!' I hiss once I'm beside him. He mumbles a bit in his sleep but doesn't wake up, so I grab his arm and shake him. Maybe a bit too violently, as he nearly topples off the stool.

'Ugh, wha'?' he grunts at me, grabbing for something in his pocket.

'Gus, no! - listen it's Maisie, I'm one of Polly's guests,' I tell him before he bashes me with whatever's in his pocket.

'Ugh,' he says again, and then he shakes himself into action. 'Is something wrong?'

'Someone was in my room. They tried to hurt me,' I say, blinking back the tears and trying not to be so lame about it, but it did frighten me, and telling Gus has made me realise how much.

Gus is on his feet in the next breath, opening the door to Polly's room in a rush, but, as the dim light from the corridor floods into her room, we can just make out the hills and valleys in the bedspread made by her sleeping body, and the bright gold of her hair on the pillow. He closes the door carefully and goes to check Mary's room. When he comes back, he's a lot less pale.

'They all seem fine,' he says. 'Are you sure it wasn't just a bad dream?'

I show him the scratch on my arm. 'They were holding my arm when I woke up, and I found this mark. My door's closest to the main exit to the Inn. Maybe mine was the first room the intruder went into.'

He doesn't look sure, and I don't know whether it's because he's a good guy that wants to make me feel better, or because he's a Guard reacting to the concerns of a Weyfare, but he nods and starts to jog up to the main exit himself. 'I'll go and see if Barry and Clive have seen or heard anything. Go back to bed. We'll handle this.'

As he disappears out into the corridor of the Inn, I'm surprised that he doesn't check in on Ani and Tracy, or the boys in the main lounge, and if he thinks I was targeted because I'm Weyfare, why isn't he more concerned? I know what I think. I've seen that mark inside my elbow before, when Helen took some of my blood to put in the vial that Rob now has. It's a puncture wound from a needle. Someone crept into my room in the middle of the night and *tried to take my fucking blood* when I was sleeping. There is no way I'm going back to that room on my own tonight.

The door to the main lounge is wide open since Gus just went through it, but none of the boys is moving. Jasper is flat out on his back, one arm hanging over the edge of one of the sofas, dangerously close to sending a half-empty mug of cocoa on the coffee table flying. Ian is curled up on cushions on the floor, and Rob is on another sofa, head propped up by more velvet cushions, his dark hair flopped over his face. Even though Gus came through here, switching the light on before heading out into the main part of the Inn, these guys haven't stirred. Just how much did they have to drink last night, and why is it I seem to be the only one who's not been laid out cold with a bad case of alcoholic coma? Just as well I did wake up back in my room before they did me any damage because none of these tools was ever going to come to my rescue.

I sit down on the edge of Jasper's sofa and shake him gently. 'Wake up, blud, I need to talk to you.' He groans and rolls over. I'm not happy. 'Jasper bloody wake up, will you?' I yell, and this time, when he still doesn't wake up, a sick feeling washes through me. I'm convinced I'm going to hurl until a voice calls out behind me.

'Bleeding hell, Maisie, who replaced you with an alarm

clock?' Ian is sitting up, and I'm so relieved that I rush over and hug him. He hugs me back, a bit awkwardly, and we part quickly. 'Are you all right? Shit, my head hurts.'

'Nobody else will wake up,' I exclaim, 'and someone tried to attack me in my bed, and everyone's so drunk that I can't wake them up!'

'Hey! Hey, come on,' he says, shifting around on the sofa so I can sit shakily beside him. He puts a less awkward, comforting arm across my shoulders. 'What d'you mean by someone tried to attack you?'

'I mean what I say.' I show him my arm. 'That's a needle mark. Someone came into my room and tried to steal my blood while I was sleeping.'

'Christ on a Bike!' He turns me to face him. '*Steal* your blood? What is this – a rerun of *Fright Night*?'

'Well, I don't remember giving them permission,' I say, wiping the back of my hand over my damp cheeks. 'So yes, stealing. And why are you all so bladdered? We only had a couple of drinks each.'

'I don't know.' Ian wipes his own hand over his forehead, and it comes back sweaty. 'But I feel like crap. Maybe it was extra strong lager or something? I could do with a couple of aspirin.'

It's clear neither of us wants to start rummaging around

in pretty-much-a-stranger's bathroom, but, before we say anything else, Gus has thundered back into the room, with Clive beside him.

'Someone decked Barry by the entrance to the hotel,' he says. 'Is everyone still all right in here?'

'Apart from the fact that they won't wake up,' I say glumly.

Gus looks at them, but he doesn't seem too concerned. 'It's probably exhaustion, but maybe I should give my mother a call to come and check the Weyfare,' he says.

'Everyone, surely?' I countered. 'Why call your mother?'

'The Weyfarere are the ones who need the most protection here,' Gus says, following Clive out of the room, 'and my mother is Polly's healer.'

I'm a bit pissed off with him, saying all that in front of Ian. I don't consider myself any more or less important than other people just because I'm Weyfare. I don't treat anyone differently either, but the two Guard have gone again before I can say anything out loud about it.

'I don't suppose you've got any headache pills in your belt purse,' Ian says, putting his head in his hands.

'Bumbag,' I say absent-mindedly. 'Only one pill, and you don't want that.'

Fifteen minutes later, Jasper and Rob are still sleeping. I've left Ian's side to sit with Rob. He doesn't look ill, he just won't wake up, and as I stroke the hair away from his face, I'm beginning to wonder – did we leave our drinks unattended at the disco? Did people spike drinks in the 1970s, and if they did, why did they do it to everyone except me, and then attempt to take *my* blood?

Gus has obviously used a phone in another room, because a woman appears from the Inn corridor with a big black leather bag that reminds me of doctors in black-and-white films. Her greying hair is wound up on her head in a messy bun, and she's wearing a flowery trouser suit, that I realise are her pyjamas. Gus must have literally dragged the poor woman from her bed.

'Who's in charge here?' she asks, sounding like she is. This is no poor woman after all.

'In charge?' Ian repeats. 'No one's in charge.'

'Are any of the Weyfarere awake?' the woman asks him slowly.

I put my hand up, and then lower it again. This bloody woman makes me feel like I'm back in class at Drake's. 'I am,' I say, pointlessly.

Ian looks pissed off, and I don't blame him really. He's not used to this whole female power thing that the Weyfarere have going on, and 1987 wasn't all that far advanced when it comes to equality. I remember the arse slaps and the boob banter clearly enough the first time I was there. 'I'm going for a slash if I'm not needed,' he says.

The woman comes and sits beside me, ignoring him. 'My name is Janice. I help Polly, if someone is ill and it's not advisable to take them to a modern hospital.'

'You're the healer,' I say.

She nods. 'If you like. Now, can you tell me exactly what happened here?'

'We were out at a disco in town,' I tell her. 'We didn't have much to drink, not really. Came back here, had a hot drink, went to bed. I woke up, and someone was sitting on the edge of my bed, and my arm was stinging.'

'Did you leave your drinks unattended at the disco?' Janice asks, jotting down some notes in a thin black notebook she takes from her bag.

'When we were dancing, I guess. Don't you want to look at my arm?'

She nods. 'Okay. I will run some tests, but I think I know what's likely gone on here.' She takes a fresh syringe from her bag. When I flinch, she scowls at me. 'I can hardly treat you if I don't know what you've taken, can I?'

'No, but –'

'The Witan at the Mermaid trusts me, so I'm sure a little junior like you shouldn't need to worry about anything I do.'

She takes hold of my arm and pushes the needle pretty much into the place where I was scratched. Helen was much more gentle; it's a good job I don't get squeamish about needles and injections. 'There, you see? Nothing to worry about. Where have you come from?'

'The future,' I say. ' 2019. About 40 years or thereabouts.'

'Heavens. Are drugs are easily available in your future?'

'I guess - if you know who to ask.'

'The drug scene amongst the disco community is rife,' Janice says, removing the syringe and dabbing the dot of blood half-heartedly with a tissue. I take it from her, frowning, and hold it down on the small bleed. 'My belief is that your drinks were drugged at the disco, and you all made it back here before they took effect. Everyone will be fighting fit once they've slept it off.'

'Why would they do that?'

'Dealers often give a freebie to newcomers in the hope that they'll enjoy the experience and come back for more,' she says.

'And the person in my room?' I ask.

'Figment of your imagination brought on by the drugs,' she says dismissively, dropping the syringe full of my blood into her open bag. 'Gus could find no evidence that there had been an intruder here.'

'But he said Barry had been hit by somebody,' I tell her,

staring at the syringe. Surely she knows she should remove the needle?

'Did he? Knowing Barry, he probably had too much to drink himself,' she says, standing up.

'And Gus was asleep as well, even though I screamed. He was on duty outside Polly's room. And what about the mark on my arm?'

'What mark?' she asks, and as I hold it out to show her, I realise that it's been replaced by the scratch she made when she openly took my blood for testing, with my permission. 'I must go and tend to Polly and her other guests. No need to worry. Everyone will be right as rain by breakfast.'

'What about Ian and these boys?' I say, hearing the annoyance in my head transfer into my question. 'Don't you want to make sure they're okay? Don't you want to take a sample of Ian's blood as well?'

'No need,' Janice says breezily from the door to the rest of Polly's quarters, 'I'm quite sure you were all given the same substance.'

And she vanishes into the corridor as if she can't get away from me quick enough, before I have a chance to ask her the other question I have, which is; why are me and Ian are awake already if we were all given the same dose?

Ian comes back into the main lounge, frowning. 'She's in a

hurry,' he says. 'So what was the outcome of the big pow-wow?'

'You're going to have to translate,' I say.

'Why does she think these peeps are all still sleeping?' he asks, sitting back down beside me.

'She thinks someone drugged our drinks at the disco.'

He pulls a face. 'Why would someone want to drug all of us, and why aren't we still out of it?'

'I'm not the only one who thought that was weird, then.' I watch as he pulls a slightly squashed packet of cigarettes out of his pocket. 'She told me she thought the person in my room was in my head.'

He lights a cigarette and blows the smoke away from my face. 'Do you?'

I shake my head, no.

'I have to say, you've not come across so far as an empty-headed bimbo like some of the girls I know.'

It's a compliment of sorts. 'Thanks, I think.'

'I mean it,' he assures me. 'I'd ask you out myself if I didn't think you already had your hands full.'

'Yeah, well, right now I have my hands full trying to work out what happened last night. I do believe there was someone in my room, and if we were drugged at the disco, it doesn't ex-plain why Gus was still asleep when I came out of my room. It took a massive shake to wake him, but he wasn't at the disco with us.'

'Maybe this will answer that question.' He reaches into another pocket and pulls out a small green bottle of something powdery. 'I found this on the floor near to Polly's door by the stool when I was going to the bathroom.' He hands it to me. 'I don't know what it is. Do you?'

The label says 'valerian root', and it's written by hand. I don't know what it is, but the fact that it's been found in the corridor makes me wonder whether what's in this little bottle has got far more to do with everyone sleeping so deeply than some random doper in a disco in the back of beyond.

'Is it important, you think?' Ian asks, his voice all-keen.

'I think it probably is,' I say, slipping the small bottle into my bumbag and getting to my feet. It's a good job Jasper bought the large size bag for me that day. 'Let's go and find Janice and ask her what it is. She's bound to know.'

Chapter Seventeen – New Dawn Fades (Joy Division, 1979)

In the corridor leading down to Mary and Polly's rooms, it is creepy and silent, apart from the occasional creaks coming from the old building. There's a glow in the sky that I can see through the windows over the uneven rooftops of the town. I've had about three hours' sleep, but I'm wide-awake. I'm sure I'll hit a wall at some point, but for now, I'm too wired to rest. I push open the door to Mary's room, knowing Tommy and Helen are in there as well, and me and Ian peer into the room.

I'm surprised to see Gus in there as well, next to the sofa with Janice, and they don't look very happy. Gus is speaking so quietly I can't hear a word, but before he finishes his sentence, he sees us in the doorway, and he's instantly smiley, and suddenly, it feels bare fake.

'She's fine!' he says brightly. 'Mum's just checking her over.'

'What about Helen and Tommy then?' Ian asks, looking at the two of them, curled up on the sofa and an armchair, completely oblivious to what's going on.

'They'll come round soon enough. Those kinds of drugs

aren't designed to do you any lasting damage,' Janice says.

'But they didn't go to the disco, so how come they've been drugged?' I ask, much more loudly than I need to. In fact, I pretty much yell it.

As the tumbleweed blows past the doorway, I step further into the room. Mary is sleeping on the bed as before, showing no signs of stirring. I don't think Helen and Tommy would wake up even if Fallen Angel came in and play a set, any more than the guys in the lounge would.

'It must be exhaustion,' Janice says snappily, and I don't miss the irritated glance she gives Gus. 'They're worried about Mary. A night of good sleep is what everyone needs, and frankly, I'm going home now to see if I can get some more.'

'Have you had a chance to check on Barry?' Ian asks.

'Barry?'

'The Guard. You said he'd been knocked out, Gus.'

Gus shrugs. 'Well, he'd probably just had one too many pints last night.'

'What about you though, Gus? You were sleeping on duty, and you didn't wake up when I screamed,' I persist.

Gus looks uncomfortable. 'Maybe we both had one too many pints then.'

'What if someone broke in here and put something in our drinks?' I go on. 'It would explain why everyone is so out of it. Ian found this bottle on the floor next to Gus' stool. I think someone tried to drug all of us, Gus included.' I take the little bottle of powdered valerian root from my bumbag and show it to Janice.

She takes the bottle from my hands. 'This has nothing to do with deep sleep,' she says brightly, pocketing the bottle, 'it's a powder for settling the stomach.' She smiles up at us. 'Go back to bed, and get some rest. There is nothing to be done. None of your friends is in danger. A few more hours' sleep will do us all a world of good.'

'I'm not going back to my room,' I say firmly. 'I'll go back to the lounge with the boys.'

'As you wish,' she says, stepping forward so that me and Ian have to step back. Should this feel threatening? Should she feel like she's not on our side? Or is it just because out of the four Weyfarere in the place, I'm the only one who's not Witan? Like she says, I'm just a junior here. We turn around and walk out the door into the corridor, and I swear that, if we hadn't left, she would've pushed us out.

They follow us back into the lounge, where she frowns, but I doubt it's for the same reasons I do. 'This place is a disgrace,' she exclaims, glaring at Gus. 'How is your Witan going to feel when she wakes up to this sorry mess?'

Gus grunts something untranslatable and starts gathering

mugs, plates and dishes onto a tray. I get the feeling that tidying up after Polly and her guests isn't necessarily on his to-do list, but, as he's rattling around the room, there's a shuffling from one of the sofas, and Jasper rolls over to face us. His face is all crumpled from the tassels on the edges on the cushions, and his eyes are bloodshot and watery, but they are open, finally.

'Do you have to do that so loudly?' he grumbles, trying to wrap one of the cushions from behind him up over his ears. 'What's the time? I think an elephant has been roller skating on my skull.'

Gus scowls and leaves the room with every scrap of crockery, cutlery and food waste piled high on one small tray. Janice stands in the doorway and looks back at us. Her face is calmer now; maybe now she's satisfied all the Witan are safe, she's not so stressed out. I'm far from calm. None of this is making any sense.

'Does anyone have any ibuprofen?' Jasper asks faintly.

I shake my head, no. 'Jasper, I need you to get it together, blud.'

He sits up and winces. 'Something's wrong?' he asks.

'We couldn't wake you up,' I tell him.

'Someone got into Maisie's room and attacked her,' Ian says.

Jasper's on his feet now, but still holding his head like he's worried the contents are going to fall out of his ears. 'Attacked!'

'I'm fine, really,' I say, sitting him back down.

'Attacked?' he says.

'Someone tried to shove a needle in my arm –'

'What the *fuck*? –'

'It's okay,' I say, settling him back against the sofa yet again, 'I'm okay. I woke up before they did any damage, but weirdass things have been happening. We couldn't wake anyone up.'

'Janice thinks someone slipped us all a Mickey at the disco, but you were all out for the count, including the ones who didn't come dancing,' Ian says.

'Janice?'

'Polly's healer. She's a bit alpha, but I guess it's her job to make sure Polly's safe.'

Jasper rubs his knuckles into his eyes. 'And is she? Safe? Polly?'

'Janice seemed to think so.' I look around the lounge, to where Rob is still out cold. I'm not going to get all high key about it. He'll come round when he's ready, like Jasper has. 'She only checked the Weyfarere. She wasn't bothered with you guys.'

'Seems to be a thing with these women,' Ian adds.

'And you're sure you're okay?' Jasper asks, looking at me with a bit more focus. A slight smile crosses his eyes. 'Nice PJs.'

I look down at myself and realise I'm still in the embarrassingly extra silk bedclothes Polly left out for me. 'I'm going to have a quick shower and change,' I tell the boys. 'Keep an eye on Rob for me.'

Opening the door to my room makes me a bit nervy, but I know there's not going to be anyone in here now. I shower quickly, wash and blow dry my hair, socks and undies and change back into my clothes, grabbing a covered elastic band from the bathroom cabinet, along with a box of Disprin, and forcing my still damp hair back into a messy pony. There's no sign of any trouble in here, apart from an overturned photograph frame on the bedside table next to the mug of cocoa that I remember abandoning last night in my desperation for some sleep ...

I pick up the mug and its cold contents and leave the room.

In the lounge, the pale light of dawn is brighter now through the window, but Rob is still asleep. I put the box of painkillers and the cup of cold cocoa on the table.

'I couldn't stomach a thing right now. Thanks anyway,' Jasper says.

'I don't want you to drink it.' I look at them, waiting for them to see what I saw, but I realise I'm going to have to help. 'I *didn't* drink it.'

'Well, obvs,' Jasper replies.

'Did you drink yours?' I ask Ian. His lips thin as he considers the question.

'Not all of it, I don't think. Blimey!'

'Blimey?' Jasper puts his head in his hands. 'Please explain this like I'm five.'

'I figure we were drugged, but not at the disco. What if the cocoa was drugged, but I didn't drink it? I slept normally. Ian didn't finish his, so he woke up before the rest of you.'

'Why would someone drug the cocoa?' Ian asks, peering at the contents of my mug as if it contains dog muck.

'Because they didn't want me to wake up when they stuck a needle in my arm,' I say, and my whole body shivers like someone turned the temperature in the room down by ten degrees. 'Or Polly's, Helen's or Mary's, at a guess.'

'Weyfarere blood.' Jasper swings his legs around and pushes the hair back from his face. 'They were trying to steal Weyfarere blood.'

'Who would want to do something skanky like that?' Ian asks.

'Weyleighers,' I say quietly. 'Everyone who drank the cocoa was drugged, including Gus. They weren't taking any chances.'

'Have you told Polly?'

'She's still conked out,' Ian replies. 'Everyone's conked out.'

'Who's still conked out?' We all turn and look at Rob, who is shaking his head as if he's shedding cobwebs and pushing his gorgeous floppy hair out of his pink eyes. I can't help it; I rush across the room and fling my arms around his neck. I know I said I wasn't worried. So I lied. He reaches up and takes me by the waist into a really uncomfortable hug.

'Totes awkward,' Jasper says. 'Where's the bathroom? I need some water for these tablets.'

'You don't have to leave,' I say, pulling myself reluctantly away from Rob; this is not the time or the place. 'Tell Rob what's been going on. I'll go and get you some water, and see if all the others are waking up.'

Half an hour later, the lounge looks like the waiting room at a really posh doctors' surgery, since most of the people in here look like they need medical help. We've told them all we know. Ani and Tracy's eyes are heavy-lidded, and their cheeks are flushed. Tommy is pretending he's recovered, but he's sweating in his black roll neck jumper, sitting on the floor in front of Helen and Mary like an obedient Rottweiler. Mary is pale, but talking; Helen is also pale, but the hand that grips her eldest daughter's arm is even whiter at the knuckles. Me and Rob sit on the floor in front of my cold mug of cocoa. Jasper and Ian were feeding everyone headache tablets and glasses of water, but Polly's run out of headache tablets now. She's pacing the floor so much she's going to wear track marks in the carpet.

'I think it would be prudent to be productive,' Helen says. 'Sitting around here inactive won't do us any good whatsoever. Will your tests be ready on the Weydoor pills yet, Polly?'

Polly glances at a black plastic Casio digital wristwatch. 'It's only six. They'll probably need a couple more hours, but we can check.'

'Then maybe we can take a look at what's in this.' I point at the cocoa mug.

We all stare at it like it's a bomb waiting to go off. 'Good thinking,' Polly says, picking it up. 'Is everyone up to a mosey down to the lab?'

Up to it is probably an exaggeration, but we all follow her down the corridor anyway. Polly keeps the door to the lab locked, and we file into the white clinical atmosphere that's completely different to the rest of her apartment.

'Obviously I don't know what was in the tablet, so I did two different types of tests,' Polly says. 'One test is looking for trace elements of the crushed tablet Maisie gave us. The other was comparing the structure of Helen's blood with Mary's. Then there's the Weyfare versus Bystander tests I was doing. I don't expect to have any clear results from any of them, but we might have more luck finding something dodgy in the cocoa.'

'Could a stomach remedy make you sleep for hours?' Ian

asks. 'Like if you take too much of it or something? Like if you take too many headache pills, it's really bad for your liver?'

'Why d'you ask?' Polly says, drawing some of the cocoa out of the mug with a clean syringe and putting a little into the first of five new test tubes.

'Well, it's just I found a bottle of powder on the floor and Janice said it was stomach medicine,' Ian says.

'Could be,' Polly says. 'Though I never heard of anyone over-dosing on liver salts. Did she say what type?'

'Valerian root,' I say. I remember because the name reminds me of Valerie.

Polly stares at me and overfills the third test tube so that the cocoa spills onto the surface. 'Valerian? Are you sure? Where's the bottle?'

'She took it from us,' Ian says.

'Valerian is a powerful sleep aid,' Mary says. 'It's not an antacid.'

'Janice is a healer, so wouldn't she know that?' Ani asks.

'Why would she lie about it?' Tracy asks.

We all turn to look at Polly like we're in an episode of *Scooby-Doo* where those pesky kids foil the dastardly plot.

'She must've misheard you,' Polly says, but her usually open, happy face is darkened by doubt as she sprays down the spill with a yellow plastic spray bottle labelled Jif. 'Janice has no reason to lie.'

'Unless she's a Weyleigher,' Rob says. As everyone's eyes turn back to look at him like they're watching a slow motion tennis match, he sighs. 'It's not like you aren't all thinking it. Don't shoot the messenger. Who else would want to steal Weyfarere blood?'

'That's completely bonkers,' Polly says, as the last traces of colour drain from her cheeks. 'Janice has been the healer at the Mermaid for years. She worked for my mother. I'd know if she was a Weyleigher.'

'How would you know?' Jasper asks. 'They don't even have silver keys to identify them like you do.'

Polly sits down abruptly; luckily, there's a high stool right behind her to stop her sprawling onto the floor. 'There has to be another explanation,' she mutters.

'It would help if we could speak to Gus,' I say.

'Gus doesn't start work at the Inn until seven.'

'If this stuff in the cocoa is valerian root, Gus could explain why the bottle Ian found by his stool contained the same stuff when he was on duty outside your bedroom door.'

Polly switches sharply to face me. 'Gus doesn't keep watch at my bedroom door,' she says. 'None of my Guard does.'

'Well, he was last night,' I say, 'because I found him there. Except he wasn't on duty, he was sleeping –'

'Maybe that's just what he wanted you to think,' Tommy says thinly.

I stare at the little glass tubes of brown liquid, containing Sod knows what, as the fog clears. 'If it was Gus in my room, he had just enough time to get down to that stool and pretend to be out cold,' I think out loud. 'Maybe the valerian fell from his pocket.'

Polly leans forward and puts her head in her hands, and Helen goes over and puts an arm around her shoulders. 'I don't believe this,' Polly mutters. 'This can't be real. This is an utter disaster.'

'We don't know it's the truth yet. But if it is, you won't be the first Weyfare to be targeted by Weyleighers, and I'm sure you won't be the last,' Helen says, in her lullaby-comforting voice.

'But I'm Witan! I'm supposed to be someone that the Weyfarere come to for help! I protect one of the Great Weys! How can I be expected to protect the Weys if I can't protect myself?' Polly says, her voice getting higher and higher until it's virtually at shriek level. 'You came to me for help!'

'We aren't expected to be perfect, Poll,' Mary says.

'Gus and Janice are supposed to be my friends! They're supposed to have my back! At least you woke up, Maisie, before he could do any real damage to any of us.'

I close my eyes, and touch the pinprick wound on the inside of my elbow. When I open my eyes again, I look at Ian.

'Except that's not quite true,' Ian says. 'Janice took some of Maisie's blood, supposedly to test for drugs.'

Images of Janice and Gus arguing at Helen's side flash back across my memory. 'And I'm willing to bet a pair of red satin drainpipes that she took blood from Helen as well,' I say.

'Gobshite's knackerbag,' Tracy exclaims into the silence. 'You weren't kidding about this time travel lark being complicated, were you?'

Chapter Eighteen – Girls Talk
(Dave Edmunds, 1979)

'It's not as if we never warned you.' Ani says.

Tracy shrugs.

Helen and Mary check their arms, and I can see by the way they try hard not to react that they have the same marks.

I shake my head, and I look at my feet. Complicated? Stephen Hawking never knew the meaning of the word. I came here for answers, not more questions. Every step I take forward seems to be three steps back. So I'm standing here surrounded by white and steel which feels clinical, logical and completely the bloody opposite to my life.

Before I got here it was bad enough, and all we can do is hope that the other Witan in 1987 were able to get their hands on Valerie and Scott and lock them away in the Bergh forever. But if Mary can't ride the Weys any more, who is going to be the Witan at the Dials in 1987 if we can't get her home? Lizzy still isn't speaking to me. Joan has been thrown through the Drake's Weydoor unless we can go back and prevent it from happening. How much of a threat to us is Vix? I've hurt Tommy. I'm kissing Rob for five minutes knowing soon he's going to disappear off to find his real family. The Mermaid has been compromised by Polly's Guard, Tracy and Ian are here like lab rats and yet by my side are still my crew, Jasper and Ani, even if she's not the BFF I began this bloody journey with. If I ever have a Guard, they'll always be my only choice to have my back. If I have a back left after my dad moves to London, and never gets asked out by my mum.

'What do I do?' Polly says quietly, echoing my thoughts. I feel for her; she was larger than life when we arrived, and now she's a shadow like the sunken spaces below her dull eyes. 'I don't know what to do. If they are Weyleighers, they have Weyfare blood. They will use it, and they could put the Master Timeline at risk. They could already have been putting it at risk.'

Helen straightens her back. 'There are four Weyfarere in this room. I refuse to believe that, between us, we can't solve all of our problems, including the ones we came with.'

There she goes again with the mind reading.

'It's a matter of priorities,' she continues. 'We set priorities, and we work through our problems methodically.'

'It's like being back in Chem. class,' Ian says, pulling a high stool towards him, and sitting on it.

'So what's the biggest problem here? Jasper asks.

I nod at Mary. 'Getting Mary back to 1987 safely.'

Mary shakes her head, no. 'I'm safer here in the past until we know whether the Witan from my future were able to restrain those Weyleighers and take them to the Bergh,' she says. 'Polly's tests on the tablet will need at least 24 hours before they give us any useful information as to whether I can risk a ride. I threw up most of the pill, hopefully. We are all here now. We go after these people of Polly's and see what they're up to.'

'And if they're Weyleighers, they'll run like the wind as soon as they get a whiff of the fact that you're onto them,' Tracy says.

'So we don't tell them we're onto them,' I say. 'As far as they know, we've swallowed the script about stomach meds and hallucinations.'

'What time did you say Gus usually starts work?' Helen asks.

'Seven,' Polly says glumly. 'Barry was on night duty last night.' She glances at her watch. 'Gus will be here in half an hour or so.'

'Do we get the Guard from the Dials down to come and help?' Jasper asks.

'Too much of a risk of another paradox,' Ani says, looking at Helen. 'Am I right?'

Helen nods, yes. 'I'm the Witan of the Dials in 1979. We must not involve my Guard, but Polly should alert the nearest Witans and ask for assistance.'

'You must be there as well then, mate,' Ian says to Tommy.

Tommy shrugs. 'I don't know. This is my future. The end of my natural timeline is 1972. It's different for Mary. She's from 1987.'

'I'm getting a headache,' Tracy says.

'Happens to me regularly,' I say, trying to be reassuring.

'What happens when you guys find a Weyleigher?' Jasper asks. 'I mean normally – not when Tommy goes all vigilante? No offence.'

'None taken,' Tommy replies. 'It depends. All the Witan residences have a direct alarm to their nearest neighbours. The alarm at the Dials alerts the Witan at Dial Post, here, Trinity Hall and the Tor if there's an attack. When I sounded the alarm, the Witan would have kept a skeleton level of protection and sent the remainder of their Guard to help.'

'Using the blood to travel the Weys?' Ian asks.

'No. Weyfare blood takes you to the Weyfare. They'd have all ended up here if they'd done that.' He looks a bit shame-faced. 'They drive. It probably sounds positively archaic to you dudes,' he adds, looking at me, Ani and Jasper.

Jasper shakes his head, no. 'We may have a lot of technology in our time, and a lot of it gets stuff done quickly, but no one's invented supersonic public transport yet.'

'Well, they have. It was a plane, but they retired the fleet when one crashed.' Ani looks at the little tubes of cold cocoa, so far resting redundant in their rack. 'Surely we should check these samples for valerian before we make any decisions about going after anyone.'

'Sooner rather than later,' Helen says. 'The Witan should still be warned of a potential breach, though.'

Ian has his nose in one of the heavy books lined up at the back of a shelf behind the rack of tubes. 'According to this, you need to run GC/MS for the presence of valerenic acid,' he says. 'It's only found in valerian root.'

Polly says nothing. I step over towards her and put a hand on her shoulder. I've only just worked out that responsibility means more than remembering to take your empty mugs from your room to the dishwasher before you're asked. She's responsible for one of the Great Weys, and people she thought were her crew are likely not at all.

Then Tommy is on her other side. 'Come on, Poll,' he says gently. 'We need you, chica. Let's get this done, and maybe once the tests are complete, we'll all be able to celebrate.'

She looks at him, and a faint light flickers back into her eyes. 'I'll need the big white machine at the back of the lab.'

'Is it worth checking the results of the other tests yet?' Tracy asks.

'We can have a look at whether anything toxic has been introduced to Mary's blood to damage the DNA. I thought the only way those pills could work would be if they contained something that affected the chromosome that connects Wey-farere to the energies of the Weys.' Polly takes two of the cocoa samples to the back of the room, where a massive white plastic box sits on a polished chrome table. 'You said the girl who gave you these said it would act as an alarm if you rode the Weys again?'

'Something like that,' Jasper says. 'She suggested strongly that it would hurt. A lot.'

'Which suggests a poison marker activated by crossing the fourth dimension.' She looks back at me. 'It's potentially very sophisticated chemistry. The people of your time must all be brilliant scientists.'

I scrunch up my nose. 'We take a lot on trust, I guess.'

A lot can happen in forty minutes. By the time Gus comes back in his smart uniform to check on Polly, we are all sitting in the lounge listening to a guy called Andy Peebles on Radio One. There's no FM or Xtra. There's no TV at seven in the morning, Polly says, unless you want to watch the Open University. I'm getting better at not giving too much away. So, when Gus asks us if we'd like some tea, we smile politely, and Polly says she already made some for us, nodding at the teapot on the low table and the mugs firmly in our hands.

'Are you feeling better, Polly?' he asks hesitantly.

'Much,' Polly says. 'I don't think I'll be going to that disco again, Gus. Not if they're going to put downers in the drinks.'

He nods and looks reassured. 'That might be wise.'

'Defo,' Jasper says. 'Can't be doing with that every week.'

'Has Barry recovered from his sore head?' I ask lightly. 'From the hangover, I mean?'

Gus blinks. 'I haven't seen him, but he's not due at work until two.'

'That'll give him a chance to sleep it off,' Tracy says kindly.

'Nothing worse than a hangover when you've got an early start,' Tommy says knowingly.

'Tell us about it,' Rob says. The hand at his side is occasionally stroking my arm, but it's too subtle for anyone else to notice. I'm glad he's not the kind of guy to make Tommy feel awkward, even if he is giving me goosebumps.

'I may have to have a word with him about drinking on the night shift,' Polly says. 'It's just as well the intruder in Maisie's room was a figment of her imagination. What if someone had really been set on doing us harm?'

Gus has the grace to colour up a bit. 'Would you like me to have a quiet word with him, Polly? Save you the job?'

Polly bobs her head from side to side a couple of times and then smiles. 'That's probably the right thing for now. Don't want to come over all heavy-handed. You'll know the right things to say, Gus.'

What Gus doesn't know is that Polly's tests on the cocoa came out positive for valerenic acid, the compound present in valerian root. Not only that, but the levels in my cocoa were five times the dose of a normal sleeping aid. Gus also doesn't know that Polly is pretty sure that Mary's DNA hasn't been compromised by the blocking tablet, due to her swift puking on arrival in 1979, so she should still be able to ride the Weys. We don't know yet is what's in the tablet, but we're going to help Polly get Gus and his mother gone on their way to the Bergh. Polly spoke on the phone to the Witan at Dial Post. She is sending as many Guard as she can spare. Gus doesn't know that, either.

'I am a bit worried about my friend.' Polly points at the prone figure of Helen, laid out on one of the sofas with Mary holding her hand. 'She doesn't seem to have recovered as well as the rest of us.'

'We wondered whether she might have been given a stronger dose than the rest of us,' Ani says. 'At the disco, I mean.'

Gus takes a step or two closer to Helen; I hold my breath. If he gets too close, he might realise she's faking it. 'Did she wake up at all?' he asks Mary.

'She's opened her eyes a couple of times, but that's it.' Mary looks up into his face, her eyes huge with concern. I'm well impressed. 'She didn't seem to be able to focus on me at all. I wondered if we could take her to your mum's place to get her checked over. Make sure she's not coming down with anything more sinister.'

Gus looks shocked. 'No!' he exclaims, and then he recovers himself a little, actually shaking himself as if he's trying to re-organise his thoughts. 'No, I don't think it's a good idea to move her,' he adds a little more calmly.

'We don't normally conduct Weyfare business at Janice's home,' Polly says calmly. 'Could you ask Janice to come back here, Gus? Maisie tells me she was here until the early hours this morning, but I know she's not a great one for sleep. Maybe she could come over once she's eaten her breakfast.'

'I'm sure she'll come right away,' he says.

'I could murder a plate of toast as well,' Ian says. 'Whatever it was those gits put in our drinks last night, I'm now gagging for some grub.'

'They normally send my breakfast up about 7:30,' Polly

says. 'I told them I had guests, so there should be plenty.'

'You're not going to work today after everything that happened, are you?' Ani asks innocently.

'Not today,' Polly replies.

Gus shuffles from foot to foot. He looks like a big kid on stage in front of a panel of judges. I'm guessing he wants to ask questions to make sure we haven't latched onto what they're up to, but he knows if he does, he'll draw unwanted attention. He's likely the son of a Weyleigher, but unlike Rob, we don't know if he's happy about what his mother does.

'Maybe I'll just nip down the kitchens and see how the food is coming along,' he says into the silence.

'Good thinking,' Polly says. 'Ring your mum too. Ask her what time she can come over.'

He nods and leaves. On the radio, Babylon is burning with anxiety. I don't think Babylon is alone.

We give it a long three minutes, and then Rob gets up and walks to the door to the hotel corridor. He opens it, puts his head out and closes it again. 'All clear,' he says.

There is a shuffling from the sofa. Helen opens one eye. 'Was I convincing?' she asks.

'You didn't exactly have to do much,' Mary says, letting go of her mother's hand and poking her in the side. It strikes me that it must be difficult for them all, Helen looking into the face of her daughter as a woman of roughly the same age; Mary seeing a much younger version of her mum; Tommy accepting them both. Maybe I can ask the Davenports to help me sort things out with Lizzy.

'We gave him no reason to suspect anything was dodgy,' Polly says. 'The Dial Post Guard are ninety minutes from here, so they're still about an hour away. I did ring Trinity Hall, but they are a bit further away, and the Witan feared it would take them too long to get around London's North Circular during the rush hour to be of any help to us.'

'I hear that,' Tommy says, putting his mug on the table. 'The Ring Road's chocka until ten.'

'Can't they use the M25?' Jasper asks. As all but two sets of eyes look back at him blankly, he adds, 'My bad.'

'Where is Trinity Hall?' I ask.

'It's a college at Cambridge University.' Ani says. 'Brian's sister goes to Cambridge. At least, she used to.' She looks from Tracy to Ian. 'Is Yvonne at Trinity Hall?'

Tracy shakes her head, no. 'She's at Clare. Reading Medicine. She's a brainbox, that woman.'

Trinity Hall isn't the Trinity in Stoneford then. It's good to know that some things haven't changed in 1987, regardless of what we've been doing to the past. I wonder whether I'll ever be able to wander through the back door of Travellers' Rest in

1987 and sit down for one of Glenda's endless cups of tea with Lizzy, Paul and Henry, or whether that moment has left the station for good.

'Maisie?' Rob's hand is on mine. 'You there?'

'Sorry I was just – don't worry.'

'I was just asking if you wanted to go over the plan again before Gus comes back with the brekkie,' Polly asks.

'No, I know what I'm doing.'

Sure I do. Polly's got to stay here because she's the Witan. Helen's got to stay here because she's pretending to be ill to draw Gus and Janice away from their house. Mary's got to stay here because she would stay if her mum was sick, and so would Tommy. That leaves me and my crew to go out into a town we don't know, to find a house we've never been to, to find a way inside, find and take back any evidence that Janice stole blood from me and any others. To try and see whatever else she's been doing without Polly's knowledge; maybe getting bystanders to travel back in time to collect goods to sell on like Scott used to. Then we're going to stop her.

'She's not likely to have the blood laying around the place, is she?' asks Ani.

'No,' Helen says. 'Don't underestimate the ingenuity of the Weyleigher. In my experience, they are cunning and they play the long game. Weyleigher families will wait for a generation to locate the Weydoor, and wait for another until they've found the Weyfare.'

I think back to Valerie's family; her father the vicar and her mother serving soup with the Umbridges up at Trinity in 1972, clearly not knowing the existence of the labyrinth of passageways below them, leading from the church to the Weydoors and the Weyroom. Waiting for a day that changed everything, when Valerie fell for a bystander while she was nursing at St Peter's Hospital so that she could finally ride the Weys.

Thing is, if Janice is a Weyleigher, she knows the location of the Weydoor; she knows the Witan. She doesn't want to control the Weydoor; she wants to make hard cash from Weyfare blood. She may not give a shit about riding back in Time to alter her future, and maybe even the Master Timeline. Knowing how fragile my own existence is at the moment, Janice suddenly seems a lot more threatening than Valerie's control freakiness, or the mysterious Vix smuggling goods for resale.

It's time to put my big girl pants on.

Chapter Nineteen – Bad Girls
(Donna Summer, 1979)

Stuffed full of buttered toast, cornflakes, fried egg and crispy bacon, we step out onto the street outside the Mermaid Inn. Janice arrived with Gus as we were finishing the coffee, and everyone started making a fuss of Helen, who had 'just come around'. We'd planned for Helen to be awake by then since you can't easily fake unconsciousness in front of a healer, but Polly's going to get her involved in comparing Helen and Mary's blood. We're all hoping it'll be enough to keep her at the inn while we get into her house and look for evidence. Polly assured us that it's just Janice and Gus living in their house; there should be no one else up there. I'm not reassured at all.

Maybe if I'd read a bit more of *The Truth*, it would have tips on breaking and entering strangers' houses for the greater good of the Weys, but somehow I doubt it.

There are already people shuffling up and down the cobbled street, and the sky overhead is clear of clouds. To my right, Rob stands close; the white jacket from the disco has been abandoned, but the black shirt and trousers remain. Tracy lifts her leg, wiggles it so that the dark blue flared Lee jeans she's borrowed from Polly flap about over her purple Converse, and she giggles. Ian has swapped last night's paint-splattered collared shirt for a genderless blue T-shirt. To my left, Jasper is my twin in black jacket, tee and jeans, and Ani sleek in a floral maxi dress that wouldn't look out of place on Stoneford High Street in 2019. We're a weird-ass mixture of fashions but, to be honest, 1979 seems to be a weird-ass mixture of cheese and hippy anyway.

According to Polly, we can't miss Janice's house. It's two streets away right at the top of the citadel along from the Town Hall. It's called Castle House. As we walk around the corner, I see instantly what Polly means.

'Jeeez,' Jasper says, putting his hands on his hips. 'How the hell do a pagan healer and a hotel receptionist make enough dosh to afford a house like that?'

'You could say the same about Travellers' Rest though,' I say. My family home is impressive; built over three floors like Castle House, it's made of stone and it even has turrets like the Old Library. I used to get a lot of stick for living there when I was young – I got called a snob – but Mum was a teacher, and Dad worked in sales; we were hardly wealthy. 'Maybe it's been handed down through the generations, like my place.'

'Or maybe it's been paid for by illegally trading in goods

smuggled through Time,' Ani says, staring up at the ivy creeping all over the front of the imposing red-bricked house.

A narrow alley overgrown with purple weeds snakes its path down the left side of the building, past a tall, arched slatted door in the wall that needs another coat of paint. I try the handle, but it's locked, as we were told to expect. So Ian and Tracy go back to the end of the alley and stand there, lighting cigarettes to pass the time in keeping watch and blocking us from the street while Rob, as the tallest, kneels down so I can get on his shoulders. When he straightens up, I pull myself up and over the wall.

The garden is wild and rambling, with trees with twisted trunks hanging low over shrubs and plants overgrown across winding uneven paving slabs. I can even see a few statues dotted around; their cherubs' faces dirty from the exposure to the passing years. It's not a welcoming place.

The door is padlocked, and we don't have a key, so Ani and Jasper come over the wall the same way I did, and Rob goes back to the front of the house to keep watch with Tracy and Ian.

'Don't blink,' Jasper says with a shiver as he spots the statues. 'Don't blink. Don't even blink. Blink and you're dead.'

'Yes, thanks for that,' Ani says, thumping him. 'We all know that episode from *Doctor Who*. Try that window first.'

The ground floor windows are all old-fashioned wooden framed and they slide up instead of opening out. I try the first and second and they are either locked down or stuck fast by years of old paint, but the third has some give and with all three of us wiggling it backwards and forwards, we eventually get the window to slide up far enough for us to scramble under the opening. I land on what looks like a washing machine, but there are two openings at the top instead of at the front, and I nearly put my foot in one.

'Utility room?' Jasper points at a green and red cardboard box labelled Fairy Snow sitting on the draining board.

'At least we didn't land on anything valuable,' Ani asks.

'You and Jasper take the upstairs floors. I'll see what I can find down here,' I tell them.

The house is as big and rambling as the garden, but not untidy. In fact, it's almost clinically clean in here, like the inside of Polly's lab. Janice either has a good cleaner, or she's a bit OCD about mess herself. This is not the kind of house where people leave around incriminating evidence that they are stealing Weyfare blood. I'm not sure how successful we're going to be.

Having searched the whole place: the huge kitchen with its massive pine table and yellow-painted wall cupboards; a vast lounge with square black leather sofas and footstools, with cabinets full of expensive-looking trinkets; the study with the walls of books and a shiny black vintage typewriter with paper threaded through and the words, "TO MY VALUED" typed on it in black ink.

After a look in the dining room with yet another huge table, this time in a block of polished dark wood with carved edges, I'm no closer to finding anything I can use to prove that Janice and Gus had unpleasant intentions when they took my blood. Something about this house bothers me, but I can't put my finger on it.

Jasper comes down the wide staircase. 'They have a bloody games room up there with a full-size snooker table in it!' he exclaims. 'Can't find anything sus though.'

'Me neither.' I sit down on the last step.

'It's a weird mix though,' he says. 'Old and new stuff. Like they couldn't decide which décor to go for.'

Of course. That's what feels wrong. The whole house is furnished in items from pretty much any decade you want. This is the house of someone who travels in Time - or gets someone else to do it for them.

'There's nothing up there except massive bedrooms and two bathrooms with roll-top baths. No sign of anything skanky.' Ani says, but as she follows him down the last few steps, she freezes, and I turn back to face the door with its stained glass flowers, and the face of a guy staring in at us.

It's hard to see clearly because the glass warps his face, but I'd say he's as surprised to see us as we are him, and then he shoves something through the door. Instead of walking back down the pathway to the road where the others should have seen him and made a row loud enough to warn us, he darts left to avoid the path completely.

'Well, he wasn't acting weird at all, was he?' Jasper says, reaching the ground floor as I get up to take the envelope that hangs teetering from the letterbox. It's addressed to Jan and has the word "PRIVATE" written in huge blue capitals.

'It feels sketchy, opening someone else's post,' I say.

'We're on a mission,' Ani says firmly, coming to stand beside me. 'Are you going to open that, or am I?'

I tear open the envelope.

Inside, there's what looks like the kind of letters Mum used to call junk mail; unwanted emails but actually printed out on paper and sent through the snail mail. Complete waste of effort; no one ever reads them, do they? I'm going to read this one though, if my heart will stop thundering in my chest like it's making a bid for freedom.

Typed in the same black ink as the page in the typewriter, the paper reads:

TO MY VALUED CUSTOMERS: FOR
YOUR EYES ONLY!

Available from the 19th, I have new tonics that will enable
travel to the future!

Yes, the FUTURE!

The years 1987 and 2019!

What will you see there? Where will you holiday in Space? Men, will robots
cook dinner better than your wives? Will the robots do the ladies' housework
after a day at the typewriter or till?

Limited availability!

Also available - rediscover your inner peace and free love in 1972!

STRICTLY FIRST COME FIRST SERVED!

Please indicate below your preferences, and return to
sender. Payment on confirmation of travel dates.

NOTE: Please use the usual method for re ordering standard stock.

I require _2_ bottles of tonic for (please tick all that
apply)   1972

1987 ✓

2019 ✓

I am available for travel on the following dates: **_All of August_**

My code number is **159**

'Holy crap,' Jasper says, peering over my shoulder. 'We've got her.'

'She is selling Weyfare blood,' I say, my insides churning as I remember someone telling me on a timeline I hoped was long extinguished: *they sell Weyfarere blood to the highest bidders so that they can travel the Weys safely and change their futures.*

'She's giving people Weyfare blood as a tonic!' Ani says, shuddering at the thought beside me. 'And to at least 159 of them?'

I'm sure the whole operation she's had going on down here

will gross me out in time, but for the moment, we've nailed it, and we need to get this letter back to Polly.

Chapter Twenty – Wanted

(The Dooleys, 1979)

We run out of Castle House, slamming the front door shut behind us, waving the letter at Rob, Tracy and Ian as they chase after us up the street, past the Town Hall and back down towards the Mermaid, where Ani screeches to a halt just before I do. There is a small crowd of people standing around outside the Inn, and three guys in black standing at the entrance, preventing anyone from going inside. Despite having met Mavis, Tommy, Barry and Clive, the Guard remind me of a pack of human panthers, and my stomach cramps up.

'That bloke with Barry and Clive must be from Dial Post,' Tracy says, breathing hard. 'They must be here.'

Ani looks at her. 'We weren't running that fast,' she says. 'You should give up smoking.'

Tracy gives her the stink eye. 'I can give up any time I like.'

'As long as it's not right now,' Rob says, winking at me, and the cramps in my stomach unclench a bit.

'Why is everyone standing around outside?' Ian asks a random woman as we arrive more slowly at the back of the waiting group.

'We've been evacuated from the hotel,' the woman, dressed in a pink woollen coat tells him excitedly. 'Apparently, there's a fault with the electricity supply, and it may start a fire!'

'Bloody electrics,' the man beside her says. 'Doesn't work half the bloody time, and when it does work, it's bloody faulty!'

'Bloody terrible,' Jasper quips, but the man doesn't seem to get the sarcasm and just nods vigorously.

Luckily for us, when Barry and Clive see us, they let us in, much to the bloody annoyance of the man. Through the passage that leads to the back of the old building, I can see a dark blue van like Ed's, their drivers waiting inside, also dressed in black.

Inside the Mermaid it's like a scene from *Black Ops 4*, minus the bloodshed and the automatic rifles. Everywhere I look, someone is standing with arms crossed in a doorway, wearing black combat gear and looking like the *Terminator* or *Rambo*. Judging by the words on the paper firmly held in my hand, equality hasn't quite reached the masses any more than in 1987, but I'm pleased to see it's not only Helen that has female Guard; Mavis is not the exception.

'How are you feeling, Barry?' I ask as he escorts us to the staircase, being replaced immediately by another clone.

'They clobbered me from behind,' Barry says grimly. 'Wouldn't have got me if they'd had the balls to face me. Won't get another chance, the tossers. Polly and the others are all waiting for you upstairs.'

The door marked Bayley is wide open in the absence of any guests, but on each side, there is another Guard. Inside the lounge, it's changed from *Black Ops* to a scene from one of those old *Poirot* movies they show on ITV3 at the weekends. The Guard's serious faces and sharp black clothes contrast with the bright colours and faded fabrics of Polly's home. Polly, Helen, Mary and Tommy are sitting cross-legged on the plush chairs, looking serious. Two more Guard are sitting either side of each of Janice and Gus, one sofa each, with two more Guard behind them.

Polly stands up, and she's flushed, but her voice is calm. Maybe she's been taking notes from Helen and Mary. 'Did you find what I sent you for?' she says, making it very clear that she's in charge; that this is her manor.

'We found this.' I hold out the letter, and she takes it, reads it, and the flush in her face deepens with anger while she takes in the enormity of what these people have been doing to her.

She turns to face Janice and Gus. Gus is looking at the carpet, but Janice is defiant, staring straight at Polly with a smirk on her lips that's almost goading the Witan into losing her shit. Sitting there, Janice reminds me of Valerie at St Peter's Hotel in another 1987, as proud of her heritage as a Weyleigher as the Weyfarere are of theirs. There's no chance this woman isn't a Weyleigher; I can see it in her eyes. I hope to whichever God is listening that the Guard in 1987 have got to the Dials in time to deal with Valerie and Scott.

'I trusted you,' Polly says, her voice quiet and steely. 'I trusted you, and my mother trusted you, and you violated us, and now you hurt my guests.'

Janice snorts. 'Violate is a bit over the top -'

'You are stealing Weyfare blood and you are selling it to by-standers!' Polly says, a little more loudly. Helen reaches out an arm like ivory and gently touches the younger woman's. Polly looks at it and nods. 'How long have you been profiting from the Weys?' She waves her hand at the paper. 'Code Number 159. Are there 159 people in this town who have ridden the Weys using mine and my mother's blood as an anchor?'

'Not any more,' Janice says smoothly. 'Ingesting blood regularly isn't exactly good for the liver. I warn them, but at the end of the day, these people are paying consenting adults.'

'You evil son of a -,' Polly says, the calm voice wobbling a little. She straightens her back and takes a breath. When she speaks again, her voice is controlled. 'As Witan of the Mermaid, I have the right based on this evidence to order a thorough search of your home, on suspicion of your Weyleigher status. I commit you to the trustees of the Bergh until a full trial can be held to determine which of the laws of the Weys you have breached, as well as any of the laws of the land, and detain you accordingly. Get them out of my home,' she finishes and slumps back into her armchair.

Gus looks at her, and I wonder if he's about to speak, but if he is, he thinks better of it.

In the end, it is a quiet ending to the nastiness. Janice and Gus are led in silence from the room, surrounded by black figures.

Two that were downstairs come in with Barry and Clive.

'With your permission, Miss Frobisher, once the detainees are in the wagon, we'll be on our way back to our Witan,' one says. 'Unless you have further need of assistance?'

'What I have need of,' Polly says sadly, 'is more Guard. I never considered myself a target down here in the back of beyond.' She smiles at Barry. 'You need more backup.'

Barry smiles, but he doesn't comment. They leave the room with the others until the room feels empty and a lot more colourful again.

'Well, at least I know I can keep on boogying at the discothèque,' Polly says into the silence. 'No bugger there is going to be sticking a needle in my arm.'

We spend the rest of the day watching golf on the TV of all things, and chillaxing. Helen wants to wait and be certain that Mary's well enough to attempt a ride back to 1987, but thankfully Mary has other plans - we've just survived two Weyleigher attacks, the last thing we need is death by sport.

'I can't just sit around here, not knowing whether the future is a nightmare,' she says. Her face is white like fresh snow, but her voice is hard like sheet ice. 'I'm ready as I'll ever be.'

After Helen has been convinced, we follow Polly through to the hidden room, past the round table to an unimportant-looking cupboard on the back wall. She opens it up, and we are faced with more shelves of vials and tokens, like in the Wey-room. To the side of the shelves on the left, there is a brass metal plate, a bit like the ones you see on school passageway doors, but a lot smaller. Polly pushes on it, and the whole shelf swings backwards to reveal a very narrow wooden spiral staircase, winding sharply down.

'It's a bit steep, so watch your footing,' Polly says and, as she moves onto the top step, I can see it's a bit tight as well; her shoulders are as wide as the space between the stairwell even though she's fit and slim, and the steps are narrower on one side than the other. One by one, they begin to follow her down, hanging onto the bit of rope that is posing as a handrail.

Jasper, in front of me, doesn't move. Jasper isn't impressed. 'When I signed up to ride the Weys with you, I did not sign an agreement to face my claustrophobia on a regular basis!' he wails.

'You signed nothing,' I remind him, giving him an encouraging shove, 'and still you came because we're fam. Come on, Jas, I'm right with you.'

After about ten stairs down though, I've stumbled more than he has. 'Polly, how do your bystanders ever find you?' I call down, as my foot slips for the third time. 'These stairs are lethal!'

'Why d'you think we don't get many 'ghost' sightings in the Inn?' she says. 'Plus there's another passage from the Weydoor out to the harbour.'

'Now she tells us,' Jasper says irritably.

'We're not beside the sea,' Tracy points out. 'That must be a hell of a long passage.'

'No, but the area that used to be underwater in the Dark Ages is still called the Harbour,' Polly says. 'My only other Guard lives in a cottage near to the exit, and he contacts me when he sees anyone appear looking bewildered. Only another ten or so steps.'

It's definitely nearer twenty, and it's a massive relief to leave the tiny stairwell and put my trainers on flat ground.

'Are we underground?' Helen asks, looking around her at the brick walls forming a square-ish space. In the middle, there is a circular glow like a tie-dyed pattern hanging in mid-air with no obvious means of support, and it's the shade of purple I've come to know so well.

'We're in the basement of an outhouse at the side of the Inn,' Polly says. 'From the outside, it just looks like a wall, and there's only one access point from the Inn itself, which is the one we just used.'

Mary holds out her hand. 'I owe you a great favour,' she says.

'Hold that thought until we see whether or not you get back to 1987 in one piece,' Polly says, taking the hand. 'Seriously, I can't guarantee that you won't puke on arrival, but I'm pretty sure whatever it is in Weyfarere DNA that controls our rides, it's still intact in yours.'

'I too owe you a debt,' Helen says, also shaking Polly's hand. 'It will be repaid shortly.'

'Aww shucks,' Polly says. 'My first crisis and I was a spaz, and you know it.'

'No one ever told us being Witan would be easy,' Mary says, with a smile. 'I assume you're going home, Mum?' Helen nods, yes. 'See you in about eight years then.'

They look at me, and for a minute I wonder whether they're

expecting me to be all adulty with the handshaking and the debt owing, but I feel the tear on my cheek that's sneaked out of my eye, and Helen steps forward.

'We are used to this life, Maisie. Lizzy will come to understand how to deal with meeting her pasts and her futures. Even if it's only because she has to.' She touches my shoulder, and I feel like a small kid. Then she turns to face Tommy.

Tommy is looking at Rob. Rob is looking back. I'm hoping there's not going to be a face-off, and then unexpectedly, Tommy holds his hand out to Rob. They shake hands, and although they don't say a word, it's as if they've had a whole conversation that we couldn't hear.

Tommy turns to me. 'I have to go back to 1972 with Mum. I'm her Guard. But I will always be by your side if you need me, Maisie Weyfare. All you ever have to do is ask.' He reaches into his pocket and draws out a small vial. 'You should have this back now.'

I hold out my hand. The label on the glass reads L - 2/1/72. It's Lizzy's blood token, from the night we sat around in Glenda and Henry's bedsit with Helen. It seems like weeks ago. 'Thank you,' I say, lost for anything more meaningful.

'I lost yours,' he says bluntly, turning back to look again at Rob. 'You?'

Rob nods once.

'Thought as much. At least I know it's in safe hands, dude.'
Words seem crass just now.

I look back at Rob. 'I'm coming with you,' he says.

'What about the question you wanted to ask Helen?'

'I can ask Mary,' he says. As I go to ask him if he's sure, he reaches out and takes my hand. 'Maisie. I'm coming with you.'

'Well, I don't know about you, but it's been a bare lit time,' Jasper says brightly. 'Where are we going then, Doc? Back to the future?'

I nod, yes. 'Not as far forward as we can go, though,' I say. 'I want to make sure Valerie and Scott are banged to rights in 1987, and then I want to sort things out with Lizzy so we can help Joan.'

Ani nods firmly in agreement. Of course she knows and I know that, if we can sort things out with Lizzy, she can be with Brian again. If that's what she wants.

'Well, I vote 1987 if I get any say in this,' Tracy says. 'I'm actually standing here thinking a day in Granty Esmé's garden revising sounds like a relaxing way to spend an afternoon right now. Who'd have expected that?'

Helen pulls out the silver teardrop locket that hangs next to her silver key. Inside is a now-familiar vial. 'Take a little of this on your fingers to return you to Mary.'

'We're only going forward eight years. Will you still be

Witan here?' Ian asks Polly.

Polly shrugs. 'I have no clue. Where's the end of your time-line?'

'May 26th 1987,' Mary says.

'Then if I'm still Witan, I'll make sure I'm here waiting for you all, and I'll leave a note for the new girl if I'm not. Maisie.' Polly holds her hand out for me. Awks. This is all a bit old for me. I'm still at the high-five fist bump level. Having daubed everyone's fingers, I return the vial to Helen, who puts it safely back in the locket.

'Good to meet you,' I say, holding my other hand out to Polly.

We shake. 'Good luck. I'd like to say it gets easier, but I'm not sure it does.' Polly steps back as if formally ending the meeting. 'And I'd like to say it's been a pleasure, but not to worry.'

Everyone laughs politely.

Helen and Tommy leave first. It's totally cray to think of him effectively disappearing from my timeline. In 1987, he'll be 35. In 2019, he'll be – FML. Really not thinking about this for any more seconds.

Mary's mouth is set in a straight line, and she looks like someone who's about to walk into a cage fight. We all link hands. Tracy and Ian follow Mary so that I don't drag them back to 2019 with me, but Rob, Jasper and Ani stick behind me regardless, and as we step forward, there's white heat, purple light, black – nothing.

No one is at the Mermaid Weydoor in 2019, so I jump straight back through, making sure to hold the hand with Mary's blood on the Weydoor, just in case. The Weydoor in 1987 looks like a London train station in the rush hour.

Tracy and Ian are scrambling to their feet. Mary, as you'd expect from a Witan, is on her feet, but bent over holding her stomach, and supporting her is Polly Frobisher, blonde hair all backcombed now in a scrunchie, wearing a shiny pink and black striped leotard. Her leggings and purple legwarmers are the same shade as the Weydoor; there are a few lines around her mouth and eyes. There are several Guard in the brick room, plus a guy in jeans and a white T-shirt printed with the word Whitesnake above the image of a gold seal.

Mary lifts herself up and puts her hands on her hips. She's breathing heavily, but she's not jet washing the floor with vomit, so that's got to be a good thing. 'I'm okay,' she says. I'm not the only one watching her. 'It's all right. Nothing worse than a medicine ball to the guts.'

'Great to see you all again!' Polly looks up at Tracy, and then across to me and winks. 'Betting you're completely freaked out, aren't you? What do you think of my Guard?' She waves an arm back at them. 'Helen sent them down from 1972 to tide me over, and they've been with me ever since.'

'You're still the Witan then,' Jasper says.

'Yeah. The Moot actually thought I did a good job with stopping Janice and Gus. You got an honourable mention in my report though.' She grins.

I'm not sure whether I'm pleased about the recognition or not, when I am completely blown away by the sight of a little girl in a short denim dress over red and black stripy tights, peering out from behind the Whitesnake guy.

Polly looks at what I'm looking at, and beams. 'That, my friends, is Charlotte, my brightest star and the next Mermaid. And her dad, Rich. Say hello to everyone, chicken.'

Charlotte hides behind her dad and everyone giggles. 'Hello everyone,' Rich says cheerfully, and everyone giggles again.

'Now, as lovely as this reunion is, you can't stay.' Polly puts her hand out, and one of the Guard steps forward with a piece of paper that's perforated at the edges. 'We had a fax through from Dial Post requesting immediate assistance from all Guard at the Seven Dials about an hour ago. There's trouble, so that'll be your Weyleigher and her sidekick. You better get back up there, Mary, and start kicking some butt.'

We are taken to London in a long, sleek silver car that looks like a bullet. The Guard driving it tells us that the Citroën CX is the only seven-seater car in Polly's fleet. Sounds like the boogie-loving Mermaid of 1979 has grown quite an empire here in the last few years. With eight of us, it's still a squeeze, but a lot more comfortable than the black van similar to Ed's behind us, carrying a cargo of Polly's Guard in the back. They are taking the trouble at the Dials seriously. Just as well, really.

I'm exhausted. Really trashed. I've not had any decent sleep since we were in 1987 at Esmé's house, and I can't work out how long ago that was in real hours. When I wake up with my head on Rob's shoulder and his arm along the bench seat behind me, the roads are busier, and there's even an M25 now, weirdly much to Jasper's delight, which we drive on for a junction or two before plunging into the depths of the London suburbs.

It's Tuesday evening, and the roads into London are gridlocked, but Polly's driver knows a few shortcuts and we arrive in one of the loading bays on Earlham Street to find lots of people in black outside Mary's apartment. There is a definite police presence, but the Guard seem to be convincing them the trouble is under control. Maybe the police think they're the SAS.

271

'Looks like a Goth convention,' Ian says.

The Guard are talking to people who look very much like the witch hunters who were baying for Mary's blood last time we were here.

I reach forward and touch her arm. 'I'm not sure you should be going outside until we know what's going on,' I say.

'I have to agree with that, Miss Davenport,' Polly's driver says. 'I'll radio the Guard to give us a ground report, and we'll park a little further away from the fracas until we have a better measure of the situation.'

He drives past the centre of the Dials and parks down past the Cambridge Theatre, before jumping out of the front seat and pulling a big brick of a two-way radio from a clip on his belt. I turn around, and in the rear window, I can see Polly's Guard piling out of the van that followed us, and immediately taking some of the people in the street by the arm. They don't appear violent, just firm as they take each one towards the row of Black Mariah type vehicles parked up on the road that leads down to Leicester Square. Quite a few people are watching, and some are taking photographs with boxy black and silver cameras.

'Surely if they're grabbing the witch hunters from the street, they'll have already dealt with Valerie and Scott,' Tracy says from the bench seat behind me.

'You'd have hoped so,' Jasper says. 'Not all of those people are the Lost, either.'

He's right. The Guard seem to be asking everyone nearby about their reasons for being in the Seven Dials, and some of them are just being sent on their way, probably being told there's a terror alert or whatever they call it in 1987.

'We should still stay here until we're given the all-clear,' Rob says.

'You sound like a Guard,' Tracy says, grinning back at him.

'That's not such a bad thing, is it?' Ani asks.

'I'm not Witan. I don't need a Guard,' I say firmly.

'You need people who know your secrets, and will look out for you,' Mary says. 'Otherwise being Weyfare can become nothing but a burden that isolates you from your current world.'

'There you go,' Ani says. 'Listen to your boss.'

I look at Mary in surprise. I've never seen her in that light. 'Are you my boss?' I ask.

She laughs. 'Strictly speaking, no, as you are anchored further down the timeline. I'm your mother's boss, I guess.'

'Interesting imagery.' I say. 'She's not all that good at taking orders.'

'The Witan don't work that way,' Mary says. 'I'm just the person she can come to if she has problems.'

'Thank Sod for that,' Jasper replies, and I guess he's remembering the almost militarian set-up that we witnessed Valerie running in an alternative 1987.

Polly's driver comes back to the car. Mary presses a button on the roof and the window comes down. At least it doesn't open with those winding levers that Ed's shagmobile has.

'We have your Guard here as well as some from Dial Post, Trinity Hall, and us,' he says. 'The initial danger is over. The Weyleigher and her abettor are on the road North to the Bergh. We are also detaining the Weyleigher's followers, and taking them to the Bergh for further questioning.' He pauses. 'The threat is past, but the Guard inside say that you will need some assistance in restoring your home to its original state, and you need to be prepared for that.'

'You mean they trashed it,' I say dejectedly, remembering the noise the Lost made as they climbed over chairs and sofas, breaking off anything that could be used as a weapon against Mary and Tommy.

We all get out of the car, my legs aching from being cramped up on such a long drive up from the Mermaid. As we approach Number Seven, several men and women run forward and encase Mary in a massive bear hug. I can hear her laughing and complaining from inside the cocoon, as they shower her with apologies and love.

'Mary's Guard, at a guess,' Jasper says, with a smile.

'They were all off duty, remember?' Ani says. 'I bet they won't leave her attended again.'

'Maybe they should consider a shift system like ours,' Polly's driver says. 'Nothing like finding your Witan in danger to stir up some change.'

We're attracting a fair bit of attention, but the Guard manage to get us through to the door of Number Seven, which is wide open, and from nowhere, there is a figure standing in front of it. She's held securely either side by Guard, which makes my heart lurch.

'Oh, I forgot to mention,' Polly's driver says. 'This young woman turned up, and she's been saying most forcefully that she's the Stoneford Weyfare and that you could verify that.'

'I showed you my fucking key, you wanker!'

'Hello again, Lizzy,' Mary says, with a smile.

Chapter Twenty-One – Alone
Again, Or (The Damned, 1987)

'This is Lizzy Brookes. She is one of the Stoneford Weyfarere. There's no need to restrain her,' Mary says, with a smile.

Looking at the expression on my mother-to-be's face, I'm not so sure.

'Perhaps you'll take your great meathooks off me *now*?' Lizzy snaps, and both Guard drop their hold on her.

'I'm sorry, Miss, but there's been a serious incident here, and we had to be certain you weren't a threat,' one of the Guard says.

'Not to Mary here, no.' Lizzy rubs her arms and then registers the group of people staring at her. '*Tracy*?'

Ian puts a finger up. 'Hey, Lizzy.'

Tracy steps forward. 'You're the Stoneford Weyfare!' she exclaims. 'Gobshite's ballbag, Brookes! You told me we don't keep secrets from one another, and then they tell me you're the guardian of some kind of mystic doorway? Patchouli is one thing, but this?' She waves her arms around. At all of us, I guess.

I am not saying aloud the thoughts going through my head. Déjà vu-ish.

Lizzy looks at her, then me, then Rob, then Mary. Her shoulders slump. 'Don't give me a hard time, Rutherford; I've only known myself for five minutes. What in the name of Sod has been going on up here?' she grumbles. 'What's he doing back?' she adds, pointing at Rob. 'And where's Tommy? I was looking forward to getting myself another eyeful of that fine goodness. Assuming I can get a crack at him, since *she* can't make her mind up?'

'Tommy's back in 1972. Rob is sound. Let's all go inside and have a cuppa,' Mary says, and we all walk through the battered remains of the door to Number Seven.

As soon as we're inside, it's obvious that a cup of tea might not be that easy a thing to make. The plastered walls are damaged by the dents and holes that Tommy and Mary's struggling feet made when the mob was carrying them down to the Weydoor. The paintings that aren't smashed on the floor are hanging broken at weird angles, and the light shade is gone.

Before we can take another step, I'm almost knocked flat by a skittle topped with blonde curls, and hugged to within an inch of my lung capacity. Out of the corner of my eye over Kim's shoulder, I can see Brian approaching Ani slowly and respectfully, and I can't help but smile as she flings her arms around his neck. Lizzy tuts like a teacher.

'I missed you so much,' Kim whispers.

I hug her tightly back. 'It's good to see you.'

'We've managed to secure the passage to the Weydoor, Mary,' one of her Guard says, as Kim continues her hugs with Jasper, and Brian shakes a few hands. 'We thought you'd want that done before we did anything else.'

'You thought right.' Mary leads us up the staircase to where the table with the old telephone is on the floor with two remaining legs, into more of the same carnage in the lounge: overturned sofas, smashed armchairs trampled under rioting feet, sticks and bits of furniture abandoned next to the fake sheep's rug, who is staring at it all as if nothing happened here today. The cabinet of china next to the television has fallen forward, spilling its cracked contents. The television seems intact, but the record player stack is on its side, and all of the plastic cassettes have tipped onto the carpet.

'I'll say something for you; you Witan sure know how to throw a party,' Lizzy says.

If this were Travellers' Rest, I'd be in pieces. 'Mary, we'll help you get it straight,' I say, feeling pathetic that it's all I can offer her.

She smiles back at me. 'This isn't my home,' she says. 'This is the home of the Seven Dials Witan. I just live here. My home is with Mum and my family in Totleigh. It always will be. All the same, this is a bloody mess.' She turns to the Guard. 'Would you go see if there's any alcohol or ciggies left in the kitchen? I think we're going to need something stronger than tea to deal with this.'

It doesn't take long to turn some of the sofas up the right way; some cushions have dirty footprints on them, but they're still useable. We gather up the shattered furniture pieces and put them in a pile at the foot of the staircase. Mary, Rob and Ani manage to get the record player and its stand back upright. Mary picks one of the small cases from the debris at the bottom of the stack and slots a grey plastic cassette it into the player. It still works. I recognise Bono's voice. Mum likes U2; she used to play this album a lot.

The Guard return with glasses and spirit bottles; apparently, the rioting hordes never made it as far as Mary's kitchen. While Bono is telling us he can't live with or without you, we sit down, sipping vodka with orange squash or whisky and ginger ale, and I for one am wondering who's going to begin. Someone needs to.

Mary takes a cigarette from one of the black boxes and passes it on. 'Can I ask why you're here, Lizzy?'

'I need your help,' Lizzy says, 'but frankly, it looks like you need mine more. What happened here?'

'Valerie,' I say.

'I was asking the Witan,' she says as if she's spitting the words at me.

'Maisie is in as good a position as me to supply you with the information you need, Lizzy. She is Weyfare as well,' Mary says evenly.

'Not right now she's not,' Lizzy says, and the words come out like a snarl. 'In her future, she might be, but I'm the Stoneford Weyfare here and now, not her.'

'Lizzy,' Mary says, as if she's talking to a frightened pony, 'no one is disputing that you are a Stoneford Weyfare, but you have to accept as part of your duties that you will meet your past and your future.'

'We know you're Maisie's mum, Lizzy,' Tracy says.

'Fucking Hellfire!' Lizzy cries out, pointing at me. 'You had no right to tell them ...'

'She didn't tell me, I worked it out,' Tracy interrupted. 'Don't get your knickers in a twist, Brookes. It was fairly obvious.'

'Not to me it wasn't.' In the silence, I wonder if Lizzy's face of fear is the one Bono can see.

'We have to keep enough secrets because of our birthright, Lizzy,' Mary says gently. 'What's the point in keeping secrets needlessly from those who care about us?'

I can see why they thought Mary Davenport would make a good replacement for her mother. She lifts an ashtray from the collapsed table, puts it on the arm of the sofa and flicks ash into it.

'Two or three hours ago here in 1987, I was drugged and thrown through my own Weydoor. I've just spent four days in 1979, with my mother and brother from 1972.' She leans forward. 'I knew things about them. I knew what would happen to them, and they knew I knew their futures too. But I told them nothing, and they asked no questions. This is how the Weyfarere and their families have to live. This is how you both have to live.' She waves the smoking cigarette at me. 'Maisie, you know Lizzy's future and you can't tell her, any more than she can ask you about it. But you need each other. You need to accept that you can appear on each other's timelines at any point.'

'I'd never tell her anything about the future,' I say.

'I don't want to know,' Lizzy snaps back. 'I never asked.'

'No, you just had a major benny and stormed off –'

'You lied to me!' she yells.

'I didn't lie! I just didn't tell you who I was, and do you fucking blame me?' I yell back. 'Look at how you've reacted! You think this is easy for me, travelling back in time and meeting my freaking mother?'

Everyone looks at Lizzy, and it makes me feel bad. I do get her reaction, really, no matter how much it hurts me. We are both coming to terms with something far bigger than either of us ever thought we'd have to deal with.

'You lied to us too,' Brian says, his voice calm, 'but I get why, and I'm good with it.'

'If you'd showed up in the Common Room on Friday and said you were time travellers, we would've just thought you were a bunch of loonies and told a teacher.' Kim adds. 'But once we knew, it would've been really hard to then tell us that you were related to Lizzy as well.'

'And you never even told me you were Weyfare. I'm one of your best buds,' Tracy says. 'But I'm not going to get shirty about it Brookes, because you need me, and I know everything now. Maisie found an entrance to a Weydoor in the road at the bottom of my Granty Esmé's garden. She might even be a Weyfare.'

Lizzy turns to look at me, finally distracted. 'Another tunnel from the Old Library?'

I shake my head, no. 'From the new Weydoor that's linked to the Weyroom under Drake's,' I tell her.

'I've ridden the Weys with Maisie back to 1979. Hell, I even went to a proper disco and wore satin drainpipe trousers, and we helped to put away a 1970s Weyleigher.' Tracy takes a mouthful of vodka and orange. 'So if I can get my head around this, Brookes, I'm sure you can.'

'There was another Weyleigher in the 1970s?' Lizzy asks, blowing blue smoke across the room.

'There are Weyleighers everywhere, Lizzy. The problems begin if they know the location of the Weydoor or the identity of the Weyfare,' Mary explains.

'While we're on the subject, maybe someone can explain to me why we're sharing your whisky with one,' Lizzy asks, glaring at Rob.

'Maybe if you promise not to bite Maisie's head off, she'll get a chance to bring you up to speed,' Jasper says.

Since Lizzy scowls at him but doesn't reply, I take a breath, and fill her in on all the events that have happened since she stormed away from me, Ani and Jasper in Stoneford: the ride to 1994 and the revelation about Rob's parentage; the discovery that the new Weydoor is possibly linked to a female line of Tracy's family; the trip to London to stop Tommy taking Rob to the Bergh; Valerie and Scott's attempted coup; Polly, the Mermaid and Janice, and Mary's lucky escape from the still unidentified drug.

'Did we really do all that in a couple of days?' Ian asks faintly.

'So Valerie's not your mum,' Lizzy says to Rob.

He shrugs. 'It's no biggie.'

Kim exhales sharply. 'It's a massive biggie!' she says.

'I mean – yes okay, it's a biggie that I'm not her son, but being part of that family isn't important to me. I never felt like I belonged there anyway.' Rob puts his cigarette out in the ashtray next to the whisky bottle. 'I'm glad she's banged up.'

'They definitely are locked up?' I ask one of Mary's Guard, sitting on the floor a discreet distance from us, also enjoying a drink. 'The Weyleigher and her … partner?'

'Well, we don't lock people up, Miss. We aren't the police,' one of them says. 'But they will be taken to the Bergh and kept there while evidence is gathered about their activities, and then they will be put on trial.'

'And if the trial decides their activities are crimes against the Weys community, then they will be detained indefinitely,' another Guard adds.

'Doesn't detained mean locked up?' Ani asks.

'No, it just means that they won't be allowed to leave the Bergh,' the Guard says, with a smile.

'You always did have shit taste in boys,' Tracy says to Lizzy. 'Remember when you fancied the arse off Mark McQueen in the third year? He was a real knob. And I told you Patchouli was a nasty piece of work, but did you listen to me? Did you buggery.

When are you going to learn, Brookes?'

Lizzy switches quickly to face her as if she's going to react badly; then she looks first at me and then at Mary, and she puts her hands over her face and bursts into unexpected tears.

It's instinctive to go to comfort her, but I'm not out of my seat quick enough. Tracy is in front of her in a second, stroking her hair and holding her close, telling her she's a soft touch, but everything will be all right.

Rob takes my hand and squeezes it. Ani and Brian are close together on one of the other sofas, and Jasper is at my side like he always is. Mary is smiling at us all. Ian is smoking, looking peaceful despite the circumstances. I catch Kim's eye, and I get the feeling that Tracy's right, as she sits at Lizzy's feet. We're all here. The Witan and her Guard, Weyfarere from now and the future, surrounded by all their friends. All the tea's been spilt. Valerie and Scott won't be leaving the Bergh any time soon. Maybe there are no more secrets left to keep. It might take a bit of time for the dust to settle, but maybe, just maybe everything's going to be okay after all.

'I need your help, Mary,' Lizzy sniffles into a hanky that Mary has passed across to her. She swallows a sob. 'Okay, okay - and your help as well, Maisie. Rob's grandma – I mean Valerie's mum has moved in and she's living at Travellers' Rest.'

Or not okay, then.

Chapter Twenty-Two – I Still Haven't Found What I'm Looking For (U2, 1987)

'Eve Bennett's living at your house?' Rob asks. 'Now?'

All but two of the Guard nod towards Mary and leave the room.

One says, 'We'll take our leave, Mary. Radio down if you need us.'

She nods.

Of course, Rob would know this woman; she was his grandmother for 18 years. Last time we saw her, she was ladling out vile soup to the street communities of Stoneford at Trinity Church in 1972, hoping to find some of the Lost who might tell her the location of the Weydoor. Lizzy nods.

'What did you do after the row?' Jasper asks. 'Did you go straight home, and she was just there?'

Lizzy dabs at her eyes. Tracy sits at her feet. 'I used Mum's vial and went back to 1972 to fetch her, Dad and Paul. It all seemed to go smoothly enough. We said goodbye to Nora, Dillon and little Scott, and we rode back. Brian went home, and

Kim stayed with us. I could've gone straight back to check on Joan, but I wanted a really nice evening like we used to have when me and Paul were kids. We had Findus crispy pancakes and waffles on our laps in front of *Bob's Full House* and *Ever Decreasing Circles*, then we watched *Staying Alive* with John Revolting from *Grease*.'

'Yeah, we watched that as well,' Tracy says, smiling up at her. 'Then last night we were at a disco where most of the blokes were dressed like him in *Saturday Night Fever*. It's nuts.'

'So what happened?' I ask.

'The front door opened, and Eve came in,' Lizzy says. 'I didn't recognise her at first, but Mum did, and Dad jumped up and asked her what the hell she was doing letting herself into our house, and she laughed and called him a card, and said she was going to bed.'

'Freaky,' Ian says.

'You're telling me. So me and Mum went upstairs and, sure enough, her room looked like it had been there a long time. There were pictures of me and Paul growing up on her wall.' She shivers. 'Me and Mum think Valerie must've gone back to 1972 at some point and changed events.' She looks at Mary, and then at me. 'It took me all morning to convince Mum to let me come to you for help, and when I got here, I thought there'd been a bomb alert. Do either of you know anything about where Valerie went after 1972?'

'Wherever she went, she'd made a token with Scott, so she rode straight back to Stoneford earlier that day. Tommy had a couple of Guard watching the house. Glenda didn't take any notice of Helen's warning. She still met Valerie for coffee regularly and, one day, she took *The Truth* with her.' I take a large mouthful of vodka. The orange squash is really sweet; I think I prefer drowning it in Coke Zero. Or drowning myself, since I don't really want to tell Lizzy about the next bit.

'No more secrets, Maisie,' Mary says gently. I swear the Davenport women can read minds.

'We know she went back to 1972 to stop something happening to her son, Robin,' I say.

'Robin?' Lizzy looks at Rob.

'Valerie's first son. When Robin died, Valerie adopted Rob from a young unmarried mum,' I say, putting a hand on Rob's knee. 'Back then, a lot of women just didn't have kids if they didn't have a husband. It was like some kind of disgrace. Valerie saved her son; we don't know how. The thing is before she left 1972, the Guard with Tommy saw someone take your grandma to the Weydoor at the Old Library, and when Joan came out, she was different. Confused. She looked ill. You said she had dementia. I don't think she did. I think she was thrown, by this person, and she got herself trapped somewhere.'

'Trapped?' Lizzy asks, looking as if she's going to choke on her vodka.

'For years, probably. Long enough to mess with her mind. It would only be a blink on her natural timeline, of course.'

Lizzy looks at Mary. 'Is this possible?'

'It's possible to spend years off your natural timeline, yes, but the body still ages, so it's not recommended,' Mary says.

Lizzy needs to know this, since I once saw how the consequences of constant time travel affected her. 'And you think it was Valerie that threw her?' she asks.

'The Guard couldn't be sure, but I don't see who else would want to do it. Valerie knew she had Glenda under her thumb. She needed to get rid of Joan.'

'Or maybe Rob's grandma did,' Jasper says. 'Valerie had set her sights on the Seven Dials by then, but – what's her name? – Eve would've wanted control of Stoneford.'

'Eve Bennett is nothing to do with me,' Rob says. 'I'm not a Bennett, remember? At some point, I need to find out exactly who I am. I wanted to talk to you about that, Mary.' He looks at Lizzy. 'Maybe not right this minute though.'

'Mum wanted to stay at Travellers' Rest to monitor the Weydoor,' Lizzy says, ' but, when I finally convinced her to ring this number in *The Truth*, there was no reply, so me and Kim met Brian, and caught the train up here.' She looks around at the pile of debris in the doorway. 'Course, I wasn't expecting to find a set from *Lethal Weapon* when I got here, but it explains why no one answered the phone.'

'So what do you and Glenda want from me?' Mary asks.

'We know Eve's a Weyleigher now, so can you just send some of your Guard down to take her to the Bergh?' Lizzy asks.

Mary stubs her cigarette out and immediately lights another. 'It's not that straight forward. It's not a crime against the Weys community to be descended from Egil or Slagfiðr. Unless you can obtain proof that Eve is using the Weys to further her own interests, then there's little I can do.'

'She's moved into Travellers' Rest!' Lizzy says, her temper flaring again. 'A Weyleigher has moved into a Weyfare home! What more frigging proof do you need?'

'A lot more. There could be all sorts of circumstances in which Eve could be there. You will need to monitor her.'

'Or maybe go back to the time before she moved in, and stop it happening?' I ask.

'That may also be difficult,' Mary replies. 'Weyleighers play the long game. The family may have been working towards their goal for some time.' She gets up and pours herself another generous whisky and ginger ale. 'You want my advice? Prioritise. The first thing I would do is find out when your grandmother becomes unwell, and see if you can prevent her from approaching the Weydoor.'

'Would Glenda remember the date?' Rob asks. 'It's potentially a long time ago.'

'She'll remember,' Lizzy says bleakly.

'If she doesn't, I'll check the ledgers in the Heritage Room. Tommy should've made a note of his observations at some point.'

'But how will we get back without a token?' Ani asks.

'Maisie still has my mother's vial from 1972. I may also have vials from later in 1972 stored away,' Mary tells her, sipping the amber drink.

'It might be worth a look in the Weyroom at Drake's,' Kim says. 'There were loads of tokens and vials in there.'

Some of them are still in my bumbag, I think.

'I would also see if your dad or brother's memories adjust. Weyfarere brains are more primed to hold multiple timelines, and so you and your Mum may only have a hazy sense of events changing, and Eve moving in, but it may be clearer to them.'

'And if Henry and Paul don't remember?' Jasper asks.

'Arrange a family meal. Is it anyone's birthday any time soon? Have a lovely meal with everyone present, to sit down a chat about 'the old days'.' Mary uses finger speech marks. 'Get the talk around to the wonderful day Eve came to live with you.'

'Wonderful?' Lizzy snaps.

'She's being sarky, Lizzy,' Tracy says smoothly. 'Keep up.' She turns to face Mary. 'Shouldn't we all be at this meal? I mean, I don't know about you lot, but I consider myself one of Lizzy and Maisie's Guard.'

'Dogtanian,' Ian says, saluting randomly like he's a soldier.

'We're not Witan,' I tell him.

'You may not be Witan, but your Weydoor seems to be attracting a lot of attention at the moment, and it's a good idea to keep your friends close,' Mary says. 'You don't need to do the training to look after your mates.'

'So we find out when Eve moved in, and then what?' Lizzy asks. 'Go back and hide her suitcase?'

'I can't predict how your rides will change events,' Mary says. 'You asked for my advice, and I have given it.' She finishes her drink and stretches her arms above her head. 'I'm shattered. I need to go to bed. Would anyone like a nightcap?' A few of us raise our hands. I don't want a hangover in the morning. 'I'll set the percolator off – if those bastards haven't wrecked it.' It's the first time she's hinted at how traumatic this has all been for her. 'Rob? Would you come and give me a hand?'

If he's surprised at being singled out like this, he doesn't show it. She obviously wants to talk to him about the question he wants to ask her. She obviously doesn't want us to hear, which is fair; it is his private business, but I'm still unsettled, and without her in the room, the atmosphere feels slightly less stable.

'You'd love the Mermaid, Brian,' Ian says, putting his empty glass on the floor. 'The Witan Polly is a chemist, and she has a full working lab in her flat.'

'He'd have hated the disco though,' Ani says. 'There were men there. Dancing!'

Brian pulls a face. 'So Mary took one of those pills, and Polly crushed one up for testing. There should've been three? One for Tommy, one for Jasper and one for you?' he asks me.

I nod, yes. 'I'm not giving it to Valerie's Mum, though. I'm not risking a repeat performance of what happened here.'

'So, you're the same as Lizzy,' Kim says carefully. 'Descended from Valkyrie. That must be weird.'

That is the understatement of the millennium.

'I got used to it.'

That is the lie of the millennium.

'Don't go asking her stuff about the future, Kim,' Tracy says.

'I wasn't! What kind of a moron do you think I am?' Kim retorts. Tracy looks so shocked that she doesn't have a clapback; I wonder how much of this Kim she's seen before now. Her Kim was a victim of a sociopathic stepmother and would never openly confront anyone. This Kim left home and is discovering that her cahones are as big as the next person's.

Mary comes in with the percolator (thankfully not broken), several cups and a jug of milk. Rob isn't with her, and she says goodnight. Looks like Rob's question wasn't a quick one to answer.

Despite drinking the coffee, after a bit of light banter avoiding anything that's going to upset anyone, we start to fall asleep where we sit. I'm the last awake, mainly because Rob hasn't come back, and Mary's been in her room for ages.

He wouldn't have just walked out on me again without saying goodbye, would he? I know I've been dreading the moment we have to part again; I totally get the fact that he needs to meet his birth family and find himself, but I thought we would do it properly this time. I don't want another note scribbled on telephone notebook paper telling me it was for the best. By the time I leave the lounge, making sure not to wake Jasper who is snoring softly at my side, I have worked myself up to bare highkey.

So that when I storm into the kitchen, flicking three switches down and flooding the room with artificial light, expecting to find another note left for me leaning against Mary's brown teapot, I freeze when I see not a note, but Rob, sitting quietly at the table, eyes open but somehow vacant.

Why has he been sitting here in the darkness?

I flick all the switches back up, apart from one, which leaves one big lamp that hangs down over the centre of the table, eerily making Rob looks like he's under a spotlight.

As I walk over to the table, he looks at me, and I can clearly see track marks down his cheeks. FML. What did Mary tell him? I pull out a high-backed wooden chair, sit down, and put my hands over his clasped ones.

'What's the matter?' I move my head, trying to get him to look at me.

When he does, it's like looking into an empty grave. 'I don't have a home, Maisie,' he says. 'I don't have a family. I don't exist.'

Chapter Twenty-Three – Invisible Touch (Genesis, 1987)

'Of course you exist!' I tell him. It's not like either of the Rob's that I've cared for to be so down on themselves. 'I wouldn't be able to do this if you didn't exist.' I lean across the corner of the table and put a soft kiss on his wet cheek.

'I don't belong then.' He still stares forward into the empty space between the table and the door I closed behind me.

'Not to the Simmons, no,' I agree. 'But that's a good thing, isn't it? You said it was a good thing. We knew you weren't Valerie and Ted's son. Now we know that you've never been part of that family. Just like you never wanted to be.' I gaze into his green eyes and see nothing but pain. 'Rob, what's changed? What am I missing here? Help me understand?'

He turns to face me then, and I am shocked by how gaunt he looks under the unforgiving light above, as if all the life has been sucked out of him.

Before he can say anything, I suddenly grab onto his hands, a chilly fear washing over me like being doused in Eve's cold gravy soup. 'No. No, don't tell me that. Please don't tell me –'

'I'm not extinguishing,' he says calmly. 'I'm an anomaly, according to Mary.'

I try not to breathe too heavy a sigh of relief because he's clearly not happy about it. 'What's one of those?'

'You know the first time we were here? Well, it wasn't your first time; I'm not sure how many times you've been here.'

'You and me both, bae.'

If he doesn't understand me, he doesn't say so. 'When we met, I was Scott's stepson. He'd been living with Valerie since she left my dad in 1972.'

'That's right.'

'But there was another Scott, wasn't there? He was already alive.'

'He was a little boy. His family lived next door to the Hippy Shop or the Stoneford Healthy Blah Blah Blah as his dad called it. Why are we talking about Scott? He's on the road to the Bergh. We don't need to worry about him any more.'

'I thought his parents were dead,' he says emptily. 'That's what he told us.'

'Maybe they were,' I reply, but I'm starting to feel uneasy again. It's hard to remember multiple memories from time-lines, but I'm sure Scott told me that the Kelly family had been given a big payment to leave Stoneford, so that there was less chance of the Scott from 1987 ever meeting his younger self.

'No, I don't think they were,' Rob says interrupting my thoughts. 'But they were dead to *him*.' I must be suffering from lack of sleep because I still can't see what he's driving at. He tugs my hands closer to him, pulling me out of my seat and onto his lap. 'I can't go home, Maisie. I can't meet my real family. Not ever. Because I'm already *there*.'

The enormity of what he's saying hits me like the train I caught in 1940, and I can't even.

'Mary said that when Valerie went back to save Robin, she created a paradox. Me. Because Robin never died, Valerie never went to the mother and baby unit, and she never adopted me. So the me that Valerie never adopted stayed with my mum until my brother and sister came along and, as far as we know, he's still there.'

I thought I knew how it feels to be lost in Time, with no way of telling what I'll find if I go to the end of my timeline, travelling backwards and forwards through the decades trying to put out fires. But there's only one Maisie Wharton, born June 2001, at the end of my timeline. There are now two Robs. I can only guess how he must be feeling. He had a home and a family, even if he hated it. Now he has nothing; that family doesn't exist, and he can't meet the other one.

'What else did Mary say about it?'

'Mary said she has some contacts who might be able to locate the mother and baby home my mum was in. But we have almost nothing to go on and, even if we do find the place and even if they do tell us where she went afterwards, it won't tell me where they are now. And even if it did, I can't go and meet them. I can never meet them.' Rob swallows down a deep breath and puts his head against my shoulder. 'I don't even know my name, Maisie. Mary said I may not even have been named Robert.'

'You are Rob,' I tell him determinedly. 'You can be whoever you want to be. Take a new family name. Call yourself Abercrombie or Fitch. Call yourself Wharton if you want; it doesn't change who you are to the people who care about you. And if Mary finds out your family name, we'll call you that, but it won't make us love you any more or any less.'

He moves his head from my shoulder. I can feel the damp through the jacket. 'I couldn't call myself Wharton,' he says, with the first light of a dawning smile.

'Why not? What's the matter with it?' I ask, mock-bothered.

'People will assume I'm your brother, and then I couldn't do this,' he says, and the kiss is like the sun breaking through the dark clouds of doom that seem to follow us both.

We are still sitting on the chair when Mary comes in.

'If I followed a religion, I'd think the two of you looked spiritual, lit up under the lamp like that,' she says. 'Coffee? I'll just do instant, it's quicker than waiting for that infernal machine to produce the wake-up juice.'

She pulls on a looped string at the side of the huge bay window overlooking Earlham Street, opening some plastic blinds, and, as natural light floods into the room, she turns off the light still shining over us. I have a crick in my neck from sleeping on Rob's lap all night.

'Rob, your legs are going to be blue,' I say, realising I've been sitting there for hours.

He proves me wrong by wiggling his legs beneath me. 'I do need a slash though,' he admits, so I move aside to let him leave, rubbing my neck and going over to where Mary is already spooning dark coffee granules into a mixed bag of mugs.

'He told you then,' she says simply.

I nod, yes. 'Can he really never meet his birth mother?'

Mary puts the jar of Mellow Birds back in a high cupboard. 'Never isn't really a Weyfarere word,' she replies. 'Although this is a tough case, because Robin would have to die in 1972 for Rob to be adopted under the same circumstances.'

'No one wants that,' I say, toying with a mug with a fat

orange tabby cat on it holding a mug with steam coming out of his ears, labelled "I like my coffee hot."

'Precisely. Can you get the milk for me from the fridge over there? Thanks.'

'It's harsh, though.'

'Time travel is harsh,' Mary says. 'Bystanders think it's all nostalgia and old music, but surely you've already seen enough to know that it's a much darker experience than that.'

I pass her the milk bottle and think for a moment. I lost Ani. I lost Rob. It seems to have worked out, but so many other things may not have. I still don't know whether Mum will be there when I go back to 2019. Joan's illness might never have been an illness at all. Mary nearly lost her ability to ride the Weys, and Polly was being drained by her Guard. How much of it has been my fault? How much would still have happened if Brian hadn't made me stumble in the Old Library that day?

'I'll never get back to the timeline I left, will I?' I ask Mary out loud.

She puts the milk bottle down on the worktop, stops and places her hands on my arms. 'Never isn't really a Weyfarere word, remember? Neither is self-pity. There literally isn't time for it in our world.' She lays a palm gently across my cheek. 'Go and grab us a couple of trays from the rack over there by the Welsh Dresser.'

As we walk into the lounge with the coffees, everyone is waking up. Lizzy, Kim and Tracy are propping themselves up on the largest sofa; Ani and Brian are on another. Ian's on his back on the sheep rug, and Jasper's wide-awake in one of the vast armchairs.

His face collapses with relief when he sees me. 'You need to stop wandering off in the middle of the night, blud,' he says, adding as he sees Rob coming back into the room with a jar of Coffeemate and a plate of Viscount biscuits in their green foil, 'or at least let me know where you're going.'

One of the Guard comes up the stairs with several newspapers and hands them to Mary once she's put her tray on the wobbly coffee table: *The Independent*, the *Daily Mail*, *The Guardian* and a copy of *Private Eye*. 'Thanks, angel. Be a darling and fix us some toast,' Mary says to her. 'Help yourself as well. There are Sugar Puffs and Ricicles in the cupboard.'

Brian lets Ani ease back gently against one of the cushions as he leans forward. 'Why buy so many papers? Isn't one set of bad news enough?'

'First, it's a failsafe, to make absolutely sure of my position in Time,' Mary says, handing him a red mug with KitKat printed on it. 'Second, I don't conform to any political persuasion, so I get a selection of left, right and satire. Third, and most importantly, I track the major events and make sure there are no anomalies.'

There's that word again. 'Anomalies?' Brian asks, passing his mug to Ani as she sits up and wipes the grit from her eyes.

'Did Mum tell you about the Master Timeline?' Mary asks.

'She told some of us,' I say, sitting down between Rob's raised knees with the orange cat mug. On the bottom, it says his name is Garfield. 'Can't remember who was there.'

'The Master Timeline is the backbone of History, the one that links all the major world events.' Mary passes a mug printed with Choose Life to Ian. 'It has to be preserved. I check today's news with the ledgers, to make sure they match. If they don't, there's an anomaly that needs to be investigated. Fortunately, it's rare.'

'So what about all the events you've been changing?' Brian asks me.

'Our lives don't affect the Master Timeline,' I tell him.

'Well, we don't know that for certain,' Mary picks up the CoffeeMate and spoons it into her mug, this one with blue and white stripes. 'Sometimes, ordinary people flick a switch and, three months down the Master Timeline, the whole world lights up. Like, what would've happened if those random travelling players hadn't invited William Shakespeare to come to London with them?'

'I wouldn't have had to bother learning any quotes for

Hamlet,' Kim says, shaking the hair out of her eyes and holding her hands out for some coffee, which she passes to Lizzy.

'You might not need to have bothered anyway,' Tracy says. 'We can just ride the Weys forward and nick the test papers.'

There is a noticeable breeze in the room as several of us breathe in sharply. Kim pulls a face, and takes her own mug, labelled "I shot J.R".

'You have got to be kidding me,' Lizzy says. 'If that's how you think, you can go back to Stoneford right now and bloody stay there! Do you know how much of a mess Scott Kelly made when he started fooling about on the Weys?'

You don't know the half of it, I think, but I save that nugget of info for another day.

'I was joking, all right?' Tracy says, her face flushed; maybe from the embarrassment that she just made a really massive gaffe, maybe from the embarrassment that she thought it was funny. 'I wouldn't really do it!'

'Good because that's how Weyleighers think, and I've had a gutful of those lately,' I say, so sternly that I surprise myself at how seriously I've taken her comment. But if Tracy starts thinking in those sorts of terms, who's to say what damage she could do, if only to herself? And I'm the one who told her about the passage to the Weydoor from Esmé's road. FML. Have I been a complete tool? Again?

'I didn't mean it,' she says, more apologetic now. 'Keep your hair on.'

Jasper reaches over for his mug, looking a bit dazed at waking up into a full-blown row. Mary tactfully switches on the TV in the corner, which was somehow left intact by Valerie's flash mob. TV listings in the papers tell her BBC1 is showing a cartoon called the *Pink Panther*, followed by the news and something called *Breakfast Time*, which sounds a whole lot like *Good Morning Britain* without Piers Morgan.

'Telly in the mornings? It's almost like being back home,' Jasper says.

'Since when do you watch mainstream in the mornings?' I ask.

'I catch up with my channels on *YouTube*,' he says. 'That counts.'

I'm not sure it does, but hey.

The *Pink Panther* is entertaining like cartoons always are, and the weather's still going to be okay. We can only stomach five minutes of a woman called Sally on *Breakfast Time* telling us about the election that's coming up before Mary turns it off.

'So what are your plans for today?' she asks. 'What's the priority to be? Lizzy?'

'I need to get that Weyleigher bitch out of my house,' Lizzy says.

'You need to find out who throws Joan through the Wey-door,' I say.

'That too. I'm going to stop that happening,' Lizzy says.

'But won't that change the future again, if Joan doesn't get ill?' Ani asks.

'What happened to her can't be right,' I say decisively.

Lizzy sips at her coffee for a moment or two then nods in agreement. 'D'you think they're connected? Joan becoming ill and Eve moving in?'

Is she asking my opinion as Weyfare, or just asking my opinion? 'Well, it's not a bare crazy idea. They were all friends. Maybe Glenda asked Eve to help care for Joan.'

Mary looks around at us all; Rob and me; Jasper; Ani and Brian; Lizzy, Kim, Ian and Tracy. She looks back at me. I get her meaning straight off. 'If you do ride back, you shouldn't all go, Lizzy. Even the Witan travel with a very limited Guard and only then in the case of an emergency,' she says, looking apologetic. 'As cool as you all are, there are only three Weyfarere in this room.'

'Isn't having a Weyleigher move in classed as an emergency?' Lizzy asks.

'It's a cause for concern until you have evidence of the Weys being abused.'

'Or the Weyfare,' I say. She nods, understanding my point.

'Rob stays with me,' I say, 'wherever I go.'

'You know he's 50 years old on your timeline,' Lizzy says, and I can sense that she's still a little salty with me.

'Don't be a moron your whole life, Lizzy,' he says. 'Take a day off.'

'I know. I met him, remember?' I say quickly before she can reply, going to show her the signet ring on my necklace. Shocked, I realise the only thing hanging there is my silver key. 'Shit! Where is it?'

'I reckon it's extinguished,' Rob says sadly, holding up his own bare hand. He looks at Mary. 'Isn't it?'

'It was never given to you on this timeline,' she says, her kind face drawn with lines of sympathy. 'It doesn't exist here.'

'Woah,' Tracy says. 'What's extinguished when it's at home?'

'When you change a point in the past that affects the existence of a person or an object.' Suddenly, I'm burrowing into my bumbag, and from amongst the vials, small objects, and Tommy's hanky, I pull two books. Not one. Two. *The Book of the Witan* is still here. What the feck have I got to do to get rid of it? 'It hasn't extinguished.' I hold it out to Lizzy, who looks at it as if I'm handing her dog muck on a plate, and doesn't take it.

'What does that mean?' Kim asks.

'It means someone had this made after Valerie found out

about *The Truth*,' I say, putting the purple leather book back into its safe place. 'Which is sometime between March 1972, and whenever she went back to stop Robin from dying.'

'Which is around the time that Tommy thought Joan was abducted,' Jasper says.

'You have to help me, Maisie,' Lizzy says. 'Much as I hate to admit it, you know shed loads more about all this than me.'

'I come with Rob and Jasper,' I say, looking at Ani, holding Brian's hand. 'Ani?'

They look at each other and Brian nods. 'I'm with you,' she says.

'It's okay because I'm with Lizzy,' Brian says.

'Lizzy does not leave my timeline,' Kim says.

'You seem to have both developed a Guard despite not being Witan,' Mary says, sighing, but she's smiling as well. 'And Tracy? Ian?'

'It's been a ball, but I think maybe I'd like a break from the quantum stuff for now,' Ian says.

Tracy pulls a face. 'Lizzy, we're s'posed to be bestest buds.'

Lizzy turns and hugs her unexpectedly. 'It's not about favourites, Trace. It's my job, kind of. Mary's right. It's probably best we don't all keep riding.'

'So how come Kim gets to play time travel and I don't?'

Tracy's starting to sound like a whiny kid, and Kim's looking more and more uncomfortable.

'You need to make sure the other Weydoor is protected,' I say, suddenly inspired. 'Find out whether Esmé and Angela are Weyfarere, and help them come to terms with it.'

'I can show them the Weydoor and that creepy little room!' Tracy exclaims. Totally distracted from her disappointment, like Dory in the films.

'That is first on my agenda for today,' Mary says. 'You are to say nothing to either of them about the Weys until their birthright is confirmed. You are to say nothing to anyone else of its existence. The Weydoor is not public property, and it needs to be protected.'

Tracy nods glumly. I guess in her eyes, there's no fun in having a secret if you can't spill it.

'Lizzy and Maisie – I'd like to take a token from you both so that I can locate you again if you ride out. I will give you my own – I know Maisie has my mother's. Tracy, you and Ian stay here with me first while I go through the Heritage Room and see if I can find a trace of the lost Weydoor and its Weyfarere lineage. We can travel down to Stoneford together.' She pauses. 'You do realise we could end up changing your great-aunt's life forever, Tracy.'

'Granty,' Tracy corrects her. 'She hates being called Great-Aunt.'

'Let's hope she doesn't mind being called Weyfare if it turns out that she is descended from Wayland,' Mary says dryly.

'Hell. What's another few hours from revision?' Ian says cheerfully.

Ani's nose crinkles. 'If we go back to 1972, I'm not wearing that shitty woollen coat again.'

'Unless you specifically want to glam up, regular riders of the Weys should dress under the radar,' Mary says. 'Wear dark clothing. Girls should keep a long skirt for time periods where women didn't wear trousers. I have some clothes you can keep. Wear a hat if you need to disguise long hair, or cut it short.' She lights another cigarette, and passes the packet straight to Lizzy. 'You should also be prepared for what to do if you are separated from your Weyfare.'

'Streets ahead of you there,' Brian says. 'Go find the Weyfare on that timeline.'

'See if there's a Weyroom linked to the door? Find a token?' Ani suggests.

Mary shrugs. 'Fair enough. For now though, my advice is stay here in 1987. The first thing I would do is find out whether Eve moved into Travellers' Rest before Joan became ill. Locate a token or vial that gets you close to that date. There may be something in the Weyroom under your school.' Mary walks over to one of the upturned cabinets, and, pulling out a small, solid-looking carved wooden chest, she reveals a stash of syringes and empty vials. 'You should head back to Stoneford right away. Convince Glenda to host a dinner party, or somewhere you can chat about the old days.' She turns to face me. 'And before you ride out to the past again, you need to tell her that you're her granddaughter. Get everything out in the open with your family, once and for all.'

'Now that'll be a conversation worth hearing,' Lizzy says.

'Do you think she'll take the news as well as you did?' Ani asks in her sweetest voice.

Lizzy is over the news well enough to give her a sarcastic smile.

Chapter Twenty-Four – Big Love
(Fleetwood Mac, 1987)

It feels weird leaving Tracy and Ian with Mary at the Dials, but for now, we've got a different party to go to. We're driven home by one of Mary's Guard in a cream VW camper van; it doesn't look like the ones the surfers used to drive in the '60s films, but it's still cool, and there are seats for all of us if we squish up. It's a lot more comfortable than the back of Ed's van, and it's a lot less smelly than the train carriages.

When we arrive at the gate of Travellers' Rest, I have a quick reassuring look around me as I climb out of the back of the van. Across the road, there are people walking dogs and kids into the bottom part of the Park, which looks ordered and tidy. A little further down the road, I can see the first houses in the Saints' Estate where Brian and Ian live, where Lizzy's friend Claire lives and where Rob used to live on another timeline. Behind Travellers' Rest, orchards lead to the recently built Stoneford General Hospital, instead of the Poets' Estate where Jasper will live in 2019, and the land also leads down to the River

Stone, and the pillbox that was built in the Second World War.

It's Wednesday 27th May 1987, and it isn't even a week since I stumbled over Brian and dragged Ani and Jasper through the Weydoor with me, but it's been a whole lot longer than that. And it's this place that feels more like coming home now. I know it always has been my home; it's just that my family didn't know who I was.

'You're not just going to walk in there and say "Hi Granny!" are you?' Lizzy asks.

'What kind of a tool do you take me for?' I say.

'The kind that is stirring bucket loads of shite through my life,' she snaps.

'Oh, what's this then?' Jasper comes to stand next to me. 'Changed the script now the Witan can't hear how you really feel?'

'You can't alter who Maisie is, Lizzy,' Ani says.

'Surely it's a good thing?' Kim suggests. 'Two Weyfarere heads are better than one?'

'You need each other,' Rob says. 'Your crew is important.'

'Well said that man.' Brian plays his imaginary trumpet.

Lizzy glares at them all, sighs and pulls the ever-present golden pack of cigarettes from her pocket. 'Get off my back. I'm okay with it, but you can't blame a girl for needing a bit of time to get her head around a bombshell like that, and Mum and Dad won't find it easy to swallow, either.' She offers one to everyone except me, Ani and Jasper, peers in the packet and sighs before crumpling it in her hand. 'Or Paul. Maybe we shouldn't say anything until we've sorted out what's going on there.'

'I'm not carrying secrets around any longer,' I tell her.

'No, I get that,' she says. 'But let's get some booze down their necks first, okay? I might've coped a bit better if you'd told me after a couple of 1080s.'

There are no guys in black talking into boxy two-way radios in the front garden, and maybe more importantly, no sign of Valerie or Scott. I know they're probably in Edinburgh by now, but half of me still expects them to leap out of a bush at us.

The back door is open, and the multi-coloured plastic ribbons that keep the flies from getting into the kitchen are flapping in the light breeze. My nan, Glenda, is sitting at the big round pine table, drinking a cup of tea and reading the newspapers with her husband, my granddad Henry. That table has seen some action over the past few days. My uncle, Lizzy's brother Paul, is not in the room.

As we walk in, Glenda lowers the paper, and her face is a mask of tension. 'Hello, Lizzy darling!' she says loudly and brightly. 'Auntie Mary rang and said you were on your way back!'

Henry lowers his paper as well, and beams, but there is a

warning in his eyes. I have never heard Glenda call Lizzy darling, and Mary is not her Aunt. Eve alert.

'She said she was going to call,' Lizzy says. She's getting quicker at following a change of script. 'One of her friends gave us a lift home.'

'Auntie Mary didn't come back with you?' Glenda asks. 'How disappointing.'

'Auntie Mary has to do some chores,' Lizzy says. 'She'll come as soon as she's finished. Where's Paul?'

'Out,' Henry says. 'With Dave on the bikes. He has to go back to University tomorrow. And Grandma Eve is having a bath.'

Grandma Eve?

The jackhammer clock on the wall drops a minute into the silence. 'Lizzy, I must show you the new portable telly we've put in the caravan,' Henry says in a strained voice.

'Oh yes! Let's all go down and look at the new telly,' Glenda says, almost throwing the newspaper down on the table. I swear she nearly claps her hands, she's acting so lit.

'That sounds like a lot of fun,' Lizzy says, not so lit, but appreciating, like I think we all do, that Glenda and Henry are trying to get us to a place where they can't be overheard by rogue grandmas.

We walk down the garden path, past the pond, the greenhouse, and Henry's vegetable plot, down the side of the garage to the caravan and pile in. It's supposed to hold four, but there are now nine of us crushed inside.

'This isn't going to look at all sus if she sees us,' Jasper says, as he crams his slim body into the corner of the van. 'So where's the new telly? Jokes,' he says quickly as Ani, Lizzy and Brian turn on him.

'We don't have long,' Henry says. 'We don't know much. She had breakfast with us, and when I called her Eve, she tapped me on the arm with her knife and said '*Grandma* Eve, please Henry,' as if I was six. It'd be funny if it wasn't so serious.'

'She's having a bath; and she has an appointment with a client at midday,' Glenda says. 'She said it like it happens all the time, so I couldn't ask for more information. I hoped Mary would come down with her Guard so that they could detain her if she's doing anything dodgy with the Weydoor. What's so important that she couldn't come to intercept a Weyleigher?'

'Don't throw a wobbly, Mum. She's got other business in Stoneford. We found another Weydoor.'

'Another Weydoor?' Glenda's jaw nearly hits her blue Jeffrey Rogers T-shirt. 'In Stoneford? That's impossible.'

'Well, actually it is possible because there is potentially an infinite number of times a fracture can occur in an energy flow,' Brian says.

'It's true, Glenda. We've ridden from it,' Ani says.

'Which family is responsible for this other Weydoor?' Glenda asks. 'We can't be expected to protect two of them!'

Lizzy pulls out the scrunched up golden packet. 'That's Mary's other business. She's trying to locate the family responsible for it. Don't s'pose you've got a smoke?'

'You can't smoke in here with us all, we'll choke,' Ani retorts, from Brian's lap.

'You want her to hear the rest of the news without alcohol or nicotine?' Lizzy exclaims. 'What kind of sadist are you?'

'The rest of the news?' Glenda says, taking her own packet from her jeans and offering it to Lizzy regardless. 'There's more? Why didn't you tell me any of this last night?'

'Well, maybe I thought riding the Weys back from 1972 to find a Weyleigher shacked up in Nan's old bedroom was enough to be going on with!'

'She does have a point,' Kim says helpfully, squashed up next to Jasper.

'I couldn't tell you the rest of the news, anyway,' Lizzy says innocently, lighting up. 'Not my story to tell.'

Kim, Ani and Brian look at me. Jasper pats my leg. Rob, whose lap I'm crushing again, squeezes my middle. Talk about under pressure to perform.

'Lizzy's my mum,' I just blurt out. 'Except she's not, obviously, because we're the same age. But she will be, assuming she meets my dad. But we're not allowed to talk about that -'

'Stop! Ow bugger!' Henry stands up sharply and bashes his head on an overhead storage cupboard. 'Are you telling us you're our granddaughter?' he asks as if I've told him I'm Carol Danvers.

I turn to Glenda, expecting her to look like she's going to puke everywhere or hit someone, but she doesn't look at all like Lizzy did when I spilt the tea. There's a small, shy smile on her face, and I realise, to my relief, that Lizzy's reaction to me wasn't anything to do with me personally, it was all about the concept of having your future thrust into your face, which is something Weyfarere deal with a lot. Glenda's been Weyfare a lot longer than Lizzy.

'It's the truth,' I say, pulling the silver key on its chain from around my neck. 'This is my key. It belongs to Great Grandma Joan. Lizzy gave it to me in 2019. I had no idea who I was until you told Lizzy about the Weyfarere. I didn't know how to tell you. Any of you,' I say, looking at Lizzy, and then back to Glenda.

'I've been expecting you,' she says quietly. 'I should've realised who you are. I've often thought you had Lizzy's eyes.'

Lizzy is the one who looks more shocked, and she's known for a while now. 'That's it?' she asks, and she's more than a bit salty. 'That's all you're going to say? You aren't going to take her apart for all the time she spent lying to us about who she really was?'

'Well, what would you have done, smart arse?' Brian suddenly says. 'Lizzy, I love you, you're one of my dearest, oldest mates, but you need to get over this already. If you'd found yourself on her timeline and you knew who she was, would you have gone waltzing over to her at the Fundraiser saying, "Hey girl, guess what? I'm your mother?" These people are part of the gang now. Don't make it harder than it is.' He puts his head on Ani's shoulder, and she pats him like he's her favourite dog.

'Chicken, Brian is right,' Henry says to his sullen daughter. 'Maisie is no threat to us. She's family. She was in a very difficult situation.'

I could break down in that caravan right here and sob my eighteen-year-old heart out. It feels like weeks and months that I've had to tiptoe around these people, first pretending I was a runaway, then admitting we'd come through the Weydoor, pretending I was lent a silver key by Lizzy, pretending I didn't ride back to 2019 every time we rode out – now finally, I can be who I am. I just need to stay Maisie Weyfare. Lizzy isn't stupid - well, not most of the time - and if she hears my family name is Wharton, she'll make assumptions about her future, and that can't happen.

Glenda reaches and takes Lizzy's hand, and then she takes mine. 'My girls,' she says as if she's the happiest woman in her world, and Rob reaches around and rubs the tears from my cheeks. 'It was only the other day I thought I lost my Lizzy, and now I have you both.'

'Rob, Ani and Jasper are my fam too,' I say to her urgently. 'Just like Kim is to you. We stick together. They've all lost their Wey.'

'As lovely as this is,' Ani says, her eyes glistening,' we need to make plans before Eve finishes her bath and comes looking for you all.'

Kim wipes the stray tear from Jasper's cheek. 'Mary said that we needed to find out when Eve moved in with you, and why,' he says, with a sniff.

'How do we do that?' Glenda asks. 'Ask her over the fish fingers at dinner?'

'Mary said something about using nostalgia,' Lizzy says, snuggling next to Kim.

'Talking about the old days over a proper family dinner could work,' Glenda says. ' I usually do the roast on a Sunday though.'

'You said Paul's got to go back to Exeter tomorrow. We could have a fondue,' Lizzy says. 'One of those cheese ones. I like those. It could be to wish him a safe journey, or happy new term or something soppy like that.'

'That's a good idea,' Henry says. 'You could say you'd been given a load of cheese that was nearly out of date from school, Glennie.'

'When? I'm not even at work today.'

'Can't you say you have to go in to check the school's deep clean is all being done properly?' Lizzy asks.

'I could. But I was going to follow Eve and see what this client business was all about,' Glenda says.

'Nancy Drew and the Hardy boys and girls have turned up,' Henry says, beaming at us all. 'They can follow her instead, and if you're at Drake's, you're closer to the Weydoor, and you can watch it better.'

'All right. We'd better scoot,' Glenda says, sounding like she's lost several decades. 'Henry, you'll have to get the cheese. Get Gruyère and Gouda.'

'Yes, ma'am!' he says, saluting her like she's a soldier, and plopping a big wet kiss on Lizzy's head, which makes her squeak. He looks at me then, and suddenly I'm really shy, and we just smile at each other, before he tumbles out the door and into the garage.

'You lot go up the track and around into the front again,' Glenda says. 'Lizzy and Kim come with me the back way. Just play along with whatever she says. She's a bit –' she struggles to find the words as she steps out of the caravan, '- quaint.'

'Quaint? What in the name of Sod does that mean?' Lizzy asks, following her.

'You'll see,' I hear Glenda say as the three of them begin to walk back up the path towards the house.

When they are gone, Jasper reaches for me and plants me with a huge hug. 'You did it! You can stay here now they know you're family!'

'We're all home,' I insist, 'unless I can find a way of ever getting you back to our original one.'

'Home is where your BFF is,' he says, not letting me go.

My shoulder feels a bit damp. Poor Jasper. He's really been through it with me. I don't know what I did to deserve such an amazing bruh, but I'm glad I did it.

I look at Ani. She'll never be quite as extra or quite as quirky as the one I left on another timeline, but she's had my back through some rough spots as well, and of course, now she's got Brian. 'I've got no great urge to go rushing back to 2019 unless we're sure it's pretty much like I left it,' she agrees.

'Home is where your heart is,' Rob says. Jasper lets me go, and Rob kisses my cheek. 'We need to get gone before my ex-grandmother comes looking for us.'

'Ex- grand monster,' Brian says as we leave the caravan, echoing Kim's name for her father's biatch of a second wife.

'Race you to the end of the track,' Jasper says, and we all hurtle off like little kids let loose at the start of the summer holidays.

Chapter Twenty-Five – Respectable

(Mel And Kim, 1987)

By the time we arrive at the back door for a second time, the dining room is a bit more crowded. Glenda and Henry are still sitting down at the pine table reading the papers, but Lizzy and Kim are sitting next to a tall, slim woman in a navy blue jacket with shoulder pads that make her look like an American footballer, matching trousers and a pale pink blouse with a double string of pearls under the embroidered collar. Her nails are painted neon pink, but her hands aren't young; there are lines around her eyes and deeper ones either side of her mouth. Her hair is silver grey.

Lizzy goes across to the white cube of a portable television on a pedestal in the corner next to the dresser that used to hold *The Truth*.

The woman tuts sharply. 'Can't we have a peaceful morning without that idiot box making a racket in the corner?' she says. 'You know I don't like it, Elizabeth. Television rots the brain. Are you feeling well, Kimberley? You look peaky.'

I'm not surprised; this woman sounds like a doppelganger for her stepmother. 'I'm well, thank you, Mrs Bennett,' Kim replies, the image of perfect polite teen.

It's probably just as well Lizzy notices us in the doorway; I'm not sure she would've kept her cool. 'Hey! Come on in, peeps; Mum just put the kettle on.'

Eve Bennett is far more glam than she was at Trinity, the time when she served us soup. As she turns her head to take us in, I worry for a second that she'll recognise us, even though we must make up only a tiny percentage of the people that she would've seen pass through the doors of her husband's church. Rob has frozen at my side. I squeeze his hand, and we take a few steps into the kitchen.

'Who's this?' she asks. 'Introduce us, Elizabeth. You know I like things done properly.'

Did we just step into a copy of *Pride and Prejudice*?

'These are my mates. Maisie and Rob, Jasper, Ani and Brian.'

'I'm very pleased to make your acquaintance,' Eve says. 'I'm Elizabeth's Grandma Eve, but you can call me Mrs Bennett. I don't believe we've met.'

'I thought Lizzy's Nan was called Joan,' Ani says bluntly.

Eve blinks twice and frowns deeply. 'We do not talk of family tragedies at the breakfast table, young woman.'

'Do we not?'

Glenda coughs and puts down her newspaper. 'Breakfast is over, anyway, but Lizzy's right, the kettle's only just boiled. Sit down, and I'll refill the pot.'

'Are you young people here to study?' Eve asks. 'Elizabeth has important exams coming up.'

'Absolutely,' I say. 'A-levels. Big deal. Massive.'

'There's not much time left for revision,' she says, in a sing-song of a voice.

'Who knows where that pesky time goes?' Brian sings back with a grin, which vanishes as Ani elbows him in the side.

Eve's gaze drips with disapproval. She finishes her cup of tea (and it is a cup as well, a little dainty thing on a matching saucer that looks like it came from the top of Glenda's dresser) and places her hands together on the table. Glenda takes the cup and saucer away to the sink and puts four steaming mugs of tea on the table.

Rob is still fixated on Eve, and I have to nudge him twice before he realises he's staring at her like she's the tiger who came to tea. I sit down next to Lizzy, and he stands behind me. I can feel the tension streaming from his body as he rests both hands on my shoulder.

'What are your plans for the day, dear?' she asks Glenda.

'Oh – I have to pop into work,' Glenda replies, sitting back down. 'There's been a problem with one of the floor polishers, and I want to make sure the Main Hall's been buffed properly before the girls go back next Monday.'

'So you're going to be up at the school all day?' Eve asks, and she definitely doesn't look happy about it.

'No, no. Just for an hour or so,' Glenda says, smiling. I'd be convinced if it was me she was messing with. 'Harry's working on a project in the garage today, and Paul's out on the bikes with his friend.'

'I don't know why you continue to let the boy chase all over the countryside on that death trap. He'll meet his end on a motorbike, you mark my words.' As if to make a point, she stands up, and all the mugs shiver and shake as if they're scared of her. 'Well, we can't sit around here, all day, can we?'

She stares at Glenda, whose eyes are darting about all over the room as if she's missed an obvious cue. Eventually, she stands up, and that seems to satisfy Eve, who then turns to face those of us who are still seated.

'Polite young people stand when an adult leaves the room,' she says primly.

'They're still drinking their tea, Grandma Eve,' Glenda says.

'They'll never learn good manners if people keep making excuses for them, Glenda. I don't know what's got into you this past couple of days. ' She glares at us and leaves the room, and I have to look away quickly after watching Lizzy raise her mug towards Eve's back, smiling with her middle finger prone. Glenda coughs again and virtually runs from the room after Eve.

'Since when did Valerie's mother turn into the Dowager Countess of Grantham?' Jasper hisses over the rim of his mug.

I snort into my coffee.

'Definite delusions of grandeur,' Brian mutters.

'The whole Bennett family's the same,' Rob says. 'All the women think they're Maggie Thatcher.'

Ani gives a noticeable shudder. 'So, what now? We have a study date in your room to keep up appearances?'

Lizzy shakes her head, no. 'A J P Taylor can wait another day. We'll stay here until Elvis has left the building, and then we follow her from a safe distance.'

'You don't think she'll notice a big crowd of teens behind her?' I ask. 'Maybe some of us should follow her, and the others can hang around the Weydoor.'

'Mum's doing that,' Lizzy says dismissively.

'Not the Drake's Weydoor. The other one,' I say.

Lizzy's mouth makes a textbook 'o' shape. 'You mean the underground one! That's – actually, that's a really good point,' she says as if it's just occurred to her. 'Mum wouldn't even know where to check if that's where Eve's been going.' She eyes me shrewdly. 'Maybe it is a good thing having you around after all. But don't expect any lovey-dovey mummy stuff, okay?'

'I think you'd get a smack in the mouth if you tried it,' Jasper says smoothly.

'Hush your gums, tool,' Ani says. 'Borderline too much information.'

Jasper is about to give her some clap back when his face shows he's realised she's right, and he just nods and finishes his tea. 'So who's going to follow Eve and who's going underground?'

'I like the Jam,' Brian says.

'Random,' Jasper replies. 'I like Cheerios.'

'Never heard of them,' Brian says. 'Are they one of those new House acts? Can't bear the stuff.'

'I got pretty good at following you lot before, and you never noticed,' Rob says. 'I followed Scott and Valerie too. Maybe me and Maisie could follow her, and maybe Jasper and Ani too?'

'If it's okay with you, Maisie, I'll go with Brian,' Ani asks.

'You don't have to ask me, Ani; I'm not the boss of you,' I tell her.

'No, but – well, we're fam, aren't we?'

That question means more to me than probably anything she's said since she followed Lizzy through the trapdoor of the Old Shed and we realised she wasn't the person we thought she was.

'Yeah. We're fam,' I say with a smile. 'But you go with Brian. It's all cool.'

'I do so enjoy being the third wheel,' Jasper says. I thump him. He grins. We both know we would refuse to be parted now.

'Me and Kim can watch to see if Eve shows up at St Pete's, and Ani and Brian can hang out at the back of Tracy's aunt's gaff because Ani knows where that is,' Lizzy says. 'We're all over this like a rash.'

'You better get going,' I say. 'Otherwise, we'll all going to be tailing Eve down Town Hill.'

They go, and the door slams again about ten minutes' later.

Jasper rushes into the front room. 'She's gone,' he calls back to us. ' We need to go now, or we'll lose her.'

We wait until she's walked some distance along the road in the direction of the Saints' Estate and go out of the front door, but, as Jasper is pulling the garden gate closed behind us, a blue double-decker bus goes past, heading towards where Eve is now waiting.

'Bugger! She's waiting at the bus stop,' Rob says.

FML. I hadn't considered that Eve might not walk into Town. The buses don't even come this way in 2019. 'Where does that bus go?' I ask Rob.

'I didn't see the number. If it turns into the estate, it's the 71 and it goes all around the houses and ends up at the bus station down by St Pete's,' he says.

We watch helplessly as the bus stops next to Eve, letting her board before indicating right and heading into the Saints' Estate.

'Shall we just head for the bus station then?' Jasper asks.

'She could get off anywhere between here and there,' I say. 'Does it drop off anywhere important?'

Rob thinks for a moment. 'It goes out the back of Town past Trinity.'

'We should go there,' I say. Jasper nods.

'Would she be meeting a client at Trinity?' Rob asks.

'It's 1987,' I remind him. 'Trinity's not a church any more. There's a canteen for the street community.'

'Street community?' Rob asks. 'You mean the soup kitchen for the homeless?'

'A lot of them are the Lost,' Jasper tells him. 'Trinity would be the perfect place to meet a client, if her clients are by-standers.'

I see the idea dawning as Rob thinks about it. 'We should take a look then. It's as good a place as any to start. We might even get there before the bus does.'

By the time we've walked down Town Hill, pointing Granty Esmé's house out to Rob, and stopping off at the water fountain on the edge of the Railway Gardens, we reckon the bus has long since left Trinity. I still get a shiver of expectation as I walk through the lych gate and past the bench where Rob and me got pretty extra at Lizzy's party. It's still weird to think the guy holding my hand now doesn't have the same memory.

The canteen at the back of Trinity isn't busy. There are a few people dotted around the tables: a man and a woman wearing grubby coats and scarves despite the sunshine outside, hunched over mugs of hot something and paper plates of pink sponge cake; a guy in a blue Parka with the fur-trimmed hood up, stuffing chips into his face; a group of women dressed in '50s full flowery dresses, frilly white petticoats and ponytails tied with ribbon giggling over a magazine. I may be Weyfare, but I couldn't tell you which of these people are lost, which ones live on the street and which ones are just offbeat. Luckily Rob still has some money that works in 1987, and it's enough to buy us all a cup of tea and one plate of chips. Eve is nowhere.

'Well, I thought it was a good idea to come here,' I say when Rob notices the same.

'It's the only other obvious place we hadn't got marked,' Jasper says, squirting sauce from a red bottle onto the side of the plate. 'Apart from squatting like a vagrant in the caves near the other Weydoor, there was nowhere else we could go.'

The petticoat girls all laugh loudly and make me jump,

nearly sending the coffee mug flying over Rob's hands. He still has drummer's arms, even if he's never been a drummer on this timeline. If I try hard, I can just about imagine Fallen Angel on the stage at the front of Trinity, stagelights searing down on them as they perform at Lizzy's birthday: Lizzy herself, singing rock songs into the heavy black microphone; Brian on one side playing guitar; bass player Will, his older brother, on the other side; behind them, glowing under the lights like a god on a pedestal, Rob at the rack of drums. It was a good night, up to the point where Ani was extinguished. We know why Rob is different. I wonder if we'll ever work out what happened to Ani.

'You're miles away,' Rob says, touching the end of my nose. It tickles.

'Not miles. Maybe a few timelines,' I say, taking a chip. 'What are we going to do now? We can't sit here all afternoon. Shall we try the Amber Teapot?'

'We're going to keep our heads down real low and hope that we're far enough away that she doesn't recognise us from this morning,' Jasper says, cupping his hands over the lower part of his face like a mask, and nodding towards the main doors.

I bob my head up. Eve is walking in. I can hardly believe it. Why don't they have bloody mobile phones in 1987? How do we communicate this to the others?

'Bingo,' Rob mutters, slumping down so that his chin is on the table, hidden by his folded arms.

Eve takes a seat by the guy in the Parka. His plate of chips is empty. They speak a few words to each other, but they're over the other side of the seating area, and I can't hear anything they say. Eve goes to the serving hatch and speaks to the girl behind the counter; minutes later, she accepts two mugs of something steaming and returns to the hooded figure. She sits back down beside him.

'So her client is a homeless bloke,' Rob says.

'I don't know about you, Maisie, but my spider-sense is tingling. They are looking bare sus,' Jasper says, sneaking a couple of chips under his hands.

Both of them are right. There's something shady about the way she's sitting with the guy; as if she's threatening him, or at least he's threatened by her, even if she's not trying to intimidate. He takes some things out from the inside of his Parka and places them on the table. Because we've all got our heads down, I don't think any of us can get a clear look, but Eve seems to be unwrapping a package, and then she holds the contents out in front of her. It's just a lunchbox; a metal one with a curved lid, like soldiers used to use, except it's decorated with pictures of what looks like a band.

'Why in the name of Sod is he giving her his lunchbox?' Rob

asks.

Eve then picks up a large cardboard envelope covered in pictures of what look like people from this distance.

'That's Sergeant Pepper's Lonely Hearts Club Band,' Jasper says. 'On vinyl. My mum has a copy of that. She always says it's her pension because it's a first pressing.'

Before I can reply, the guy takes his fur-trimmed hood down and accepts the cigarette that Eve is offering him and I'm so shocked, I cry out and nearly send my half-drunk murky coffee water spiralling across the plastic tablecloth.

'What's the matter?' Jasper hisses. 'What's with the freak-out? Don't you like the Beatles?'

'Forget the bloody Beatles,' I hiss back. 'Look at that guy, Jas! That's Blake! My brother!'

Chapter Twenty-Six – Control

(Janet Jackson, 1987 (1986))

I'm on my feet; the two guys either side of me have me by the arms and are pulling me back down under the radar.

'Let me go,' I tell them. 'Jasper. It's Blake. Listen to me!' I'm causing a bit of a stir amongst the tea drinkers nearby, but Blake and Eve are too preoccupied with their own business to be worried about some high-key girl flexing on the other side of the canteen.

'It can't be him,' Jasper says calmly. He bobs his head up, and when he comes back down to our level, his eyes are wide. 'Crap. It is him. But it's 1987!'

'So? We're here, aren't we?'

'Are you sure it's your brother?' Rob asks.

'Of course I'm sure,' I snap, and the look on his face shocks me out of myself. 'Sorry. But that is my brother, here in 1987 and he's sitting with Eve Bennett!'

'Don't go all extra again, but he's also giving Eve Bennett presents,' Jasper points out, giving me a meaningful look.

'I can see that,' I say, more quietly. The onlookers go back to their own concerns, now I've stopped being so entertaining.

'Scott used to give presents as well. *To Vix*,' he adds, dropping the last two words like they are made of lead.

I thump him then. 'I know this already!'

'Vix? Who's Vix? Valerie?' Rob asks.

'We don't know who Vix is. Scott said he used to work for her as some kind of mule, carrying valuables back from the past to flog for big money,' I say. 'It's a long story.'

'Your long stories are never long,' Rob says, nudging me, his eyes twinkling. 'How do you say it? Explain it like I'm six?'

'Five,' I correct him. 'Okay. Scott knew about the Weydoor and Travellers' Rest a long time before we thought he did. He worked for a woman called Vix who gave him a blood token so he could ride the Weys, collect valuable stuff from the past and bring it back for her to sell. He found out about *The Truth*, so he hooked up with Lizzy so he could steal it. He thought it would be worth a bit.' I take a breath. 'We will never tell her that.'

'I thought you weren't keeping any more secrets,' Jasper says.

'You think we should tell my mother that her buff boyfriend only wanted her for her old book?' I ask. 'Go right ahead. You first.'

'Point taken,' Jasper says flatly.

'Buff boyfriend?' Rob asks, eyebrows raised. Thankfully, his eyes are still twinkling.

I drop a brief kiss across to his smirking lips and peer across the room towards Eve and Blake, and my stomach twists. 'Blake shouldn't be here.'

Blake is my youngest brother; he's two years older than me, and he should be in his second year at Exeter University. Lucas, my other brother, is two years older than him, and training to be a History teacher. Both my brothers inherited my mum's love of history. I was the disappointment; I took GCSE History and didn't pass, knowing I'd be dropping the subject I hated before I'd even taken the exam. Lucas graduated in History and Archaeology, and Blake is studying Ancient History. At least he was. I suddenly remember the text I received from Lucas. I didn't contact him, because I didn't want more bad news about Mum, but was it actually bad news about Blake instead?

Jasper pokes his head up again like a meercat, before coming back down to table level. 'Shit. Maisie. You don't think Eve is Vix, do you?'

A chill spreads across my back like an ice blanket. 'I have to get him away from her.'

'Babe, if you go over there now, all hell will break loose,' Rob says. 'Mary said you need evidence that Eve is abusing the Weydoor before you can get the Witan involved, and you can't risk her discovering you're Weyfare as well. She'll start watching you like a hawk if she finds out.'

'I've got enough evidence in front of me that she's abusing my brother and that's good enough for me,' I say, lurching to my feet again as the anger soars up my body. Jasper and Rob pull me down again.

The couple about to take the empty table next to us glance over, change their minds and choose another at a safe distance.

'She's not abusing him. He gave her an old lunch box and an LP,' Rob says. 'Maisie, if that woman knows about the Weydoor and you go stomping over there and yelling your head off about your brother, she's going to ride out like Valerie did, and you won't know where she went or what she's going to do next.'

'You can't expect me to sit here watching her gaslighting my brother,' I say, and to my irritation, there are tears prickling at the corners of my eyes.

'Haven't you ridden enough Weys yet to know you need a little patience as well as big cahones?' Jasper asks. 'I've ridden the Weys with you enough to have a couple of ideas about what we can do.'

'Go for it,' I sniff, wiping moisture on my black jacket sleeve that I hope won't dry out as snot.

'Okay.' Jasper eats another chip, and I wince: they must be

stone cold by now. 'We can leave now, go and find Lizzy and the others and tell them what we've seen. I haven't finished!' he whispers. I close my mouth. 'I know it means leaving Blake here, but be fair, Maisie, you haven't known where the hell he was or what was happening to him until just now. We tell Lizzy, and Glenda can call Mary and see what she suggests.'

'But now I know he's here,' I say, and wipe my wet cheek roughly with the other sleeve. 'I know Blake's here, but I don't know *why* or *how* he's here. I can't just leave him.'

'If we ring Mary and tell her we saw Eve receiving gifts from a young guy, she'd think it was skanky, but not necessarily a crime against the Weys community,' Rob shrugs. 'He could've found them for her in any old emporium up the back of Town.'

'So how do we prove she's no good?' I ask.

'We stick to the original plan. Glenda keeps watching the Weys; we go back to 1972,' Jasper says. 'We find out what happened to Joan, and who was responsible.'

'That means we've got to let it happen,' I say. 'I thought we were aiming to prevent it.'

'But if Joan is thrown into the Weys by someone other than Eve, we've still got no evidence that she's corrupting the Weys,' Rob says.

'I know.' Jasper leans his chin on his clasped hands. 'I didn't say the plans were any good. I thought I did okay, for a Guard.'

I giggle at him, and then I stop because I realise he's not laughing, and his face is bare serious. 'Jasper, I'm not Witan, and you're not Guard.'

'You're my bae. I don't mean I'm into you or anything. You know that.' He turns to Rob. 'I like guys.'

'Fair enough,' Rob says.

'I just mean right now you are the most important person in my life, Maisie. Not just because we share the same memories and we come from the same timeline. You'd be that person to me anyway. I am going nowhere that you don't go. I figure that makes me your Guard.'

I watch as Rob smiles at him, reaches out a hand and they clasp and bump fists. 'Good call, mate,' he says, and he turns to me. 'I have nowhere I would rather be than by your side so you can call me your boyfriend, your bloke or your Guard – you are my forevermore.'

This is all a bit much to deal with over three half-drunk mugs of murky coffee, two half-baked plans and a half-eaten plate of cold chips, but I squeeze both their hands.

'You don't know how long your brother's known Eve,' Rob says. 'You know how it is with time travel. Maybe the best way we can help him is to go back in Time and change events so that she's not here for him when we come back. If we get an idea of how she ended up living with your family, we could stop it from happening.'

'And when we come back?' I ask. 'What happens to him then?'

'Maisie, we don't know if our 2019 still exists,' Jasper says. 'What makes you think Blake's does?'

I take another look at Blake. His hair's longer than I remember, hanging limply around his grubby face. I wonder how long it is since he had a decent wash or a change of clothes. Did he fall through the Weydoor after me? What was he doing in the Old Library at Drake's in the first place? I have listened to everything Rob and Jasper have told me, and my head knows they are right, but Blake is my brother, and I can't even.

I just have to do something. I have to.

'Okay,' I say aloud. 'Let's go and find Lizzy and get planning the cheesefund so we can ride back to find out how Eve wormed her way into my family, and maybe help Joan as well.'

'Cheese fondue,' Rob says. He tilts his head to one side. 'You sure you're okay with this?'

'Peachy,' I say. Where did that come from?

We tip the remaining cold chips and the paper plate into a metal cage lined with black plastic, and walk casually back towards the main doors of Trinity.

Neither of them is expecting my next move.

As we walk past their table, I channel every Drama class I ever attended and throw my arms up in the air. 'Billy! Is that you! I can't believe it!' I reach down and yank his slender frame onto its feet and, before he can say anything, I hug him close and push my mouth close to his ear, whispering urgently, 'I don't know how you're here or why, but if you're half as intelligent as Mum thinks you are, then you need to bloody play along and fast.' I push him away from me, holding his arms and beaming into his face. 'It's Maisie. Remember me?'

I don't look at Rob and Jasper in case I lose my nerve.

'Maisie?' Blake says, his eyes huge. 'Is that really you?'

'It's really me!' I say, my voice deliberately all light and fluffy. 'Fancy you knowing Grandma Eve!'

'Grandma Eve?' Blake says, glancing at the silent woman. 'Oh, we go back a long way. I haven't seen you in forever, Maisie.'

'We can catch up real soon,' I say, linking my arm through his.

Eve isn't happy. She gets to her feet, and I can feel Rob and Jasper bracing themselves. 'Aren't you young people friends of Glenda's girl?' she asks. 'Didn't I see you back at Travellers' Rest?'

'Yes, you did,' Jasper says, 'but we just couldn't resist a bit of carb-loading before we started our study schedule.'

'Carb loading?' she asks as if we are speaking a foreign language.

'We wanted some chips,' Jasper replies.

'Chips are good for study?' she asks.

'Got me through my GCSEs,' he replies happily.

'O' levels,' Rob says, bumping Jasper's side a little harder than necessary.

'How do you know Billy?' Eve asks, her eyes narrowed.

Nope. Not playing 20 questions with you, Eve. The more I talk to this woman, the less I like her. Clearly Blake didn't trust her either, since he never told her his name. 'Billy. We're having a cheesy fondle tonight at our friend's house. She's called Lizzy. You must come and meet her,' I say cheerfully.

The colour drains from Blake's face. 'Lizzy?'

'Cheese fondue,' Rob points out.

'Yeah, one of those. Her brother Paul is going back to Uni tomorrow,' I say. 'Come and join us. I'm sure it'll be okay with her mother. Glenda. It's okay with you, isn't it Grandma Eve, if Billy comes along?'

Blake looks as if he's going to barf all over the plastic table-cloth. Jasper punches him lightly on the arm. 'Sure is good to see you after all this time, blud,' he says.

Rob holds his hand out. 'Rob. Maisie's bloke.' I like the sound of this but it isn't the time to get all sappy.

Blake shakes his hand, but he still looks ill. 'A cheese fondue?' he asks.

'What's all this about a cheese fondue? I know nothing about a cheese fondue. Glenda never agreed anything with me about having a dinner party this evening.' Eve says. I can almost see the silver hairs bristling on the back of her neck.

'Oh, we talked about it after you left,' I tell her with what I hope is coming across as complete conviction. 'Drake's rang and said they had a load of fondue cheese and did she want it?'

'Drake's had a surplus of gruyère? Since when does a school canteen have gruyère on the menu?'

I shrug. 'It's a mystery. You'll have to ask Glenda.'

'I'm not sure that Wednesday is a suitable evening for hosting a dinner party,' she says primly.

'That's okay. You're not hosting it. Glenda and Henry are.' I smile so broadly that my cheeks hurt. 'Come on, Billy. It's been such a long time. I have *so* much to tell you,' I say. Linking my arm through his, I go to march him away from Eve and out of her hearing, but although Blake may be skinny right now, he's still strong, and he stands his ground and looks back at her.

'Are we done here?' he asks. Eve passes him a brown envelope, which he pockets.

'Ooh, what you been doing?' Jasper asks, linking through his other arm.

'Billy runs errands for me occasionally,' Eve says, patting her tote bag. 'You children run along. Another of my errand boys is due to meet me shortly. Remember our agreement, Billy.'

'I remember,' he says coldly.

Another errand boy? What kind of scam is she running here? As Blake finally allows us to walk him away, I think about Vix and Scott, and the woman in the Hippy Shop that cut my Dad. The way she patted her bag gives me the shivers. Could Eve, Vix and the attacker *really* be the same person?

No one says a word until we are through the lych gate, when Blake steps in front of us and stops. 'Would someone please tell me what the fuck is going on?' he asks, sounding as desperate as he looks.

'It's not really safe to talk this close to Trinity,' I say, 'but I promise, as soon as we're home, I'll tell you everything I know.'

'Home. You mentioned Lizzy. Surely –'

'Home. Yes. Lizzy. Mum. Yes. And Glenda. And Henry. Nan and Granddad.'

He is still for at least a minute as he takes this all in, and we wait, respectfully. 'But Great Grandma was called Joan, not Eve.'

'If you think that's the most messed-up thing you're going to hear today, you're going to need a stiff drink,' Rob says.

'We need to get away from here,' I insist, and this time, Blake moves.

As we are walking away from Trinity, I hear a bus coming around the corner behind us, and it's another 71, going back the other way. Blake has more than enough money in his brown envelope to pay for our fares, so we run to the bus stop and get on it.

The bus is filthy inside. The blue-green fabric seats look as if they've been washed in dust, and there are cigarette butts and suspicious-looking sticky patches all over the floor at the back where we take our seats.

Blake stares out of the dirty window. I'm pretty sure what he's thinking – much the same as I did the first few times I saw Stoneford in 1987. Rob puts an arm around my shoulder, and Jasper sits in front of us. The bus is quite full, of old ladies with tartan trolley bags and teenagers like us, but no one acknowledges us. Why would they? We may look a little similar, but we're nothing like. Our lives are completely alien to theirs. Do I envy them their endless days of studying and partying? No, I don't. These guys don't have Google to help them with their homework. Or Alexa. They can't even DM their blud with the smarts to help. It'd be cool to only have those things to worry about again. Wouldn't it?

'When did you last get a shower?' I ask Blake.

'I can't remember. When I'm here, I've been washing in that toilet block in the Railway Gardens.'

'When you're here?'

He sighs. 'I come and I go.'

'I know,' I say. 'So do we.'

Blake turns away from the view of Stoneford Station and rolls his eyes at me. 'This is not possible. You're all figments of my imagination. I'm going to wake up eventually and you'll be sitting at my bedside sobbing into a tissue, like the wuss you are.'

He's still trying to look so arrogant with his grubby face and coat, and I can't help but burst out laughing. Blake used to put his little sister down all the time, but I'm not that little sister any more, and he looks a bit shocked.

'You don't know the half of it,' Rob says, and I'm pleased to see him smiling. 'And you might want to start treating your sister with a bit more respect.'

'Amen to that,' Jasper says, with a grin. 'Since she's the only one who can get you out of this shituation.'

'Well, not just me.' I put a hand on his shoulder. 'Wait until Glenda and Lizzy get a load of you.'

Lizzy's only just got her head around her daughter showing up. How's she going to react when I walk through the back door with one of her sons? FML.

Chapter Twenty-Seven – Rat In Mi Kitchen (Ub40, 1987 (1986))

By the time the bus drops us up the road from Travellers' Rest, I give Blake a couple of minutes to take in his surroundings. Once inside the kitchen, he stares wordlessly at the unfamiliar décor before we go into the front room, where Henry is watching cricket on the television in the front room.

When Blake sees him, sitting in his favourite armchair, he freezes in his tracks. 'Granddad?' he blurts out.

Henry looks up, startled.

'Henry, this is my brother,' I tell him quickly. 'His name's Blake. We found him at Trinity at the soup kitchen. He was with Eve.'

Henry stands up, wipes his hands on his trousers and holds one out for Blake to shake, as though he meets unborn relatives every day of the week. 'Good to see you, son. You look like you could do with a drink.'

Blake steps forward and shakes his granddad's hand as if he's being introduced to the Duke of Cambridge.

'First rule of time travel. Never talk to your rellies from the past about the future,' Jasper says, sitting down on the end of the brown embroidered sofa.

'Is that what this is then?' Blake asks. 'Time travel?'

'What did you think it was?' I ask him.

'Rohypnol?' he replies. 'A coma?'

'So you starting riding the Weys as a smuggler in the pay of a strange woman because it's a figment of your drug-fuelled imagination?' Rob asks.

'And now you've conjured up your entire fam,' Jasper adds.

'I always was creative,' Blake says.

'Bull,' I say abruptly, and he stares at me. 'This is real, Blake. We're real. It's 1987. There's a rift in the fourth dimension in the Old Library at my school. It's called a Weydoor and it lets you travel through Time. There are lots of them. The girls in our family get to protect them from cringys like the woman you were with, Eve Bennett. We're called Weyfarere.'

'Now that's one hell of a long story cut short,' Rob adds, grinning at me.

'That's all he needs to know for now,' I say.

Blake just stares at me. I guess he's not used to his little sister being in his face.

'How did you end up here, son?' Henry asks, managing to release his hand from Blake's and going over to the glass drinks cabinet at the back of the lounge.

'Everything's so screwed up,' Blake says eventually. He starts to sway on his feet, and me and Rob manage to get him onto the sofa next to Jasper before he falls down.

'Screwed up how?'

'Ever since you ran away.'

'I ran away?' I repeat.

'I think so. My memory's failing. I don't remember things any more. Or I think I remember something, and then the next day, it's gone. I forget people's names. I even forget people. We thought someone abducted you. Ani and Jasper too. There was talk of intruders breaking into the Old Library on the night of the Fundraiser Disco when you were in Year Thirteen. I went in there to see if I could find any sign that you'd been there, which was a long shot since the police had been over it with a fine-tooth comb, and then ... and then ...' He stops, and Henry puts a glass with a very generous shot of what looks like whisky into his shaking hands.

'Drink that, son. It'll put hairs on your chest,' Henry says helpfully.

'I've already got — what?' Blake asks, his face crinkled in confusion. Guess it's going to take him a while to get used to some of the goofy things they say here. I don't think we're helping, and then Lizzy, Kim, Ani and Brian appear in the doorway from the hall.

'Thought we heard voices. Did you find her? There was no sign at the other Weydoor or St Pete's. Who's this?' Lizzy asks.

Blake looks at her. He stands up. He sits down. He stands up again and throws the entire contents of the glass down his throat.

'Think we're going to need another one of those,' I say. Henry goes obediently to the drinks cabinet.

'Long time since I've had that reaction on anyone,' Lizzy smirks.

Eww. No. No *Back to the Future* icky on my Night's Watch. No time for breaking the news gently. 'Lizzy, this is Blake. My brother.'

Kim's eyes nearly fall out of her head.

Brian stares at Lizzy, then at Blake. 'Same nose,' he says.

'Random.' Ani looks at me, and I just shrug like the incapable tard I feel like right now. 'You were supposed to be following Eve, and you come back with another family member?'

'He was with Eve,' I say. 'Lizzy, are you cool with this?'

Blake has her dark red hair, and Henry's; everyone always says that he's the child that most resembles her. They are just staring at each other. Henry brings the whisky bottle from the cabinet, puts a glass in Lizzy's hand and fills it, sloshes another couple of centimetres into Blake's glass and then fills two more.

Lizzy drinks about half of the whisky with her eyes closed.

She shakes her head violently from side to side. 'Dad, that's fucking rank. You could at least put some ginger ale in it.'

Blake's jaw hits his chest.

'Yeah, she's a bit different,' I say.

Lizzy scowls at me and steps towards him. 'Have they told you that you are not to tell me anything at all about my future?' she asks. He nods slowly. 'Good. At least I know I knock out a couple of lookers. I need a seat.'

'He was smuggling goods for Eve. He'd just started telling us about it. Where's Glenda?' I ask. 'She needs to hear this.'

'I'm here – I was stripping the beds,' Glenda replies, arriving behind them with a huge armful of multi-coloured laundry. 'We're going to need fresh linen on all the beds tonight. There's another pile on the second floor landing, Lizzy — could you please go and bring it down for me?'

Lizzy finishes the whisky and stares up at her. 'Drop the laundry, Mum. Meet Blake. Maisie's brother. He's been smuggling goods from the past for Eve.'

Henry puts the other already filled glass of whisky in Glenda's hands as she drops the dirty sheets. I don't think she was following Lizzy's orders.

'Blake? This is Glenda.'

Blake looks at Glenda as if she's just slapped his face.

'Right, well now we're all up to speed,' Rob says, 'maybe

Blake can finish his story.'

'How did you end up smuggling for Eve?' I ask.

'I don't think he can speak,' Brian says, peering into Blake's glazed eyes.

'He needs to tell us before Eve comes back,' I say. 'Come on, Blake. Get a grip. You can freak out later.'

'I didn't know her name. I made one up. She never knew mine,' he says, after taking another gulp of whisky. 'I was in the Library the next evening looking for stuff that might help us find you, and then someone pushed me into a bookcase at the back of the room. Except it wasn't a bookcase.' He stops.

'We call it a Weydoor. You'll catch on,' Kim says kindly.

'When I came around, I thought someone had knocked me out, but I could hear kids' voices outside, and it was daylight. I hid all day by the door, thinking maybe I was concussed. I was convinced I was going to die. The Library looked the same, but it felt different. It must've been hours later when a caretaker came because it was getting dark again. I managed to creep out as he walked in.'

'When did you realise you were in 1987?' Ani asks.

'It must've been days. I came here first and saw … strangers in our garden.' He stops, and points at Glenda and Henry. 'I think it must have been you two. Then I found an old paper. That was when I thought I was seriously ill. I slept in the Park for a bit and I just wandered down into Town one day, for no other reason than finding something different to eat in the bins. She found me in the Railway Gardens. Said if I came up to Trinity with her, she'd buy me something to eat. I had a half-thought about trafficking but to be honest with you, I was too bloody hungry and I didn't give a shit. She asked me what year it was and stuff like that. Then she asked me if I wanted a job as a courier.'

'A courier?' I say.

'Well, that's one word for it,' Jasper replies.

I'm beginning to wish Henry had poured me a whisky as well. Poor Blake. At least when we first came through the Wey-door, there was me, Ani and Jasper. We were all confused and disbelieving too, but we had each other. Blake had been alone, living rough.

'And now you've shown up,' he says, taking another sip from the glass. The whisky's making him chill. 'This is really good stuff, Gra —' He stops and looks at me. 'Henry.'

'So Eve's been sending you through the Weydoor to collect items from the past that are worth her flogging today,' Rob says.

Blake shrugs. 'That's about it. Caretaker checks the Old Library every day at about seven. I slip in behind him, wait for him to leave and fall through the bookcase. When I come back,

I wait in the Library until he opens up. I leave a message at Trinity with the girl who works the canteen, and Rose lets me know when she'll meet me. She gives me enough money to buy a bit of food, and I saved up for this coat.'

'Why Rose?' Brian asks.

'That's what I call her. Because of this?' He puts a hand in a pocket and pulls out something small enough to fit in his fist. We all peer down when he opens his hand to reveal an oval of pink enamel framed by fancy gold twirls, with the impression of a rose carved in a creamy stone on top.

'That's a cameo brooch,' Kim says. 'My step monster had one of those.'

'No, it's a pocket watch compact, actually,' Glenda says angrily, finding her voice again. 'And that one is *mine*. She must've stolen it from my dressing table.'

'Can I see it?' I ask.

Blake passes it to me. 'Be careful, there's something fragile inside,' he says. 'She said I should never break it. Not that I guess it matters much now.'

I click the little compact open to find a small piece of cream paper, folded carefully in half. I unfold it, heart racing, and find what I'm expecting. There is a tiny thin bottle inside, containing a drop of dark liquid. 'Your blood token too, I'm guessing,' I say, passing the compact back to her. 'It would explain why

Blake's been able to ride back and forwards from 1987 without causing a paradox.'

'She stole my compact *and* my blood?' Glenda asks, anger raging in her eyes as she takes the pink oval from me. 'She's been stealing my *blood*?'

'Ratchet, I know,' I say, 'but sadly, not as rare than you'd think. We had a case of it at the Mermaid in nineteen - a while ago.'

'You've met the Mermaid?' Glenda asks.

'Met her, boogied with her and helped to catch a Weyleigher who was stealing her blood,' Ani says.

'You met a Mermaid?' Blake asks faintly.

'They've been busy,' Brian says.

'We never stop,' Jasper says. 'At least it doesn't look like Eve's stooped to selling it on yet.'

'Eww!' Kim exclaims. 'Are you serious? You met a Weyleigher who was trading in Weyfarere blood?'

'Sent them to the Bergh. Like Brian says, we've been busy,' Rob tells her.

'This is all far worse than I thought,' Glenda says, slumping down so heavily onto the only other chair that she nearly spills her whisky. 'We need to stop this. I'm going to call the Witan right away and have that bitch taken to the Bergh.'

'Probably for the best. I'm all over a cheese fondue tonight, but I'm not convinced now that Eve is going to buckle under a grilling and tell us when she moved in, based on what I've seen so far today,' Jasper says. 'Woman's like a tombstone.'

'Oh, good one,' Henry says, giggling. 'Fondue; grilling – get it?'

'No. Put the whisky down, Dad, this is serious,' Lizzy scolds.

'I still want to find out whether Eve moved in before Joan became ill. Do you remember showing Valerie *The Truth?*' I ask. 'Like an inherited memory?'

Glenda sips at her whisky. 'Vaguely. It feels a bit like when someone tells you about something you did as a kid, and you remember it because they told you it happened. I remember Eve was around when Mum got sick ... ' Her voice tails off as she loses her way in her thoughts. 'Why do we need to know this now? I've got enough evidence to get rid of her right here in my hand.'

'Bear with us, Mum,' Lizzy says. 'We may be able to kill two birds with one stone. Do you remember Robin Simmons becoming sick when he was a little boy?'

'That's a bit left field,' Brian remarks.

'Valerie went back to 1972 make sure Robin never died, didn't she? ' Lizzy asks me.

I nod, yes.

'She told Eve about us and the Weydoor, and then she rode

out again.'

'Someone died?' Blake asks.

I pat him on the shoulder. 'Not any more.' I look at Glenda. 'Is he?'

'Not unless I've been sharing my Breithaupt with a ghost,' Brian adds.

'Say what?' Jasper asks.

'Physics textbook,' Brian explains. 'He's in my Physics set.'

'That author's name is more tricky than the subject,' Jasper remarks.

'If you're talking about Eve's grandson, Robin, of course he's still alive,' Glenda says.

'You'll have inherited memories about him,' I say. 'But Robin might still have had the accident, or illness, or whatever it was that saw him off the first time.'

Lizzy looks at Glenda. 'Mum? Can you try to think? Was Robin ill? Do you remember when?'

'Robin was ill when he was a little boy,' Henry says, scrunching his eyes up. 'I remember him being ill. He had a nasty cough and a temperature. Ria didn't think it was any-thing to worry about at first, but then she changed her mind.'

'That's right. We were going to a party — but her and Ted took him up Casualty instead, and it was serious,' Glenda says, gazing forward as if the cork-tiled wall is going to give her clear hindsight. 'It was pneumonia. They kept him in for a few days. He was only a nipper and they put him on a drip. I remember this now!' Glenda says. 'And it was *your* birthday, Harry! It was! We were celebrating your birthday!'

Henry toys with his silver bracelet. 'Bugger me,' he says, 'so it was. August 15th.'

Blake is going a funny shade of grey. I'm not sure whether it's the conversation or the whisky.

'Do you still remember what happened at St Pete's the other day, Mum?' Lizzy asks. 'It's a different timeline but you've been on them both. Do you remember Scott Kelly, and Valerie being Witan?'

'Do you remember me?' Rob asks, but his tone is so sad I don't think he's holding out much hope.

'Do you remember Eve moving in now? Was it after Joan was ill?' I ask.

'I … I'm —' Glenda stops talking and drinks her whisky. 'I don't know any more. I'm getting one of my heads.' She clutches at her temple with her free hand. 'One thing I do remember is that time travel is a bloody dangerous pastime, and this is precisely why!'

There is a respectful pause, but this is too important to stay quiet for long.

'It's fair to say that Valerie told Eve about the Weyfarere

sometime before she saved Robin,' I say. 'She didn't hang around much after, did she?'

'No, she ran off with some bloke she'd met in hospital,' Glenda says sourly. 'I remember that very well. Poor Ted. Still, he's happy enough these days.'

'Do you remember when Grandma became ill?' Lizzy asks.

'August 17th,' Glenda says flatly. 'I've never forgotten that date. Although I had forgotten it was so close to the party.'

'Me too, Glennie, but it's understandable.' Henry says, stroking her hair.

'Looks like it's back to 1972 then.' Ani starts pulling the few vials she took from the Weyroom at Drake's from her pockets, as Jasper and me start emptying pockets and my bumbag of the vials and tokens we took, onto the floor in front of the gas fire with the fake coals.

Lizzy's face is a picture of disgust. 'You two-faced gits! All that grief you gave me about not taking things from that room, when you were up to the same tricks!'

'Not exactly; we did it another time,' Ani says. 'All of this needs to be stored somewhere safe anyway.'

'And what exactly is all *this*?' Glenda asks.

'Weyfarere stuff,' Lizzy says. 'You know we told you about the other Weydoor? Well, there's a bit more.'

'Not more grandchildren?' Glenda asks.

'No more kids. We found something we called a Weyroom down a partially-blocked passage that links Drake's to the other Weydoor.'

'Perhaps I should go and open that bottle of single malt I was saving for Christmas,' Henry says, peering down at the sparkle and shine of glass, metal, papers and gemstones on his carpet.

'What an excellent idea,' Blake mutters.

'The Weyroom is like the Heritage Room at the Mermaid,' I say. 'Passages lead down to the other Weydoor. It's in a kind of cave system under Stoneford.'

'Why would there be a Heritage Room here? Stoneford isn't on the Great Weys,' Glenda says.

The telephone on the stand in the hallway starts ringing.

'Leave it, Glennie,' Henry says, but she is already on her feet.

'I can't — it might be important.'

She pulls the hallway door closed behind her. We all stare down at the little treasure trove we've gathered on the carpet.

'What are the chances of having a token or vial here that takes us back to the right point in 1972?' Rob asks.

'Somewhere in the region of a gazillion to one,' Brian replies. 'Infinite years; 365 days. The combinations are endless.'

'That's right, blud. Stay positive,' Jasper says, rolling his eyes.

'We need to be back in 1972 just before Grandma Joan goes through the Weydoor,' Lizzy says. 'Do we have any tokens for August 1972?'

'You want to go back to *August* 1972? Why didn't you say so?' Henry takes the silver bracelet from his wrist and hands it to Lizzy. 'I was 25 in 1972. That was my birthday present from your other grandparents. If you promise me you'll get it back to me, you can use it if it helps.'

I stare down at the mess on the floor. 'Big time, yes.'

'Perhaps we should hang onto this stuff with Eve living here for the time being,' Brian suggests. 'I'm sure there are a few trinkets here that she'd flog for outrageous prices.'

We are sharing the items out more equally, although I still keep the pill, the books, Lizzy and Helen's vials and Tommy's hanky, when Glenda comes back into the room.

'That was Eve calling from the phone box at Trinity,' she says. 'Apparently, she's been delayed, and she won't be home in time for the fondue.'

'Surprised much,' Jasper says, glancing down at where Blake is handling one of the small vials of blood from the carpet.

'Well, I still want cheese fondue anyway,' Lizzy says. 'Dad bought the cheese so we might as well eat it. Then we can ride out in the morning. Dad's given us his bracelet as a token.'

Glenda nods. 'I'm going to ring the Witan now.'

'Let's hope Eve doesn't do a runner in the meantime,' Rob says.

'If she thinks we've got wind of what she's up to and who she is, she may not stick around to wait for the Guard to take her on a road trip north,' Ani agrees.

'What are you suggesting we do then?' Glenda asks.

Rob turns to me, and then Lizzy, and then back again. 'Maybe we take things into our own hands.'

Chapter Twenty-Eight – Stay Out
Of My Life (Five Star, 1987)

'You don't think *we* should be taking Eve to the Bergh?' Brian asks, the colour draining from his cheeks.

'You don't think she *genuinely* got delayed at Trinity this evening?' Rob replies.

Brian bobs his head from side to side and shrugs. 'Well, no. But I don't *genuinely* believe we can convince her to come quietly, either.'

'Anything's possible, Rob,' Jasper says. ' She could've been delayed tonight. She was meeting another errand boy, as she so delicately put it. He might've been late.'

'She knows Maisie and Blake are friends though. Won't she wonder why Lizzy has a friend who's on talking terms with one of her street kids? Does she know when you came through the Weydoor, Blake?' Ani asks him.

'She doesn't really know anything about me,' Blake says, staring into the dregs of the whisky glass. 'When she asked me what year it was, I told her 1987 because I'd seen it on an old paper someone left in the bin up the Park. I didn't know how I got here, so I didn't tell her.'

'Well, that's one thing less to worry about then,' Rob says. 'She shouldn't connect Maisie with the Weydoor.'

'All the same, she knows Blake is here. If I were her, I wouldn't be hanging around to find out if he spills the tea,' Jasper says.

'I have told you everything,' Blake says.

'Exactly,' Jasper says. They look at each other and both pull a face.

'Jasper's right. If Eve's been handing my blood token around her bystander army like acid tabs, she could have a stash of my blood stored so she can ride out any time she likes,' Glenda says with a shudder. 'The sooner we stop her, the better. But you can't just say you're going to pretend to be Guard. The Guard are trained. It's not like joining a youth club.'

'First rule of joining Guard Club is you do not talk about joining Guard Club,' Jasper says, grinning.

'No, you don't,' Glenda says, completely missing the reference; it's an old film, but I guess it's not been released yet. 'The Guard keep their business as secret as we do. I'll ring Mary Davenport, explain what we know and ask her to dispatch a team.'

'Mary's got business in Stoneford already,' Lizzy says. 'You might be better off ringing the Mermaid since you know her.

Surely we can protect the Weydoor until she gets here.'

'Polly owes us a favour,' I say. 'It's probably just as far up to the Dials from here as it is down to the Mermaid.'

'What's gone so wrong?' Henry says suddenly, emptying his glass of whisky. 'Stoneford was a sleepy little town. We didn't use to have Witan rushing in to save the day from Wey-leighers.'

'Doesn't matter, Pop – you do now,' Lizzy says unhappily, and I can see in her face that she knows, one way or another, that each of us has got to take some blame for changing events.

'Someone has to stay here and protect the Weydoor,' I say. 'Even if she doesn't make a ride for it herself, Eve's got people running back and forth smuggling things through Time.'

'You really need to put a stop to that, Mum. It's our job to make sure no one abuses the Weys,' Lizzy says.

Glenda frowns, rolls her eyes and goes out to the hallway, pulling the door closed.

'Get you with the responsibility,' Brian says, with a grin. She fixes him with a stink eye.

'Glenda shouldn't go anyway, and neither should you, Henry, because you're both already living at Travellers' Rest in 1972.' I look at my brother, who now has his elbows on his knees and his head in his hands. 'I think Blake's done enough riding on the Weys for now.'

'You think?' he mutters. Just how much is still up for discussion. He could be years older than he ought to be, like Scott was when he rode the Weys for Vix.

'You're not wrong there.' Henry pours another whisky. 'Mum's in charge here, of course, but probably me, Mum and Blake here should go over to Drake's as soon as Paul gets back, and make sure there are no more entrances or exits from the Old Library.'

'I'm already in 1972 but I'm going again anyhow,,' Lizzy says, 'and Kim and Brian always come with me.'

'So you can include Ani in that list now,' Jasper says. 'And me and Rob are with Maisie.'

'Do you want to borrow some of Mum's old gear from the 70s?' Henry asks. 'It's all upstairs.'

Ani looks as if he's just asked her to wear his cat. 'It's fine. We'll manage.'

Glenda comes back into the room more quickly than I expected. 'I can't get an answer at the Dials or the Mermaid,' she says, lines creased on her forehead.

'Even more reason for you to guard the Weydoor,' Lizzy says. 'Don't let Eve get away.'

'Mary might already be on the road down here with Tracy and Ian,' I say. 'I'm sure she'll come here as soon as she arrives.'

'Paul can stay here and wait for her,' Glenda says. 'We need to eat. Get the fondue set out of the larder, Harry.'

'Hope it works with Edam,' Henry says, 'I couldn't get any of that fancy cheese you wanted in Safeways.'

True to her word, Eve doesn't show up for the fondue, which is like a baked Camembert minus the skin, melted in a little saucepan over a camping stove. Paul and Dave turn up while we're dunking bits of white, fluffy bread in the gooey yummy mixture. After the now familiar double-takes and whisky requirements while Blake and Paul are introduced and the situation explained, Paul rings a few friends and invites them over for bevvies in case Eve comes back. The rest of us head into the Old Shed in the back garden, where the trap door leads down into the tunnel linking to the Old Library.

'Let's hope that if Eve turns up in here, she doesn't bring any of the lost boys,' I say, looking doubtfully at Glenda, Henry and Blake as we arrive in the Old Library, and they pull out the chairs from the long, carved central reading table.

'Eve looks nothing like David,' Jasper says, 'but then these three don't look a lot like the Frog brothers either.' He looks around at their blank faces. '*The Lost Boys* is obviously not on release yet.'

'Stop wittering, and let's get a move on,' Lizzy says. 'Pop, I promise I'll bring back your bracelet soon.'

'I know you will, sugarbush,' Henry says. 'We'll hold the fort. Off you go and be smart for me and your mother.'

'Let's see what's going on. Link up.' Lizzy reaches her hand out for Kim and hesitates, looking back at me. 'Will you be going to 2019 first?'

'It'll be an inward ride for me, so yes.' I pat my bumbag. 'It's okay. I've got your vial. Tommy gave it to me.'

'I feel like I should be pissed off about my blood being handed around like a joint, but I don't have the time for that now,' Lizzy says, as she holds out Henry's bracelet, and Kim, Brian and Ani follow. I take Rob's hand, and Jasper links arms with him, and as we step forward, there's white heat, purple light, black – nothing.

We don't hang around in 2019, but I'm relieved to see there's no Guard or any sign of fake Witan presence here. I dab a little of Lizzy's vial onto Rob and Jasper's fingers, just to be sure, and we ride out again, to find the others just staggering to their feet. The sun is beaming in through the high windows in the Old Library like so many laser beams, and you can feel the heat humming through the stone walls.

'Welcome to the summer of '72,' Lizzy says, pocketing the precious bracelet, and pulling the silver key from the chain around her neck. Like us, she's adopted a kind of uniform now: black denim jacket, plain black T, jeans and black Converse All-

Stars. Even Kim has abandoned her preferred '80s neon for more subtle whites and blue denims. None of us would look on point at the Crypt at Trinity, but I'm okay with not fitting in these days. My hair has completely forgotten the feel of a pair of straighteners.

'Isn't it a bit of a risk to go through the tunnel?' I ask.

'How else are we going to get out? It's the summer holidays. I doubt that even a caretaker is on site.'

'Jasper still has his keys,' I say. He pats his jacket pocket. 'It's Henry's birthday. They'll be having a party with loads of people who saw us at Glenda's 21st.'

'Not another bloody rents party at Travellers' Rest,' Jasper moans.

'Keep your knickers on. Even if they do recognise us, it makes sense that we'd be at both parties, doesn't it? Anyway, we're not stopping. We're going up to Trinity to find Eve.'

'Eve will be at the party if she's already a friend of Joan's,' Rob says.

'So we might have to listen to that weirdass Gnome song again,' Jasper wails.

'What would you rather us be doing? Going up to Trinity to drink beef tea with Professor Umbridge?' Ani says. 'Or watching Lizzy and Maisie's faces when they realise they haven't saved their sick grandmother.'

'Great,' I point out.

'Do you have to lay it on so thick with your shovel?' Jasper mutters indignantly.

'No, I just meant Joan is my great- grandmother.'

'Valerie will be at the hospital. Glenda said she took Robin to Casualty instead of going to Henry's party,' Brian says. 'Wouldn't Eve be with them if her grandson's that ill?'

'Shouldn't we be going to St Pete's then?' Jasper asks.

'Bloody hell,' Lizzy says, her eyes darkening as she begins to lose it, 'you're all doing my head in!' She pushes her hands into her pockets. 'Bugger. No smokes! How do I cope with all this and no smokes?

Rob throws her the packet I saw back in 2019, with the plain packaging and the disgusting photos.

Lizzy looks at them. 'What in the name of Sod's brand is this?' she cries.

'Search me. I asked for B&H in a shop in 2019, and that's what they gave me,' he tells her.

Lizzy looks at me. 'You people are sick,' she mutters, but she takes one anyway.

'So much for smoking prevention,' I sigh. 'Look, I can't be sure of this, but, like I said before, if Robin's ill, and Joan's ill two days from now, surely Valerie must've already told Eve about the Weydoor,' I say. 'She wouldn't have time to do it any later if her son is in hospital.'

'Joan is not going to get ill,' Lizzy says firmly. 'Not this time. Whatever happened here, we're going to make it right. My grandma is not getting thrown through the Weydoor, and Eve is not shacking up with us because I'm going to ring Helen as soon as I get inside, and get the Bennetts off our backs for once and for all time. Got it?'

'You're the Weyfare,' I say shortly.

'So are you.' Her face softens.

She pulls the usual leather-bound rune-covered fake book from the bookcase, locating the hidden lock inside with her silver key. As she turns the key, the bookcase creaks inwards, showing us the way to the underground tunnel, another party at Travellers' Rest and hopefully a final conclusion to the Bennett family's twisted history with us in Stoneford.

Do I really feel hopeful about that? Do I think that after this, I might get the chance to sit down and work out what I'm going to do about Rob, Ani and Brian, and Jasper? Jasper and Ani's 2019 is long gone. Rob and Brian are still 50 in anyone's 2019.

As Lizzy would say, bugger. Probably she'd say something else.

Chapter Twenty-Nine – All The Young Dudes (Mott The Hoople, 1972)

'Déjà vu or what?' Jasper says as we peer through the window in the Old Shed on the scene outside.

'Or what,' I say. 'It's a different party.'

'Could've fooled me,' Jasper says.

I know what he means. The evening is warm, people are sitting in circles on the grass sharing spliffs like before, and the garden is covered in empty bottles labelled Double Diamond and Bass. The music coming from the house itself is thumping through my body like a second pulse. It could be Glenda's 21st, or even Lizzy's 18th, except there's no marquee and no olds snogging in the bushes. I shudder at the memory.

'I know this song,' Rob says, looking up at the house. 'This is Alice Cooper. School's Out for summer.'

'Unofficial end of year anthem at FCAB,' Brian agrees.

'Be careful when you go in,' I say. 'Remember Joan's met most of us before. She knows we're from the future, and it'll be a bit of a shock for her to see us again.'

'And Mum?' Lizzy asks. 'Won't she remember meeting you at her own party?'

'I doubt that,' Ani replies. 'It's Henry's birthday. She'll be too wasted to remember her own name.'

Lizzy turns sharply as if to defend Glenda's reputation, but stops and shrugs. 'Fair comment.'

Inside Travellers' Rest, it's the familiar haze of blue smoke and the stench of ash paired with sweat; there are masses of bottles of wine and beer on the table in the dining room, and people dancing with their hands in the air to the record player in its place in the corner. The guy standing next to it is holding a cardboard vinyl album cover with a photo of a graffiti-covered school desk on it. I'm guessing it's Alice Cooper's album. Everyone knows School's Out. I shiver in the heat; I have the craziest weird feeling someone is watching us.

Lizzy grabs a bottle of Worthington 'E' from the table, takes a mouthful, pulls a face and puts it back down.

'Sugar!' A loud voice booms behind me, and to my horror, I'm lifted up and twirled around by something resembling Wolverine wearing a beaded collarless shirt and uber-flared trousers. 'It's me! Mick!' He beams at me, revealing the gold tooth.

'Mick!' I squeak, since he's crushing all the available air out of my lungs. 'Good to see you again!'

'Far out! Hey Johnno! Look who it is! It's the beatnik chicks from Glen's bash!'

The short, tubby guy who appears through the crowd is just as high key about our arrival. 'Right on! Foxy! Babs, it's Foxy!' he says, stumbling slightly and sloshing a mug of what I hope is beer over my foot. Thank whichever god is listening that I'm only wearing cheap black kicks. 'Man, what happened to you guys at our pad on New Year? One minute you were there, and the next – Poof!' He claps his hands together, and Kim takes the mug and puts it down on the edge of the table. 'Thanks, little lady,' he winks.

'Needed some sleep,' Lizzy says.

Rob coughs. He's getting better at not playing my knight in shining denim.

'I don't s'pose you could put me down, could you?' I ask.

Mick laughs and places me on the floor. 'You dudes need a drink. We got a couple kegs in the upstairs and a doozy of a doobie. Wanna come hang?'

'It would give us a chance to look for Joan,' Ani says.

'Glen's old lady Joan?' Mick says. 'She's up in the lav. Bust her hand on a tin opener getting into a Red Barrel. I told her you only need the two holes; one for the beer out, one for the air in.' He rolls his eyes as if it's the most obvious thing in the world. 'These old folks are not switched on.'

I smile, and deliberately put my hand around Rob's waist. He puts his arm across my shoulders.

'Peace out. I dig this,' Mick says, with a grin at Rob. 'Be cool, brother.' He holds out a heavily ringed hand to shake, and Rob takes it. 'Let's go party on down.'

It's not as bad as when we went to Lizzy's 18th, and all the rents were sitting around. The people here are much younger, and now we've got over the eye-melting wallpaper patterns and the weirdass fashions, it doesn't feel so different from any house party in Time.

Lizzy can't make her phonecall as there's already someone using the burgundy house phone in the hallway. We get to the top of the first staircase, the third step from the top squeaking underfoot as I pass over it, to find the bathroom door open and the room full of people. One girl is sitting on the loo, smoking, her short flowery mini skirt barely hiding her girlie bits. As we look into the room, she waves cheerfully at us. Another girl is sitting sideways on the edge of the bath, holding back the long hair of a guy who is puking into the bath itself. Joan is leaning over the sink, grimacing as an older man tosses a yellow blood-stained flannel on the floor at our feet and wraps a thin white bandage around her hand. Mick and John sink into the crowd at the foot of the second staircase, already having forgotten about us. I glance across at Lizzy, but she seems to have finally got a grip on meeting older rellies when they are younger.

'You might need a tetanus jab,' the older guy says to Joan. 'That's a nasty cut. Maybe you should go to Casualty.'

'I don't need Casualty,' Joan snaps, and then she sees us in the open doorway, and she grabs hold of the guy and shoves him past us. 'I need a drink. Go and get me a drink, Arthur. Something strong. Now!'

'Okay, okay!' Arthur staggers from the force of the push and almost falls down the staircase. Jasper picks up the flannel and passes it to me. I fold it up as if it were a piece of paper.

Joan steadies herself on the sink and looks at me. 'I know you.'

I nod. 'We had to come back. I can't tell you why.'

'To help me? Or Glennie? Or Lizzy?' she asks. Then she spots the red-haired girl in the room and she covers her mouth with her good hand. 'Oh my giddy aunt.'

'Not even close,' Lizzy says, her eyes glistening under the harsh white of the strip lights above us. 'Hey, Grandma.' Both women step forward uncertainly, and they hug.

'Glennie isn't here,' Joan says. 'She's taken the kids to St Pete's to be with her best friends Ria and Ted. Their boy is sickening for something.' She looks at Lizzy again. 'You aren't here in the house, at least.'

'And you're holding the fort,' Brian says.

'Someone has to keep an eye on these youngsters,' Joan says.

'Grandma, listen -' Lizzy begins, but her voice, already dampened by the partying around us, is almost drowned out completely by the loud ringing at the bottom of the stairs. It stops abruptly. 'Grandma, I need you to promise me something. I need you to -'

'Where's Joan Bishop?' someone shouts up from the hallway.

'I'm here. What's the matter?' Joan slips past us to the top of the staircase and leans on the banister.

'Telephone call for you. Says it's urgent,' the voice replies.

'Wait here for me,' Joan says to Lizzy. 'I won't be a moment.'

I put the folded flannel in my bumbag as Joan goes down to the hallway. A tickle of unease patters down my spine, and I get that weird feeling we're being watched again.

'Insurance?' Lizzy asks, looking at the bag. I nod. 'At least we didn't have to find a syringe to stab her with. You never know what's going to happen – Can we help you?' she adds sarcastically, staring over my shoulder.

'Holy crap,' Jasper says, having already turned.

I turn to find Polly Frobisher standing behind me. Barry and Clive are standing to each side of her.

'Hello, Polly,' Rob says. 'This is a surprise.'

'Thank God I found you all, Maisie,' she says, looking from face to face. 'But where is she?'

'Where is who? And who are you?' Lizzy asks, laying her palms out in front of her in frustration as she glares at me. 'And why is it that every bloody person we meet lately already knows you?'

I shrug. 'Polly, meet Lizzy. Polly is the Mermaid. Lizzy's a Stoneford Weyfare. She'll be my mum one day,' I add.

Lizzy shivers all over as if someone has doused her in ice water. 'I wish you wouldn't say that word; it gives me the willies. Polly the Mermaid. I know it's 1972, but I'm not into acid tabs, and you've got legs.'

'Lizzy,' Ani says, disapprovingly. 'Get a grip. Polly's the Witan from the Mermaid.'

'Oh!' Lizzy has the smarts to look uncomfortable. '*That* Mermaid.'

'Is she always this clueless?' Polly asks.

Brian splutters into Ani's shoulder. Jasper stares pointedly at the longhaired guy behind us, now sitting on the bathroom lino wiping puke from his mouth using a pristine white towel. Kim looks from Lizzy to Polly and back again. Me and Rob glance at each other, but I have to look away.

'Bloody cheeky cow,' Lizzy says. She stares at Polly for a moment, and then inexplicably they both laugh.

'I like you,' Polly says. 'You should come down to the Mermaid and we'll go for a boogie. But not now,' she adds, her face growing serious again. 'Business first. Where's Tracy?'

'Tracy?' I repeat. 'She's not here. Why?'

'Is there somewhere we can talk privately?' Polly asks.

'It's a house party,' Jasper says. 'It's not really Privacy Central here tonight.'

'Go up to Joan's bedroom,' Lizzy says. 'She won't mind if it's - business.'

The bedroom on the second floor is quiet, so we go in and close the door. Barry and Clive lean against it. Jasper and Kim sit on the floor with Ani and Brian, and me, Rob and Lizzy perch on the edge of the big quilted double bed. Polly stands between us as if she's about to give a speech.

'What's the matter with Tracy?' I ask. 'Why do you need to see her?'

'It's not really protocol to tell others first,' Polly says, 'but, oh hell, you'll find out sooner or later. You know I took samples of her blood, and yours,' she nods over at Ani, 'to compare Weyfarere blood to bystander blood?'

'Ooh. Are you building a new Weyfare?' Brian asks with a grin. Ani puts a hand over her face. Polly gives him a look that would wilt a spider plant. 'Sorry. Bad Frankenstein joke.'

'I'm a chemist, ' Polly says. 'I found the Weyfare marker.'

'You found the difference?' Ani asks, impressed.

'I think so. It matches markers I found in myself, Mary, Helen and Maisie.' She stops, and looks at us all. 'And Tracy.'

The windows in the room are open, and a familiar voice from downstairs is faintly singing that someone called Layla has got him on his knees, but I can't name the singer. An old favourite of Mum's I think.

'Are you telling us that you think Rutherford is Weyfare?' Lizzy exclaims into the void between us all.

'She can't be,' I say. 'Can she?'

'I thought her aunts would be the Weyfarere, I must admit,' Ani says. 'The other Weydoor is linked to their house.'

'Did Tracy ever live there?' Rob asks.

We all look at Lizzy. 'You've known her the longest time of all of us,' Kim says.

'I don't remember her living anywhere other than the top of King Street.' Lizzy replies.

'You don't think she could be like me?' Rob asks. 'I mean, could she be adopted?'

'No. This is nuts.' Lizzy shakes her head. 'We don't keep big secrets like that.'

'Like you never told her you were Weyfare?' Jasper asks.

'That's different,' she snaps. 'I only just found out myself.'

'Maybe she doesn't know. Like Rob.' I reach over and

squeeze his hand.

'Tracy can't be Weyfare,' Lizzy says. 'It's just ridiculous. She's way too hot-headed to handle the pressure of time travel. I just can't believe it. You must've made a mistake when you were analysing the blood.'

The hard thumps of a drumbeat below us vibrate through the ceiling as I consider the irony.

'Why are you all here, anyway?' Polly asks, ignoring the opportunity to give Lizzy clap back. 'I drove up here from 1979 to use your Weydoor. It's likely I'm still Witan in 1987, and I didn't want to meet myself coming forward. I was expecting Tracy's blood to track her to 1987, but it bought me here. I'm no historian, but they're playing Slade downstairs, and every-one's dressed like Woodstock.'

'Snoopy's sidekick?' Kim asks, her nose wrinkling.

'American music festival,' Polly says. 'So where are we, and why are you here?'

'Well, that proves you're wrong,' Lizzy says. 'Sorry – I know you're the Witan and everything, but Tracy's not here.'

'This is August 1972,' I tell her. 'You remember me saying that we thought Lizzy's grandma got thrown through the Wey-door and trapped somewhere in Time? We managed to track it to happening in the next couple of days.'

'We've come here to stop it happening,' Lizzy says firmly.

'No one throws my grandma back in Time.'

'What happened to her again?' Polly asks me.

'Something happened to her mind,' I say.

'She couldn't remember how to do things. She couldn't remember any one's name in the family. She would shriek the house down in the middle of the night. She died a few years later.' Lizzy takes a deep breath. 'They said she was senile.'

'So you think she was trapped off her timeline?' Polly asks, looking at me again.

'It ages the brain prematurely, doesn't it?' I say. 'On the outside, you don't look much different, but on the inside –'

I remember Glenda telling me; " ... in Wey years, the medics think internally your Mum was well over 100 when she collapsed." I'm still haunted by events on that timeline. I hope I've changed enough of the past to make sure that future never exists for me or Lizzy.

'As Maisie says, the organs age quicker than the outer body.' Polly finishes for me. 'It's a strange phenomenon that's mentioned in some later versions of *The Truth*, but not in any great detail.' She pulls a familiar red and white packet from her jacket, black with a zipped front and an elasticated waist and collar, and offers them to us. 'Marly?'

'So you're here because you thought Tracy was here?' Ani asks as Lizzy takes one.

Polly nods as she lights all the cigarettes taken and almost vanishes behind more blue waves of smoke. 'This is where the token bought me.'

'But Tracy's in 1987 with Mary Davenport,' I say. 'Mary was researching the other Stoneford Weydoor using the archives in her Heritage Room, and she wanted Tracy to stay with her because it affected her family.'

'Big understatement,' Ani suggests.

'So it seems,' Polly agrees. 'It doesn't explain why I'm here though.'

'What if you got the bloods muddled up?' Jasper says, and he turns very slowly to look at the dark-eyed girl standing with her back to the door. 'What if you thought the blood you were using was a token for Tracy when actually, it was a token for —' He stops speaking, but his mouth stays open.

'But that would mean —' I can't finish my sentence either. I almost can't look at her, but I see she is becoming paler beneath the coffee tones of her skin, as one by one everybody in the room is looking at her, and as it dawns on her what we're all thinking, she crosses her arms defiantly.

'Don't be so fucking ridiculous,' she says indignantly. 'I'm not a bloody Weyfare!'

'I'm sure I didn't get the tokens confused,' Polly says.

'Then why did it bring you here to Ani, and not to Tracy?' I ask.

Chapter Thirty – Take Me Bak
'Ome (Slade, 1972)

'Do you travel back to 2019 after every ride out?' Polly asks her.

'I — I don't know,' Ani says, her defiance starting to look a little shaky. 'I always follow Maisie, and she always goes back there first anyway.'

'Gobshite's ballbag,' Brian says, his voice all breathy, 'am I going out with a Weyfare?'

'You'll get used to it,' Rob says.

'No. No! I don't believe this! My family have nothing to do with any of this!' Ani says incredulously. 'My mother is a bloody solicitor! She doesn't have time to be Weyfare! And we live nowhere near the other Weydoor!'

'Don't get upset about it now, blud,' Jasper says. 'Maybe in a couple of days, we can go back with Polly and run a few more tests, but right now we've got to look out for Joan.'

I think it's the first time that Jasper's said anything that kind to Ani, and she obviously thinks so too because she blinks twice and then, brushing at her eyes roughly, she nods once and gives him a small smile.

'It's just as well you came through to us, Polly, as it saves waiting until Helen can get down here,' Lizzy says.

'Talk to me,' Polly says, and we bring her up to date on the situation that brought us to 1972. Again.

'Where is Joan now?' Polly asks once we've finished.

'She took a phone call. She said she'd come straight back,' Kim says.

'How long ago was that?' Polly asks. When we don't reply, she nods at Barry and Clive, who step away and open the door. 'We'd better go find her. I need to introduce myself anyway; I expect she knows my mother.'

But when we get to the first floor, the bathroom door is closed again and, when Brian tries to open it, a female voice tells him to sling his hook. At the bottom of the next staircase, the hallway is crammed full of people standing around, drinking and talking, but none of them is Joan, and the phone isn't in use. A slightly sick feeling grumbles in my stomach, until we see her, pushing towards us from the kitchen. The music is eardrum-shattering loud.

'ZoSo!' Brian shouts. 'They had some great music back here. Got to love me a bit of Zeppelin.' This time, he plays air guitar.

'There you are! I have to go and sort out a group of bystanders at the Weydoor,' she shouts, not seeming to care that anyone could overhear, but to be honest, with Led Zeppelin powering their ways through the walls, even I can barely hear her, and the sick feeling isn't going away. 'We can talk more when I get back.'

My instinct kicks in. 'I don't think you should go,' I cry back.

Joan frowns. 'Don't be daft, girl. I have to go. It's what we do.'

'How did you find out that bystanders were needing your help?' Lizzy cries.

'I got a tip-off,' Joan nods at the telephone on its stand.

'Is that normal practice here?' Polly shouts. She holds out her hand. 'Polly Frobisher. Future Witan at the Mermaid. These are my Guard, Barry and Clive. You'll know of my mother, Margaret.'

Joan takes Polly's hand, but her cheeks have gone a deeper shade of red. 'A Witan? At Travellers' Rest? Is something wrong?'

'Potentially, yes,' Polly cries. 'Can we please go somewhere that we don't have to keep bellowing at each other?'

The garden is quieter, but there's more opportunity for someone to hear us, so we walk a little further away from the buzz of the party and stand by the greenhouse.

'I came here to speak to Maisie and Lizzy,' Polly explains,

'but now I'm here, it would appear that you might be in very serious danger from a Weyleigher.'

I don't think any of us expected Joan to laugh. 'A Weyleigher?' she repeats, through the giggles. 'We haven't had any Weyleighers in Stoneford for centuries. It's a quiet little place. We aren't on the Great Weys. We don't ride out on the Weys. We just do our duty to the bystanders.'

'Do you know Eve Bennett?' Rob asks.

Joan nods. 'Her husband's the Vicar of The Blessed Holy Trinity in Town. My Glennie is very close to her daughter. Why?'

'She's a Weyleigher, Grandma, and we think someone from their family is going to try and hurt you,' Lizzy says. 'Possibly even her. Please don't go to the Weydoor.'

The laughter on Joan's face melts away as she realises how serious we're all looking.

'You think Eve Bennett's a Weyleigher? I'm sorry, but that's just silly. I can't just ignore a group of bystanders in distress,' she says. 'I must've missed the alarm with all the commotion of the party.'

'The alarm?'

'There's a sensor pad under the floor that sets off a light alarm in the Old Shed, and a sound alarm in the kitchen,' Joan says.

'Mum never said anything to me about any alarms,' Lizzy says.

'The Old Library is perfect for containing the bystanders until we can send them back on their Weys,' Joan says, 'but if the main door is left open for any reason, the bystanders can sometimes elude us, and they end up goodness knows where.'

'Eve has a band of old biddies scouting Stoneford's tramps for bystanders who can tell her where the Weydoor is,' Lizzy tells her. 'Valerie's been to the future. She knows what's in the Old Library and we think she came back and told Eve.'

For a second, I think Joan's going to accept what we're saying, but then she shakes her head. 'No. No, I'm sorry, I won't have it. I have to act on the information I'm given. You can all come with me if you must, but I'm going to Drake's.'

And she storms up the garden path towards the Old Shed, and we have no choice but to follow her. If there is anything shady going down tonight, we can make sure Eve doesn't get the chance to throw Joan through the Weydoor, and, if she does, I now have a bumbag with a bloody flannel inside that means I can hopefully get Joan back before any damage is done.

No one at the party seems to notice when we all pile into the shed, and I don't expect they'll notice when we all come out again. The tunnel, as always, is not an easy walk but it's August, and the ground underfoot is hard and dry.

When we get to the Old Library, my fears are realised. Joan pushes a switch on the wall next to the glowing Weydoor, and the empty room is flooded with a pale light.

'Where are they?' Joan asks, as if the question is going to make a group of people leap out at her from one of the alcoves.

'There's no one here, Grandma,' Lizzy says.

'Uncomfortable much,' Jasper says, looking around.

'It looks like someone has played a trick on you,' Polly agrees. 'This is not a good sign. Could the bystanders have got out of this library?'

'Only if the door has been left open,' Joan says.

Rob goes to the front of the room and tries the heavy iron handle. It twists in his hands and opens. 'I'm going to have a shufty around,' he says; 'see if anyone's wandering around out here. Anyone coming?'

'I'll come,' Kim says. 'It feels strange in here tonight.'

'Should we go with them, Polly?' Barry asks.

'Nothing's going to happen in here that I can't deal with,' Polly says. 'It's just a Weydoor. You two go and scout out the place with them.'

Kim goes out with Rob, Barry and Clive, and they disappear into the night.

'This doesn't feel right,' I say, staring at the open door. 'Why is it open? Why is no one here?'

'Did you recognise the voice on the phone?' Jasper asks.

Joan shakes her head, no. 'The school groundsman will sometimes call if he hears a disturbance, as I'm in charge of the school interiors. It wasn't him that called tonight though.'

'Who else would notice anyone acting sus around Drake's in the middle of August?' Ani asks.

The bookcase that leads to the tunnel swings open wide to reveal a younger Eve Bennett, brushing dust from her clothes, her face alight with excitement and triumph as she steps blinking into the room.

'Of course, it would be in here!' she says as if she's talking to someone else. 'It's the only original building left standing after the War!' She turns and gazes at the glowing purple of the Weydoor as if she's seen an angel. 'I can't believe it.'

'What in Hell's name are you doing here, Eve?' Joan asks in shock.

Eve, far less polished than the version we left in 1987, looks embarrassed. 'I followed you.'

'And why would you do that?' I ask, stalling for a few more seconds. Eve is too close to Joan, not to mention the Weydoor.

'Val told me there's a time portal in Stoneford, and that Joan knew where it was. She said it was here at the school, but I thought she was having me on. So I asked one of my friends to ring Joan and tell her there was a ruckus in the Old Library, and

I watched to see what she did next.'

I bloody knew someone was watching us at the party.

'Why would you be interested in the location of a time portal in Stoneford?' Polly asks her.

'Well, honestly. Wouldn't anybody be?' Eve asks, looking innocent. 'And you've obviously told these people about it, or they wouldn't be here. Why shouldn't I know as well? This is a goldmine, Joanie! Think of what you can do! Things that cost tuppence ha'penny thirty years ago could be worth several quid by now!'

'The Wey ... The time portal isn't to be used for ill-gotten gains,' Joan says, pulling herself up to her full height.

'Nor is it to be used for disposing of people you don't want around,' Lizzy says gravely.

'You wouldn't catch me going anywhere near it.' Eve says, folding her arms and looking decidedly pissed off. 'What an awful thing to say! I thought we were friends, Joan Bishop, and all this time you've been keeping a secret like this from me, while these kids seem to know all about it. How do you think that makes me feel?'

'Plus ça change,' Brian says lightly.

'The more they stay the same,' Ani says. Her voice has gone all tight and scratchy. When I turn to find out why she sounds so frightened, a cold blanket of fear drapes itself over my shoulders until all I feel is panic.

A tall, slender figure stands beside Ani. It's dressed from head to foot in black, complete with a black mask that covers the whole face apart from its eyes. It towers over her, and I can see it's holding a short serrated knife to her neck. At first, I think it must be Valerie's Guard, somehow escaped through Time; then I look more closely. This figure is caped, material flowing over floor-length fitted narrow tunics. A hood covers its head but a sheet of black material covers its face, not a mask.

There are more of the figures now, appearing from the shadowy alcoves. I'm pretty sure they are all women.

The one holding Ani must have been hiding behind one of the alcoves, but, as I watch on, stuck to the spot like one of the statues in Trafalgar Square, more still step into the open doorway of the Old Library. One is holding Rob, one other is holding Kim and two more are holding Barry and Clive, and I can see the steel of the blades against skin reflecting in the light from the room.

'Call them off!' I shriek, snapping my head back. 'Call them off right now, Eve —' My sentence runs out of juice as I see Eve's face.

She's as terrified as the rest of us.

Fuck.

'I don't know what you mean,' she mumbles, her voice hushed in terror. 'I don't know who these people are. You think I know them? Why would you think I know them?'

Is she bullshitting me? She gabbles on a bit more, and I realise the bitter, hard truth. Eve Bennett doesn't know who these creeps are anymore than we do, and that means we are in a far worse situation than we imagined when we rode here. Have we been wrong all along about Eve? We know she's a Weyleigher, so if she's on the level, who the hell are these guys?

Before I can help myself, the words are out of my mouth. 'Do you know anyone called Vix?'

The laughter that fills the Old Library is high-pitched, like something inhuman.

'We have come for the Weyfare that dares to change the fates of men,' one of them rasps.

Without consulting each other, Polly, Joan, me and Lizzy stay completely still, guarding the Weydoor behind. In front of us, the strange figures have taken hold of everyone else until the four of us are the only ones without restraint.

'You will put the knives down, and return our friends to us,' Polly says. She's trying to pull rank, but her voice is wobbly. On her timeline, she's only just found out about Janice and Gus' betrayal. What a couple of days she's having.

'You will ride the Weys, and you will not return to this

place,' the figure holding Rob says. 'Or there will be consequences.'

Kim whimpers. I don't blame her. Lizzy balls her hands into a fist beside me.

'Please don't be a hero,' Ani says as if she's asking what time it is.

"I'm sick of people pushing me around,' Lizzy snaps. 'Let go of our friends or we'll have the whole lot of you taken to the Bergh.'

The figure next to Rob turns and thrusts a fist hard into Clive's side. He crumples to the floor.

Polly cries out; Joan puts her hands across her face, hiding her eyes. Kim is breathing hard now, and Jasper looks as if he's about to vomit. Eve is crying. Lizzy is silenced. I'm too shocked to speak. Please, no. Was she holding her knife? Has Clive just been stabbed in front of our eyes?

'I will make sure the next blow truly disables him,' the figure says, her scratchy voice calm. 'The bystanders will leave now. We only require the Weyfare who changes the fates of men.'

FML. It's not us they are forcing to ride. I look at Rob, who's already been through more than most people could take. He's lost his family, he's lost his timeline, and now someone is threatening his life because of me, and he still gives me a small smile.

I thought if Eve or Valerie attacked Joan, there would be enough of us to stop it happening, but we weren't ready for multiple bastards with knives threatening all of our friends. I don't want Rob, Jasper or Ani to ride the Weys without us. Lizzy wouldn't want Brian or Kim to ride. Polly wouldn't want her Guard to ride.

But we have to let it happen.

'There's no choice,' Jasper says clearly. 'We'll work a way out of this. We always do.'

I mentally go through the contents of my bumbag: *The Truth;* Valerie's fake version, still not extinguished; vials and tokens from unknown times and people; Tommy's hanky, Lizzy and Helen's vials and now Joan's blood token on the abandoned flannel.

I've never been a leader.

I don't have complete belief that I can work this out, but one of us has got to step up.

I turn to Polly. 'Do you trust me?'

Her cheeks are colourless. 'Yes,' she whispers.

'We have to let them ride.'

'No!' Lizzy yells. 'Not without us!'

'It's the only way to save them,' I tell her. I swing around to face Joan. She nods.

'Ready for lift-off,' Brian says.

'Forevermore.' Rob says, and he pats his pocket to remind me.

I already remembered.

The four of us move away from the Weydoor. I have to drag Lizzy back, and I can't watch as one by one the Women bring our friends to the glowing purple light, and they step through into who knows where.

The one who attacked Clive bends down to haul him to his feet at the back of the Library. I'm thinking these people are exceptionally strong.

'You will also leave with your Witan,' she says. 'Your presence is not required. We only require the Weyfare who dares to alter the fates of men.'

Without further encouragement, Clive is running down the middle of the Old Library at full Usain Bolt. Barry, also released, thunders after him. I realise what's happening at the same time as Polly.

'What? No!' Polly yells, 'I'm not leaving them -'

Clive pushes Polly through the Weydoor, grabbing Barry who seizes Joan who's nearest to him, and she clutches at Eve.

'What are you doing?' Eve cries, her voice shrill, and her pink cheeks streaked with mascara.

'Giving you a taste of what you came for,' Joan says, and

they all disappear through the Weydoor with a blinding flare of violet lightning.

Beside me, Lizzy takes my hand. 'Looks like it's just you and me, kid,' she says. 'Here's looking at you.' I know it's supposed to be her joke, but it's a lame one and I don't feel like laughing.

I'm wondering which of me and Lizzy is the Weyfare who changes the fates of men. Whatever that means, I think we're about to find out.

The Women begin to circle around us, closing in, herding us like sheep. But I am not sheep. I am not even just Maisie Wharton any more.

I am Maisie Weyfare.

'Don't even begin to think that we're finished here,' I say to Lizzy, as the bodies of the Women hem us in at the edge of the Weydoor.

Lizzy squeezes my hand tightly. Wherever we end up, at least we'll be together. We will find our family and friends again. I have to believe this.

I smile bravely into the face of my terrified mother as the women step forward around us and there's white heat, purple light, black – nothing.

So, how did Lizzy end up in 2019?

To receive your FREE short story, *The Wey We Were*, all you have to do is tell me where to send it.

I'll also send you details of other events, such as book deals, new launches, and other freebies, but I promise I won't overload your mailbox!

Grab your free story today!

Did you enjoy this book?

*Do you want to make an
author happy today?*

Reviews are one of the most effective ways for me to attract new readers for my books.

Honest reviews help other readers to make the decision to give the Weys a try.

If you enjoyed this book, I would be forever grateful if you could leave a review. It doesn't have to be long, but it might make all the difference.

Thank you

If you want to know more about me, click here for all the places you can find out.

ACKNOWLEDGEMENTS

With special thanks to Vicky at
www.virtualofficegenie.co.uk

ABOUT THE AUTHOR

S. J. Blackwell

I'm a British author with a passion for writing time travel adventure sprinkled with British nostalgia, romance and fantasy. Unlike Maisie, I love History!
My favourite thing (after Salted Caramel Puddles from Hotel Chocolat) is writing in the magical den at the bottom of my garden with the elves and hedgehogs, but sometimes you will find me adventuring in my vintage camper van with my husband, or playing with my two soppy greyhounds.

READY FOR THE NEXT
PART OF THE JOURNEY?

Wey Back in Time - where 20th century time travel adventure meets enduring love and English folklore

Wey Back When - Book 1

Meet Maisie Wharton. She's invited to a party this weekend but it's in 1987, and it's her mother's 18th birthday ...

No Wey Of Knowing - Book 2

It's 1987 and Maisie now has a secret she wants to keep from her mother, but first she has to fix her family's future ...

Long Wey Round - Book 3

It's New Year's Eve 1971 and, just like 1972, Maisie's journey through time is just beginning when a shock revelation about her boyfriend leaves everyone reeling ...

Works Both Weys - Book 4

More problems, more choices - now Maisie's back in time, dancing with the Mermaid in 1979 ...

Any Which Wey - Book 5

The past, present and future are catching up with her, but 1987 hasn't finished with Maisie yet ...

Jingle All The Wey - Novella 5.5

A seasonal standalone novella that sits between books 5 and 6. When a cherished family keepsake goes missing, Lizzy and Kim take a new recruit back to 1973 to find it. But it's Christmas, and maybe a few other wishes will be coming true ...

One Wey Or Another - Book 6

She thought she was safe and sound, time travelling days all done. Now trouble's chasing Maisie down in 1981 ...

Look The Other Wey - Book 7

Is returning to 1981 worth the cost, when Maisie's future is bleak and so much has been lost?

Wey Past Caring - Book 8

Will love prevail for Maisie in 1974? Will she ever manage to settle the score?

Weys And Means - Book 9

Expected Summer 2022!

Printed in Great Britain
by Amazon